A Tiger's Heart

A Jake Fleming Investigation

Other books by E. C. Ayres

Tony Lowell Mysteries
Hour of the Manatee
Eye of the Gator
Night of the Panther
Lair of the Lizard
Day of the Red Tide

Jake Fleming Investigations
A Tigers Heart
When Darkness Falls
Black Dragon River

Young Adult
Toon Man

Non-Fiction
The Shakespeare Conundrum
Inside the New China

A Tiger's Heart

A Jake Fleming Investigation

E. C. Ayres

SPEAKING VOLUMES, LLC
NAPLES, FLORIDA
2021

A Tiger's Heart

Cover design by Hannah Linder

ISBN 978-1-64540-355-5

This book is dedicated to those who spent much of their lives and careers researching the content material in this novel.

Prologue

Outside London, late November,
11:51 p.m., present day

The pallid sliver of moon drooped low over the London night sky, the city's sullen glow giving way to the onward creep of fog rising from the river as the witching hour drew closer. Abruptly, the moon vanished as the mist closed in on the churchyard. The ancient stone edifice and dark bell tower loomed above and behind the two intruders as they dug: a black pit before them, darkness at their backs. The man shivered, pulled the drawstring tighter on his military surplus parka, and plunged the shovel once more into the sodden, moldy earth. So far so good. They were nearly six feet down and had collected a dozen or so bones of different sizes and functions, some with ancient, dried organic matter still clinging to them. They'd even found a pale staring skull, its ancient jaw clenched in a perpetual scream as if yearning to tell a tale of horror that would remain forever untold. The man who so frantically dug could only hope they had gotten enough evidence to make their case.

"Oh shit. C'mon, hurry up, please!" the young woman called out anxiously as she stopped a moment to listen. "I think someone heard us!"

The man heaved another scoop of loam from the burrow they had dug along the wall. He could tell she was losing her resolve by the minute. "Hang on. We have to know one way or the other!" His stomach emitted a growl of displeasure. Shit, he thought. Bad time to run out of Mylanta.

As with most old English churches, the rear of the churchyard had lain in silent vigil over the worn and weathered stones for ages, some of the crusted markers many centuries old, with names long lost or forgotten. Such was the case with the name engraved on the bronze plaque above their heads, on the vine-and moss-covered brick wall. The plaque was ancient, yet it appeared to be the newest object in the vicinity, suggesting that some lonesome devotee somewhere had assumed responsibility for its care, perhaps not unlike the longtime faithful nocturnal visitor to the tomb of Edgar Allen Poe. *'Cut is the branch'* it read in letters still clearly etched in the dim night glow from the city's distant lights. The man had seen it once before, recently, and heard the words uttered long ago and far from here by a dying man on a theater stage: *Cut is the branch that might have grown full straight.* And above the inscription, a name that had languished in infamy for more than four hundred years.

By this time, he was convinced that the dead poet was not buried here but rather another man entirely. Possibly a stranger or derelict, or even a true victim of murder rested below. But not the name on the plaque. Ironically, the only way to prove that was to fail to dig him up. Yet dig he would, fully aware that he was engaging in a crime: stealing bones from a church cemetery! But it was the only way he could think of—that any of them could think of—to know the truth for certain.

They had access to forensics. They could DNA any bone marrow or tissue they found. It would be enough, he believed, at least to eliminate the line. It would be a much harder task, he knew, to assign these bones to Penry. But that wouldn't matter; it wasn't whose bones they were, so much as whose they were *not* that counted.

A light went on upstairs in the rectory, at the far end of the church. "Damn!" he muttered, and his stomach sounded its own second warning. He dug faster.

The young woman stopped digging, more urgency in her voice than before: "Jesus, let's go! Someone's coming!"

He heard the rectory door open in the distance. He heard it slam, then the sound of footsteps approaching. The graveyard filled with shadows that came alive like creeping ghosts, swooping and weaving before the uneven gleam of a hand-held lantern as it came bobbing towards them.

"Who's there?" a gnarled voice shouted out. *"Curst be he that moves my bones!"*

"Fuck this," declared the young woman. "I'm outta here."

The man gave in at last. "OK, I'm coming." Quickly, he helped her out of the hole and scrambled up after her. By then he knew they'd been seen. His stomach churned again in open rebellion as he grabbed the shovels, threw them over the wall, and dove after them.

But his companion's feet slipped, and she fell back into the graveyard. That was when he heard the scream.

Chapter One

Uneasy Lies the Head

San Francisco International Airport, three weeks earlier, 1:45 p.m.

The thin-set, gray-haired man in a custom pinstriped gray suit stood in the shadows of the concourse and waited with growing impatience for his former protege to arrive. It wouldn't be long now. The young upstart celebrity scholar was landing at any moment on British Airways flight 285, and according to the airline, the flight was on time.

He checked his watch. He would have to play this scene to perfection, he knew, or all would be lost. At least he'd managed to buy some time. The university had arranged for a committee to greet their esteemed guest, but he'd delayed them temporarily with a simple phone call, masquerading as a British Airways agent with word that their expected guest had missed his plane and would be on the next flight. That should allow enough time, he felt confident, to do what needed to be done.

What had gotten to him at last had been the sheer magnitude of his young rival's betrayal. And to what end? To discredit four hundred years of scholarship and tradition—not to mention his own life's work and writings? It was untenable, unbearable, and must not be allowed to continue. His final blasphemy was this new book he was about to announce. A book that would surely be the most serious imperilment yet to The Name. *Even the devil can cite scripture for his purpose*, the thin man knew. And this above all must be prevented.

His upper lip began to perspire. He fretfully wiped it with his Seville Row sleeve, took a deep breath and continued his watch. He would have to put on a good performance, he knew, or all was lost.

A loudspeaker blared the announcement: "British Airways Flight 285, now arriving at Gate 7." It wouldn't be long now.

If only that searing pain in his skull would cease and desist. It was beginning to drive him mad!

Berkeley, California, 2:00 p.m.

Melissa Fleming was troubled. The day was gorgeous, the sunlight slanting down in broad golden beams like the stays of a vast celestial bridge, the sparkling bay spread out below in all its magnificence, with the gray silhouettes of the San Francisco skyline clearly etched out beyond. Yet her thoughts and feelings were dark, and at times lately, almost tenebrous. For one thing, she hadn't been allowed to join the greeting committee, for the simple, stupid reason being that she was no longer an English Major, having switched in graduate school to Theater.

Angrily, as she wended her way under the soaring redwoods to lecture her English Literature class, her mind raced with questions she had wanted to present to the man as soon as she had the chance. She'd read Desmond Lewis's first book, *The Problems with Bacon,* several times and disagreed with most of it. Now a rumor was sweeping the campus that Lewis had a new bombshell to unleash. What it was about was a topic of frenzied speculation on and even off campus. Oscar Wilde? No, he'd already written extensively about him, and the gay community had been sharply divided about a lot of it and would have probably successfully fought any invitation to the man. Unfairly, in her opinion. No, it had to be something else.

As a graduate Theater major at The University of California at Berkeley, Melissa was fully accustomed to controversy in all its various manifestations. She had played most of the parts, as it were. What had provoked her interest now was the fact that Professor Lewis was a rarity among academics: a bona fide trend setter who had dared to break ranks with his peers—something that was rarely done in university English departments, and strictly frowned upon as a rule in Academe, as she herself had learned firsthand more than once. Not that she entirely approved of him, or most of his work. In fact, she didn't. Still, on the other hand, he was relatively young for a full professor, and hot-looking to boot. So now that he was coming to Berkeley this very evening for a sold-out lecture in Sproul Hall, she had wrestled with her conscience, which had been soundly defeated, and, forced to the outside, as it were, she had joined the throng to hear what this new Outlier had to say. In more ways than one, if she had the chance, she could hardly wait to get her hands on him. So to speak. She blushed at her own boldness and blasphemy and hurried to catch the Dwight Avenue bus.

First thing after class, however, she'd promised her father she'd bring dinner for him. It was the least she could do, at least once in a while, since her mother had died. Not that they got along. Not that they'd ever gotten along. Why was that? Granted, she had a tendency to want to remake his life for him, starting with his dismal eating habits. But that aside, she'd pretty much kept her distance since her mother had died. Maybe it just had to do with her own need for independence. Was this why she had decided to become an actor? She shook her head, her flaxen blond hair flying, drawing wishful looks from nearby passing students, including several leering frat boys whom she thoroughly ignored. Maybe she should have become a psych major instead, she thought wryly, as she climbed the stairs to her lecture hall. At least that way she'd stand a small chance, at least, of landing a paying job someday. But if it wasn't in her blood, acting was most certainly in her soul, and she was determined to persist.

Besides, she was not without resources. She had been gifted with natural beauty, thanks to her mother and, at least so she'd so often been told, considerable talent. Again, thanks to her mother. Still, was that enough to survive in this ever-more-competitive and materialistic world? She knew that her only chance of success would be to remain confident that she could overcome all obstacles and, at the end of the day seize her moment upon life's stage, literally.

As she reached the building's elevated entrance, she turned and looked back at the tree-lined path she had just taken and once more at the bay glimmering in the distance beyond. Something about it sent a shiver down her spine. It was a beautiful day. So why couldn't she enjoy it?

Berkeley, California, 3:00 p.m.

On Benvenue Avenue not far from the U.C. campus, Jake Fleming was having one of those days. First, the water pipe had burst in the basement of his beloved three story Victorian ('basement' being a shallow excuse for a hole in the ground not much deeper, as his daughter liked to remind him, than a grave). Then his computer had frozen, possibly one of those fucking viruses, he feared, leaving his latest *Tribune* article in limbo. Just my luck, he thought. He was having a hard enough time as it was focusing on a story about the governor's latest flap with women at a time when politicians couldn't possibly sink lower in repute in any case, so who cared? Then there was that cryptic call from an old acquaintance from London, Desmond Lewis. What was that all about?

He'd just come into the kitchen earlier that morning from his customary jog up in the Berkeley Hills above the campus and had caught the phone on the sixth ring.

The voice was British, clipped and concise, and vaguely familiar. It also sounded strained. There was noise in the background suggesting an airport.

"Is this Jake Fleming of *The San Francisco Tribune*?"

"Who's calling?"

"Jake, this is Professor Desmond Lewis of London University. We met at the research symposium two years ago at the Poynter Institute?"

"Yes, of course." They had spent a week at a conference together at the Renaissance Vinoy hotel in St. Petersburg, Florida. The sponsoring Poynter Institute was one of the last truly independent journalism think tanks, a non-profit organization affiliated with *The Tampa Bay Times*, also one of the last independent publishers in the news business. The subject had been Truth and Power, an interesting paradox. Desmond Lewis had been one of the guest speakers on the subject of academic freedom. Apparently, he was of the view that such a thing was a myth. Perhaps not unlike what passed for "truth," given recent history on the home front.

"I'm calling from JFK in New York, actually. I am coming to Berkeley tonight, and wonder if we could have dinner? I've just finished a new book which I'd like you to look at before I send it on to my publishers."

Jake sometimes reviewed books, but only rarely–usually hard-hitting political exposes and such. "What's it about?"

"I can't tell you over the phone," the Briton said, lowering his voice. "Too many ears about. I'll explain when I see you."

"Sure, but is this really up my alley?" Fleming had asked in puzzlement, a touch of irritation creeping into his voice which he would regret later. The water was boiling, and he hadn't had his customary second cup of coffee yet. "I mean, no offense Des, but I'm not exactly an expert in your field."

There was a momentary pause on the other end. "No matter. For one thing, I feel I can trust you. For another, you have an international readership, have won two Pulitzer Prizes, been nominated for three others, are respected for your accuracy, and most of all, you are not beholden to the Ayatollahs of Academe." He wouldn't say more.

Jake thought hard. *Ayatollahs of Academe*? Melissa would love that one. This Englishman was something of an eccentric, from what he remembered. He'd be happy to have a meal with the man and hash over old times, but this request sounded way out of his league. On the other hand, he recalled a certain debt he owed to the man that Lewis had had the grace not to mention.

"Look," Jake said, finally. "I'd like to help you out, but I have to tell you I am not the right person for this. I really don't have the kind of qualifications you're talking about and need, frankly. So, whatever I had to say would probably be dismissed outright by whoever it is you are trying to persuade."

"Even so," came the reply, "I'd like your opinion."

Jake sighed. "OK, sure. Maybe I could ask one of the people in the Books section to—."

Lewis cut him off, as though rushed for time. Maybe his plane was about to leave. "I appreciate that Jake, but, in any case, I really do need to speak with you."

"Sure, sure, OK." Jake sighed, feeling trapped between obligation and dismissal. "Look, meanwhile I'll talk to my daughter. She's a graduate student at the university here, and maybe she'll have some idea who else might be better than me to show this to."

"We can discuss that when I get there. I'll call you when I land."

"Absolutely. Give me a call."

Jake hung up and gave the conversation no further thought until Melissa had come and gone bearing some kind of rice and tofu concoction he could barely choke down, claiming there was no time to cook. She had done her best to distract him with the scenes she was currently working on, from—what was it, George Bernard Shaw? He couldn't even remember, his mind on other things.

Finally leaving in exasperation like the drama queen she aspired to be, she had thrown a comment over her shoulder to the effect of "Thanks for listening, Dad. As usual." Throwing up his hands, he'd called it a day and turned in early, and had slept soundly until the phone woke him at around one a.m.

"What?" he grumbled, his voice cracked and edgy with sleep and annoyance.

"Dad? It's Melissa. Sorry to wake you. I thought you'd be up, it's Saturday night."

"It's Sunday morning and I wasn't. Can't it wait?" He sighed. Once again, he'd gotten off on the wrong foot with her.

"Dad, you know that English guy, the professor who was supposed to speak this eve–last night?"

"Desmond Lewis," he grumbled, struggling awake. "What about him?"

"He never showed. So much for his great 'revelations.' "

That got his attention. "What revelations?"

"Who knows. But nobody can find him. It's like he just up and disappeared."

"Melissa, can't this wait? It's one o'clock in the morning."

"Yeah, I know. Sorry to bother you, Dad. Guy's probably a flake anyway, according to the department heads. Go back to sleep."

"Hold on," he said, now fully alert and sitting up. "He called me earlier, actually. Said he wanted me to read something. A manuscript or something. I told him I'd ask you for some suggestions, it's really not my bailiwick."

"You *know* him?"

"From Florida. A conference a couple years back."

"And he called *you*?" She sounded mystified at this unlikelihood, which didn't improve his mood.

"Yes. Sounded like he was at the airport and seemed in some sort of a rush. Anyway, I told him I'd ask around. Look, is that why you woke me up?"

"But why didn't he show up, if he called you to say he was coming? That doesn't make sense."

"Maybe he had a last-minute change of plans. Maybe he's just absent minded and forgot he had a dinner date in Barcelona."

"Ha ha. Right. The 'absent minded professor' syndrome." Her tone turned serious. "Dad this was a major campus event. We even canceled a performance of *Pygmalion* for it. Plus, he was paid a serious honorarium and, if you ask me, he has a lot of nerve skipping out like that."

"Maybe he just missed the flight and got stuck somewhere."

"No, I talked to my friends on the committee. They checked with the airline. He was on that flight, they said. And he would have called."

"Well, maybe he hooked up with a flight attendant and headed for Stinson Beach."

"Yeah, right. In October?"

Normally Jake would have shrugged off the whole incident as inconsequential in the greater scheme of things. At least in terms of his own priorities. Still, something bothered him, enough to take closer note of his daughter's apparent concern than usual. "What about the University? Has anyone checked with them?"

"Yes, of course. Neither the Dean nor the Student Activities prez has heard from him since he left London."

"Strange. Well, let me know if you hear anything. But please, not before I've had my morning coffee?"

She sighed. "Dad. You call that stuff you drink coffee?"

Berkeley, California, 7:40 a.m.

As daylight broke over the Berkeley hills, Jake awoke from a fitful night of tossing and turning, something gnawing at the back of his mind. He got up, washed his face, and went down to the kitchen for his customary Folgers instant coffee and Snickers bar. He'd forgotten all about the incident of the day before until he picked up the morning *Chronicle* from the front stoop. He liked to read the competition, just to stay on his toes. The usual grim headlines were nothing to give pause, and he knew his own newspaper would have the same coverage. Then a smaller item on page two caught his eye: *Controversial Professor a No-Show at UCB*. So who filed that? He'd have to call Flannigan. He skimmed through the story over breakfast, which shed no new light on what he already knew. He moved on to other more relevant topics, like the Niners' already faltering new season. Then the phone rang.

He checked the caller I.D. It was Flannigan, speak of the devil. Tom Flannigan was his features editor at *The San Francisco Tribune*.

"Yeah, Tom, I was just going to call you."

"Jureadthithit?" Shouted Flannigan, above the roar of traffic in the background. As usual, the editor was in his car, driving, talking on his cell phone and consuming large quantities of carbohydrates all at the same time. Which he somehow washed down with copious amounts of coffee between expletives. Tom Flannigan was single-handedly doing his best to keep Dunkin Donuts afloat with a waistline to prove it.

"Which shit? I just got up."

"Thithit about theroidths again. I thought that wathall put to reth!" Flannigan splattered.

"Yeah, I know. Listen, if you're calling about my piece I faxed last night, it should be waiting for you when you get to the office."

"Ath good. We need to keep thoth polls on their toeths!"

Once again, something jabbed at the back of Fleming's mind, relating to yesterday. Normally he would have dismissed the whole matter, but for that page two article he'd just read. "Tom, while you're on the phone, did you see the story about the British professor?"

"Whowut?"

"Desmond Lewis. There was supposed to be a big hoodoo at UCB, and he was the guest of honor last night. Except he never showed up."

"Look, that's nice, but I got some acthual fith to fry right now."

"Yeah, I know. I wouldn't have mentioned it, except that he called me en-route, saying he wanted to talk to me."

"You? A profethor?" Flannigan snorted some more donut crumbs. "What for?"

"That's what I want to know. He said it was serious. I told him I'd talk to him when he got here, then he never made it. There was a piece in the *Chronicle* about it."

Flannigan paused at a traffic light to flush his gullet with a splash of coffee. “Listen, Jake. That’s not our kind of story, it’s a little, I don’t know, pedestrian, wouldn’t you say, to take up your valuable time? A professor gone AWOL, for Chrissake. Gimme a break.”

“Yeah, I guess you’re right. If anybody asks, I’ll tell ’em to call Homeland Security.”

“They won’t. Look, I’ll call you when I’ve finished cutting up your weekly doily.”

“Ha ha. Bye, Tom.”

Jake finished his Snickers, refilled his cup, and gazed out through the back window at his garden. The roses were looking good, better than they had since Beverly. . .he shook off the thought. He wasn’t ready to reminisce yet about Beverly. The pain was still too fresh, like an early spring bud, still vulnerable to frost, in whatever form.

Returning to the phone, he dialed ‘011’ followed by an overseas number.

“It’s Jake. There’s been a disappearance.”

“So what else is new? Unless you think it’s related to the Middle East, I don’t—”

“Have you ever heard of a university professor named Desmond Lewis?”

“Why would I?”

Jake knew it was a long shot, but still, there was something more here than met the eye, he was sure of it. “He’s been making waves, I gather.”

There was a pause. “Professor at London U.?”

“That’s the one. I met him a few years back.”

“Man, you know how to pick ’em.”

“Yeah, well he was supposed to be here in Berkeley last night and never showed. I’m wondering if it’s related to those recent kidnappings in the U.K.”

“I doubt that. They don’t usually target English professors. But I’ll check it out.”

“Thanks. He’s kind of an old friend, and I’m wishing now I hadn’t blown him off.”

“I’ll get back to you.”

Jake hung up, went outside, and turned on the sprinklers. The hydrangea was looking a little peaked, he thought. About ten minutes later he was just adjusting the faucet when he heard the phone ring in the kitchen. He hurried inside to answer. The number on caller I.D. was from London.

"Jake here," he answered. "What'd you find?"

"It was supposed to be a big deal, Jake. He's not my cuppa tea, but the man's supposed to be a celebrity in academic circles, and according to my sources he was definitely on the flight. Which means he vanished somewhere between SFO and the Berkeley campus. It's in your court, old boy."

"Shit." Jake had sworn to himself that he'd done his last investigative work years ago when he'd run up against Hezbollah in the Bekaa Valley. Jake had been a freelancer with AP in those days, frequently called upon from overseas, especially by his less-constrained counterpart at Reuters.

"You check for accidents, that sort of thing?" his Reuters colleague inquired, still on the phone.

"Not yet. I will. I just wondered, why'd he call me?"

"Wonks and weirdos are your department, Fleming. Good luck with it." With that he hung up.

The hotel Dr. Lewis had been scheduled to stay at, the Claremont, confirmed that he was a no-show. The room had been paid for in advance for one night, but Lewis had never checked in. Jake called his usual sources at SFPD, EMS, the Berkeley cops, even the Oakland authorities, all of which came up empty. He then called his friend and rival Bill Emory at the *Chronicle*, who had nothing to offer beyond the morning story that had come, it turned out, from the AP. It was as though the man had vanished from the planet.

Chapter Two

His Faults Lie Gently on Him

The thin man was faced with a dilemma. While perhaps not as dire as that of Hamlet, it nonetheless required some unpleasant choices. He would do his part, like any player on the stage. But the task at hand would have been much easier had a new complication not arisen he'd only just learned about through his connections at the university. The problem was that because his prisoner had contacted a certain well-known journalist prior to his arrival, if there was any hint of foul play, the whole situation could backfire. *A little fire is quickly trodden out; which, being suffered, rivers cannot quench!* he knew.

He'd devised a reasonable "suicide" cover for his captive, but it wouldn't hold up for long under careful scrutiny. There was simply insufficient motive for it. Quite to the contrary, Desmond Lewis had been eager to tell the world what he'd found out and publish his book as soon as possible. The book that the thin man now had in his possession.

This would take some thought.

Until now things had gone smoothly. He'd met his surprised former protege at the gate, and assuring him that bygones were bygones and all was well, explained that the university committee had been delayed, but that he himself would escort him to a very special accommodation he knew Lewis would not be able to resist: a floating houseboat on San Francisco Bay. He had seen the whimsical photos on his rival's office wall. Lewis loved houseboats. It was his dream to own one, he had learned, to cruise in retirement along England's numerous canals. And now he would be invited to stay in one. If not quite in the manner he'd expected.

Lewis had been suspicious at first, given their relationship of late, but the thin man had played the gracious host well, won him over, and brought him aboard. And having accepted the invitation, in proper British style Lewis had dutifully joined his host for tea, as expected. Which he had cheerfully sipped, along with an unnoticed dram of the sleeping potion henbane, which was not expected. And now he had become a prisoner instead of a guest and was only beginning to show some awareness of what was to come.

What the thin man still needed to find out, and had not done so, was how Lewis had learned what he claimed to know, and where he had learned it, so that, if possible, those sources themselves could be better dealt with. Clearly, he had gotten access to certain inconvenient information that had never before been uncovered until now. But how? And where? How had this been allowed to happen? The one thing he'd taken upon himself to guard against, the worst possible scenario, could still be averted. But now the headstrong young professor had refused to talk. Why couldn't he understand that any unseemly information jeopardizing *The Name* had to be kept from the public–the wellspring of all things profitable and enduring–at all costs? Didn't Lewis understand that he was simply trying to protect England's most cherished icon from the tremendous cultural and economic damage such disclosures could cause?

Meanwhile, he had other matters to tend to that, if not handled carefully and quickly, might prove equally irksome, as well as perilous. There was no time to lose. He'd managed to destroy the only other copy: that CD at Lewis's office in London, along with the hard drive. But as for the manuscript, he had no choice now but to burn it. And part of him recoiled at such an act. It was a part of history, a part of the whole, and just as the Vatican had preserved heathen gospels never seen, he would rather preserve this artifact along with the others if only for safe keeping, or perhaps posterity. But he couldn't risk it. Not with that journalist out there preparing to stir up even more trouble.

As he parked the rental car and returned to the houseboat, he nodded brusquely to one or two of the other owners of that fabled floating community that dated back to the Sixties, and kept his head low. He had been able to rent the houseboat on short notice because the Sausalito live-aboard community had a tradition of personal freedom. People minded their own business and didn't ask questions. Plus, he'd paid in cash.

One fire burns out another's burning, One pain is lessened by another's anguish, he reminded himself. He opened the gate to the ramp, strode on board the cedar-shingled floating box, and unlocked the entry into the main cabin.

Somewhere in the dark, he heard the muffled sound of cursing coming from the interior. By now he had decided what he would do if this forthcoming confrontation didn't bear fruit. He was fearful that it would not and had taken preparations accordingly. After all, the man had held out now for two days and time was running short.

He stepped into the salon, flipped on the light, and contemplated the bound and gagged scholar slumped half prone, half seated on the sofa, his tweed jacket soiled and crumpled, his eyes glaring in rage and indignation at his unseemly condition.

"Are you hungry?" the thin man asked, as though nothing untoward had occurred. "I have some bangers in the fridge. And perhaps some more tea?"

His captive, eyes wide and now wary, nodded, vigorously.

"If I remove the gag will you promise not to shout?"

More nods. Equal vigor.

The thin man shrugged. "Very well, I doubt if anyone would hear you here anyway, especially in your weakened state and with all that traffic noise out there." Which was another reason for his choice of this location, just east of U.S. 101. He removed the gag, and his prisoner gasped.

"Water!" pleaded Lewis.

The thin man shuffled to the little-used kitchenette to fetch the near-moldy sausages and prepared a cup of tea on the small burner. In keeping with Shakespearean tradition, he took from his jacket a small vial and dropped three drops into the cup, along with the English Breakfast teabag, which quickly absorbed the yellowish liquid. "You know, we've both been through a lot in our day," he said, putting the tea and bangers on a tray. "And as the old sovereign put it, we have *'seen the best of our time: machinations, hollowness, treachery, and all ruinous disorders.'* "

He spoke sorrowfully, as he carried the tray to his prisoner. "I never thought this would come, however, from you." Grudgingly, he extended the cup and allowed his captive a sip before pulling it away. Then, as if relenting, he fed him a bigger sip, and then the bangers with his own fingers, which Lewis quickly wolfed down, followed by the remainder of the tea. The thin man nodded in satisfaction and wiped his hands on a napkin. "Excellent. It is done."

"What? *'And the noble and true-hearted Kent banished! His offense, honesty! 'Tis strange,' "* muttered Lewis, stretching his jaw, and glaring at his captor.

"You see yourself as Kent? I think not. Goneril, more likely. Or York."

"Look, I'm sorry I didn't acknowledge your contributions and all. But where's my book?" demanded Lewis, harshly. "Do you really expect to get away with kidnapping and theft by force?" Then he paled, and gasped in abrupt abdominal pain, suddenly sweating.

The thin man's brows narrowed. "Theft? You dare speak of theft?" He regarded his captive with a frown. Lewis's eyes widened as he felt his throat constricting. "Actually, if you don't mind, I need the names of any persons who share this hypothesis of yours."

Lewis shook his head, defiantly. *" 'Croak not, black angel; I have no food for thee!' "* he gasped again, as another surge of pain seized his midsection.

"It seems that you, my friend, are the one about to 'croak,' " noted his captor.

The thin man leaned forward and studied him thoughtfully as Lewis's face turned blue, and he began to shudder. *" 'Nothing will come of nothing: speak again,' "* he said, reaching for his coat pocket for the vial. "It's Hebenon, a distillation of the bark and leaves of a yew tree. I do have the antidote in here somewhere, if you'll just tell me the name. Let's see, where is it?"

Gasping, his eyes bulging in horror, Lewis gave up a single name, and had to spell it out, each letter a torture in itself.

Damn it to hell, thought the thin man, writing the name down. Another bloody foreigner. What business was it of these outsiders anyway?

Lewis was choking now, unable to breathe. "Surely, after all these years," he gasped.

The older man looked at his dying rival with a strange expression of sorrow in his eyes. "Why did you do this fell thing? Do you hate me that much?" He added, almost apologetically: "Actually, sorry to say old chap, there is no antidote. Unlike the version Romeo got to take."

Lewis stared, his life seeping now swiftly away, and then his eyes went blank, and watched unseeing as his rival and killer arose and began to pace the floor. He could no longer hear, as the soft murmur slowly rose in cadence and intensity. He would have recognized the words, however. Like those spoken earlier, they were from King Lear:

"By the sacred radiance of the sun,
The mysteries of Hecate, and the night;
By all the operation of the orbs
From whom we do exist, and cease to be;
Here I disclaim all my paternal care,
Propinquity and property of blood,
And as a stranger to my heart and me
Hold thee, from this, forever."

And then, like the Jews who beheld the rivers of Babylon, the thin man sat down and wept at what he had lost. He felt no satisfaction for this retribution, only grief. Justice had been rendered, but that was all. And the worst part was that this wasn't over. To the contrary, it was just beginning.

Gathering himself together, he went outside to the rail, vomited over the side, and then turned to fetch the benzene from the dock. It was time to burn the evidence: manuscript, author, and all. *Our remedies oft in ourselves do lie!*

Late that evening, the fire that erupted on the cedar shake tinder box at the end of the pier was so spectacular it was said later that nothing like it had been seen on the Sausolito waterfront for at least forty years. Not since the old floating PCP lab had gone up like a Redstone rocket, some of the older salts insisted.

During the next few hours, the police were quick to pinpoint the cause: arson. A search for the anonymous renter began immediately but with little success. The thin man was long gone by then. As was his victim. Along with the missing manuscript.

Chapter Three

If the Sun Breed Maggots

The Golden Gate Bridge, San Francisco Bay, 4:00 a.m.

Already forced to cope with one emergency and en route to another, a California State Police cruiser was first to spot the rented Lincoln Town Car abandoned in the middle of the Golden Gate Bridge with the doors open and the engine running. There was no sign of a struggle. According to the papers in the glove box, the car had been rented in the name of a Professor Desmond Lewis of London, England.

Jake Fleming took the call from one of his contacts at the Marin County Sheriff's Department, in whose jurisdiction the car had been found. "You were asking about a missing Brit?" Jake recognized the slightly squeaky voice of Deputy Hank Carter, an up-and-coming young African American on the force. "We just found his car."

Jake's errant stomach lurched and gurgled as he sat up. "What car?" A check with the university had confirmed that the professor was being met at the airport, which a call to his office in London also confirmed. Drivers had been arranged for the entire visit, which had been scheduled for just over 24 hours. Desmond Lewis would have had no use for a rented car. "I'll be over as soon as I can," he said, fumbling for a fresh pack of Ultra Cool Mints in his nightstand. "Let me know if it's impounded before I get there."

He headed over the Richmond Bridge, where traffic was usually still light at that hour but was backing up quickly, and he could see the flashing lights on 101 well before reaching the police barricade. There had been a major fire just off 101 in Sausalito, the flames and smoke of which were still visible on the waterfront as he inched past. Southbound traffic was already near gridlock on the Golden Gate, and, when he got to the scene, the tow truck was just hooking up the rental car's bumper.

Deputy Carter waved him over. "Took long enough."

"No shit. Find anything?" asked Jake.

"The trunk contained a small travel bag with several changes of clothes and personal toiletries. That's pretty much it. We'll have forensics go over the car at the impound lot."

Jake thought for a moment. "Any sign of a book or a manuscript of any kind?"

"No sir. Nothing like that. The car was totally clean. Looked like it hadn't been driven at all, hardly. Usually we find ashes, or a candy wrapper, or shoe mud, something. In this case, nada. Zilch."

"Don't you find that strange?"

Carter shrugged. "It's not for me to judge, sir."

"Anybody check the rental agreement for the mileage? Also, the time and day of rental?"

"Not yet. We're working on it."

Jake went to the guard rail and stared out at the fog-bound sea beyond the bay, just visible in the early light. Carter joined him after a moment. "So whaddaya think?" asked the deputy, unwrapping a stick of gum.

"I think it's a set piece. Put here for show. It's way too neat."

Carter shrugged. "Tell that to the Sheriff," he said.

"You tell him for me. Maybe you'll get a promotion."

"Yeah, right."

Jake thanked Carter and walked back to his car, ignoring the expletives of some of the less tolerant backed-up drivers, and the more ominous grumblings of his own stomach, also backed-up. His doctors had warned him years ago of the likelihood of an ulcer if he didn't moderate his work, diet, and lifestyle. He'd had no trouble ignoring the doctors. As for the ulcer that followed in due time, he was doing his best to ignore that as well with a little help from a steady diet of Mylanta and Ultra Cool Mints.

The first light of day was just glimmering to the east, and the early-bird commuters, unaccustomed to such holdups at this hour, were getting increasingly impatient. Jake felt no sympathy for them as he stopped at an all-night pharmacy to stock up on antacids and headed back to the East Bay, noting that the marina fire off to the right was now just smoke and ashes.

The "hot" story in the morning news was the fire in Sausalito with some dramatic video footage of the soaring flames. Aside from arson, the police had no further leads. As the morning went by, the news shows dutifully reported the traffic on the bridge, then the abandoned car. But only the later editions mentioned the vanished professor. No one made any connection between Desmond Lewis and the burned houseboat in Sausalito.

Something about his conversation with Lewis compelled Jake to focus on the missing book. To double-check, he called the SFPD, which confirmed what he had already concluded: no manuscript had been found at the airport, hotel or anywhere else in between. Another call to Lewis' publisher revealed that they too had seen and heard nothing from their unpredictable client. After some prodding, the editor admitted that they had, in fact, been expecting an "explosive" new tome from Desmond Lewis, which had not been received. Interestingly, the young editor he spoke to confided that he'd expressed some doubts as to whether it would even be publishable.

By late morning the Sheriff's Department, in consultation with the San Francisco Police in consultation with Scotland Yard, announced their sad conclusion. Professor Desmond Lewis, of London, England, for reasons unknown, had apparently taken his own life. No body had been recovered, nor a suicide note, but then that was not uncommon with Golden Gate suicides. The currents were powerful in the waters below, and bodies were often swept out to sea never to be seen again. Sometimes people jumped on the spur of the moment due to some crisis or catastrophe in their lives. Such must have been the case with Dr. Lewis, was the official story that made the midday news on both sides of the bay.

Jake Fleming found that conclusion presumptive and unsettling. Which was to say, bullshit. Ignoring the objections of his gastric sector, he finished a hurried lunch of a frozen burrito and a Coke, checked the time, and dialed his London contact again.

"It's me," he said, when the call went through. "Did you find out anything?"

The answer was negative. Apparently, word of Dr. Lewis's disappearance had not made the news back in the UK. He wondered why and said so.

Again, the answer was negative. "Your lad is not really popular here; it's hard to get much cooperation."

"He's not my lad, he's yours," Jake reminded him. "Hasn't anybody spoken with his people there in London? At the university or wherever?"

His counterpart sighed. "Look, I'd like to help you, but there's a situation developing in the West Bank, we've had a lot of layoffs, and I'm not sure about my availability in the next week or so. You'll have to call me back."

"Right. Well thanks for checking. I'll be in touch."

Jake hung up, went online for the hell of it, and Googled Desmond Lewis. 4782 sites came up, varying from mostly hostile reviews of his many books to denunciations of his viewpoints by his many peer critics. There was one overlying theme, he noticed, about the man which he remembered now from their week in Florida: he was a consummate skeptic and iconoclast.

By this time, his interest was piqued. Especially when Flannigan called him back at midafternoon. "Jake, you're gonna love this."

"You got married?" That had been a running gag back in the old days, at the paper. Actually, he'd never even seen the gender-neutral Flannigan so much as go out on a date.

"Don't remind me of my age, Fleming. The car the university sent to meet Lewis at the airport?"

"What about it?"

"Somebody called the office and reported he'd missed his flight. Except funny thing is, he hadn't. So they got there two hours late."

"Really." Jake thought for a moment. "So it was a ruse. Which means someone else met him, maybe? Someone he knew."

"We're working on that. Or the cops are, anyway. They said the caller had an 'English' accent, for whatever that's worth."

It had to be the book, thought Jake. There was something in the book somebody was desperate to suppress. But wouldn't there be at least a backup copy, for safekeeping? Somewhere back in London, presumably? Writers nowadays used computers and flash drives and CD ROMs. Everything was easy to back up. Unless. . .

He didn't want to discuss any of this with Flannigan just yet. Let alone his real reason for taking this sudden new interest. Not until he had more to go on. Still, there was something increasingly unsettling about the whole thing. "I don't buy the suicide story, Tom. The man was about to deliver a bombshell of some kind to his public. Also, his publisher. I smell an abduction. To silence him, or worse." It was the 'worse' part that worried him the most.

"Look, maybe he just despaired at his lack of respect. Maybe his book sucked, and he threw it off the bridge before jumping," Flannigan suggested. "You never know."

"Like I said. I don't buy it. The rental car is all wrong. Now you say somebody must have met him who may have abducted him. So now we have a missing person, and also a missing book. Tom, I need to go to London." I owe Lewis that much, he wanted to add. Instead, he said: "There's something bigger here than meets the eye. I want to find out what it is."

There was a long pause on the other end of the line. Then, as usual Flannigan fumed and fussed and fretted and in the end gave in and authorized the London flat and travel vouchers. "I'm warning you though, Fleming. We are getting squeezed hard upstairs in finance, and you had better come up with something to justify this or it comes out of your pay."

"No problem." If only, thought Jake.

That evening Jake called his daughter to say goodbye—not, he thought, that she'd miss him all that much. But their exchange was courteous, if not warm. "Be careful, Dad," she told him. "There's something creepy about this."

It made him wonder, how cannily she seemed able to read his thoughts. Close or not, she was definitely a chip off Beverly's old block, he thought, wryly. "Why do you think so?"

"I don't know. Just a feeling."

One thing Jake Fleming had learned over the years was never to dismiss a woman for her "feelings." Especially when he sensed she was right. He assured his daughter he would be careful.

Not that he would, of course.

Chapter Four

Against a Sea of Troubles

London, late October:

A chill wind was blowing in out of the north, stirring up eddies of leaves along the pavement. Pulling his collar tighter as he climbed out of his cab in front of the small, tidy boutique apartment hotel on Denmark Street, Jake noted the seemingly random movements and thought about thermodynamics, and that led to reflections on the nature of things. It made for a good distraction from more troubling thoughts.

One reason he loved this great sprawling city was because it was such a passel of contradictions, ancient and modern. Its streets wound irrationally from no place in particular to no place else in particular, perhaps etched into the landscape over centuries by the random wanderings of direction-challenged peddlers and pilgrims. Narrow and cobbled, traversed by absurdly modern expressways. Steampunk railways and riders. The amazing and terrifying Underground. Ancient stone, abutted to modern steel, smells of old urine and bacon grease, industrial outfall and offal, car exhaust, blending with the sharp sweet aromas of hops, and kitchen smoke, West Indian food, and baking bread. Darkened architectural angles hiding long-lost secrets. London, like New York and a few other places, was an amalgam of everything and everyone rather than one surging mass of mostly a single people, like Beijing or New Delhi. It represented ages of history and achievement, of course. And vast power, over the centuries. And money. It was also one of the two great seaports of the Old World, the other being Rotterdam. So, having been here many times before, Jake was accustomed to the extraordinary diversity of its people and offerings, its architecture, the incredible and unremitting level of energy that sizzled beneath the dark clouds like a constant electrical storm. London never ceased to surprise him. And sometimes, as on this occasion, to dismay him.

Meanwhile, he had learned nothing yet of consequence from his regular sources, and was feeling more than a bit puckish, with growing misgivings that something was seriously wrong in regards to his missing acquaintance (did he dare even want to think of Lewis as a friend?). Jake had lost three longtime friends and colleagues in the so-called 'War on Terror' in the past decade, and they had been missed. They'd also not been replaced, due to "budgetary constraints," much to the futile outrage of the editorial department. Fewer and fewer people read newspapers anymore, and that was the way it was. So, he knew his employer's tolerances for his stay in London would be limited, for much the same reason.

As he returned from checking in at the Reuters office in a taxi, Jake discerned something unsettling he'd never noticed before: an almost palpable tension in the atmosphere. Surely it was his imagination, he decided, shrugging it off. He was one of a million foreigners at any given moment in London, foreign correspondent or no. As such, he was usually anonymous and unnoticed. And yet . . . And yet—he glanced around warily at nearby darkened doorways and windows that suddenly felt like they had hidden eyes. With a quick nod to the doorman, he hurried into the building.

The flat was small but expensive, long ago acquired by *The Tribune* for the then-increasingly demanding needs of their once-flourishing staff of traveling foreign correspondents, including Jake Fleming. While clean—even stylish—it had all the personality and charm of a hotel suite, which he supposed in a way was all it was. The furniture was Scandinavian, the kind of bare wood Ikea minimalism that had been trendy in the 80s, still good quality, rarely used. The appliances were basic but adequate, the fridge disconcertingly empty, although the *Tribune* had thoughtfully provided several bottles of white wine, Perrier, and a hard wedge of cheese, perhaps leftover from a previous occupant. On the sideboard there was also a small wine rack with mostly Australian red varietals (was this a donation from the host country, or just a function of the economy?). There was a working telephone, and a very serviceable desktop computer, by means of which he was able to access the Web and get Email. The art on the walls was competent and original but inexpensive, probably selected by a staging decorator rather than a collector. When he'd first used this flat some years earlier, he'd spent a few moments studying it and decided that this unhappy assortment of Caribbean and African prints was destined to remain essentially unseen. Sort of like the tree that falls in the forest, he supposed. The flat was in a great location, though, just off Oxford Street and Charing Cross Road, within walking distance of shopping, Trafalgar Square, the University district, the British Museum, and Westminster, if his feet held out and he developed a sudden yearning to revisit Big Ben or salute Lord Nelson. He wondered how much it was costing his employers, and whether he should be feeling guilty about using it for primarily (he now understood) personal reasons.

Jake tossed his coat on a chair, picked up the house phone and dialed Tom Flannigan's direct contact number, ignoring the nine-hour time difference. It rang seven times with no answer, which meant he was still in the sack, so he dialed his cell number, which was answered with an angry grumble.

"Yeahwhassit?"

"Tom. Any news on Lewis at your end?" asked Jake.

"Lewis who?" Flannigan managed to respond without spitting crumbs, but his reply was still negative. "Oh, that missing college guy?"

"University professor, actually."

"Look, your little personal quest is not real high on my priority list, Fleming, so the answer is no, and I am gonna need to hear some justification for your little escapade and quick, or it's coming out of both our hides. I can't believe I let you go off on this wild goose chase of yours. I must have been outta my mind. You still haven't told me what you expect to find over there, anyway."

"I'll let you know," said Jake, "I'm checking some leads." He disconnected, hoping it was true. He also hoped he'd remembered to pack extra Cool Mints. He was going to need them.

Desmond Lewis had seemed uncharacteristically anxious, even worried, when he'd called. And he'd really wanted Jake to read his now missing book. Why would he suddenly change his plans with no explanation? And even if he had, he wouldn't just disappear like that. The last time something like this had happened to a personal source had been in Beirut. A defector from Hezbollah had called him, offering him a first look at some crucial documents linking the terrorist organization to a recent bombing in Kenya. That man had been found a week later with his head cut off.

The London police had been less than helpful, and he was beginning to wonder if his inquiries were on the wrong side of the globe. But if so, whatever the cause, and whoever had been behind it, Lewis had started out in London. And another factor still troubled him: why had there been no demands, no statements? Most abductions, if this was one, were political and to make a point. But this case, if it was such a case, was chilling in its silence. And what would motivate anyone to abduct a literary scholar, who specialized in Elizabethan obscurities? Could it be personal? He realized then that he actually knew very little about Lewis's personal life other than what he'd shared in Florida. Even so, Jake decided he could wait no longer. If his friend had been taken and there was a chance he was still alive, every hour could be crucial. He owed him that much.

Still, cautioning himself not to jump too soon to conclusions, Jake's first order of business was to talk to his now missing friend's secretary, for Lewis most certainly had one, and interview his colleagues at London University to try and find out what they might know about his sudden disappearance. Maybe he was overreacting after all, and it was just a last-minute change of plans, a misunderstanding or miscommunication after all that could quickly be cleared up. He hoped so. But he'd seen situations like this before, and they had never turned out well.

And what was he doing here in London, in October for Chrissake, when the fog sticks to your skin and penetrates to your bones? Could it be he was trying to escape more meaningful engagement back home in Berkeley? Such as making amends with his distant and detached daughter? Or was he simply hoping to avoid taking on yet another assignment somewhere he was notably unwelcome, to report on news of a religious war that was centuries old by now? And yet just now, for reasons he could not yet comprehend, he was feeling notably unwelcome in London, even now.

Not that anyone had been openly impolite or hostile. This was Great Britain, after all, where cheerful euphemism, compulsive denial and jaw-clenched courtesies were deeply ingrained.

He checked his watch. It was late morning Greenwich time, and dawn back home. Fighting off a feeling of growing apprehension, he bolstered himself with two cups of black java and a fistful of Cool Mints and set out on foot for the London University center.

Desmond Lewis's university office was in a nondescript gray stone building just off Tottenham Court Road. It was at the end of a long, presently empty hallway, and his name was prominently displayed in brass letters on the door. Jake hesitated a moment, glanced around, and tried the handle. To his surprise, it swung open. As he peered cautiously into the room, the woman sitting at the desk glanced up, startled and possibly even a bit frightened to see him. Or perhaps anyone. The secretary, he supposed, giving her a discreet once-over. She was in her mid-forties, somewhat obese, and had a round pink face adorned with turtle-shell glasses. Her name was on a brass wedge on the desktop: Gloria Peckham. He was surprised. Somehow he'd expected that a youthful semi-celebrity like Lewis would keep a hot young babe on hand, if only for image purposes. So much for assumptions.

"Sorry to bother you. Are you Dr. Lewis's secretary?"

"I'm his assistant," she replied, curtly. "May I help you?"

He stepped into the office and handed her his card. "My name is Jake Fleming. I'm a reporter from *The San Francisco Tribune* and a friend of his." He glanced around. "Do you have a moment?"

She looked alarmed. "I suppose so. I remember he mentioned you. Is there trouble?"

"I don't know. He called me two days ago in Berkeley saying he was on his way there for a lecture and asked me to review a new book of his. But he never showed. I've checked his cell and home numbers and there's no answer. I was hoping you might've heard from him."

Gloria looked at him, bewildered. "He never got to San Francisco? Surely there must be some mistake."

He decided the edited version would be best, for now. "Well, he arrived there, according to the airline. But never checked into his hotel, and no one has seen him since."

Her jaw dropped open in a moment of perhaps rare candor, then closed up quickly again. "I haven't heard from him since Friday," she sniffed. "He should have been back by now. I was wondering where he was, this morning. Have you contacted the university in California?"

"I have. The University of California hasn't heard from him either."

"Oh dear. This isn't good. This isn't good at all, is it?"

The outer office was amply furnished in heavy dark oak, and neatly kept. A heavy oaken connecting door, probably to Lewis' private inner sanctum, dominated the wall opposite a long row of book cases and file cabinets behind her prim secretarial desk. "Can you tell me what his book was about? It was something controversial, I gather, although I guess that goes without saying."

Her brow knitted as she glanced towards the inner door. "He has been working on his book for several years. He's been very secretive about it. When I left Friday, he was still making last-minute corrections. That's all I can tell you."

"But you know what it was about, right?"

She looked away. "Sorry, but that's highly confidential, sir. Like I said, he was keeping it very much under wraps, even from the department, and since you evidently have spoken with him since I have, far be it from me to disclose confidentialities." She sniffed.

"But by asking me to read it, it seems rather likely he wanted me to know the content," he pointed out.

She shrugged. "Perhaps so, but I'm afraid he will have to confirm that for himself, Mr., er," she glanced at his card, "Fleming. I'll be happy to tell him you called when I hear from him."

If you hear from him, he thought but didn't say.

As Jake left the office, he gave a quick glance back, sensing a lot had gone unspoken, in true British fashion. Sure enough, he caught her off guard, staring after him with what could only be a look of sheer terror. She hid it quickly, with a game attempt at a smile and parting wave. He wondered what she was afraid of. Surely not him?

He had no better luck with anyone else he could find who had any sort of connection to the missing professor. Was Desmond Lewis some sort of cipher? And yet he'd befriended the man and knew him to be real. Very real and very human, with an irreverent sense of humor, a penchant for seafood, and an aversion to righteous punditry. They'd actually had a great time together that week in Florida. Even apart from the rescue. Lewis had even rented a houseboat at the hotel marina as an alternative to more conventional accommodations, because, he'd cheerfully confided, "I always wanted to live on one of these."

"Like that detective character, Travis McGee?" Jake had suggested.

"Who?" had been Lewis's innocent response. "Slumming," Des had called it, with his infectious grin. Which reminded Jake of that houseboat fire in Sausalito, that same night of Lewis's disappearance. Something was definitely amiss. He made a note to call his contacts back home first thing in the morning.

Jake's phone rang the next morning just as he was stirring a spoonful of fake creamer into his customary instant coffee. The voice was thin and frightened. "Mr. Lewis? This is Gloria Peckham. Dr. Lewis's assistant?"

"Yes, Gloria. Have you heard from him?"

"No sir. But something has happened."

"What is it?"

Her voice trembled, and she could barely speak. "Please, just—can you come over to the office, right away?"

"OK. Hang tight. I'll be right there."

Gloria met him at the hallway door, her eyes red and face strained. "Come in, quickly," she pleaded, with a furtive glance around.

He entered and surveyed the room, quickly. Nothing seemed out of the ordinary. "What is it?"

"In here." She closed the hallway entry, bolted it shut, then crossed the room to the inner office connecting door, and opened it cautiously.

The room was dark. Reaching around the door jamb, she groped for the light switch and flipped it on. Jake glanced into the room and felt sick. The entire once-elegant oak paneled inner office looked like it had been run through a shredding machine. The last time he'd seen so much destruction had been at a refinery installation in Libya during the rebellion, when Khadaffi's loyalists had executed their own version of Guernica. He didn't like to think about it. At least, for the moment, here in the inner office there was no sign of blood.

Gloria, doubtless unaccustomed to such violence so close at hand, put her own trembling hand on her ample breast and leaned against the door jamb to steady herself. Books were torn from the shelves, the mahogany file cabinet ripped open and the files strewn about, the desk drawers yanked out and unceremoniously dumped onto the green Afghan carpet. An older model desktop computer lay on the floor, its housing pried open, the hard drive gone. CDs were scattered about in pieces, carefully and thoroughly smashed. It was immediately clear to Jake that if there was something here Desmond Lewis had been keeping under wraps, it was long gone now.

On the other hand, sometimes even professionals missed something. And this looked like the work of a madman. He turned and looked at her questioningly. "Have you called the police?"

She shook her head. "Only you. Sh-should I call them now, then?"

"Listen, Ms. Peckham, there's a good chance whoever did this is responsible for Dr. Lewis's disappearance. Would it be all right with you if I looked through this mess first? Maybe there's something they overlooked, or a clue to who or what we're dealing with. Once the police are involved, the first thing they are going to do is rake you over the coals, and the second thing they're going to do is seal off the entire office, which puts you in the street."

She hesitated, then nodded, doubtfully. "He's a good man, you know. No one understands what he is trying to do. But his colleagues all treat him like an outcast, just because he takes the road less traveled, perhaps."

"Road to where?"

She ignored the question. "They're all hypocrites, if you ask me," she sniffed. "Isn't a university supposed to be a place for the discovery of new knowledge? Yet it's like they all have something to protect."

Which reminded him of Lewis's own cryptic comment over the telephone. "The Ayatollahs of Academe," he murmured, glancing around once more, as if in hope of some ready explanation for all this if he could just see it.

"What did you say?" asked Gloria, giving him a strange look.

"Nothing, just thinking out loud." And, he thought, ungenerously, if it was Gloria's job to protect Desmond Lewis's interests, she had seriously failed.

Gloria looked like she needed to sit down, so he cleared some space on the nearest slashed leather armchair and she poured into it like spilled Jello. Fortifying himself with a couple of Cool Mints, he began with the strewn files, looking for an overlooked SD card, flash drive or CD, stray papers or even scraps of paper with writing–anything. He sorted the papers by topic according to their folders, checked the empty cabinets, rummaged through the clutter of keys, pens, pencils, odd coins, staple remover, scotch tape holder, white-out, obsolete pen cartridges–in short all the junk on the floor, careful not to disturb the crime scene any more than necessary.

With great care, while at the same time trying to keep Ms. Peckham distracted and at bay, he pored through the remainders of the no-longer-complete works of Desmond Lewis, searching for something–anything, that might indicate what he might have been up to, what he'd found, what he was writing. Even the paintings had been removed from the walls—good Renaissance prints—and smashed, along with his diplomas, which, as Jake glanced through them, included an undergraduate degree from Cambridge and a Masters and PhD from Oxford. Most of his published books–the bulk of the materials in the room–were esoteric: studies with titles like *The Muddled History of Blank Verse*, or *Sir Walter Raleigh and the School of Night*. What the hell was that? He could find nothing that might offer a clue as to the man's recent activities or interests, apart from routine curriculum materials.

That, and something Jake had almost missed: a framed photograph by the door, of the houseboat Des had so happily rented in St. Petersburg, Florida. And there they were—the two of them—seated on deck, waving cocktail glasses at the hotel photographer.

Jake told Gloria to wait a moment and made a call to San Francisco, reverse charges.

"Tom? Check out that houseboat fire in Sausalito, last week. There may be a connection."

"Connecthun to what?" came the glib reply.

"To the disappearance of Professor Desmond Lewis. He may have been on that barge."

He hung up. It was nearly noon.

"OK, so chances are whoever broke in here was after the book. Do you know if there are any other copies around? I'm sure he must have made more than one copy, in addition to computer backups."

"Only the one he left with me. But it's gone, too. I looked for it first thing this morning when I—when I—" she sniffled and couldn't finish her sentence. "I'm sorry," she sniffled, and wiped away a tear with a well-used handkerchief. "You're not the first to ask about that book, you know."

He looked at her sharply. "Oh? Who else has asked?"

She frowned, trying to remember. "It was last week. An older man. I told him to go away. It was a day or two before Dr. Lewis called you, I think."

"I see. He didn't leave his name?"

"He wouldn't say. He left and good riddance, if you ask me. He made me nervous."

"Can you describe him?"

She frowned. "He was kind of mousy. Thinnish, late fifties or sixties, graying hair. Average looking, but for his eyes. There was something odd about him, I'd say, although he spoke well, so I'd guess he was probably a scholarly type. He acted like he knew Dr. Lewis pretty well, but I'd never seen him before. He asked about that picture, now that you mentioned it."

"Gloria," Jake said, finally. "Not to state the obvious, but do you have access to Dr. Lewis's residence?"

Her mouth fell open. "Oh, sir, I couldn't do that."

"So you do have a key, and the address?"

"Yes, but that's private, sir."

"Don't you think it's possible that whoever did this and waylaid him last Friday in California may have already destroyed what might be left of his privacy?"

She gasped, plainly distressed. Finally, she agreed to let him into Dr. Lewis's flat, provided he swore he would tell no one. "But we must wait until dark," she insisted. "I could lose my job, you know."

He didn't have the heart to tell her that had probably already happened, and she just didn't know it yet.

Nor was she ready to disclose the subject matter of his missing book.

Chapter Five

Ask Your Heart What It Doth Know

London, late October, six p.m.

Darkness was closing in when Jake Fleming and Gloria Peckham set out from the university center. Desmond Lewis' home was close by the campus on Bedford Square, in a sturdy four-story brick town house dating from Dickens' time. Looking absurdly furtive, Gloria fumbled with her set of keys to open the outer door and led the way up the stairs to the second floor. With a quick glance back to confirm that there was no one in cloaks lurking about brandishing daggers, she unlocked the flat and pushed the door slowly open. The interior was dark, musty, and silent.

Gloria switched on the light and gasped. The flat, like the office, had been savagely torn apart, as if mere rampant destruction was nowhere near savage enough to satisfy whoever (or whatever, Jake couldn't help thinking) had done this. Letting forth a low moan, she seemed too overcome to do anything beyond collapse into the nearest ripped up formerly leather-upholstered arm chair. After checking to make sure the perpetrator, or perpetrators had left the premises, Jake popped a mint and grimly surveyed the damage. It would take a team of experts days to sort through the mess and determine what was missing, if anything.

Gloria shuddered, and fought back tears. "What is happening here? What does all this mean?"

"I wish I knew. But I have to think it has something to do with that mysterious missing book of his."

Unlike the campus office, there were no papers on the floor or other debris. "What about a computer?" he asked, noting there was none present. "Maybe he had one here at home. A laptop, or notebook?"

"He always had it with him," she said, now plainly frightened.

With as much care as he could muster, Jake fought off a sense of hopelessness at the task, and proceeded to sort through the wreckage, waving off her insistence that she help. She'd just make things worse by undervaluing or missing something crucial, in her state.

He thought of something else. "What about email? Does he use email?"

"Probably. But I don't know his screen name or password."

He seemed to recall that Lewis was unmarried. "What about friends or family? There must be someone he's close to."

"Not that I know of. He was rather a loner. Elderly parents in Cambridge is all, but he never spoke to them. No sisters or brothers I know of."

"How about a girlfriend?" He felt reasonably certain Lewis wasn't gay, although life was full of surprises. "Was he seeing anyone?" He wondered if Gloria Peckham had aspirations in that regard, perhaps a would-be latter day Jane Eyre. Or Austen. She blushed and shook her head.

"I know nothing about his private life, sir," she said, simply. "But I never saw anyone here when I came by, which was perhaps once or twice a week. Usually to deliver something from the office, and sometimes pick up his dry cleaning." She made a face and snapped her fingers. "That reminds me. I promised I'd pick up his suits. I should do it before he gets back."

Jake didn't know what to say. That she needn't bother? He couldn't be certain of that, or of anything else relating to this situation. "If you think of something else, call me. Anything at all, even if it seems inconsequential. Sometimes the smallest details can be hugely important, when it comes to finding a missing person. Or finding out what happened to them. Do you understand?"

She nodded, tearfully.

"And if anyone bothers you, or in any way frightens you, call the police. In fact, you'd better go ahead and call them now, they're going to find out sooner or later."

Much to Jake's surprise, she called him two hours later. "Mr. Fleming? This is Gloria Peckham, from Dr. Lewis's office?"

"Yes, Gloria. Are you OK?"

"I'm all right, but I've been thinking about what you said. About how any information that might lead to Dr. Lewis's whereabouts could be significant?"

"Yes? What is it?"

"Well, there is one thing. I found something. Or rather the cleaners did. He left a small notebook in the pocket of one of his suits. He often forgets things, even left his passport one time, so I've had to alert the cleaners to be on the lookout, you see."

"So what's in this notebook? Any names, addresses, anything like that?"

"Well, I don't normally feel it's my business to be snooping into my employer's personal affairs, Mr. Fleming, but since the police have sealed the office just like you predicted, I thought I should have a look, just in case."

"And?"

"Well, it is a bit odd. There are only a few little entries on the first page. Sort of a list, I think. The rest of it is blank."

"Can you read it to me?" He reached for a pen and his notepad from the kitchen desktop.

"The first one is 'Ox.' Underlined three times."

"Did he underline anything else?"

"No, sir."

"That could be significant." He jotted that down " 'Ox.' Is it capitalized?"

"All of them are capitalized, but that was Dr. Lewis's style."

He pondered that. "Are there still oxen in England?"

"I wouldn't know, sir. I seldom visit the countryside."

He sighed. "OK. What else?"

The next is 'Lamb'."

"As in roast?"

"Or Mary had a little."

He jotted it down. "Go on."

"Then 'Herb.'

"This is starting to sound like a recipe. Or a menu."

"I wouldn't know, sir. Then 'Crow.'

"Crow." He wrote it down and circled it. "Not so tasty in a recipe. Any idea what that might mean?"

"It's similar to a raven, I think."

That he knew. "Right, but does it have any special significance to him, do you know?"

"Sorry. I really can't say."

He sighed. "Anything else?"

"Yes. The next entry is 'MT.' No periods."

He wracked his brain. "MT? I assume those are initials?"

"I don't know. Could be, I suppose."

"Yeah. It could also be 'motor transport' or 'multi-task' for all we know," he fretted. "Can you think of anyone he knew or had an interest in with those initials?"

She sniffed and thought for a moment. "Well, there's always Margaret Thatcher, I suppose. But he hardly knew her."

"Margaret Thatcher?" he wrote that down. Could Lewis have stumbled across some kind of political scandal or controversy that might have gotten him into trouble?

He sighed. "Okay. What else?"

"Three more letters: 'LWT'."

He jotted it down. "That could be anything or anyone. A name, a corporation, an abbreviation? How about a location?" He made a note to check stock abbreviations and also airport letter codes. It sounded familiar. LWT?

"I really can't say, sir."

"Can't or won't?" She didn't respond. "OK, sorry, forget it. Anything more?"

"Looks like a foreign name, or word of some kind. 'Hoff.' "

"Hoff'?"

"Yes. Maybe another abbreviation?"

He thought a moment. "Like for Hoffbrau?"

"Pardon?"

It's a German beer. Never mind."

"Dr. Lewis didn't drink much beer, I think. He preferred hard liquors and wine."

Actually, Jake remembered this, from their Florida adventure together. "OK, go on."

"Next is 'Inq.' " She spelled it.

" 'Inq.' Not 'Ink' or 'Inc.'?"

"Correct."

"And that sets off no messages, signals, or alarms in your head either?" By this time, he was feeling more than a little frustrated with her obtuseness, but she didn't seem to notice.

"Nothing that comes to mind."

"Is that it?"

"No, there's more. Two more letters: 'V.A.' With periods."

"V.A.? Was he a veteran, do you know?"

"I don't think so."

He wrote it down. "Anything else?"

"One more entry. A strange-looking word or term. 'A-p-o-c.' "

"Hmm. Another abbreviation, maybe. Again, this doesn't ring a bell?"

"Sorry. Some kind of tree, perhaps?"

"You're thinking of Kapoc." A Florida tree, come to think of it. "So, nothing else?"

"That's all."

"And you have no clue what any of this means?" He found her incorrigible loyalty touching, actually, and gave Lewis extra credit for having chosen her over a countless labor pool of more decorative women willing to assist him.

"I'm afraid I can't say, sir. Sorry. As you say, 'Herb' and 'Lamb' certainly go together. Also 'ox,' maybe. You know, that Indian oxtail soup dish. If you enjoy that sort of thing."

Jake didn't doubt that Desmond Lewis enjoyed food, but he wouldn't eat crow. Not even in the proverbial sense. "Right. Was there anything else you can think of that might be useful?"

She hesitated once more. "Well, there was a business card."

That caught his attention. "Where?"

"Tucked inside the back cover. He always gets cards from people, then they end up in a pile somewhere, or thrown out, so I didn't give it much thought."

"Do you have it there?"

"Yes, but I don't think—"

"Could you just read what's on the card, please?"

She muttered something sounding faintly like a complaint, then fumbled a moment. "Very well, here it is. It's a colleague of his, I assume. It has the University logo and a name. But he's from the Physics Department. Why would Dr. Lewis know someone from the Physics Department?"

"Beats me. Maybe they both like Hoffbrau." She didn't laugh. He waited. "Could you give me the name, please?" he said, finally.

She cleared her throat. "It looks foreign. I think it's that man who comes to his office sometimes. I do hope Dr. Lewis hasn't gotten himself in hot water. Oh, dear me."

He held back his irritation. Weren't disappearing and having his home and office ransacked hot water enough? "What man?"

"The foreign one. He frightens me, I'm sure he's from one of those terrorist countries in Africa or Asia somewhere. The Middle East. And a physicist?"

Was Gloria implying that Lewis might have fallen prey to Middle Eastern terrorists? Could that have something to do with his book? It might explain why he'd choose Jake, instead of an academic writer to review it, he thought, worriedly. But it just didn't seem likely. It was too far from his field of interest or expertise. On the other hand, people often stumbled into or became involved with nefarious doings they never planned for. "All right, just spell it, and give me the contact information, could you please? And I'll check him out."

With what was now evidently characteristic reluctance, she read out the name: "First name is S-u-n-i-r. I wouldn't presume as to how to pronounce that. The second name is 'B-a-l-s-a-v-a-r. PhD.' I might venture a guess as to say it's pronounced—"

"That's all right, thank you. Just give me the contact information."

"It's just an office here on campus, in another building, and the phone number." She read him the address and number, once more with grudging reluctance.

"Anything else?"

"I can't think of anything. I only hope I'm doing the right thing giving you this information."

"I'm confident Dr. Lewis would agree you did the right thing, Gloria. Take care of yourself."

"Please, sir," she begged him, before ringing off. "If you find him, just don't tell him I looked in his notebook."

Jake promised he wouldn't. It was the least he could do.

After a quick dinner of woefully greasy fish and chips on Tottenham Court Road, Jake hurried back to the flat on Denmark Street, determined to disregard the growing unrest in his mind, not to mention his mid-section. He popped down the last of his Cool Mints, and made a mental note to track down some more. The weather had turned typically dismal, and a cold, steady drizzle had begun to fall. As he crossed the wide road and turned down a narrow byway towards Denmark Street, he glanced back and noticed, in the glare of a passing taxi's headlights, a large man in a raincoat keeping pace with him, hunched over against the rain. Something about the man's bearing and demeanor triggered an instinctive alarm, and a warning jolt surged down his spine. Hurrying his pace, he glanced back as he cut through another side street, and sure enough, the man was still there, a block or so behind him.

OK, he thought. So I'm being followed. It wouldn't be the first time. He hesitated, wondering whether he was just being paranoid. After all, he was not dealing with religion or espionage, was he? There were always people on the streets of London. And some of them were bound to be looking his way or going his way. But he'd also spent enough time on assignment in Beirut, in Baghdad and Kabul to know that being followed was no laughing matter. Denmark Street was just a block away now, so he hurried his pace for the remaining hundred meters to his building, and this time was gratified to see the stocky, forty-something doorman waiting for him, holding the door.

Once inside the lobby, he turned and quickly scanned the street in the direction he'd come from. He could see nothing but the lights of a passing taxi. If anyone was out there, they were well hidden in the darkness.

Again feeling unsettled, he took the elevator up to his flat, let himself in, and switched on the lights. Hanging up his coat, he hurried to the computer and logged on. Then he took out the list he'd gotten from Gloria, the list of Desmond Lewis, and placed it carefully on the table before him, along with a glass of Austrian red he'd found in a cupboard and his last bottle of Mylanta. Something on this list might hold the key to what had happened to the man, he knew.

But what? Or who? The entries were eclectic, if mostly unremarkable in themselves:

Ox
Lamb
Herb
Crow
M T
LWT
Hoff
Inq
V.A.
Apoc

Ten abbreviations. Or words. Or initials. Or phrases. What did they have in common apart from the mind of the man who'd written them down?

Starting with the first entry, he pondered 'Ox' for a while. It could be a stand-alone word for a beast of burden still in common use in Asia. Certainly, seldom seen in the West anymore. Could there be a connection between an Asian ox and the Asian physicist? He shook his head in dismay and moved on.

'Lamb.' Obviously, a common meat dish. Or farm animal. Or term of endearment. The kind of term he never could bring himself to call his daughter, for instance? Or Beverly? But this had nothing to do with Desmond Lewis, and he forced himself back to his task, momentarily shaken by the distraction. It was clear he was not yet over the loss of his wife. As for 'Herb,' since all the terms on the list had been capitalized, it could be a plant, or a person. No way of knowing without more information. On a hunch, he focused on the next entry, 'Crow.' Whether it was because 'crow' seemed out of place among the prior food-related entries or triggered some darker image in the back of his mind, his reporter's instincts told him this was the key.

Running a search for 'crow' on Google, thousands of hits came up, ranging from Edgar Allen Poe websites to movie lists. Dutifully he followed the links one by one, looking for some kind of indication as to what an English professor might be after. But the Middle Eastern inference threw a new ominous shadow over everything. Was crow a metaphor, or a code name for something? Or someone? What had Lewis gotten himself into?

To narrow his search, he eliminated ornithology and film subjects or titles. As he continued to check the sites, he noticed a name that came up more than once: Robert Greene. OK, he thought. Running an advanced search on the name, he felt he was onto something. Robert Greene, he learned, was an Elizabethan poet who'd written a number of plays, and an infamous pamphlet called *A Groatsworth of Wit*. This would certainly be on Professor Lewis's home ground. He was too tired to read on and made a note to check into that further in the morning. Then, signing off, he located Gloria Peckham's number, which he'd managed to squeeze out of her, and punched the keys, unmindful of the fact that it was almost eleven.

"Sorry to bother you, Gloria. Does the name Robert Greene mean anything to you?"

After registering her litany of complaints about the time, her health, the weather, Lewis's absence and Jake Fleming's existence, she grudgingly admitted one thing. "I do know he has been doing a lot of reading of Robert Greene's essays."

"Why? For his book?"

"I really can't say, sir." He had to admire her continuing fidelity to her cause as Keeper of the Flame, seemingly still unaware that it had been extinguished some time ago and the Saxons had already come and sacked the city and gone, leaving her still standing alone, and breathless.

"Do you remember any essay in particular? *A Groatsworth of Wit*, for example?"

"No, I don't think so. Though now you mention it, there was something though, about a crow."

"A crow? As in the fourth item on the list?" If she'd developed a sense of irony since their last conversation, it wasn't yet evident.

"Quite right. Now that you mention it. I think he was very disturbed about some sort of business involving a 'crow.' "

"Do you think that could be connected with this Dr. Balsavar in some way?"

"Who?"

"The Middle Eastern or Asian professor. The one whose card you found, the one you say was visiting his office on occasion?"

"Oh. Him." He sensed her frown over the phone. "More than just 'on occasion,' I should say. But being a foreigner and all, I never spoke to him."

"I see. Did you presume, perhaps, that he didn't speak English?" Changing the subject away from her provincial shortcomings, he went on: "Didn't you say you picked up books for Professor Lewis on occasion?"

"I did."

"Can you tell me the name of the bookstore he frequented?"

She hesitated. "Well, his favorite was one of the old used bookstores on Charing Cross Road." She couldn't remember the address, but knew the name: Henry Blodgett, Bookseller. Jake noted that she'd also referred to Desmond Lewis, for the first time, in the past tense. Why would she do that? Did she now believe he was dead? Or was her unwavering loyalty now bending under the strain of so much mayhem at her very feet?

The next morning, while waiting for the shops to open in Charing Cross, Jake tried the phone number for the physicist on the card, Sunir Balsavar. A man answered in brusque, sharp tones.

"Yes, what is it you're wanting?" From his accent he was South Asian; either Indian or Pakistani.

"Is this Dr. Sunir Balsavar?"

"Who is this calling?" Jake noted what could be an undertone of fear in his voice.

"My name is Jake Fleming. I'm a reporter from *The San Francisco Tribune*, in the States."

"What do you want? I'm very busy, you know?" To Jake he sounded audibly afraid.

"I was wondering if I could speak to you about a colleague of yours at the university, Professor Desmond Lewis? Do you know him?"

There was a distinct pause. "Why are you asking?"

"Well, he seems to have disappeared, and I was hoping you might know something about his whereabouts."

There came an audible gasp over the line. "Sorry. I have nothing to say to you," he said, and hung up.

Chapter Six

What's Yours is Mine

London, Late October
Mid-morning

The bookstore was in an old townhouse on lower Charing Cross Road, just north of St. Martin-in-the-Fields. Cloth and leather bound volumes were stacked to the high ceilings on all sides, as well as in the middle aisles. It appeared to Jake as old as London itself as he entered and looked around. The well-traveled-looking bookseller didn't appear much younger: bald, paunchy, with a wicked twinkle in his bespectacled eye that intimated vast stores of secret and highly amusing knowledge.

"Excuse me. I understand you have a London University professor name of Desmond Lewis as a regular customer," said Jake, for openers.

"Yes, of course. Professor Lewis. One of my best customers. And you are?" The gentleman had a Scottish accent, perhaps Edinburgh, and Jake liked him at once.

"I'm a journalist, actually. Also, a friend of his."

The man's bushy Scottish eyebrows lifted, which took some effort. "I see. A member of the Fourth Estate, you say?"

"The name's Fleming. Jake Fleming. *San Francisco Tribune*." Jake took out his notepad, flipped it open, and removed his card, first crossing out the Berkeley phone number and writing in the London one before handing it to the bookseller.

"Ah. The Golden Gate. Jack London, Bret Harte, Dashiel Hammett, and all that. Welcome to London," the clerk said, putting the card in a drawer. "I'm Blodgett. So how can I be of assistance?"

Jake glanced down at his notepad, wondering whether to show him the list. He decided to hold off, for now. One of his own shortcomings, one which had cost him dearly in the fading eyes of Beverly, and the very alert eyes of Melissa too, he had to admit, was a lack of trust in his fellow man. Or woman. "To be honest, I'm trying to locate him. He never showed up for a lecture he was scheduled to give last Friday in California, and I'm worried something may have happened. Has he been in your store in the last few days, by any chance?"

Blodgett hoisted his weighty white eyebrows once again. "No sir. Why do you ask?"

Jake took in the proprietor, then his environs, and sensed he wouldn't get very far without establishing some sort of a rapport beyond interviewer-interviewee. He picked up the nearest book—a tattered Thomas Hardy, as it happened—and leafed through a few pages with a frown. Victorian literature had never been his cup of coffee, but he had a gnawing sense that he was entering unknown territory in which he should leave no page unturned, so to speak. He glanced back up at the bookseller.

"Did Professor Lewis have any particular field of study he was pursuing that you know of?"

The bookseller snorted. "He's a professor. And a writer. They are always chasing literary ghosts and demons and what not of one sort or another, down through the annals of history and all. He was no different. Well, I take it back, he was a bit different, I suppose. But then," he reflected, "who isn't?"

"How do you mean?"

The bookseller looked at him and blinked. "Well, it's hardly for me to divulge, sir, given that he is an old customer and wanted to keep it close to the vest, shall we say? But then, he isn't the first."

"First what?"

"First to question a certain authority, shall we say?"

"I see." Jake enjoyed word games about as much as the next investigator, but he did like this feisty old curmudgeon, so he played along. He turned another page of Hardy's *Jude the Obscure*. "Can I ask which authority we're talking about here?"

"No sir, until I'm told otherwise by my very good patron Dr. Lewis, I'm afraid that's off the table, as it were."

Jake nodded. "I see. Well, there are authorities and there are Authorities. Did you ever hear him use the term 'Ayatollahs of Academe?' "

Blodgett's eyes lit up at once, then the heavy blinds came down once more. "In respect to what, exactly?" he asked, but Jake could tell he'd struck a nerve.

"I don't know. I was hoping you could tell me," he said, with a shrug. Then, having been distracted by some of Hardy's more ponderous descriptions, he realized with admiration that the bookseller was studying his notepad where it lay on the counter, and on which he'd written 'crow,' then in large letters: 'Robert Greene???' Apparently, Blodgett had the ability, which he himself had cultivated with a certain degree of pride, of reading upside down. He reached to close it, but Blodgett stayed his hand, and glanced around the shop with a conspiratorial look. "So you know about the crow, then?"

Jake felt like the farmer contemplating his open barn door while the horse canters gleefully over the horizon. "Not actually. But I gather Dr. Lewis was researching an Elizabethan writer by the name of Robert Greene. Is that a fair assumption?" And if so, why, he wanted to ask, but didn't, might such an interest be possibly fatal?

"Very good, sir, very good. You are clearly a man of discernment." Blodgett tapped the open page of Jake's notepad, which Jake saw no point in closing now. "This chap Robert Greene was the one who first challenged that Authority I mentioned. Very disgruntled, that one." As he spoke, the old man skillfully maneuvered his ladder to a particularly perilous section of the high wall of books and began to climb, to Jake's growing dismay. "—Ah, here it is." He reached out a full arm's length and then some, teetered precariously on his ladder, and somehow managed to acquire, then secure, an ancient, dusty leather-bound volume. In triumph, he started back down, while Jake held his breath, powerless, watching with the fascination of someone waiting for an inevitable disaster to happen.

"Here we are. Robert Greene," Blodgett announced, alighting safely on the floor once more, to Jake's considerable relief. "You do know the scholars cite him as proof their man was the author," he said. "Apparently they haven't read his invective very carefully."

"Author of what?" Jake was feeling thoroughly mystified.

The clerk slid the book across the counter. Jake recognized the title immediately:

A Groatsworth of Wit, and Other Essays by Robert Greene. A chord sounded in the back of his mind–something Desmond Lewis had said to him, that night they'd met at the Poynter Institute in Florida two years before. He wished he could remember what it was. It had been late in the evening, and they'd gone through quite a bit of the hotel's best Chardonnay by then.

"It's right in there, in *Groatsworth.*" The aged clerk lowered his voice and his gaze meandered toward something unseen and impossibly distant: "You are familiar with the parable of The Jackdaw and the Birds? I'm sure you read Aesop as a schoolboy."

"I think so. What about it?"

"The jackdaw is a crow, you know. This chap Greene knew all about the entity in question."

The alarm in the back of Jake's head grew louder. " 'The entity in question'? What the hell is that?"

"That, sir, is the rub. I am sworn to secrecy, to put it to you straight, as it were." Blodgett lowered his voice. "But I'll divulge to you this much. That book you are holding there contains extraordinary and explosive material about a certain beloved countryman, including the only written description of actual personal contact with said entity by anyone in his lifetime. That book, if one were to study it carefully, could blow the casket lid off one of our foremost national treasures. Put that in your tea and stir it."

Jake frowned, deep in thought. Where was this going? "OK, I'll bite. How much?" he asked, tapping the book.

The clerk looked pained. "As I told the professor, Greene is not for sale, sir. This is a Routledge, Warne and Routledge first edition from 1861."

Jake nodded. "Look, a dime-store reprint would do. Can I just read it here?"

The clerk shook his head in alarm. "Oh no, sir. The pages are fragile, and I'm afraid they might be damaged, no offense." He scratched his head. "I did used to have a reprint in the back somewhere, but I haven't had time to find it." He thought for a moment. "If I were you, I'd try the British Library."

"The British Library. Right. Thanks." Jake jotted a note. He could have thought of that himself.

"Pride of the Mother Tongue. Home of the Gutenberg Bible, the Magna Carta, and the beloved First Folio. Plus an odd assortment of every single book, map, publication and pamphlet ever published in the U.K. Or at least those that weren't burned baking pies."

Jake bit. "Pies?"

"Yes, which, alas, seems to have been most of them. Relentless bakers, those Elizabethan pie ladies were, and required a lot of paper, sad to say." Jake stared, blankly. "For the ovens. As I said, the British Library should do you. It's worth a visit in any case."

Jake nodded. This library was in fact something he had been meaning to see. He'd always wanted to get a look at some of the early bits and scraps of English reportage: who dined with the Queen last night, how many troops were being mustered for the Boer campaign, how many caskets of wine for the King's coronation, and so on. "How do I get there?"

"It's up past Euston by King's Cross/St. Pancras. You can't miss it." He frowned a moment. "You'll need a letter, though."

Jake glanced up from a quick perusal of Robert Greene and blinked. "Excuse me?"

"A letter of introduction. Here, I'll be happy to write you one." With some effort, the bookseller rummaged in his desk and produced a pad of bookstore stationary. He dashed off a quick note, and signed it 'Henry Blodgett,' with a Hancock-like flourish, and folded it neatly into thirds. "There you go. You are hereby assigned the position as official research scholar for Blodgett's Books, a well-known bookseller and scholarship emporium par excellence, if I do say so myself." With a wry chuckle, Blodgett carefully tucked the letter into an embossed white envelope with his shoppe's logo in its proper corner and started to hand it over. As Jake reached for it, he withdrew it slightly. "There is one condition, of course."

"Which is?"

"You do me the courtesy of imparting all the salacious details you can muster as to the doings and whereabouts of my erstwhile client. Do you agree?"

"I'll keep it in mind." Jake secured the envelope before Blodgett backed out altogether. "What's the fastest way to get there?"

"Well, aside from a taxi, assuming you could find one, that would be the bus to Euston Station, I suspect," Blodgett thought for a moment. "You can walk from there."

Jake nodded, and tucked away the notepad and envelope.

"Good, then." Blodgett extended his hand and Jake accepted a firm handshake. "Pleasure to know you, sir. And best of luck with your inquiry."

Inquiry. That was a good word for it, Jake thought, as he reached for the door. But inquiry into what? As he opened the door and stepped out into the blustery autumn day, Blodgett called after him, as though in afterthought. "Mr. Fleming? Tell you what. If you can't find Greene's Essays in the library, give me a call and I'll see if I can locate a trade copy for you."

Jake stopped, genuinely touched. "You would do that?"

"I'm expecting I won't have to," said Blodgett, with a wry smile.

Jake stepped out onto Charing Cross Road, wondering if he shouldn't have shown Blodgett the rest of Lewis's list after all. This could take some time. He turned his collar to the chill wind and began to walk. A few blocks north, he stopped at a small drug store to pick up some Mylanta, which he was relieved to find was in plentiful stock. As he paid and turned towards the door, he stopped abruptly. Just across the street, ostensibly busy at a news stand, stood the same large man in the London Fog he'd spotted following him last night. He had an excellent memory for forms and faces—a skill that had saved his life on more than one occasion, and this was too much for coincidence. Heart pounding, he pondered the next move.

The large man tugged on his jowl, thoughtfully. He was a patient man– to a degree. He had been very interested to learn of this American journalist's possible involvement with the Lewis affair, and needed to assess the matter very carefully before deciding what, if anything, needed to be done about it. The bookseller would require a visit, but that could wait. He might not know anything useful in any case.

It didn't improve his state of mind that this American interloper seemed inclined to walk everywhere. What was he, some sort of naturist? Ah, well. Increasingly aware that he himself was becoming more bulk than brawn with each passing year, he supposed he could use a bit of a nudge in the direction of fitness. That had once been his forte, even part of the job description. At least in the old days. Perhaps it was time to seize this newly loose bull by the horns, as it were.

On the other hand, he hoped he wasn't wasting his time, not to mention energy. There were other performers in this play, and at the moment his resources were such that he could not yet cover them all. Choices had to be made, and he could only hope he made the right ones. There was too much at stake, he knew, to make a wrong move. And this play would not play out this day.

Just as a precaution, however, he patted his jacket where his special issue Sig Sauer P226 was tucked away. He might no longer be able to leap fences in a single bound. But he was very capable of blowing someone's head off if necessary. And this new target might be a greater threat than early warnings had suggested. It was just a feeling he had. A bad feeling. . .

Jake missed the bus to Euston and the next one, according to the sign, was not for twenty minutes, so he had elected to walk the whole mile or so, enjoying the now-sunny late autumn afternoon. As he crossed through yet another small city park, the prickling sensation on the back of his neck—his sixth sense or whatever it was—sounded its alarm loud and clear (as did his stomach): watch your back. He didn't turn around to look. He didn't need to. After years of often dangerous work as a correspondent for the *Tribune* and other papers, his senses were pretty well honed. Sure enough, a quick glance in a shop window across the street removed all doubts: he could see the large man matching his pace, and eying his back with a look of alarmingly possessive intensity. He needed to do something, and fast.

As the large man closed ranks, Jake spotted his chance an instant before his pursuer: a two-decker bus was approaching an adjacent bus stop from the east in one direction, and a second bus from the west. A cluster of tourists stood waiting for the first bus, and he hurried to join them. Then, with a quick glance back to confirm that his stalker had taken the bait, he pushed through the crowd just as the coach slowed to a stop. At the last moment, instead of boarding the bus, he darted in front of it and cut across the street, barely reaching the other side as the westbound bus rumbled past cutting him off from sight, let alone any possible pursuit, and squealed to a stop on the corner opposite. Jake jumped aboard and watched through the facing window in satisfaction as his follower pushed his way onto the east-bound coach, which pulled away taking him with it before the large man realized his mistake. Meanwhile, as the bus Jake had boarded also pulled away, they locked eyes for a fleeting moment through the tangle of passengers as the two coaches accelerated in opposite directions, and Jake knew there was no way his pursuer would make up the lost ground before he reached the library.

But then what? If the man had been following him for two days now, he undoubtedly knew where he was staying. If not where he was going.

Chapter Seven

Winding the Watch of His Wit

The vast new British Library was situated just north of the university, between two venerable old London railway stations: Eustace and St. Pancras. Jake got off the bus after a few blocks and made his way back to the library simply by pointing himself towards the easily visible modern edifice: a huge, multi-tiered, mall-like structure readily identifiable in the distance. A glance back at each corner crossing showed no sign of his erstwhile shadow.

To his surprise, Blodgett's letter was as good as dollars in Dubai. The guard quickly let him in when the passing librarian, a willowy, slender forty-ish woman with dark red hair, recognized the name of the bookseller. "Ah yes," she said, cheerfully. "You're from Mr. Blodgett's. He called." Her name tag, he noted, read Ms. Armwood. "Here's your reading pass, sir. It will be good for the duration of your stay."

"Thank you, Ms. Armwood. You're very kind." She blushed as he turned to study the layout of the building and location of the various collections.

As he entered the main gallery, Jake quickly saw that the library was everything Blodgett had promised, and more. He could easily spend days, even weeks here, just perusing the displays. He edged past an impromptu mime performance in the lobby and found his way to the already legendary John Ritblatt Gallery, where the real treasures were kept. There he contemplated the origin of English Common Law–the first Bill of Rights–and the first book ever published outside of China. There was enough knowledge—and enigma—in this room, he knew, to ponder for a lifetime, and still not have all the answers to life's persistent questions. He moved on.

As it turned out, Mr. Blodgett's investment was secure. A helpful young library assistant, a pudgy postgraduate male with unruly blond curls, located Robert Greene in the computer data base in a matter of moments and steered Jake to the correct section. He explained apologetically that guest researchers couldn't check anything out, but he was welcome to stay all day at one of the many kiosks or tables or even use a soundproof study carrel, if he wished. "The British Library is for serious scholars only, you see," he explained. "It isn't a lending library."

To Jake's astonishment, having scarcely heard of the man before last night, they had more than two dozen volumes of the plays and essays of Robert Greene. Brushing aside a gnawing concern that he might be wasting his time, he located *A Groatsworth of Wit* easily enough–there were half a dozen copies–and found a vacant carrel where he sat down at the table, laid out his notepad and pen and began to read, still mystified as to why such a pedestrian-seeming pursuit of apparently common knowledge should be so dangerous—if in fact it was.

Groatsworth was a parable about two brothers: one a businessman, the other a 'scholler.' On their father's deathbed the former was given all the assets except a single 'groat,' with which the scholar was told to acquire at least that amount's worth of wit, presumably because he had none. Instead, the 'better' brother squandered the money with the complicity of a 'madam.' A witless attempt at revenge backfired, leaving both brothers bereft. At the moment of discovery, a rustic, ruddy-faced traveler turned up and began to make a pitch: "You are a scholler, and pittie it is men of learning should live in lack," he told them. The brother Roberto (presumably Greene himself) then asked how he might be employed. "Why, easily," quoth hee, "and greatly to your benefit: for men of my profession get by schollers their whole living." Jake made some notes. Who would make a living by exploiting scholars? Was this what Dr. Lewis had been in a twist about? Was the traveler some sort of schoolmaster? This character didn't seem like one. He read on: "What is your profession?" asked Roberto. "Truely sir" said he, "I am a player." Player? In other words, actor, Jake noted. The Player then described how he was "a substantial man, able to afford at my proper cost, to build a Windmill."

Jake pondered the significance of this. How would a 'poor player' become a "substantial man?" How could he get "by scholars (his) whole living?" Let alone get rich? He'd always heard most actors, then and now with few exceptions, lived close to the poverty line. And what about the windmill reference? Was this some sort of allusion to Cervantes? He lived around the same time, he felt certain ("note to self: check on Cervantes," he wrote). He continued reading: "What though the worlde once went hard with mee, when I was faine to carrie my playing Fardle a footebacke." What the hell was a fardle? Jake made a quick side trip to the nearest dictionary and found it in Johnson's: "a Medieval and pre-Renaissance stringed musical instrument, similar to a mandolin." The Player went on to explain that he'd once been a "poor puppeteer," but was better off now; "for my very share in playing apparrell will not be solde for two hundred pounds." That was interesting. That would be many thousands in today's money. Did actors usually acquire large wardrobes, or was that the domain of the theater company? He wished he knew more about Elizabethan culture and couture. Meanwhile, the intrepid Robert questioned The Player further, to which The Player enumerated his credentials:

"I am as famous for Delphrigus, and the king of Fairies, as ever was any of my time. The twelve labors of Hercules have I terribly thundered on the stage and placed three scenes of the devill on the highway to heaven." He then boasted that "I can serve to make a prettie speech, for I was a countrie Author, passing at a morall, for it was I that pende the Moral of mans wit, the Dialogue of Dives, and for seaven yeeres space was absolute interpreter of the puppets." As proof, he recited as follows:

> " 'The people make no estimation,
> Of Morrals teaching education.' "

"Great stuff," Jake muttered to himself, sarcastically. 'Morals teaching education'? The guy sounded like Jerry Falwell. He wondered why Desmond Lewis could possibly have been interested in this material. Next he read how, like a wheedling neophyte seeking praise, The Player pleaded:

"Was not this prettie for a plaine rime extempore? If ye will ye shall have more." "Nay it is enough," said Roberto, "but how meane you to use mee?" "Why sir, in making playes," said the other, "for which you shall be well paied, if you will take the paines."

OK, thought Jake, getting the hang of the language. So this guy was soliciting plays. What the Player was saying was 'Trust me, good sir. Write for me some plays and I'll make you rich.' He did not sound like much of a player, thought Jake. What he sounded like, reading this, was some sort of an Elizabethan hustler or theatrical agent. Jake began to write in shorthand in his reporter's notepad.

Could this player be someone who solicited the works of a struggling writer, promising financial reward: the daily pipe dream of your average London or Los Angeles wait-person? It was clear that Robert Greene's player imagined himself a writer of sorts. Although clearly not much of one. And he seemed perfectly willing to admit a readiness to 'use' or exploit others. But if so, so what? Jake remembered, from his media contacts, that same term 'player' was used in present-day Hollywood to describe a successful entertainment industry wheeler-dealer. That would certainly describe a theatrical agent. It also described the character in Greene's *Groatsworth*, he thought. Was Lewis working on some kind of expose, maybe the Elizabethan origins of Hollywood agents? Or even Hollywood itself?

Who from that time claimed to be a poet as well as player, as well as puppeteer? And was also "substantial"? He made a note to find out, and read on:

"Yes, trust them not; for there is an upstart Crow, beautified with our Feathers, that, with his Tygers heart wrapped in a Players hide, supposes he is as well able to bombast out a blank verse as the best of you."

So, there it was: the Crow. But who was this "upstart," or what was this referring to? What was clear was that Robert Greene was an angry man, thought Jake, leaning back in his chair and closing his eyes, as he did when he needed to concentrate.

He checked his watch. It was time to navigate the streets of London once more, with all its impediments and obstacles.

To his relief, there was no further sign of the large man as he made his way back to Denmark Street. But it was disturbing to know that he was out there, somewhere, and almost certainly knew where he lived. Did this have something to do with the disappearance of Desmond Lewis? And if so, what, how, and why?

Chapter Eight

No Other but a Woman's Reason

Berkeley, California, Late October

Melissa Fleming left her acting workshop early and hurried off the BART, weaving her way through the early evening crowd to catch the bus home on Ashley. Tonight's rehearsal had been an education, all right. She'd been working on a lead role in a new play by a male student she despised, but the role had some good lines, she'd had to admit. But then she'd been interrupted by a call from her work-study employer, Dr. Scofield, head of the Department of Elizabethan Studies. He was someone for whom she'd already gone well beyond the call of duty, and spent hundreds of midnight hours supporting and providing the documentation for his latest book, which was due out any day, and she was very excited for him. And not a little proud of her own efforts, even if she knew she wouldn't be sharing much of the glory. At least she'd share in a little glory. After all, he had promised to mention her on the acknowledgments page, and that was a lot more than nothing.

But now, after this afternoon's meeting at his office on campus, she saw a golden new opportunity in the making: a course consistent with her own work; a course that even Dr. Scofield would support. She needed to go to London to finally see the theater in all its glory, and maybe even make some contacts, and if she was very lucky, try out for some roles. Sooner or later she would have to take a shot at it, both in London and on Broadway, because the play was the thing, and the stage was where the real art happened, and Hollywood was all well and fine, and she'd give that her best shot too, but it all began with stage work. If she couldn't cut it on the stage, why ever did she imagine she could make it on the screen? And what better time than now, while her father was there—at least long enough for her to make further connections and get settled on her own? The timing was perfect. Her advisor would be away on his book tour soon, and the city of Dickens, and Shakespeare, and all its kings and poets, with all their glorious history and mystery beckoned, and suddenly she wondered why she had delayed going before now. She couldn't wait to tell her father she'd decided to join him there. While they hadn't been close since long before her mother had died, she was sure he wouldn't mind. And they might even finally close some of those many gaps in mutual understanding that had widened between them for much too long.

As she got off the bus at College Avenue, a short walk to her apartment, she thought about her relationship with her father, and suddenly felt depressed. Why was it that they'd grown so far apart? It wasn't that anything awful had happened between them. They'd just gone in different directions and had never been that close to begin with. He hadn't even blinked when she announced her plans to become an actor (a decision that had caused her mother more than a little grief and dismay, by contrast). He'd just glanced up from his desk and said "That's great, Sweetie. You do whatever makes you happy." She'd wanted to scream, and kick him, for not at least asking her how she planned to make a living and so on, like a concerned parent was supposed to do! And even before then, he was always traveling, writing his investigative stories, and she was away in boarding school, then college, then drama school. Maybe it was just a matter of style, of her comfort zone. He was so laid-back and carefree, while she often felt as though she carried the weight of the world on her shoulders. Again, why? Did she imagine herself in some melodrama that didn't even exist? Maybe she *should* have become a psych major instead of a drama major, she thought wryly, as she reached her building. But still, there was something that nagged at her and wouldn't go away.

But then she remembered another thing. When she'd mentioned her father's involvement with the academically infamous Desmond Lewis to her advisor this afternoon, there had been a distinct chill in the room. Was her father getting in over his head? Her missionary spirit took over and settled the matter. She would kill two birds with one stone: see all the plays she could in London, attend every open call possible just for the practice if nothing else, and maybe get to know her father a little better, too, at long last. It was about time.

"Carpe diem!" she shouted into the wind, turning several heads. But then, she was accustomed to turning heads.

Chapter Nine

So Well as By Reflection

London, Late October

The sprawling urban campus of London's top university provided ample opportunity for Londoners, Englishmen, Britons and foreigners to further their education, earn degrees, and meanwhile remain anonymous and unnoticed among the ten million or so people who inhabited the London area. Bloomsbury was just another district in London; the university just another collection of institutional buildings. At least to the untrained eye.

For Jake Fleming, it was a mint-popping nightmare. He'd found Desmond Lewis' office easily enough on Monday, through the campus directory and a few well-placed questions (and in the case of one porter, a few well-placed pounds). Tracking down the professor's colleagues, however, was another matter. He'd gotten hold of a College of Arts and Sciences directory—no easy task—at one of the campus bookstores. But that was just the beginning. The building and office numbering system was nearly indecipherable, and busy students and faculty, hurrying past this way and that, did not, as a rule, tend to want to proffer much information. Plus, the various department faculty members' office locations and class hours differed sharply.

He located the English Language Department Chairperson, Diana Parker, PhD, almost by accident, while inquiring at the main campus library. The senior librarian grudgingly nodded towards a thin, gray-haired man in a bulky knitted sweater, striding across the foyer: "You might ask Dr. Childers. He's the Vice Chairman." Jake hurried to intercept him just as the professor was heading out the door.

"Excuse me, Dr. Childers?" he called over.

The professor turned and raised his eyebrows querulously as Jake caught up to him in the doorway. "Yes, what is it?"

Jake extended his business card. "Jake Fleming, *San Francisco Tribune*. Do you have a minute?" Childers glanced at the sullen weather outside the double glass doors, back at his inquisitor, and seemed to prefer the former.

"Not really, I'm on my way to a meeting. What is it you want?"

"I can't seem to find Dr. Parker, and was wondering if I could ask you a few questions about one of your faculty members, Professor Lewis?"

Childers' shoulders seemed to stiffen, and his expression became guarded. "What about him?"

"Have you seen or heard from him recently?"

"No, I haven't. But that isn't unusual. I can't speak for Dr. Parker, of course, but I don't keep close watch on our faculty, they are all adults. Most of them, anyway." He seemed to chuckle inwardly, then coughed.

Jake smiled. "Yeah. Well, Professor Lewis missed a lecture appointment in the States and has been incommunicado for several days. I was wondering if you might have any idea where he went?"

"Sorry. But that sort of unpredictability does sound like him."

"Well, that's not all. Maybe you know he was planning on delivering a new book to his publishers, and this has also disappeared."

Childers raised his eyebrows, but, what with his dour expression in general, Jake wasn't sure what it signified. Did he denote a glimmer of relief, or was it dismay in that look? "I see," he said. "So, you allege he's absconded, so to speak?"

"I'm not sure that's the right word, but anyway, he's gone."

Childers seemed suddenly fascinated with the blank wall beside the door. "I'll inform the department head and staff. Anything else I can help you with, Mr., er—?"

"Fleming. Yeah, do you know what his book was about?"

Childers smiled—a little too quickly, thought Jake. "I'm afraid not. Academic freedom allows for considerable, shall we say, independence, sometimes much to our regret. Can't help you there."

"I see. Well, do you know who he hangs out with, who might know where he went?"

"I haven't the faintest idea whom he 'hangs out with,' " said Childers, irritably. "Now, if you'll excuse me, I'm late for my meeting." With that he departed, with a single, troubled glance back as he reached the sidewalk, and pulled out his mobile phone.

Interesting, thought Jake. He didn't even know Lewis was missing. Or did he?

As he started to leave the library, he caught sight of a startlingly attractive woman watching him from the line at the check-out desk. She was, Jake would guess, in her late thirties; slender, dark brown hair in a short, slightly disheveled cut, flashing hazel eyes, dressed in a dark slightly askew woolen skirt and jacket, and a too-large mismatched sweater. An English Annie Hall, he thought, instantly drawn to her. Especially when she dropped her books, picked them up, dropped them again, then dropped her bag, with a soft curse. Throwing caution to the winds, he sauntered over, and bent down to help pick up her things.

"I'm fine, no problem," she sniffed, brusquely. "Thank you very much."

As she arose clutching her treasures, she dropped several books again, which he caught in midair and handed back with a smile. "Sorry to trouble you, but you may have overheard my conversation with Dr. Childers just now. Are you a faculty member?"

She stood and eyed him, coolly. "You're the Yank who's been asking about Des Lewis."

"Right. And you are?"

"Parker. Professor Parker. I'm Chairperson of the English Department. I was out of my office when you came by."

"Oh. Excuse me, you're just the person I've been looking for. Is there somewhere we could talk for a few minutes?"

"I have a class at one thirty, and a lunch meeting. But we can talk for a moment, when I finish here. Hello, Roberta," she said, to the librarian. "Early winter, looks like."

"It's all the same to me, Professor," sighed the librarian. "I wouldn't know what season it was, but for the calendar, much as I get out. You have everything, then?"

Parker gathered up her books. "I see you're reading about Billie Holiday," Jake commented, as she motioned for him to follow.

"It's for a class on Feminism and New World Culture."

"Ah." He groped for an intelligent, non-chauvinistic-sounding response, and came up empty. They settled in a study alcove near the entrance.

"Now, how can I help you?" Her demeanor wasn't icy, but it wasn't exactly warm, either.

"I noticed you referred to Dr. Lewis as 'Des,' " he said. "Were you close to him?"

She looked away, ever so briefly, then back. "Not really," she said. "Nobody was close to him. But I try to be on a first name basis with my faculty. And 'Desmond' is, well, rather, I don't know, a bit fusty, don't you think?"

"I hadn't thought about it. So, you and 'Des' weren't close. Were you close enough to know what he was working on before he left?"

Again, he noted a quick nervous hesitation, and glance to her left, just above his right shoulder. He'd read somewhere that when people responded to a question by looking upward and to the left, they were lying. "Sorry," she said, flatly. "Can't help you there."

"Ah. Well." He was tempted, very tempted, to ask her to lunch. He sensed she knew more than she was saying. Also, she was, after all, damned attractive. Not that he was in the market, these days. Not since Beverly—he shook that thought off. "I really must be going," she said, gathering her books and picking up her coat. "Will there be anything else?"

"Do you have a card, or number, in case I think of something?"

"Sorry," she said, getting to her feet. "I suppose you could try the directory."

"Under Parker?" He called after her. She was already halfway out the door, but dropped her gloves and had to stop to pick them up.

"Diana Parker." She retrieved her gloves and was gone.

Well, that was something, anyway. He knew a brush-off when he got one. It wasn't that he was vain—far from it—but he'd always been considered by the women in his life, or at least the one he'd loved and pursued and married and then neglected and now had lost, to have been a handsome man, in a scruffy, rumpled sort of way. At least in the old days. His straight nose had only been broken a couple of times in his travels and had remained reasonably intact, his longish wavy blond hair was graying but still mostly there, and his gray eyes and laugh lines bespoke a sensuality that women often detected even when he himself had lost touch with it years ago. But rejection was par for the course, for a journalist. He took it in stride.

For the next several hours Jake roamed the halls and corridors of London University looking for someone–anyone–willing to talk to him about Professor Lewis, and also for any clues as to what he'd been working on that might place him in peril. Again and again he came up empty. He saw no more of Diana Parker, and saw no further reason to look for her, aside from her personal appeal.

Regarding Desmond Lewis, the picture was increasingly clear. Apparently, he was one of those academics too lofty in stature to need to lower himself to the unseemly task of actually teaching class. So there were no students to question. At least none he could find on short notice. Lewis's colleagues in the English Department feigned ignorance as to his activities or whereabouts, and, when pressed, expressed quotidian sorrow at his disappearance, but the hostility he felt all around him was tangible. From some of them he sensed a certain grim satisfaction, a *sang froid* over the man's apparent dissolution. All of which reconfirmed what Gloria Peckham had said: that Professor Desmond Lewis was very much a pariah, in academic circles. Which reminded him of Lewis's strange comment over the phone. That he had been censured, in some way, by his peers?

And what about this Balsavar character, this physicist? He, too, seemed elusive, and somewhat of a cipher. All Jake could learn about him from the security-prone Physics Department was that yes, the man taught there, and an admission that he was "possibly" from India or Pakistan. Late in the afternoon, having gotten nowhere, Jake took refuge from the oncoming nighttime chill in a Bloomsbury hotel bar: a satisfyingly dark and woody room with old smoke stains on the ceiling and spill-darkened hardwood floors. He ordered a beer the very name of which he couldn't resist: a Wychwood Hobgoblin—a name worthy of Tolkien if ever there was one.

He felt a shock, followed by an odd sense of vindication when the evening newspaper headline jumped out at him from the Metro section: *Controversial Professor Missing*. The article, which was from Reuters, repeated pretty much what he already knew, and he wondered who had filed it. A quick call confirmed an old rival, and he suppressed the urge to call the woman. Instead, he went to the nearest phone and punched zero. "Get me the London Police," he said.

A quick check back with Missing Persons gave him nothing new, and he hung up, thinking hard. What he found interesting, as well as troubling, was his distinct feeling that some of Lewis's colleagues seemed to know more about his alleged disappearance than the police did.

To distract himself, Jake pondered Robert Greene once more, and what he could recall of Elizabethan history, wondering again what possible connection to the present could place a man in danger. Unfortunately, the images that kept coming to mind were deeply disquieting: flotillas of sailing ships being blown apart by cannon fire; bodies writhing in agony tied to burning stakes, screaming with their last breath from seared lungs; black-clad friars chanting death eulogies as men of conscience were torn into pieces fiber from fiber, muscle from bone, tissue from organ, by horses at the four points of a compass; axes being swung and severed heads tumbling with jaws gaping in a silent scream; gallows doors dropping down and bodies slumping into their final writhing throes of death. Thus had people paid with their lives back then for their beliefs. The more things changed, he thought, irritably.

Procrastination won the day, and he had another beer instead. He dug out the list Gloria Peckham had given him, and read it through once more:

Ox
Lamb
Herb
Crow
M T

LWT
Hoff
Inq
V.A.
Apoc

What the hell? What had Lewis been up to? He'd barely scratched the surface with 'crow,' and hardly knew where to go from there. He opened a new pack of Cool Mints. This was going to require a lot of Cool Mints. Either that or G.I. surgery. He preferred Cool Mints.

He scowled at the list like an unwilling student eying his exam. What now? What kind of herbs had Lewis been smoking, anyway? 'Apoc' caught his eye. Could that be 'apocalypse?' Had Lewis been planning on some kind of 'End Times' revelation or other? That was chilling. He sighed, gave up, went to bed, and had nightmares about large black birds wearing turbans and surgical coats, pursuing him through dark hospital corridors, brandishing gleaming knives. Meanwhile, an ancient chant reverberated in the back of his mind: *Hell, and Night, must bring this monstrous Birth, to the world's light.*

"What is that? What is that?" He kept shouting, but to no avail.

Chapter Ten

Be Both the Plaintiff and the Judge

The next morning, finally fed up with stale coffee and greasy leftover bangers from the nearby deli on Denmark Street, Jake stopped for a slice of stale Sicilian pizza from a street vendor, then repaid a visit to the venerable bookstore of Henry Blodgett of Charing Cross Road. Blodgett greeted him with typical British reserve.

"Ah. Mr. Fleming. You're back," he said, with a glint in his eye.

"Couldn't stay away. Looks like your rare books will remain safe a while longer, Mr. Blodgett. Thanks for the access to the British Library. Interesting place."

"Indeed. I find it a place of solace and respite at times, much as others might find, say, a chapel."

"Or a well-lighted bookstore?" suggested Jake, with a grin.

Blodgett smiled, appreciatively. "Hmm, yes, although I'm afraid one could hardly call this one well lighted. So, did you find what you were looking for?"

Jake shrugged. "I have no idea. Robert Greene sure as hell was mad about something. Or someone. That's pretty clear. Question is, who? And more importantly, what's the relevance?"

"Indeed." Blodgett changed the subject. "So, what can I do for you today?"

Jake clutched the list in his pocket. "You said Dr. Lewis was a regular customer, right?"

Blodgett took on a wary look, once again. "Look, Mr., er Fleming, as I said, I take the privacy of my clientèle quite seriously."

"Even when they're missing and presumed dead?"

That got his attention. Blodgett paled and his eyes narrowed. "Beg pardon?"

"I hate to tell you, but when people disappear without a trace, it usually means one of two things, neither of them good: either they have reason to vanish, such as when they are wanted for embezzlement or a paternity suit, or they have run into foul play."

The ancient white eyebrows shot up. "Foul play, you say?"

"Yes. I'm sorry to say this, but given that university English departments are not exactly rife with opportunities for high crimes or misdemeanors, combined with the fact that Lewis was about to publish a book which seems to make a lot of people very twitchy including yourself, the man who swore you to all this secrecy is probably dead."

The bookseller looked at him in open dismay. Then he frowned and turned away, evidently still unconvinced. He shook his head vigorously. "I don't believe it. Not him. He was young and fit. Had the constitution of a frigate. And he was wary, too."

"Even, say, to the point of paranoia?"

Blodgett bit his lip. "Perhaps you'd best get to the point, Mr. Fleming."

Jake leaned towards him. "It's now been five days since he vanished, and he hasn't been heard from since. His home and office were both essentially destroyed, to which his personal assistant was witness, as was I. You're welcome to check with his office. Or the police, for that matter. Or would that be Scotland Yard?"

Blodgett paced the floor, scratching his sparsely covered scalp. "This is most disturbing. And you think he may have met with some sort of unpleasantness?"

Unpleasantness. Yet another charming example of English understatement, he thought. "Yes, I am certain that is so."

The bookseller paced a moment longer, fretfully. "Well, that would be another kettle of fish to boil, wouldn't it? Terrible thing, if so. Terrible. I'd need to check on that, though, wouldn't I?" He shook his head, darkly.

Jake handed him a slip of paper. "Here. You can start with his administrative assistant. You can also check with London Metropolitan Police. Better yet, check the *London Times*."

He showed Blodgett the newspaper story. The bookseller frowned, then nodded. "I see. But that puts me on the horns of a dilemma, all the same. He may be dead, as you say. But what if he's merely been misplaced, as it were? Sometimes even the most punctilious of us have cause to divert, or digress, or even," he glanced about dramatically, "go into hiding?"

Jake had thought about that, was in fact somewhat of an expert on that subject, and the man had a point. But hiding from what? Or whom? And again, why? He considered the Lewis list, and whether to disclose it yet. But the bookseller's own reticence ruled against that approach just yet. Instead he tried another tack. The bookstore environs had given him another hunch. "All right. In the meantime, maybe you can tell me this: did he ever discuss or ask about anyone with the initials 'M.T.'?"

Blodgett hoisted his brows once more. "M.T.? As in our beloved former P.M. Lady Thatcher?"

"Right. Did he ever express any interest in her? Order any books by or about her?"

"I don't think she wrote any books worth reading. No, sorry. The only other book he asked for before he left was—" a look of dawning comprehension came over his face. "Ah, but that would be telling, wouldn't it?"

"You're really not going to help me with this, are you?"

Blodgett seemed to relent, slightly. "I'll tell you this much. Dame Margaret isn't the only M.T. of some distinction. And I think I can safely say that Dr. Lewis had expressed some interest in someone closer to your own heart, perhaps. If not under your own nose."

"What? Who?"

"M.T.? Your own American bard, as it were. Of course, it was a pseudonym, but often the truth is hidden in plain sight like that. Oh, my goodness yes." He let forth an ancient chuckle.

Jake was ready to strangle him. American Bard? Pseudonym? Then it hit him like a two-by-four in a hurricane. "Oh," he said, nodding in recognition. "Of course. M.T. Mark Twain. You mean Mark Twain, don't you?"

"Who else? We don't do much trade in the way of American authors, I'm afraid," Blodgett added. Jake's expression changed to one of disappointment.

"I don't suppose you can tell me why Lewis was interested in Mark Twain?"

"No, and I couldn't dissuade him, alas," chuckled the bookseller. "Even though the chap was a Yank, mind you." He winked as he said it. "However,"

Blodgett went on, "I do have something in the back I was holding for him. And since he, er—"

"You're holding a book for him?"

"Well, he didn't know about it. I found it after his last inquiry, which puts it in the public domain, so to speak. And that being the case, I suppose you'd want to see it, wouldn't you?"

"Yes, I would, if you don't mind."

"Not at all, not at all. Matter of fact, I believe I know nearly its exact approximate location," he said. "If you'll allow me."

With that the ancient bookseller shuffled to the back of the store, and Jake held his breath for fear he was going to climb that ladder—a veritable Stairway to Heaven, as it were. Luckily, instead he bent down, fussed and fumbled about, moved to another location with a mutter, and shuffled about some more.

"Aha!" he declared, triumphantly, then finally straightened up holding a bulky, battered volume and carried it back to the counter. "Here you go." He presented a stout leather-bound tome to Jake, who downed several mints and glanced at the title: *My Autobiography*, by Mark Twain.

"Isn't there a newer edition available of this?" noted Jake, in irony.

"Yes, but this is the original, unexpurgated version," Blodgett declared. "There are a lot of previously unpublished articles and essays in there. Some of his best work." He blushed, as though he'd just revealed himself. "Er, so I'm told." He smiled, gamely.

"You're saying there is something in this edition that doesn't exist in more recent ones?"

"Er, so I'm told," grinned Blodgett, with a wink.

His pulse quickening, Jake opened it up on the counter and scanned the table of contents. It contained easily a hundred or more entries, on everything from Nevada gold mining to Helen Keller. Twain wrote about Helen Keller? And this didn't even include the references to his major literary works. Still, he thought, autobiographical essays would be the best glimpse into what was on the man's mind, literally, and Desmond Lewis's most likely focus of interest as well. He noted, with surprise, that the book was a first edition, and suddenly feared he couldn't afford it.

"Uh, how much?" he asked, worriedly.

Blodgett waved his hand in dismissal. "Don't give it another thought. On the house as it were. Consider it a bit of a *lagniappe*."

"But this is a first edition!"

"Bah. The cover is battered and the pages all yellowed. Not worth the space it takes up."

Jake doubted that but saw no point in arguing. Maybe he could make it up to him later. Maybe that was the whole idea.

"As I said," said Blodgett, cheerfully, "we don't do much trade with American authors."

Clearly, he considered the matter settled. "If you insist, you can return it when you're done. Or give it to Dr. Lewis should he return, Lord willing." he shook his head. Then he looked up sharply. "What about his own book? The one he was writing? Is that missing as well?"

So, thought Jake. Our demure Mr. Blodgett did know about Lewis's book. "Also missing," he confirmed. "Not a trace."

Blodgett stroked his chin. "I'll tell you what. You take a look at Mr. Twain there and see what you can discover on your own. Meanwhile, I'll make a few calls and see what's what. And if our friend has indeed gone astray as you say, then I shall be more than delighted to assist you in whatever way I can. Does that sound fair to you?"

"More than fair," said Jake.

"Oh, and call me Henry. Er, Jake."

"Look at it this way. If he's really gone for good, as I fear, I will see to his legacy. Perhaps with your help. I intend to find out what was in this book, and then find a way to retrace his steps. Does that sound reasonable to you, Mr. Blodgett? I mean Henry."

"Reasonable indeed." Blodgett extended his hand.

Jake shook his hand and departed with the book, feeling slightly—more than slightly—guilty about his sudden wealth of literary riches. Which might hopefully provide a clue as to Desmond Lewis's whereabouts. At least in terms of his intended but now lost literary revelations.

Careful to check the vicinity for followers and spotting none, he returned to the flat, chided himself once again for being paranoid, fixed a quick snack of leftover chips and cheese, opened a beer, popped a Cool Mint, and settled down to read Mark Twain.

He knew the basics: born in Missouri as Samuel Clemens, worked as a river boat pilot, moved out west, became a journalist, then back east to Hartford, where he became a novelist and essayist. Mark Twain had taken his pseudonym from the lingo of the Mississippi River boat pilots, whose crewmen would shout out the depth readings: "Mark one. Mark twain." And so on.

Something nagged at him about that. Why was a pseudonym important, somehow? He couldn't remember the connection he was searching for and shrugged it off. But obviously Lewis had something on his mind. What was it about Mark Twain himself? His most famous novel, *Huckleberry Finn*, had often been banned, off and on, for a variety of reasons, like Salinger's *Catcher in the Rye*, and Hawthorne's *The Scarlet Letter*.

There's an irony, he thought. Poor Hawthorne was just trying to atone for the actions of his grandfather, who'd been presiding magistrate at the Salem witch trials, he'd once read. Once again proving that no good deed would go unpunished. Had that been Desmond Lewis's possibly fatal mistake as well? Or had his intentions been more nefarious? Was this the clue he was looking for, that Lewis was following up? But all this was well known. The "politically correct" scholars and librarians and so on who objected to Huck Finn had objected based on the book's overtones of racism. But Twain himself had denied this, noting that he was merely writing about how things were in those days, not condoning them. True, the language was strong for its day. Was that it, then? Twain had been a forerunner of telling it like it was, language and all. Did he have that in common, perhaps, with Robert Greene?

The volume's contents, as he'd noted in the bookstore, were capacious. Twain listed them almost at random, often repeating numerous themes, covering such diverse subject matter as General Grant and the Chinese (now that could be interesting, he thought, making a note); the Morris incident (this came up repeatedly. Who was Morris, and what incident?); a burglar alarm incident; strong language (better check that out); comments on the killing of 600 Moros (that was startling. What, when, where, and by whom, he wondered. And could that be prescient?). The list went on: interview with Tchaikovsky the revolutionist (not composer?); the drift toward centralized power; purchasing civic virtue (these topics were hot even today, he noted); the report of Twain's death being greatly exaggerated; Winston Churchill; Sidney Lee, whoever that was; and the Holy Grail.

Holy Grail? No, that had been poked at, prodded and popularized ad nauseum by Hollywood, and recent bestsellers. It must be something else, he decided. Something pertaining to England. Churchill? Twain wasn't around for most of Churchill's life, so what insights could he shake up the world with about him? It had to be something else.

Then he turned the page and sat bolt upright. Twain's preface read as follows:

PREFACE

In this Autobiography I shall keep in mind the fact that I am speaking from the grave. I am literally speaking from the grave, because I shall be dead when the book issues from the press. I speak from the grave rather than with my living tongue for a good reason: I can speak thence freely.

Words from the grave. Those always sent a chill down people's spines. His pulse quickened. This might be leading somewhere. But again, where, and to what? And to whom? Had Desmond Lewis been driven by some kind of premonition of doom, and was now, himself, speaking from the grave? He looked at the Lewis list again and made comparisons. He couldn't see any, but that didn't mean much. There were so many names and events to choose from.

Frustrated, he set the book down and opened a bottle of Australian Sauvignon Blanc, again courtesy of *The San Francisco Tribune*. As a result, he didn't hear the telephone ring two hours later, at four a.m.

Chapter Eleven

Our Doubts are Traitors

His head pounding with a world class nitrites hangover, Jake was startled awake around 7:00 the next morning by the sound of lorries outside his window growling past in the streets below, loading and unloading things wet and heavy. Nearby shops began to open, along with the cafes and several restaurants. It was the cycle of life in the city: produce in, garbage out. Trucks and taxis, buses and cars, subways and pedestrians, always in a fervent rush, moving like litter blown along the gutters, tumbled past in random powerful surges, pebbles on an ocean seabed, thrust relentlessly up against the shore, then out again, living then dead, eventually to be ground into sand. Or polished into gems. Which was it Lewis had been seeking, or may have found? That too common but elusive grain of sand, or some incalculable treasure?

He went into the bedroom to change out of yesterday's clothes and noticed that the answering machine light was blinking on the nightstand by the bed. He hadn't consciously been aware of it until now and wondered if the unheard message was for him or some reporter previously in transit. He had no idea how long it had been there. He located and pressed the "Outgoing Message" button and heard a generic voice state the phone number and ask the caller to leave a message followed by the prerequisite universal "beep." He pressed the "Incoming Messages" button, waited while the machine reset, and heard a familiar voice:

"Dad? It's Melissa. It's Tuesday night, and I wanted to get you before you went out. I've decided to come to London and wanted to see how long you were going to be there. Please call me. I'm back at the U. Everything's OK and the cat is fine. See you. Ciao for now."

So, she'd beat him to the punch. There was a note of something in her voice that puzzled him. Excitement, perhaps. But something more. He wished he knew her better; that he'd known her better growing up. She'd always been beautiful and talented, that was practically a given, considering who her mother had been. And he'd given her his full blessing to pursue her dreams, despite their ridiculously long odds against success. Why hadn't they'd gotten along better all those years? What had gone wrong? Was it that he'd devoted so much attention to his work in her formative years, and neglected, even forgotten the child? That could be so, he realized, ruefully. He had missed most of her proud performances, in middle and high school, when her future stardom, at least in her own mind, was already a given. But he could summon few memories of things they had done together since her teen years. An occasional meal out, a rare movie or play, perhaps one or two symphony concerts. Their tastes in music had long since diverged, hers from hard rock towards Baroque, and his from Folk Rock towards jazz. That was about it. She hadn't been interested in sports, or camping, or any of those "male pursuits" he'd been drawn to, and she hadn't shared her own interests with him all that much (did he even know what they were, beyond Shakespeare and Narnia and Nancy Drew?). Between them were huge gaps in their shared lives, and neither of them had found a way to fill those gaps.

Compelled by parental guilt, Jake picked up the phone and used his calling card to call through to California. It would be midnight now in Berkeley, but chances were she'd still be up.

He was in luck. Melissa answered after the second ring. "Dad? Hi. I was worried! Are you all right?" She sounded relieved to hear from him. This was not typical, he thought. But then, what did he actually know about her feelings? She was an actress, was she not?

"Yes, I'm fine. What's up? You called me?"

He felt like slapping himself. Way to go, Fleming. Why not just ask her why she's pestering him?

Fortunately, she didn't seem to notice. "I'm a little worried about you, that's all. Any word on your friend, Professor Lewis?"

"No, I'm afraid not. Which concerns me."

"That's definitely strange."

"Yes."

"You got my message, right? That I'm coming to London?"

That had startled him into returning the call, but it really hadn't sunk in. "Kiddo, this isn't a vacation. I'm trying to retrace the footsteps of a missing man who may be dead."

"I know. And I'm sorry about your friend. But I need to come there anyway, for my graduate acting class and also my theater class. London is where it's at, Dad. All due respect to Broadway, but London is where it all began."

"Not Athens?"

"OK, yes, Aeschylus and the Greeks invented the play. But it was in England where the theater truly took hold."

"Even though women weren't allowed on stage in England until the time of King Charles?" He was goading her now, he realized. Good one, Fleming!

Again, she let it pass."Well they are now, and I want to try my luck, at least for a bit part or something. And I want to see the real artists at work honing their craft. Dad. Please. This is important to me."

By this time he knew he would give in, as usual. And why wouldn't he enjoy the company of a beautiful young woman at his side, doing London town? Except for the fact that his friend had vanished without a trace, and he didn't want his daughter involved.

As though sensing his hesitation, she went on, quickly: "Besides, I could use a break after the big push for Scofield. He's publishing next week, by the way."

He vaguely remembered something about her work-study faculty supervisor having a new book coming out, something she'd apparently done some work on. But then, after all, professors publishing books were as ubiquitous as sports stars spewing endorsements. Or actresses in, well, London.

"What about your teaching position?"

"It's just part time, and I've already talked to the Dean, and she agrees I can take a research sabbatical. I only teach one movement class anyway, and there are two grad assistants just waiting for me to slip up or step aside. Just like *'All About Eve,'* Dad, but for real. But tell you the truth, I'll be more than happy to oblige them. I'd rather see London any day."

"Melissa, are you sure about this? I don't want you jeopardizing your education for the sake of a trip to London, theater or no. Especially in November. It's mid-term and this isn't exactly the Bahamas."

"Dad, you are not listening to me, as usual. I'm not talking about a 'trip,' Dad," she said, defensively. "I'm talking about furthering my career. If I am going to actually fulfill my dream, which I would really appreciate you supporting, and have any chance at all of being the next Gwyneth Paltrow, I have got to experience London, it's that simple. Besides," she added, "I have people there I'd like to catch up with." She didn't add that there was one in particular or would be soon. "Besides, from what you said last time, I think you could use some, I don't know, help and literary expertise. I used to be an English major before Theater. Plus," she added, "it would be nice to hang out a little. I miss you, Dad," she added.

He felt torn. He knew she was playing a role, even now, of the neglected daughter. But she was also right. She really was a neglected daughter, and the fault was entirely his. "I miss you, too," he managed to respond, a catch in his voice. But at the same time, he was filled with misgivings. Still, he knew she would not take no for an answer.

"OK. Here's something you can help with. What do you know about a poet and playwright of the Elizabethan era, named Robert Greene?"

There was a distinct, if momentary, pause. "Robert Greene? What's he got to do with Dr. Lewis?"

"That's what I'm trying to find out. Lewis seemed to have been researching him about something that may relate to his disappearance. So, you know him?"

"I know his work," she said, a bit taken aback. "He was one of the minor poets from the Elizabethan theater. He wrote some mediocre plays I can't recall; nobody ever does them anymore. Why do you ask?"

"He also wrote an essay called *A Groatsworth of Wit*, which alludes to some kind of theft or plagiarism going on at the time. I think it may have some connection with Dr. Lewis's missing book."

"Really? Sorry, we didn't cover Greene very much in my class. But anyway, can I come and stay with you or not?"

He laughed, in spite of his misgivings. "Only if you can help me find Dr. Lewis and compel him to explain himself," he teased.

"If only," she laughed. "So, if I send you my arrival information can you meet me at the airport?"

He hesitated once more, wondering if he might be drawing her into something risky–even dangerous. "Listen Melissa, you're welcome to stay here, but I am a bit worried whether this is such a good idea. I still don't know what happened to Lewis, and I don't want to put you in the middle of a potentially hazardous situation." He decided not to mention that he was being followed.

She scoffed. "Thank you, lecture noted, Mister Protective Parent, Sir. But I am perfectly capable of taking care of myself. Do you not remember all those Tai Kwan Do classes, to help with balance and body language and so on?"

"Sorry," he admitted. "Guess I forgot." Not that terrorist cells, if that's what Lewis had run afoul of for reasons still known, would be daunted by a Kung Fu master, girl or no.

"So now can I give you my flight info, or do I have to come there and find you by accosting strangers on street corners?"

Reluctantly, he gave in. She was probably right, he was making much ado about nothing. Maybe he *was* just being overly protective, not to mention paranoid, and like it or not, his daughter was now a grown woman. And, he realized, the only one he had left in his life, just now. Maybe this would be a blessing in disguise, an opportunity for the two of them to spend some quality time together and close some of that distance between them. He had seen way too little of her since Beverly's death.

"I guess there's no way I'm gonna talk you out of it, is there?" he asked, finally.

"Nope. I've made up my mind."

He sighed, having learned from hard experience that there was no use arguing with his daughter if she was determined to do something. "All right. I probably could use some help in the literary field," he admitted. "Maybe I can get the paper to pick up your fare."

"Dad," she said, stiffly. "I'm fully capable of paying my own way and don't expect you or your newspaper to pick up the tab, OK? Especially the way things are in the publishing business."

"Easy, Kiddo, let's not get off to a bad start here. Air fares are expensive."

"I have the money from grandma's inheritance, remember?"

Ah. He'd forgotten about her maternal grandmother's little bequest. It was supposed to pay for her ongoing education, and it sounded like this was going to be part of that. So be it. He made a note to call Tom Flannigan, later. "Fine. If you really insist that coming to London simply cannot wait until, I don't know, Spring, or some time when you can actually enjoy the place and aren't going to get chilled to the bone and have to wade through the fog, you're welcome," he said. Then added, "Long as you don't mind sharing a bath."

"Dad, I'm a college student, remember?"

He laughed. "Right. OK, let me know when you expect to arrive, and I'll meet you at the airport. Make sure to let me know which one, by the way. Heathrow or Gatwick."

"I will. See you soon." With that, she hung up.

Some people take your breath away with their decisiveness, he thought. She was one of them. On the other hand, he suspected she took a lot of people's breath away, for a lot of reasons.

Canada, the Maritime Provinces, 8 a.m. local time

As the big 767 lumbered through the skies northeastward over Greenland, Melissa stared dolefully out at the fractured, surprisingly barren landscape below: a dissonance of ice, less and less each year, she had read; patches of bottomless black water, and endless uninhabited terrain, dotted with the random, occasional barren mountain. It was empty, and alien, and matched her mood perfectly. She wondered how much she should tell her father, and when.

By now, thanks to her employer, she knew all about the Desmond Lewis manuscript and his cockeyed theories. She knew the damage they could cause. And while it might not affect her as an actress in the long run, she was no fool. She understood the economic implications; they had been told to her often enough. Although the notion of a dangerous conspiracy against Britain's most sacred Name seemed a bit much.

The only thing that troubled her was what had happened to Dr. Lewis? Her academic advisor had shared the same concern, and she had no reason to doubt him. She wished, suddenly, that she'd asked her employer more questions. He should be in London by now, she figured. He'd left the day before, in rather a hurry. Ah well, she sighed. She had a phone number "for messages," he'd told her. He also had her number, and her cell phone worked on European channels. He had promised to be in touch. She hoped he would. He'd be busy with his book, but it would be nice to have a friend in a foreign city.

Chapter Twelve

His Faults Lie Gently on Him

London, late October

As he paced the sitting room of his rented flat on Russell Square, the learned scholar pondered his next move. The one thing he'd been so careful to guard against, the worst possible scenario, had barely been averted. What he still needed to find out, and had not done so, was how Desmond Lewis had reached such shocking and devastating conclusions, let alone why he would dare to disclose them. Indeed, he had been stopped barely in time. But there was another doubt gnawing at him: what if there was another copy after all. The Heretic had denied it. But what if he had lied?

Meanwhile there was the problem of the journalist. There was no time to lose, because someone was certain to come asking questions before long: if not Fleming, then another meddling investigator. *Our remedies oft in ourselves do lie!* He reminded himself.

But there was something else working in his favor. As surely as knowledge was power, he had a secret weapon. This journalist Fleming had a daughter. And what a daughter! This budding actress, even now en route to London, was someone whom he would play, like a fine musical instrument. Yes, she would have a role to play in his drama, be it tragedy or no, whether she knew her lines or not. Thus, would she serve his interests in ways that might yet salvage this disastrous situation. He could hardly wait. Even at this very moment, she was playing straight into his hands.

Chapter Thirteen

That Which We Call A Rose

Melissa's flight was an hour late, but these days that was about par. Finally, Jake spotted her waving from the passageway leading from Customs and felt a flood of relief and apprehension at the same time.

Melissa breezed through the gate like she knew exactly where she was going and what she was about, looking as fresh and lovely as though she had just stepped off the front page of Harper's Bazaar. He had to smile in grudging admiration. She was dressed 'casual,' in faded jeans, a sweatshirt, and a yellow sailing windbreaker with a hood for rain that lay flat behind her neck, her pale blond hair tumbling loose and fine to her shoulders. She hurried toward him, turning heads as she came, stirring looks and comments that suggested that she must be "someone," or if not, soon would be. But as she drew closer to her father she slowed, as though inhibited by sudden shyness. They greeted each other with the usual brief hug, then she pulled back, and looked him over with raised eyebrows gracing her piercing green eyes. Then she seemed to soften, as she shook her head slowly, back and forth in disapproval.

"You look like hell, Dad."

"Thank you so much. You look well too," he retorted. "So, do you want to get something to eat or drink before we head back to the city? Or are you ready to crash? It's kind of a long trip."

"No thanks, I had about five meals on the plane, if you can call them that."

He laughed. "OK, suit yourself. I assume you have luggage?"

She nodded, gesturing towards the baggage claims sign. "Just a duffel bag. I've actually learned to travel light doing summer stock, believe it or not."

"That's my girl," he teased, as she started off towards the baggage claim area like she owned the place, while he contented himself with keeping abreast of her long steady strides–no easy task.

They'd almost reached the escalator when Melissa glanced off to her left and caught her breath as though startled by something. She stopped abruptly and fished into her bag. “Shit!” she exclaimed. “Damn it!”

“What is it?” Jake looked around, worriedly.

“I left something on the plane.” She turned around and hurried back towards the gate.

“Melissa! Wait!” he called, hurrying after her. “They're not going to let you just waltz back to the plane to look around!”

She glared at him. “Just you watch me.”

Jake had to smile to himself at what he and Beverly had created. Melissa's mother would have been proud of this show of confidence, he had no doubt.

She returned ten minutes later, waving a manila envelope.

“Success, I presume?”

“It was right where I left it, in the seat pocket. Thank God.”

He fell in beside her as they headed for the elevator, which would shorten their trip to the baggage claim area. “Okay. What did you bring me?”

“You'll see.”

“Come on. What is it?” he insisted, reaching for the envelope.

She pulled it away. “Not until we can sit down somewhere. Let's get a taxi.”

He feigned a sulk. “Fine. Have it your way.” The baggage claim area was just ahead.

The carousel was now almost empty except for a single black sports duffel, going round and round, which Jake recognized as Melissa's. He'd given it to her for Christmas the year before. A security guard nodded at them and tipped his hat, watching as they compared stubs. There was no one else around as they headed for the exit.

Outside, they hailed a cab and clambered in just as the rains began. Jake gave the driver the Denmark Street address in Bloomsbury and leaned back in the seat, suddenly weary. Melissa's comment at the gate reminded him that he had not slept very much in days. He fought off the onset of fatigue, wanting to enjoy the presence of his talented, lovely daughter, and not knowing quite how to go about it. He also wanted to see what presents she had brought. He managed to pry open his eyes once more.

"So, c'mon, what did you bring me?"

Melissa gave him a teasing look, which he considered a good sign, and shook her head. But she remained silent and absorbed the whole way back to London, seemingly indifferent to the water-streaked sights and scenes that passed them by. However, her eyes lit up as they entered the city on Kensington Road, and she spotted the Wellington Arch straight ahead. "Oh, man," she breathed. "I can feel the rumblings of history."

"Probably just my stomach," he countered.

She wasn't amused. "You still having ulcer problems?"

"Nothing the miracles of modern pharmacology can't handle." He unwrapped a fresh pack of mints as proof.

"Oh yeah? You really need to see a doctor, Dad, that can be serious."

He shook his head in irritation. "I'm fine. Don't worry about it."

As they passed by St. James Park, Melissa leaned forward, gazing ahead. "Omigod," she exclaimed. "Is that the London Eye?" Jake looked. She was pointing at what he knew to be the world's largest Ferris Wheel across the river.

"Yes indeed," the cabbie spoke up. " 'Tis The London Eye. Our Millennium Wheel. They say you can see everything from there. Bloody eyesore, if you ask me."

It suddenly occurred to Jake that, in his week in London, he had never even noticed it, although he knew it was there. Could it be that he'd been rushing around with his head down the whole time? Or had he been too busy looking back over his shoulder. Still, maybe he just hadn't wanted to look up, it was so ostentatiously out of character for the historic capital city.

"If that's an Eye, I'd hate to see the face," said Melissa, gazing in wonder. "Talk about Big Brother!"

"Some say 'tis the Eye of God," commented the cabbie. Jake wondered if he was being ironic.

By the time the taxicab reached Denmark Street, rain was coming down in wind-driven sheets, and the streets gleamed and shimmered in the fractured light. Fred Buttles, the doorman (as Jake now knew his name to be), hurried to open their door, large umbrella in hand. He beamed at Melissa in approval as he led them under the shelter of the building marquee. Jake introduced his daughter, got a thumbs up of approval, and had just turned towards the elevator when Fred spoke to him in a low aside. "Mr. Fleming, there was a gent askin' about you."

"Really?" Jake frowned, gesturing to Melissa to go on to the elevator. "Was he a tall heavyset fellow?"

The doorman shook his head. "No sir. Quite the opposite, actually. More of a scholarly type, I'd say. Gray hair, middle aged, looked like a ferret—sorry sir, just a moment." Another taxi had just pulled up, and he hurried to assist an elderly couple from the back.

"Dad?" Melissa called over from the elevator door, as he hurried to join her.

"Who were you talking about?" she asked.

"Just a messenger, probably. From Reuters, or the Trib." He doubted that was true even as he spoke, however, and his apprehensions returned full force as he led the way to the lift and up to the flat.

He was also wondering how this new arrangement was going to work out. Technically, the flat was a one-bedroom. But it had an alcove with a convertible sofa, which pulled open to make a reasonably adequate queen-sized bed. Adequate, that is, for people with straight spines and intact cervical discs. Which excluded Jake Fleming, old war-horse that he was. Still, one must be willing to sacrifice for one's children at times, he thought. "I'll take the sofa bed," he told her. He'd already changed the linens in expectation of this decision, in any case.

"Don't be silly, Dad, I'm young. You're prehistoric!" she teased. "Seriously, I could sleep on a floor. You need your rest. You keep the bedroom."

Jake didn't know which was worse: the implication that he was old and feeble, or the fact that he was being patronized by his own daughter. He changed the subject. "OK, we'll decide later. How about my surprise?"

Almost bashfully, she dug into her bag and took out the manila envelope. "It's some pictures," she said, softly. "Of Mom." She laid them out on the coffee table and sat down.

He sat beside her, looked them over, and caught his breath. They had never spoken about Beverly, even once, since her untidy and painful death two years before. He studied them briefly: the smiling dark-eyed woman brushing the hair out of her eyes; gazing over a magazine at the sea that summer at the Hamptons; sitting at a café that time in Prague. There, on the slopes of Zermatt. The memories flooded back, and with them the tears, which he tried to brush away. On all three of those occasions, urgent assignments had called him away and disrupted their time together. And, he now bitterly realized, she had never made the attempt to travel with him again.

Melissa arose and turned away, discreetly wandering off to explore the kitchen.

"You have any coffee?" she asked, looking back from the alcove.

He shrugged, not daring to speak.

"Look, I'm going to be up anyway. I have some reading to do," he insisted. His recent bouts of insomnia weren't going anywhere, and he knew he wouldn't sleep well tonight either. "No point in wasting a perfectly good bed. You go ahead and take the bedroom." Finally, she yielded, and, coffee forgotten, gave him a quick peck goodnight.

As Melissa passed him en route from the bath to the bedroom, wrapped in a terry robe she'd somehow managed to acquire (surely it wouldn't have fit in that bag?) she stopped for a moment, and looked at him where he sat hunched over on the sofa reading Mark Twain. Her eyes were solemn. "Dad," she said. "You know, I miss her too. She was your wife and all, but she was my mom."

He nodded and looked away. After she had closed the door, he wiped away another tear that had sprung from the corner of one eye.

I hate it when that happens, he thought.

In the morning, Melissa was up at dawn and after a quick survey of the kitchen supplies, decided to go out for some fresh coffee and provisions. Jake was snoring erratically on the sofa, half covered by a blanket, an open book on his lap. She adjusted the blanket and tiptoed to the door, after locating the apartment key on the counter, locking up carefully behind her.

She returned an hour later to find, to her dismay, that her father was already up and had made do with a cup of leftover coffee from yesterday, and a stale cruller.

"Dad, you need proper nutrition," she admonished him. "Don't you have ulcers?"

"I'm fine," he said, popping a mint.

She put her hands on her hips. "Come on. You've been living for I don't know how long on stale coffee, antacids, and a diet of what, sugar and greasy leftovers? Are you serious?" She put the bag down, opened the fridge, and pointed at the withered slice of dry pizza moldering on the shelf, alongside the half-eaten cardboard container of fish and chips from a previous lunch on the run. "I mean, look at this." She dumped them in the garbage pail with an emphatic flourish.

"Hey. I like greasy leftovers," he protested.

"You really are incorrigible."

He sulked. "So, are you interested in what I've found out about Desmond Lewis, or are you just here to reorganize my life?"

She grinned, wryly. "Maybe both. And as for Dr. Lewis, from what I hear, no offense but according to academic circles, the man's a reprobate. I really wish you would leave that to the authorities."

"But then we wouldn't be having this fun time together in London."

She held up a jar. "Do you like artichoke hearts?"

He looked at her suspiciously. "Melissa, this is what I do, investigate strange disappearances and such. And this guy was a friend. Plus, he may not be so flaky as you seem to think."

She put the jar down. "What do you mean?"

"I mean he may have been onto something."

"That's what I'm talking about. Aren't you getting in over your head with all this literary muckraking? I mean, Dad, that isn't your field."

Which, he remembered, was exactly what he'd tried to tell Lewis himself. "So, is that what you came here to tell me?"

"No, it's just that I'm concerned about you." She put two packs of cheese, some juice, and fresh milk in the fridge, and added a bunch of carrots, a bundle of asparagus, several oranges, two pears, a mango and a container of yogurt, before shutting the door and throwing up her hands. "OK, I'm sorry, I'll shut up. You were going to tell me about what you discovered, so far. So, tell me." With that, she went about putting away several boxes of granola, some fresh whole wheat bread, and, much to his horror, a package of rice cakes.

While Melissa experimented with some gaseous-looking soft English cheese on a slab of fresh dark bread she'd somehow found, along with a slice of pear, he slid a slip of paper across the breakfast bar table to her. "Take a look at this list and tell me what you think."

She picked it up and looked it over with a frown. "What's this supposed to be?"

"It was in Dr. Lewis's pocket from the cleaners. His secretary–excuse me–administrative assistant found it."

She frowned, in puzzlement. "You think this means something? Like a clue or something?"

"Your guess is as good as mine. But I think the key to Des Lewis's disappearance is somewhere on that list."

She studied it while she chewed, shaking her head, slowly. " 'Ox'. Hmm. Do they have oxen in England?"

He shrugged. "Not as far as I know. I was wondering the same thing. Ox tail soup, maybe. I was looking for a connection between 'ox' and 'lamb.' "

"Well, apart from the obvious, both are capitalized. So, they might be abbreviations and not animals at all."

He hadn't thought of that. "Right. Ox. As in 'oxygen?' "

"Or as in 'Oxford,' as in University?"

Jake snapped his fingers. "Of course! He studied there and had some kind of history there. Melissa, I think you're on to something there. How about 'Lamb?' "

"You got me." She shook her head with a frown. "Of course, 'Herb' could be a seasoning as well as a person. If it's an herb, why wouldn't he say what kind?"

"Good point, it is a pretty generic term." He paused. "It would be ironic if this was just a shopping list of some kind. Get some herbs for oxtail soup, a lamb chop, L.W.T. for lettuce with tomato, M.T. for marjoram and thyme?"

She shook her head. "Maybe. But I don't think so. Not with 'Crow.' But it could also be 'eat crow' in the non-dietary sense, or the movie, *Crow* or 'crow in delight' like maybe he's got this great recipe that people like so much it makes him crow in delight? Or–"

"All right, all right. That set of initials: 'M T.' I think it's 'Mark Twain,' and I've been reading his autobiography."

"The new one?"

"The original, actually. But Twain wrote about everything under the sun, so I'm clueless as to where he's going with that." He decided not to mention the message from the grave until he'd a chance to read said 'message.'

"Yeah, a guess is as good as a mile, and you could be a mile off. Also, for all you know it could be for Meg Tilly. Or some sports figure, like Mike whatsisname."

"Tyson."

She took another bite and continued scanning the list. "LWT could be anything, or anyone, lettuce with tomato included. Hmm. 'V.A.' as in 'Veteran's Administration?' "

"Not in England. And Lewis wasn't a veteran. Or a vegetarian, for that matter."

"Hoff and Herb could be names. But it could be anyone."

He nodded.

"And what's this 'Inq?' "

"I've been thinking about that. Only a few words begin with that spelling: inquiry, inquisitor, inquire."

"Maybe it was a note to self to inquire about the rest of the list. Or something."

"Maybe." He pondered, sensing there was something else, just out of reach.

"Inquisition!" Melissa suddenly exclaimed. "Like the Spanish Inquisition! That was a creepy period of history. Could he have been writing about that? Maybe an analogy to Guantanamo or Abu Ghraib?"

"Not English enough." He snapped his fingers. "Inquest! I bet it means inquest."

"Why? Isn't that usually a judicial inquiry into a death?"

"Exactly. I think Lewis was poking into something or somewhere he wasn't wanted. An inquiry into someone's death would be just such a place to look."

"I still like 'inquisition.' " She tapped on the last entry. " 'Apoc'? What's that?" She looked up at him. " 'Apocalypse?' "

"Yeah, I thought of that. I just don't know."

"Was he one of those conspiracy theorists? Like in 'four horsemen?' If so, that's pretty creepy."

"Maybe it's short for 'apothecary.' Maybe it is just an errands list after all."

"Maybe." She bit her lip. "Still, it's not much to go on." She went to the window and gazed out at the city lights.

"So," he said, after a while, testing a bit of the dark bread and cheese dubiously. "What would you like to do first, now that you're here?"

Melissa pondered a moment. "Dad," she said, thoughtfully. "If I am going to make it as an actor, I am going to have to start by paying a visit to the Globe."

He blinked at her, distracted by the surprisingly pungent cheese flavor. "This isn't bad. What globe?"

"Shakespeare's Globe," she repeated. "The world famous Globe Theater. Hello?" She pointed vaguely in the direction of the river. "I've waited for years for this. I read up on it in Fodor's. It's just over the bridge, near what used to be Bankside. We could take the underground, then walk from there."

"You want to see a play? Melissa, it's raining out and it's almost November. Isn't the Globe out in the open?"

"This is London, it's always raining out. That's what raincoats and umbrellas are for, you know?" As usual, he lost the argument.

The weather worsened as the day progressed, along with Jake's mood. Despite both of them being properly equipped with umbrellas, they were pretty sodden by the time they got to Bankside. The new Globe Theater in Southwark was located a short distance from the sites of the original Globe and Rose Theaters, which had since been obliterated by developers of one sort or another, over the centuries. But it certainly looked authentic enough, thought Jake, complete with wood panels and a now drenched thatched roof, although he suspected firmer underpinnings beneath. At Melissa's insistence, Jake dutifully got on the queue and purchased two tickets for the next tour, which, the ticket taker promised, they would find 'quite informative,' despite the weather.

They decided against a performance that evening, given the auditorium's open roof and rain. As they waited for their tour to begin, Jake studied the surroundings, and the other people around them who'd also decided to brave the weather. Tourists, mostly, some obviously American, others from possibly anywhere. While Melissa studied the cast lists and wandered off to inquire about any pending open casting calls ("Just in case," she had insisted), he noted among the small gathered crowd two men who were either Chinese or Japanese; a young Russian couple possibly recently wed and already a bit on edge with each other; a middle-aged, silver-gray haired Asian; an African family and a few others he couldn't identify, possibly Middle Easterners, which didn't improve his disposition any. At least they weren't young males with backpacks, he thought, then banished the thought. To the contrary, they were well-dressed business types with wives wearing hijabs.

While waiting for Melissa to return for the next tour, Jake browsed the various artworks and displays in the lobby, and perused a stylishly designed poster for the next Globe production: *Titus Andronicus,* which rang a bell in the back of his mind. He'd read it in college but couldn't remember anything about it at all.

Melissa rejoined him clutching a rehearsal schedule. "They may still have some openings for stand-ins!" she announced, as though she had just been nominated for an Oscar.

"What was this play about, anyway?" he asked her, pointing at the poster.

"Blood and gore," she said, flippantly. "Right up your alley." But there was something else about it, some connection he couldn't quite put together, if he could just remember what it was.

"Dad, did you see the cast list?" exclaimed Melissa. Indeed, the billboard featured a surprisingly long list of big name players.

"I wonder how a nonprofit like the Globe can afford such heavyweights?" he commented.

"Easy," said Melissa. "They love the prestige and would probably do it for scale. I would. Plus, they all have sponsors." She pointed to the bottom of the poster. Sure enough, there was printed, in discreet Elizabethan script: 'Brought to you by British Airways, BP, and Avena Global Partners, Ltd.'

Whoever they are, thought Jake, idly, obviously, they had money.

A cheerful middle-aged English woman in a blazer with an Oxford accent introduced herself as their guide, and the tour began. She led the way into the theater proper, where they ducked through the covered wooden seating area, basically benches, and then splashed through an open area in front of the stage.

Melissa was enthralled. "This is the 'groundlings,' " she told him, in low, reverential tones. "It's where the riff raff got to sit, or stand, and watch the plays. It was like a free-for-all. Except not free, of course."

"So, the riff raff got the orchestra, minus seats," noted Jake, with a grin. "Front and center."

"The nobility sat back there in the box seats," she explained, pointing back to the two levels beneath the thatched roof.

They moved on from the pit to the elevated stage itself. There the guide gripped a prim umbrella and, in her crisp tones and phrases, recounted to her soon-dripping audience an apocryphal tale about how the Old Globe and the nearby Rose Theater were bitter rivals

"The Globe, of course," she explained, "was the home of the Chamberlain's Men, who staged the new plays of William Shakespeare, whereas Philip Henslowe's Rose, just a block away, stuck to the old standards of Marlowe and the so-called University Wits."

Melissa nudged her father, whose attention had wandered. "Listen." she insisted. "This is awesome!"

"Some of Shakespeare's predecessors' plays had a considerable following, and there was a rivalry of sorts between the respective playgoers. As the stories go, after each evening's performances the two audiences would spill out into the streets and proceed to brawl over which theater's playwright was greater. The Shakespeare playgoers used to quote a line from Romeo and Juliet: *A Rose by any other name would smell as sweet*."

"This, of course," the guide continued, "was our Bard, poking fun at his rivals. As the legend goes, the Rose Theater emitted a foul stench, the result of excessive gutter-side urinating on the part of its patrons." The tour group laughed heartily. All except the Asian man Jake had noticed earlier, hovering in the background. He had the oddest feeling that the man was watching them. The Asian positively glowered at the comment about the gutter.

"Presumably, Shakespeare's audiences had better bladders," the Asian man muttered aloud.

"Sir, did you have a question?" Called out the tour guide, disapprovingly.

The Asian man shook his head.

The guide clucked, turned away, and the water-logged tour resumed, revealing some interesting facts regarding Shakespeare's actual fiscal interest in the plays. Shakespeare, she explained, had worked himself into a position in the company quite early on whereby he got paid *three times* for each performance: once as player; once as co-owner (he owned ten percent of the company, according to the Globe guide); and a third time as playwright.

"Pretty good deal," commented Jake, receiving an elbow in the ribs from his daughter in response. They were just leaving the theater when Jake saw something–or rather someone–that made him stop cold. A large, anapestic man stood in the crowd across the foyer. The man who had followed him home, and to the British Library. But he wasn't watching Jake. His attention seemed drawn to someone or something else entirely. Jake couldn't see who, however, because of the crowd and pillar behind him.

There, a brief transaction was taking place at that moment as a slender gray-haired man, his cold gray eyes fixed upon the Asian with malice visible even to the large man across the lobby, handed a small envelope to one of the tour guides, nodded in the Asian man's direction, and hurried away. Jake realized that something was afoot when the guide brushed past him and dutifully carried the envelope over to the Asian man, tapping him on the arm.

"Excuse me sir? This is for you." The Asian nodded absently, then reacted with a look of sudden fear when he saw the envelope. Jake, standing nearby, watched him turn pale and his hands begin to shake, as he quickly discarded the offending missive in the nearest trash bin. Jake frowned and approached the man.

"Excuse me," he said. "Are you all right?"

The Asian looked at him, with fear and anger in his eyes. "What do you want from me?" he demanded, backing away.

"Excuse me?"

The man opened his mouth to say something more, then looking beyond Jake, saw something, or someone, that seemed to either terrify or enrage him even more, and he turned and fled the theater without another word.

Jake stared after him in dismay, then, with a cautious glance around the area, he surreptitiously dipped his hand into the waste basket and removed the crumpled message. The name written on the envelope nearly floored him.

To Dr. Sunir Balsavar.

Melissa, who'd been distracted by a poster on the wall, rejoined him, curious. "What is it?"

"I think it was someone Lewis knows. Or knew. I think he may have followed us here. Maybe to contact me, or maybe just to find out what I was after. Then someone gave him this, and whatever it says, it sure as hell spooked him." Jake unfolded the paper. The note consisted of a single line. It read:

Curst be he that moves my bones.

"What the hell?" muttered Jake, downing a mint. "What is that supposed to mean?"

Melissa paled, and shook her head. "I don't know. But I think I've heard it somewhere."

Now a safe distance away and hurrying west along the promenade, the thin man considered his next move. The journalist had not been out in public since the airport the day before. Showing himself at the Denmark Street flat had been a mistake, he realized in retrospect. He knew that the doorman had reported him to the journalist, which was not good. He couldn't risk going there again for now, although he'd certainly approach the next man on duty following a change of shift. Perhaps the doorman's replacement would be more careless. Or, perhaps either doorman could be bought. Then there was the young woman's arrival to consider, and how best to exploit her talents. This would be tricky and might yet be his undoing. *Yield not thy neck to fortune's yoke*, he reminded himself. *But let thy dauntless mind still ride in triumph over all mischance.*

After all, he was not without resources. While not a patient man, he would bide his time and watch for the right moment once more. It would surely come. Meanwhile, he couldn't further risk being seen here.

If only these terrible pains in his head would cease and desist, then all might yet be well once again. If only he could place trust in medication. But it captured your soul; thus, he could not.

Chapter Fourteen

As Thy Purse Can Buy

As they rode the underground back to Charing Cross Station, Jake told Melissa about the Asian physicist.

She frowned. "You know, that guy looked Pakistani. You think Lewis was involved with Al Qaeda or the Taliban, or something like that? Whoa! Wasn't that AQ Khan nuclear physicist from Pakistan? The one that gave the formula to, like, North Korea and Iran?"

"That's a reach, but the man was definitely worried about something."

"But what?"

"Being stalked? Maybe by the same person or persons who raided Lewis's home and office?" Or, he wondered, was the Asian the actual perpetrator, fearful of being found out and wanting to know what our intentions were?

"You think someone's trying to blackmail him? Oh, this is so cool. It's almost like a real movie or something!"

He chose not to disillusion her. Movies were far safer than reality. Film audiences almost always returned home safely. Or remained safe at home watching Netflix or HBO on their sofas, regardless of the pandemonium on the screen (which granted was common and often massive).

"It's possible. Or threaten him into silence. Again, the question is why?"

Melissa frowned suddenly and looked at him askance. "Dad, I don't mean to criticize, but either way, you let that man slip right through your fingers. You should have gone after him when you had the chance and cornered him, don't you think?"

So much for playing the hero in the eyes of his daughter. "Maybe you're right. Except there was another person there I've seen before, and he's the one I wanted to follow."

"So why didn't you?" He just looked at her, wondering why he'd ever allowed her to come. Then she seemed to read his mind. "What, so it's my fault?"

He shook his head. “No, of course not. But I didn’t want to put you in any danger.” He wanted very much to change the subject, nowhere near ready to tell her about the large man. “So, what did you make of that cryptic note, *curst be he*?”

She shuddered, dramatically. “I haven’t the foggiest. It sounds like a warning of some kind.”

The train was slowing now, for Charing Cross. Jake got to his feet and moved toward the door. “Judging by his behavior at the tour, my guess is he was planning on making contact with me until that note got passed to him. If he knows who I am and how to reach me, he’ll probably try again.”

She ducked under his arm, determined to be one step ahead as the door slid open. Then, when both of them were off the train, her eyes widened. “Oh, I get it!” she said. “It’s me, isn’t it. Seeing you with me must’ve thrown him, so he didn’t know what to do.”

As they rode the escalator to the street, Jake fell silent, lost in thought. Secretly he was glad to have his daughter’s company. But he was also feeling guilty for possibly putting her in danger. Yet if anything, she seemed to be enjoying herself.

“Let’s grab a coffee!” she proposed, as they reached the busy thoroughfare.

They had Cappuccinos at a quaint little Mediterranean coffee shop off Kensington Road, and to lighten the load on his mind, Jake asked about Melissa’s plans for her stay in London.

“Nothing definite yet. I need to get a copy of the theater trades and see what’s playing where, and who I need to contact. Plus, I’m still talking to my faculty advisers.”

He could tell she was holding back but knew that pushing her would be futile.

“Ready to go?” he asked, picking up the tab.

Just as they stepped out onto the now bustling sidewalk, there was the shrill ring tone of a cell phone. “That’s mine,” said Melissa, digging into her handbag. She read a message on her screen, and snapped it shut. “I have a meeting, speaking of my dissertation,” she said. “Can I meet you later?”

“Sure,” he said. “Anyone I know?”

"No. Just an old friend who's in town," she said, and flagged down a cab. Then she added, pointedly: "Maybe we'll take in a play."

"Have fun. I'll be at home, reading Mark Twain."

As Jake entered the borrowed flat, he noticed the phone light blinking. There were two messages. The first he recognized was from the States: San Francisco.

"Hey Fleming? Where the hell are you, anyway? This is your editor, Tom Flannigan at the *Tribune*. Remember me? You need to get in touch, a.s.a.p. okay?" The message was clear. The time clock was ticking. He'd have to deliver something, and soon.

The second message was a hang-up.

Famished, Jake went to look for something to eat. It didn't improve his state of mind that all he could find in the kitchen was health food.

Chapter Fifteen

Open Locks, Whoever Knocks

London, 7:00 p.m.

The thin gray-haired man and the attractive young woman met and sat in a cafe adjacent to the university center. The man spoke expansively, gesturing at their surroundings, the library next door, at the classroom buildings beyond, at the students and teachers passing to and fro, even the city gleaming beyond, as though this was his realm; these his people. Several of whom seemed to recognize him and stopped to shake hands. They spoke deferentially for a few moments and hurried off, with scarcely a glance at the young woman, which seemed to disconcert her.

As her companion resumed his monologue, the young woman listened attentively, nodding at all the right moments like a good disciple. Or employee. But her mind seemed elsewhere, which, after a while, he began to note. He spoke some more, at length, watching her intently; and she spoke for a while, gesturing defensively, and then reassuringly. He nodded and smiled condescendingly. After a while, he rose, touched her shoulder briefly, and departed, vanishing into the midst of his evident kingdom.

She sat, alone, in fretful indecision. One or two hopeful young male students stopped and asked if she was lost, or if she was new on campus, what she was doing, and if they could join her. She brushed them off like dandruff, and finally arose, and walked back to Denmark Street.

Melissa had a lot of thinking to do.

Back in the flat, Jake, having assuaged his hunger pangs with a slice of cheese, decided to take the initiative. He picked up the phone and dialed Dr. Balsavar once more. This time the physicist answered on the first ring.

"Yes, what is it you want?"

"This is Jake Fleming again. I saw you at the Globe Theater earlier today. Somehow I don't think that was a coincidence."

There was a brief, but distinct pause. "I don't know what you are speaking of, sir."

"I think you do. Were you following me?"

Another pause. "How am I to know it wasn't you who sent me that threat?"

So, it was a threat. "I think you know it wasn't me, Dr. Balsavar."

There was a sigh of, what, resignation? "Very well, then. But I understand you have been asking questions around the campus about Dr. Lewis and myself. It's imperative that I know why."

Jake thought for a moment and decided it would be best to keep the man talking. "I met him a couple years back in Florida, and we became friends. Last week he called me in Berkeley, where I live, asked me to meet him and take a look at his new book."

"Berkeley, in California?"

"That's right."

"And did you do so?"

"I did not. He never arrived."

"So, you know about his book?"

"Only that he wanted me to read it, before he gave it to his publishers."

"So you didn't read it?"

"No. It disappeared, along with its author. What can you tell me about that? And also about that note you got today?"

Balsavar was silent, for a moment. "I cannot speak of this over the telephone. We would need to speak in person. Can you meet me tomorrow?"

"What time and where?"

"Go to the British Museum, to the exhibition of the clocks at ten o'clock. And you may bring your fiancée, if you wish."

"Dr. Balsavar, that was my daughter."

"I see. So sorry. But I'd prefer knowing whom I'm dealing with than not."

"I'll tell her," Jake replied, as Balsavar hung up.

Jake had no idea what Melissa's reaction would be to this plan, at this point. She'd probably love it, eager to play Audrey Hepburn in *Charade*, or whatever. But what if it was a trap of some kind? For all he knew Balsavar was the one who had taken Lewis. His assistant Gloria had said they had a relationship, and she was certainly jaundiced as to what sort.

Melissa returned a few minutes later. "I spoke to Balsavar," he told her.

"Who?"

"The Asian. The name on the card. He was the man at the Globe, as you thought."

"So, what did he say?"

"He wants a meeting. You can come if you want. I don't think he's dangerous, actually. But I'd rather you didn't."

She frowned. "Did he say why he was there at the Globe?"

"No. He said we needed to talk in person."

"Are you sure that's a good idea, Dad? I mean, you don't know anything about him, other than he was following us."

"Maybe he'll take me to Lewis. Maybe he can tell us what happened to him."

"Maybe he'll shoot us and feed us to the fishes."

"In which case I'd really rather you stay home, if you don't mind. Don't you have plays to attend?"

"I was just kidding, Dad. And I do mind. We're in this together."

Jake thought about that, fretfully. If there was danger, the British Museum, being a very public and popular place, was as safe a meeting place as any. It was also possible Balsavar felt the same way.

Melissa noticed what he was eating. "By the way, I brought you some acidophilus. It'll help your digestion."

"My digestion's fine, it's my ulcer that gives me trouble." But he accepted it grudgingly. Not that he planned on taking anything with 'acid' in the name.

London, 10:00 a.m.

From the outside, the British Museum looked as though it might be the drabbest slab of Greek revival concrete in the Western Hemisphere. But, thought Jake, as the saying went: it's what's inside that counts. Here were housed, he knew, the treasures of lost kingdoms that the great British explorers and mariners–from the time of the greatest monarch of all, Elizabeth I, to the mad King George III, to the timeless Victoria—had gathered, in their zeal for acquisition and empire, from throughout the world. He had spent hours there when he'd first visited London years before, contemplating the Elgin Marbles: surely the most beautiful sculptures and Athens' most heartbreaking loss of all time. Then there was the Rosetta Stone, a dazzling collection of Egyptian mummies, and so much more.

They found the exhibit on the history of clocks with no trouble, other than for the crowds. Jake was too busy watching for their erstwhile contact to pay much attention, but Melissa was fascinated by the variety of instruments and mechanisms on display. The sheer elegance of some of them, particularly the older German performance timepieces, stunned her. She found their little plays and minuets—minute intricately carved dancers, knights, monks and tinkers so engrossing that she almost forgot why they were there. Jake felt increasing impatience, however, watching each new arrival in the exhibition room. A group of Asians entered, and marveled over the displays. But the man at the Globe was not among them. Finally, after an hour, Jake glanced at his watch. It was nearly eleven.

"Let's go," he said. "He's not coming."

"So it seems," she agreed, weary at last of the clocks. "Can we get a cup of coffee?"

"I'm worried maybe something has happened."

Outside, the streets were crowded, the London lunch hour just under way. The sky was still threatening, but the rain had abated. Jake noticed a dark imposing figure standing across the street whom he'd seen before, and his heart sank, and his pulse quickened at the same time. It was the same large man he'd observed two days earlier, and again yesterday at the Globe, just before someone had sent Balsavar that warning note. Could that note have been sent by him, through a confederate he hadn't spotted?

"Melissa," he said, in a low voice. "Don't look, but I think we're being followed. I've seen that same man twice in the last few days, including at the Globe yesterday."

"Where?" Ignoring his warning, Melissa followed his glance, in alarm. "Are you sure?" So much for acting nonchalant, he thought, but didn't say. The man across the road had already turned and was moving away.

Sunir Balsavar knew he was in trouble. Someone had been following him for the last two hours, and he'd dared not risk leading his tracker to his rendez-vous point. He'd never seen him before, which was especially worrisome because the heavyset man seemed to know him and his every movement.

He had come to the end of the museum courtyard on his way to his meeting with the Americans, uncertain what to do next. Was this the person who'd sent him that note at the Globe? What could he mean, and how much did he know?

Abandoning any further thought of making his appointment, he had tried to shake the man to no avail, taking him first around the periphery of the huge complex, then when that failed, he'd tried to lose him in the crowd around the entrance. He risked a glance over his shoulder, and his heart quailed. The man was still there, less than ten paces away now and eying him with a strange and chilling look of menace which terrified him. Even worse, the man no longer seemed concerned about being spotted.

Balsavar had almost decided to accost the nearest policeman and ask for assistance, knowing full well how ridiculous that would sound, and unlikely to get results it would be. But he could think of nothing else to do, and he sensed that time was running out. On the other hand, he had many reasons to mistrust and avoid, if at all possible, involvement with the police. It was at that moment that he heard the young woman's voice: "Dad, isn't that him over there?"

It was the journalist, Fleming, and his daughter, just leaving the museum! He hurried over to them, at the same time trying to conceal his erstwhile desperation and subsequent relief. "Mr. Fleming! There you are."

"Yes. Where were you? We were just leaving."

"I'm sorry. There's trouble. Please follow me, quickly. I'm afraid I've been followed."

"You mean that big guy over there? He seems to be keeping his distance," noted Jake, nodding across the plaza to where the large man had stood, moments before.

Balsavar looked around in bewilderment. “You saw him? Where?”

But when Jake turned, there was no one in sight except for a large crowd of school children, accompanied by two nuns. He was certain, however, that it was the same large man that had been following him.

“This way,” said Balsavar, leading them through the group of schoolchildren. “I think if we stay with this group, we’ll be safe.” Jake thought about a terrorist event not that long ago involving a school in Russia but made no comment.

“Safe from what? What’s going on?” asked Melissa, not one to mince words.

Balsavar glanced at her and turned to her father. “Mr. Fleming, I fear I am in danger. Perhaps you as well. I’m sorry to get your daughter involved in this.”

“Don’t worry about it,” said Melissa, annoyed at being excluded from the conversation more than fearful of any potential danger in the courtyard of the museum. Especially in the presence of nuns. In her eyes, nuns were strictly off limits, when it came to terrorists and such. In fact, she could not think of a single play or movie she’d seen in which nuns came to harm.

Jake, keeping an eye out for the big man, looked at the Asian with a frown. “I assume this has something to do with Desmond Lewis?”

“Yes. You want to find Professor Lewis,” the Asian said, resignedly, deftly stepping aside as two young boys careened past, chasing balloons. “And so do I. We both work at the university, although different departments. He had learned of my own research and discoveries and approached me about them. He wanted them for his book, you see.”

Ironic, thought Jake. Publish or perish. And had it become, at least for Lewis, just perish?

“Professor Lewis is a renowned and legitimate Post-Renaissance scholar, as you probably know. I, on the other hand, am only a poor foreigner from Pakistan, and my discipline is physics. English is not my specialty, nor am I welcome in those hallowed quarters.”

“I find that hard to believe. You’re still a professor. And your English, by the way, is impeccable.”

"Thank you. But trust me, sir, in these matters, whether written or verbal, my opinions do not count, at least in Academe. So, I gladly gave him my notes. Now I must confess I am regretting that decision most deeply."

"How so?"

"After I helped him with his writing, he has cut me off from communication. I haven't heard from him in many weeks, and now you seem to know as much as I do. And to be honest, I feel I have a vested interest in this book, shall we say?"

"Vested interest in the publishing, in the content, royalties, what exactly?" Jake persisted.

"In all of that. In the truth."

"Truth about what?" asked Melissa, in exasperation.

Again, Balsavar turned to Jake. "Mr. Fleming, what Desmond Lewis was about to disclose may be the greatest cover-up of a crime that ever occurred, at least in the English-speaking world. And it was I who gave him that story. Perhaps because I was not schooled in the English system, I was not raised wearing blinders, although it was plain enough to see."

Melissa turned sharply, schoolchildren forgotten. "What do you mean 'cover-up'?"

"It involves murder," said Balsavar. "Wouldn't that be your field, sir?"

Startled, Jake had to admit that, as an investigative journalist, it would. At times."You're saying Lewis had uncovered some sort of crime of historic proportions, and he was about to reveal this in his book, and may have been murdered in the process?"

Balsavar stared, and his eyes shifted wildly from side to side. "No! I don't know. Why do you ask that? Do you think I had something to do with such a thing?"

Suddenly, they were alone. The children had all been hustled onto a school bus, and the lunch crowd seemed to have vanished as swiftly as a cloud of dust in a squall. The air had taken on a distinct chill.

"Let's not put the castle before the moat," said Jake. "What unspeakable crime was it you were talking about that Dr. Lewis was going to expose?"

"Theft," he said. "Theft of a great man's entire life's work!"

“What man’s life’s work?” demanded Melissa.

Balsavar looked dismayed. “That’s the problem. After I gave Dr. Lewis my notes, he went into seclusion, and would not reveal even to me what his conclusions were. Yet I know it will be something earth-shaking, and it frightens me.”

Jake surreptitiously sneaked a mint from his pocket, avoiding Melissa’s glare. He didn’t like the sound of this. “But you know there was a cover-up?”

“Very much so.”

“Do you mind if I ask one teensy little question?” Melissa finally cut in, in exasperation.

“Sorry, Miss,” apologized Balsavar.

“What is it?” asked Jake, clueless as usual about women, other than that the ones he loved best always seemed more beautiful when they were mad. Was that sexist? He wondered.

“Well, you’re talking like some horrible thing happened like, a million years ago, so, a. who cares, and b. what theft are you talking about? I mean, really, get to the point! Who was this ‘Thief for All Time’ or whatever you’re talking about?”

“I like that analogy,” said Jake, jotting it down. “This is my daughter, Melissa,” he mentioned belatedly.

The Asian hesitated a long moment, almost as if expecting he would be stricken dead by lightning or devoured by some vengeful beast straight out of Beowulf. Then he looked at the two Flemings, father and daughter, his eyes wide, perhaps as though fearing they would devour him, too. The young woman looked impatient and disbelieving, although hardly predatory. The man seemed merely skeptical. He turned away, directing his gaze towards the distant university towers, beyond. Slowly, he whispered the name like a curse, barely audible. “It was Shakespeare,” he murmured. “William Shakespeare, *The Upstart Crow*.”

Chapter Sixteen

That Now Lie Foul and Muddy

Melissa let out a sharp breath. She threw her hands into the air like the next Hepburn and turned to walk away, shaking her head, and the other two followed quickly after a moment of stunned silence.

"I assume this has to do with Robert Greene?" asked Jake, after recovering his voice.

Sunir looked surprised, stepped around some litter, then nodded, bleakly. "He was Robert Greene's nemesis, of course."

"Greene was writing about *Shakespeare*?" exclaimed Jake, stunned. Of course, he realized. 'Shake-scene.' The 'Player.'

They headed towards the museum gate, Melissa shaking her head.

"Robert Greene was just jealous of a better writer," Melissa retorted, over her shoulder. "My English Professors even talked about that, I remember now."

"A better writer who steals?" asked Balsavar.

She opened her mouth in protest and closed it again.

"Like the crow steals bright feathers," said Balsavar, simply.

Jake turned sideways for a passing crowd of Chinese students, and glanced at Balsavar, mystified. Then it hit him like a flash of lightning. "You are saying that someone else wrote the Plays and Shakespeare *stole* them?"

"That was the original basis of our book. And now you say it has disappeared, along with Dr. Lewis?"

Melissa spoke up. "That's crazy. This whole issue of the Shakespeare authorship has been raked through the coals ad nauseum, and there is nothing to it, and I should know."

"How so?" asked Jake, looking at her in confusion. She didn't answer and kept walking.

They left the Museum Square, crossed Great Russell and turned down Museum Street lined with curio shops and small restaurants and cafes.

Balsavar hurried to catch up and caught Jake's elbow. "Sir, I beg you. Consider the facts for yourself, then apply your own standard of logic," he pleaded. "Then you must help me recover my book. Dr. Lewis's and my book."

"Yeah, but what are the 'facts?' Whole governments have been known to invent or alter facts to suit a predetermined action or position. Not to mention religions. As we all well know."

"So have professors, Dr. Balsavar," noted Melissa.

"Please, call me Sunir," he insisted. "And I agree, what you say is true." As they stopped at a crossing and waited for the light, he turned towards them, gesturing intensely, focusing on Jake. "Perhaps like in politics, or from what I gather the popular media in your country, in the world of Academe conjecture often becomes entrenched as fact, and if allowed to remain unchallenged for long enough, it becomes doctrine, which then calcifies into dogma. Such is the case with Shakespeare."

The light changed. "Dad, this man is wasting your time," said Melissa, stepping off the curb and narrowly missing being hit by a taxi rounding the corner from the right with an angry honk.

"Look out!" Jake shouted way too late. She'd been looking left—a common, often fatal mistake for first-time visitors to the UK. But, being nimble, she jumped back just in time, giving her father, if not a near coronary, definite new cause for an ulcer. Melissa, however, barely missed a beat. "There's nothing new about any of this, it's all just speculative muck-raking."

Sunir winced. "I'm sorry, I shouldn't have said anything at all. If my colleague knows I am speaking to you he'll kill me."

Jake wondered how much the Asian knew. Was he being ironic?

"Who? Dr. Lewis? I doubt it, given he pleaded with me to read it."

"Perhaps he's not the only one," murmured Balsavar.

"What's *that* supposed to mean?" Melissa demanded.

"In any case, I must recover that book."

Jake looked at him. "So, I gather you don't have a copy of it?"

Sunir shook his head. "No. He promised to give me one, but alas, he did not."

"You do have your own notes though, right?"

"Yes, but it's only half the story. The rest was his own work. I can only speculate."

Jake glanced around, tensely. "From what you are saying, I'd have to agree that you may be in danger," he said. "You do know his office and apartment were ransacked?"

Melissa stared at her father. "You didn't mention that to me."

"Sorry. I didn't want to worry you." He turned back to Sunir, who had paled visibly.

"I didn't know about that either," insisted the Asian in alarm.

Melissa pulled Jake aside. "Dad, for all we know this man could be the perpetrator. He said he had a vested interest."

"How can I convince you otherwise?" pleaded Sunir, anxiously scanning the street once more.

"Tell me what you know," said Jake. Then, with a guilty glance at his daughter, still scowling, he quickly asked her: "Did you want to join us?"

"We must get away from here," pleaded Balsavar. "It isn't safe." He turned and started walking.

"Let's get back to Shakespeare for a second," said Jake, hurrying to catch up, reluctantly followed by Melissa. "Can you explain how such an alleged crime could possibly have been concealed for centuries from the thousands of scholars who have been poring over every document and writing books for all those years?"

"How many millions still believe God made the Earth in seven days?" asked Sunir. "And how many write or read books about Rapture and such, which don't even exist in the Bible? Do not seventy percent of Americans now insist, like a certain of your Presidents, that this is so? People will believe what they want to believe, or what they are told to believe, regardless of the facts or documents."

"We need to find a place to talk," said Jake, who was starting to feel the cold and damp. "Preferably a warm place out of the wind."

Melissa was now trailing behind, and Jake glanced back over his shoulder. The large man was back: a block away, biding his time. "Shit," he said. "He's still there."

"Who's there?" asked Melissa, glancing around worriedly and hurrying to catch up.

"Quickly," said Sunir, not daring to look. "This way!"

He led them down a side street, little more than an alley, which led to a small tea shop at the end.

"This is a dead end," objected Melissa.

"No, there is a back way out. And I don't think that man will dare follow us inside. It's too small for concealment, and we can call for help if it comes to it."

"Oh my God!" protested Melissa.

The tea shop, an intentional replica of another time and place like so much of London, was surprisingly warm and pleasant, complete with crackling fireplace. Balsavar proved correct. Their follower, or followers, didn't pursue them inside, suggesting confrontation or mayhem was not, at least for the moment, imminent. So, for now, at least they were safe to talk. Once they'd all warmed up by the fire with tea and scones with jam, Sunir was at last ready to explain and Jake, at least, was ready to listen.

Melissa sipped her tea and watched the door with sullen apprehension.

"So why are you telling us all this," she spoke up. "If this book is supposed to be such a big secret?"

"Because he has disappeared, didn't you just say so?" The Asian exclaimed to Jake in exasperation. "The truth about Shakespeare has been hidden for centuries, although certainly available had anyone been willing to look," he added. "And some may know it already. If this book cannot be recovered, if something has happened to my colleague, then the people, at least, should know the truth. I believe that if you, sir, as a journalist, were to examine the true facts about him, then you will see how plainly it must be that your Shakespeare was a fraud and a thief, and another man's work was purloined."

"Just don't tell me it was Robert Greene," said Melissa, practicing various expressions of scorn.

" 'A Thief for All Time,' " repeated Jake, with an admiring glance at his daughter. Smart and beautiful, he thought. As well as talented. She should go far. If she didn't step in front of a bus.

Jake banished the thought. “OK then,” he said, brandishing his notepad. “So, let’s start with Mark Twain. I have reason to believe Lewis was studying him, as well as Greene.” He wasn’t about to divulge the entire Lewis List, just yet. Like Melissa, he had no reason yet to trust this man.

“Very good. So you know about him.”

“Not really,” said Jake. “Tell me. Us,” with a glance at his daughter, now practicing tea-drinking poses and sampling the watercress sandwiches that came with the tea.

“To begin with,” Sunir began, “it was your Mark Twain who first laid out the basic facts about Shakespeare. He wrote an entire essay on the subject. He was quite the skeptic. Like yourself,” he added.

“Mark Twain wrote about Shakespeare?” Jake blinked, in surprise. “Why haven’t I heard of that?”

“That’s what I’m saying. Maybe some people didn’t want you to. It’s only in his original autobiography.”

“I have a copy of that, and there is nothing about Shakespeare in the table of contents. Which, I have to admit, I haven’t gotten very far beyond.”

Sunir shook his head. “It’s either there, or it’s been removed. Some editors have taken it upon themselves to censor Mr. Twain’s more outspoken opinions. Especially on this subject. But this isn’t just opinion. It’s based on the facts as known in his time, as well as ours.”

“Well it’s not in my book, unfortunately.”

“Are you certain? So, you read the table of contents?”

“Yes.”

“Did it mention Sir Sidney Lee? He was the preeminent Shakespeare biographer of the time.”

Jake pondered. “I’d have to recheck. It rings a bell, but I’m not sure.”

“Do go look. Do you have it with you here in London?”

“As a matter of fact, I do.”

Melissa was looking at him strangely, during this interchange. “Dad, you’re not buying into all this bullshit, are you?”

"I'm a journalist. My job is to gather the facts, present them, and let the reader reach his or her own conclusions," he said, irritably, at the same time realizing how pompous that sounded.

"You're wasting your time," she grumbled, staring into her teacup as if looking for fortunes.

"Mark Twain will give you the basics," Sunir continued, "so I won't repeat them. But there are a few other facts that aren't so well known."

"Like what?" asked Melissa, thoroughly disconcerted by this entire turn of events, which went sharply against the grain of everything she had been taught.

"To begin with, Shakespeare's father was an illiterate smuggler and a small-time politician with a prison record. Those are documented facts. Yet if you visit Stratford, they would have you believe he was a respected civic leader, educated man and worthy of knighthood."

Melissa stared at the ceiling and nibbled on a scone.

Jake frowned. "Didn't he have a coat of arms?" he asked. "I thought I read that he did."

"You can buy one of those. Shakespeare's parents did so. They were both illiterate, but he *may have* gone to the Stratford grammar school and studied all the way up to the third grade," scoffed the Asian. "Which is as far as they went."

"The books I read all say Shakespeare attended the Stratford school and received a good education there," snapped Melissa.

"Based on assumption, but not on any provable facts," responded Balsavar, finally beginning to sense that she was not in his camp. "He's not on any roster, actually."

"Third grade?" asked Jake, incredulous.

"The village school was a rural elementary school, which in those days had three grades only."

"Dr. Scofield says it was the equivalent of sixth grade, by the way." snapped Melissa.

Balsavar blinked. "Sixth grade? But is that not still primary school. Up to perhaps the age of twelve?"

"You know, my daughter is a Shakespearean actress and theater major," Jake informed Balsavar. "Are you sure you want to tangle with her about this?"

Sunir looked at her in surprise, then beamed. "But that's excellent, Melissa. May I call you Melissa?"

She shrugged. "If you want."

"And please call me Sunir."

"Fine. *Sunir.*"

Momentarily taken aback, he plows on. "If I can convince one reasonable person of the truth, then perhaps she can convince others."

"Don't hold your breath," she retorted. "It's been well established that the Latin studies at the Stratford School were very good, and perfectly adequate for the writing of the plays."

"Really. Third grade Latin?" said Jake, incredulously.

"Sixth grade equivalent," she insisted, emphatically. "It was an excellent school."

"And you actually believe that?" Sunir asked her. "In a rural farm town back then? You, a college student and daughter of a journalist actually believe that a simple rustic villager could write plays about Greece, about Rome, about Italy and France and Scotland, about love, and medicine, drama and history, with 20 fewer years of studies than yourself, with no access to professors, to libraries, no books, no travel, and basically, no sources of knowledge?"

Melissa shook her head, dismissively. "Scofield says 'genius will find a way.' "

Balsavar frowned, in confusion. "Pardon me, but who is this Scofield?"

"John Scofield. Visiting Professor of Elizabethan English at my university and my faculty mentor. I'm his graduate assistant, it's how I pay for my books," explained Melissa. "So I know what I'm talking about. He literally wrote book on Shakespeare. And I did a lot of the leg work for him."

Jake felt grateful that Sunir did not actually look at her legs, which most men, he feared, probably would.

"Whoa, whoa, whoa," he said. "Let's back this freight train up a moment. You say he had *no books*?"

"He owned and left no books. Yet he was a wealthy man," Sunir went on. "He could certainly have afforded one or two."

"Wait a sec,' " said Jake. "I took some Shakespeare in college. He wrote in *The Tempest*, 'My library was dukedom enough.' I refuse to believe he could write something like that and have no books."

Sunir spread his hands. "My point exactly." He let that sink in. "Read Mark Twain. Read Shakespeare's Last Will and Testament."

Jake stared at him a moment, groping into the back of his mind for something just within reach. "Last Will and Testament." Then it hit him. "Of course. LWT. *Last Will and Testament*." He made a hasty note: *check Twain, also Shakespeare's will*, with a quick glance at Melissa, who just shook her head and turned away.

"Just because there weren't any books in his will," said Melissa, "doesn't mean anything."

"Come now, he was a writer. How many writers do you know with no books? The actor Edward Alleyn, by contrast, left a whole library of books in his will."

"Maybe he read Edward Alleyn's books."

"Not in Stratford he didn't, and that's where he spent most of his life." He turned to face her. "As for that alleged sixth grade education at the Stratford School, there is no record he ever even attended there or anywhere," Sunir added. "Which is odd, really, because the school kept meticulous records. In fact, the Elizabethan government was one of the most compulsively anal record-keepers in history. They kept records of everything. You would be amazed by the volumes of minutely trivial records they have in the PRO. Including records of his father John Shakspur's perfidies."

"So that's why there's all this doubt about Shakespeare's education," said Jake.

"That's only the beginning. He also never enrolled at any secondary school or university, and there is no correspondence. Nor did he ever travel."

"Not true," said Melissa hotly. "Dr. Scofield cited several books showing evidence he spent time in Lancaster, and possibly even Scotland. And obviously he went to London. That's travel."

"Very well," said Balsavar. "But he never traveled to the Continent, where so many of the plays were set—especially Italy. Consider also, that Prospero educated his daughter against great odds, while Shakespeare himself did not even bother to educate his own children, despite by then considerable resources at his disposal. You'd think, being such a great writer, he might take that much trouble, at least."

"He didn't educate his children?" Jake stared, dumbfounded. He looked at Melissa, who again looked away, shaking her head.

"That was customary to the times," she insisted, hotly. "Very few rural Englanders educated their children."

"Very few rural Englanders wrote '*Hamlet,*' " noted Sunir. "The idea that such an allegedly great thinker and writer, and indeed educator, would not bother to educate his own family is not only incomprehensible and contemptible, it is patently absurd."

"And of course, not having learned beyond primary school, let alone secondary school, of course he attended no university. Unlike most other authors and playwrights." He turned back to Melissa. "May I ask what university you are attending, Melissa?"

"The University of California at Berkeley, not that that's relevant to any of this."

"A fine school. I am sure you are getting a fine education there."

"You mean unlike Shakespeare's daughters?" Jake glanced at Melissa with a twinge of guilt, mixed with pride. He'd missed out on enough of her life as it was. What if he'd never sent her to school or paid for her college? What if he'd never bought her books, or read Longfellow and Dickinson to her at night? At least he'd done that part right.

Melissa stopped and put her cup down. "You think just because a man hasn't gone to Oxford, he can't write a play. That's just plain snobbery. Admit it!"

Sunir shrugged. "Perhaps we have your Hollywood to thank for that. Your American anti-intellectualism readily embraces such notions. Joe the Plumber for President, and so on. But in any case, to write these Works would have necessitated, if not a first-rate education, at least some first-hand life experience, plus the skills to record them."

"You're saying you had to be there," said Jake.

Melissa took out her cell phone and turned away with a sullen "Whatever."

Sunir looked at Jake apologetically. "I'm sorry to upset your daughter, Mr. Fleming. But the truth must be told."

"Well, she is an actress, as I said."

"Oh, yes. I can see."

Melissa, now playing the role of aggrieved defender of truth and justice, perhaps imagining herself as the Erin Brokovich of the Arts, busied herself texting an angry message into cyber space.

"Don't mind her," said Jake, with a wry grimace. "You're just questioning and challenging her entire education and belief system, that's all."

"Well, this issue was not so paramount in Pakistan, of course. But in my own readings, I found it difficult to accept the presumption that the Bard could even read at all, let alone write, which remains in some doubt, given the way he signed those six existing documents, not to mention the 'x' on his marriage certificate."

Jake stared. "Sorry, you're getting ahead of me there. *He signed his marriage certificate with an 'x'?*"

"There are but six signatures, and his is not one of them. At the time he was married, he could not write his name."

"Jesus. The profs never talked about that in any of my classes."

Melissa was no longer listening, busily fiddling with her cell phone, with a deep frown.

What is she doing? Jake wondered. Sending an email? Checking her stocks? Watching a video? He'd left his mobile in the glove compartment of his car back in Berkeley, because it wasn't good for much else besides phone calls and was an older model that wouldn't have worked overseas in any case.

They departed the tea house through the kitchen entrance, and no one was in sight in the back street, much to their relief. Each was in a reflective (or in Melissa's case sullen) mood and spoke little as they parted company.

"Be careful," Jake warned the Pakistani, as he climbed into a cab.

As Jake and Melissa walked the short distance back to Denmark Street and the flat, Melissa stated bluntly: “I don’t trust him. He talks like a crazy man.”

Jake’s own thoughts and feelings were a jumble. What other dark secrets and surprises did this ancient modern city of contradictions have in store for him? And how was this deepening literary controversy serving to explain the disappearance of Desmond Lewis? Was someone’s ego so fragile he or she could not withstand a challenge? Or was there something more insidious afoot?

Melissa, in the meantime, was clearly not in a mood to talk about it.

Chapter Seventeen

Something Wicked This Way Comes

Bloomsbury, London, 7:35 p.m.

Safely back in the flat on Denmark Street, Melissa went to the computer and logged on without a word. With a sigh, Jake sat down in the living room and hoisted the Mark Twain autobiography into his lap once more. At least now he knew what to look for.

As he re-read the foreword and preface, sure enough, there was Sir Sidney Lee, among the random listing of topics. That led to something in the table of contents he'd completely missed before: a series of chapters, or articles, titled: *"Is Shakespeare Dead?"* Just as Balsavar had said. Of course, he hadn't known enough to be on the lookout for Shakespeare, hidden as it was among a thousand other various and sundry topics that had interested the eclectic American writer at one time or another in his lifetime.

"I found Mark Twain's essay about Shakespeare," he called over to Melissa. "Did you ever read this? *Is Shakespeare Dead?"*

"No, I didn't."

Jake began to read. Twain opened with a reference to 'claimants:' people who claimed or were claimed to be something or another that perhaps they weren't.

"He implies Shakespeare was a 'claimant.' "

"Good for him."

As he read, he came across a reference to Satan that caught his attention, and he made a note of it.

"He compares Satan to Shakespeare," he informed his daughter.

"Spare me," she muttered.

Satan and the Bard? He thought in wonder, and read on:

How curious and interesting is the parallel—as far as the poverty of biographical details is concerned—between Satan and Shakespeare.

> *It is wonderful, it is unique, it stands quite alone, there is nothing resembling it in history, nothing resembling it in romance, nothing approaching it even in tradition. How sublime is their position, and how over-topping, how sky-reaching, how supreme—the two Great Unknowns, the two Illustrious Conjecturabilities. They are the best-known unknown persons that have ever drawn breath upon the planet.*

What had provoked Mark Twain to turn against William Shakespeare? What had provoked Desmond Lewis, for that matter? He swallowed a Cool Mint and read further:

> *I haven't any idea that Shakespeare will have to vacate his pedestal this side of the year 2209. Disbelief in him cannot come swiftly, disbelief in a healthy and deeply loved tar baby has never been known to disintegrate swiftly...He ought to have explained that he was...merely a nom de plume for another man to hide behind...*

"Mark Twain believed Shakespeare was a *nom de plume*," he mentioned, out loud.

"So what? So was Mark Twain."

"No, he meant for someone else."

She wasn't interested. He turned back to the book. Twain went on to list the known facts:

> *For the instruction of the ignorant I will make a list, now, of those details of Shakespeare's history which are facts—verified facts, established facts, undisputed facts*
>
> *FACTS:*
>
> *He was born on the 23rd of April, 1564.*
>
> *Of good farmer-class parents who could not read, could not write, could not sign their names.*
>
> *At Stratford, a small back settlement which in that day was shabby and unclean, and densely illiterate. Of the nineteen important men*

charged with the government of the town, thirteen had to "make their mark" in attesting important documents, because they could not write their names.

Of the first eighteen years of his life, nothing is known. They are a blank.

Twain went on to describe his marriage to Anne Hathaway, who was pregnant at the time, and his subsequent alleged flight to London, apparently, he not being the parental type. Then:

Three pretty full years follow. Full of play-acting. Then: In 1597 he bought a New Place, Stratford. Thirteen or fourteen busy years follow; years in which he accumulated money, and also a reputation as an actor and manager.

Meantime his name, liberally and variously spelt, had become associated with a number of great plays and poems, as (ostensibly) author of the same.

Some of these, in these years and later, were pirated, but he made no protest.

Then—1610-11—he returned to Stratford and settled down for good and all, and busied himself in lending money, trading in tithes, trading in land and houses; shirking a debt of forty-one shillings, borrowed by his wife during his long desertion of his family; suing debtors for shillings and coppers; being sued himself for shillings and coppers; and acting as confederate to a neighbor who tried to rob the town of its rights in a certain common and did not succeed.

He lived five or six years—till 1616—in the joy of these elevated pursuits. Then he made a will and signed each of its three pages with his name.

It was a thoroughgoing busines man's will. It named in minute detail every item of property he owned in the world—houses, lands, sword, silver-gilt bowl, and so-on—all the way down to his "second best bed" and its furniture.

It carefully and calculatingly distributed his riches among the members of his family, overlooking no individual of it. Not even his wife; the wife he had been enabled to marry in a hurry by urgent grace of a special dispensation before he was nineteen; the wife whom he had left husbandless so many years; the wife who had had to borrow forty-one shillings in her need, and which the lender was never able to collect of the prosperous husband, but died at last with the money still lacking. No, even this wife was remembered in Shakespeare's will.

He left her that "second-best bed."

And not another thing; not even a penny to bless her lucky widowhood with.

It was eminently and conspicuously a businessman's will, not a poet's.

It mentioned not a single book.

Jake put the book down in astonishment. "So," he said. "Sunir was right. There were no books in his will."

Melissa just grunted, and kept typing her email, or blog, or whatever she was doing.

Jake jotted some notes, then read on:

Books were much more precious than swords and silver-gilt bowls and second-best beds in those days, and when a departing person owned one, he gave it a high place in his will.

The will mentioned not a play, not a poem, not an unfinished literary work, not a scrap of manuscript of any kind.

Many poets have died poor. But this is the only one in history that has died this poor; the others all left literary remains behind. Also, a book. Maybe two.

If Shakespeare had owned a dog—but we need not go into that...

He put the volume down in exasperation. Jake had been a mediocre reader and student in high school and college. But he'd sat through the lectures, and seen some of the plays, and read others, like the then-required *Romeo and Juliet,* and *Hamlet*. How was it that such potent information about Shakespeare had not even been mentioned, let alone discussed in high school or college?

"Melissa," he called over, once again. "If teachers can offer alternative views regarding global warming or evolution, or Jefferson or McCarthy or Obama or Trump for that matter, why can't they do the same about Shakespeare?"

"Who says they can't?"

"Let's put it this way. Why don't they, then?"

"Because there is no merit to any of those arguments, that's why."

"I see. So, a fiat is written, and so it shall be? Mark Twain certainly begged to differ. And apparently, so did Desmond Lewis."

"I'm going to bed."

She departed, her mood hardly improved by their brief interchange.

Jake wasn't sure what it was that awakened him five hours later. A sound in the street, perhaps. Or in the hallway or the flat above? Normally he'd have rolled over and gone back to sleep, but now he was wide awake, and thoroughly agitated. A light was beginning to glimmer to the east, reminding him for an odd moment of *Romeo and Juliet*. The man Mark Twain had described certainly didn't sound like the one who'd penned that heart-rending tale. Had Lewis bitten off so much he'd choked on the bite? And what about Balsavar? There was no way to verify anything he'd said about his alleged relationship with Lewis. What was he really up to?

He picked up the Twain biography again and read about how Shakespearean scholars have had to work backwards from a single, diaphanous piece of evidence (a name on a title page) to make their case for William Shakespeare as author of the Canon that bears his name. As Twain put it:

> *"How did he acquire these rich assets? In the usual way: by surmise."*

Twain summarized orthodox thinking roughly as follows: Shakespeare's name was on the Folio and some of the Quartos. Ergo, he *must have* written them. The author clearly had a vast store of knowledge, connections, background, talent, and wisdom to have done so. Therefore, Shakespeare *must have* had a fine education. And since he never went to any schools that anyone knew of beyond grade school (and even that is surmised), he *must have* taught himself. And since he *must have* taught himself, he *must have* had books. And since his will included no trace of or reference to any books or other literary materials among the considerable personal property accumulated in his lifetime, he must not have needed any. Moreover, since books alone would not provide the vocabulary and detailed knowledge of Europe, Scotland, England and Kent that was in the plays, he *must have* gone there. And since there was no evidence he went there, he *must have* talked to or corresponded with people who did go there. And since there was no record of him hobnobbing or corresponding with anyone about anything other than business matters, those particular records *must have* been lost. All of which somehow *proved*, beyond a shadow of a doubt, that Shakespeare *must have* written the plays.

He had to laugh, in spite of his annoyance and chagrin. He hated to think what, say, Johnny Cochrane might have done with such reasoning, on the witness stand. He could have made mincemeat of it himself. As Mark Twain put it, what they did was surmise what "must be" true, which somehow became, in their view, fact. And having taken this position, they had successfully buttressed it for nearly four centuries with a fortress of ideology that would rebuff an armada.

He read further, from Mark Twain:

> *So far as anyone knows and can prove, Shakespeare of Stratford-on-Avon never wrote a play in his life.*
>
> *So far as anyone knows and can prove, he never wrote a letter to anybody in his life.*
>
> *So far as anyone knows, he received only one letter during his life. So far as anyone knows and can prove, Shakespeare of Stratford*

wrote only one poem during his life. This one is authentic. He did write that one—a fact which stands undisputed; he wrote the whole of it; he wrote the whole of it out of his own head. He commanded that this work of art be engraved upon his tomb, and he was obeyed. There it abides to this day. This is it:

"Good friend for Iesus sake forbeare,
To digg the dust encloased heare:
Blest be ye man yt spares thes stones
And curst be he yt moves my bones. (sic)"

So that was the quote on that cryptic note that had spooked Sunir at the Globe. Jake was shocked. This was it? The final statement from the man who wrote *Othello* and *Macbeth*? How tragic. At least he could have added: *"To be or not to be."* Then the dark significance of that doggerel struck him like a speeding bus. It wasn't funny at all. It was pathetic. Those could only have been the words of an ignorant, illiterate, superstitious man. A man like Robert Greene's player/agent. How could this have happened and gone unnoticed for more than four centuries?

Once more the gravity of Desmond Lewis's apparent discoveries nagged at him.

It was increasingly clear to Jake that Lewis might well have been on the trail of something of historic importance and certainly no reprobate, as Melissa had called him, at all. But if so, then his disappearance bore a new and ominous implication. There were just too many powerful interests vested in the status quo. And again, what about Balsavar?

It was time, he decided, to run a few checks. And also revisit Robert Greene.

Chapter Eighteen

Yet Do I Fear Thy Nature

London, 10:00 a.m.

Jake decided he wanted to talk to Henry Blodgett again the next morning, and set out for the bookstore, disappointed that Melissa had shown no sign of offering assistance, and, quite to the contrary, had demonstrated renewed opposition to the entire Desmond Lewis enterprise.

"First of all," she'd complained earlier, over coffee and some tasteless rice concoction she'd urged him to try, "why do you care so much about Desmond Lewis's alleged book? All right, fine, he was your friend, but so what? Are you going to publish it for him? Are you going to rewrite it for him? What's in it for you, first of all?"

Not unfamiliar with being put on the defensive by his daughter, Jake nudged the cereal aside. "Look, my own editor would be the first to tell you 'who cares about some missing egghead professor in London and his stupid book.' I get it. In fact, that's why I've been avoiding the increasingly urgent necessity I am facing, of filing a story here. This apartment—excuse me, flat—isn't cheap, and *The San Francisco Tribune* is footing the bill, and I am going to have to earn my keep before long."

"So why don't you? I'm sure there is a scintillating explanation for the man's disappearance. Maybe he's having an affair with his secretary, and—"

"You haven't met his secretary."

"OK, fine. So, he was doing this big expose on Shakespeare, as that Sunir person claims and you seem to believe. Again, so what? I mean, I can think of some professors who would be pissed, but at the end of the day, the world will still be turning, terrorists or whoever will still be out there, we will still have global warming to worry about, and more pandemics, and I will still have roles to prepare—"

She was interrupted by the telephone ringing. "I'll get it," he said, picking it up. "Hello?"

The line went dead.

"Who was it?" she asked, a tinge of apprehension in her voice.

He shrugged, irritably. "Wrong number."

He went to the window and looked outside, not knowing what to look for, and turned back to her. "Well, Kiddo. With you or without you, I'm going to find out what it was that got Desmond Lewis abducted, his office and home trashed, and made his book go away. Obviously, someone out there," he pointed out the window, "has something to lose. Maybe enough to—"

The phone rang again. Melissa stiffened. Jake held up his hand in warning, waited two more rings and picked it up.

"Yeah, what is it?" he snapped. "Tom? Is that you?"

Again, it went dead.

"Can you check Caller I.D.?" she asked, her voice edged with increasing anxiety.

He checked the phone. "We don't have it."

"Great."

A moment later, Melissa's cell phone tweedled. She looked at him. "It just says 'out of area.' That could be anything," she whispered.

"Um, maybe you shouldn't—"

"Hello?" she asked, pressing the answer button. She listened a moment, glanced at her father, and her face turned dark.

"What?" he asked.

She shook her head. "Just some jerk," she said, and snapped the phone shut.

"Now who," he wondered out loud, "could manage to call two wrong numbers, and out of all the numbers in the world, both of them happen to be ours? Pretty amazing."

"Dad," she said, turning away. "There are some things you just don't understand."

He sat down at the kitchen counter, crossed his arms, and looked her in the eye. "Try me."

She looked away. "I can't. Not now."

That was the end of their conversation for that morning. Melissa had put on her coat and gone out a short while later and refused to say where she was going. "I have work to do, plays to see, contacts to make, remember? It's why I came to London."

As Jake headed back to Charing Cross Road, absorbed in his domestic issues and the ongoing conundrum of Desmond Lewis, the large man was waiting, and once again fell into step a half block behind him. Jake, spotting him within a block, considered whether or not to turn and confront his pursuer. He decided against it. Obviously, given they knew where he was staying and where he had been up to now, whoever it was seemed to be content, for the moment, with monitoring him as opposed to stopping him. And if he tried to confront him, from his experience there were three things that could happen. One: the man would simply bolt. Two: he would deny any knowledge of him. The third possibility he didn't want to think about. He kept walking.

There was one passage in particular from Robert Greene's *Groatsworth of Wit* that he wanted to take another look at, and, before heading for Blodgett's, he'd found it online and printed it out. It was the passage that began:

> *Base minded all three of you if by my misery you be not warned; for unto none of you, like me, sought these Burres to cleave; those Puppets, I mean, that speak from our mouths those Anticks garnished in our colours. Is it not strange that I, to whom they all have been beholden; is it not strange that you to whom they all have been beholden, shall, were you in that case I am now, be at once of them forsaken?* Then the reference to the 'tyger's heart' and 'upstart Crow', followed by: *and being an absolute Johannes Factotum is in his own conceit the only Shake-scene in a country. O that I might entreat you rare wits to be employed in more profitable courses and let those Apes imitate your past excellence and never more acquaint them with your admired inventions. I know the best husband of you all will never prooue a Userer...yet whilst you may, seeke you better Maisters; for it is pittie men of such rare wits, should be subject to the pleasures of such rude groomes.*

Blodgett greeted him cheerfully enough. "Ah, it's my friend the journalist. Still looking for another Pulitzer Prize-winning scoop?"

So, thought Jake. Blodgett's done some homework. He chuckled. "I'd settle for a good story with a beginning, a middle, and an end."

"So how can I help you in your elusive quest on this abysmally damp Autumn day? Did you enjoy your Mark Twain tome I gave you?"

"Very much, thank you. It seems that things aren't always what they seem, including your beloved Bard."

"Indeed, indeed. Well, as we all know, history is written by the victors, including your own. So how can I help you today?"

"I want to talk about Robert Greene and William Shakespeare."

Blodgett's eyebrows hoisted up and he nodded knowingly. "I see. Well, then. You have found the 'upstart crow.' "

"Yes. I ran into a man named Balsavar. From Pakistan. Another professor at the university. Did Lewis ever mention him?"

Blodgett frowned. "Can't say that he did. Why do you ask?"

"He's the one that told me about Lewis's interest in Shakespeare. Apparently Balsavar was collaborating with Dr. Lewis on the missing book. Or so he says."

"It's possible, I suppose. My client never discussed his business outside of this shop and the specific titles he was interested in. So, what did this Balsavar chap tell you?"

"Basically, that Shakespeare was a thief. He didn't elaborate and wouldn't or couldn't reveal the identity of the alleged victim or victims."

Blodgett nodded. "Well, as I said before, until I can get some sort of confirmation as to the status of my client, I cannot say more, but I will tell you this: he did not reveal to me that particular bit of information, intriguing as it sounds."

"What's your take on the theft business, then? Was it just plagiarism, or something more insidious?"

"As I said . . ."

"Let's put it this way. Would you agree that Robert Greene was calling Shakespeare a thief?"

Blodgett pursed his lips, took a deep breath, then nodded, wryly. "I'd have to say it looks that way."

"So, if Greene was speaking of Shakespeare in that diatribe of his, small wonder that Mark Twain and more recently our missing friend might have taken such a dim view of the man."

"Indeed."

"Which makes me wonder why all those professors at Oxford and Yale and so on, all these years, have refused to consider any of this?"

Blodgett shrugged. "Vested interests, shall we say?"

Jake frowned. "But who were the 'three of you' Greene was trying to warn?" He showed Blodgett his copy of the text.

"There's a great deal of speculation about that, and I suspect that's key to Dr. Lewis's thesis. But I can tell you this: most likely it was one or more of the other known playwrights of the era, probably the group known as the 'University Wits.' "

Jake nodded, and made a note. "OK, that would explain 'wits,' plural."

"Pardon?"

"I've highlighted a number of keywords in the Groatsworth text I'd like your opinion on, would you mind?"

Blodgett seemed to be warming up to the subject. "All right. I always enjoy a good puzzle. What have you got?"

"How about 'Burres?' What are those?"

"Ah. That would be a rustic pronunciation of the letter 'r.' As in 'arrrrrrrgh.' Usually by, shall we say, the less educated lot? Greene wrote 'burres to cleave,' I'd say as a criticism of the speech of certain more countrified, shall we say, actors, or players."

"Shakespeare, for example?"

Blodgett chuckled. "You said it, not I. Perhaps it's a bit like your Southern drawl. But I will confess to this. I do share a bit of Dr. Lewis's skepticism about our beloved Bard."

"I thought as much. So, help me out here. He mentioned Puppets. Any idea what that was about?"

"Good question." Blodgett squinted at the printout and nodded. "I believe he is talking about the writers being treated like puppets, but you could also infer that the players were the puppets, just mouthing lines written by others."

"Meaning in neither case was the player the writer?"

"Exactly."

Jake jotted a note. "In one of Greene's earlier diatribes, I noticed the 'Player' had boasted of being 'for seven years absolute interpreter of the puppets.' Do you think there's a connection?"

"I wouldn't doubt it. Greene was emphasizing those points he felt needed emphasis." He scratched his head. "I seem to recall an article I read somewhere about Shakespeare working in the north for a while as a puppeteer. Lancaster, I think. Which, according to some, might account for the so-called 'lost years,' when no one knows what the devil he was up to."

Jake made a note to check. "How about 'Anticks.' An actor's antics?"

"Most likely. It goes along with 'Bombast.' "

"What did he mean by that?"

"Well, plainly Mr. Greene was fulminating against a certain player for his 'bombast.' 'Bombast a blank verse' would simply refer to his acting style. Bombast also meant hot air, basically. It meant using high-sounding words with little or no meaning."

Like a certain President, thought Jake, wryly. "Hmm. I don't see how anyone could conclude that 'bombast' had to do with composing poetry or play writing, then. Isn't that what the scholars all claim this is saying?"

Blodgett nodded. "It is, indeed."

" 'Beautified with our feathers' is clear enough. He was enriching himself, or making himself look good in some way, with the 'feathers,' or works of others. Isn't that what a crow does?"

"Indeed. Very good."

"So, what's this *Johannes Factotum*?"

"Ah. That one's easy: it's a literal translation from Latin for 'Jack of all Trades.' It appears Mr. Greene is suggesting that our beloved bard was a Jack perhaps of one trade too many. It seems Shake-scene was a man with many jobs, or roles, or faces, including a puppeteer, a player, or actor, and one to whom the others were subject, or dependent."

This confirmed what Jake had already suspected: that Shake-scene was some kind of a theatrical agent. "Jesus. So, they all worked for him." Then he noticed something else. "And look at this. Greene's player/agent spoke of playing apparel valued at 200 pounds. Could he have been some kind of costume broker as well? There was clearly money in that."

Blodgett stroked his chin. "It's possible. The metaphor of the crow 'beautifying' himself with 'our feathers' could make a rather good description of a costume broker getting rich from brokering the accouterments of others, as Greene had also implied."

"So 'Johannes factotum' also translates not only to 'jack of all trades,' but also the 'Jack' in 'jackdaw,' which stole the feathers of other birds."

Image upon image, Greene had piled it on, creating the portrait of an unscrupulous operator—far more like a P. T. Barnum than a great poet, he thought. Was this Lewis's great discovery? Or was Robert Greene just a malcontent with a strong penchant for hyperbole?

"Speaking of trades, you might have a look here at this charge." Blodgett tapped the underlined word *Userer*.

"Right. 'Userer' would fit what Twain had said about suing and being sued for coppers." Willy the Shake? Yet another unsettling image that blurred history's portrait of the Bard.

"Twain noticed that, did he? Well, well, well. That raises him up a notch or two in my estimation, yes indeed!" He chuckled. "Shake-scene did, in fact, engage in more than one lawsuit over money lending. Interesting contrast to that line in *Hamlet*, wouldn't you say? *'Neither a borrower nor a lender, be?'* "

"There's definitely a pattern here. What about that comment about *'best husband?'* "

"You read the Will?"

"Not yet. But Twain said he left his wife the second best bed. Hell of a 'best husband.' "

"Greene was quite adept at little barbs and jibes. To say nothing of irony. Of course, Shakespeare was far from dead just yet, but his character was clearly evident. He abandoned his wife and family, so there's your 'best husband' bit. Greene was just being sarcastic."

"And 'Seek you better Maisters' clearly meant 'find better employers,' because Shake-scene wasn't paying Greene like he promised."

"Very likely so. As you noted, Robert Greene was a very disenchanted man indeed when he wrote this invective."

"So, what about this line: 'rude Groomes?' "

Blodgett's eyes twinkled. "Perhaps you might find the answer to that in one of the early chroniclers of our William's alleged exploits. Might I suggest John Aubrey?"

Jake wrote the name down with mounting excitement.

"How about this reference to his 'tiger's heart?' Is that a direct warning to someone in particular? And if so, who?"

"I believe our Professor Lewis was pursuing that very line of thought. I regret that I cannot tell you where it was leading him, for quite frankly, he wouldn't tell me, and I don't know."

What kind of a man was Lewis dealing with anyway, thought Jake, in wonder. And why had no one in 400 years seized upon these obvious character discrepancies?

"OK, let's back up. It's common knowledge that this pamphlet was about Shakespeare, 'the only Shake-scene in a country.' Right?"

"That's right."

"And the scholars use this as proof that Shakespeare was the true author of the plays and sonnets. Correct?"

"Correct."

"But how is this 'proof' this so-called 'Shake-scene' was author of the plays? Where does it even refer to him as a writer? I see 'jack of all trades,' and 'puppeteer,' and 'player' and 'userer,' and so on. So, where's the 'playwright' part?"

"Aye, there's the rub," agreed Blodgett. "It had our friend Lewis in quite the snit."

What he needed now, Jake realized, was more information about the Bard himself.

Just then the telephone rang in the back of the shop. Appropriately enough, it was the old fashioned rotary-dial ringer type, one that had probably been functioning in its place, like its owner, for well over fifty years. Blodgett went to answer.

"Blodgett's Books," he said, picking up the heavy black receiver. He listened a moment and his expression darkened. "Who is this?"

Meanwhile, Jake moved quietly to the front of the shop, and looked out at the busy so-called "road." Then a chilling thought occurred to him. *Charing* meant "burning." The road had been named for a burning cross! A road it may once have been, in Shakespeare's time. But now it was a busy, traffic-snarled major city thoroughfare. A long black limousine was parked on the opposite side in a bus zone, and a Bobby, in close proximity, seemed disinclined to write a ticket. Obviously, someone with clout, he thought.

Jake glanced back and noticed the old man's troubled expression as he spoke on the phone. "Yes, I know the man, and yes he is a customer of mine. And I'll be damned if I'm going to give you such a list. For your information, sir, the last I heard, the people still have a certain right to privacy in this country." With that he slammed down the phone and came back towards the front of the shop, still simmering with indignation.

"You won't believe it," he said, in agitation. "That was some twit asking about our mutual friend Professor Lewis. He seems to have become a cause celebre, of some sort."

"What about him?" Jake was suddenly torn by two distractions: Blodgett's chilling words, and an even more disturbing sight across the street. The driver of the limousine was chatting on the sidewalk with a large man in a tan trench coat, while the policeman turned pointedly away. *The Watcher*! As of now, that's what Jake decided to call him. He tore himself back to the bookseller. "You say that was someone calling about Lewis?"

"The bloody tax bureau. They wanted to see a list of all the books he's purchased or ordered in the past five years. Then they threatened an audit. Can you believe it?"

"Yes, I can. But that doesn't sound like any tax bureau. It sounds more like the Patriot Act back in the States. What are you going to do?"

"Just what I did. Tell them to go to hell. They have no right, and I know a barrister who will be happy to remind them, if push comes to shove. England is still a free country, last I heard."

Jake frowned. "I'm sorry if I've caused you any trouble," he said, with another glance out the window. The limousine was just pulling away, and The Watcher was nowhere to be seen, which he hoped was a good sign.

"No trouble. I've enjoyed our little chat," said Blodgett, seemingly unconcerned. "But perhaps we should call it a day. My wife insists upon certain routines, one of which is that I am prompt about lunch."

"You close shop for lunch?"

Blodgett chuckled. "Some authorities cannot be questioned. Are you married, by the way?"

"Was. She died of cancer two years ago."

"Ah, I see. Sorry to hear it. My condolences, sir."

Jake thanked him, got up, checked his watch, and headed for the library once more, keeping an eye out for The Watcher, who had either gone or was staying well out of sight.

He signed in and went quickly to find the Shakespeare biography section. There, from among the expected host of books on the subject, he found the one by John Aubrey, and selected the two volume work by Sir Edmund K. Chambers, titled *Shakespeare: A Study of Facts and Problems*. The librarian assured him that Chambers was considered one of the leading authorities, if not *the* authority, on Shakespeare's life. He added a few more well-known more recent biographies, lugged them back to the carrel and looked up the references to Robert Greene.

Sure enough, not only was Greene cited as proof that "The Player" was Shakespeare, the consensus indeed was that "upstart crow" meant that Greene was jealous of his writing prowess. It seemed to him, if anything, that this was evidence of quite the opposite. To Jake it looked like Balsavar might be right: that Greene was accusing the 'Upstart crow' of stealing credit for the true author's work.

Or getting rich from it. Or both.

This could also refer to his role as a Player, that he was doing the same thing a lot of modern actors did: take credit for the writer's lines. Would Melissa do such a thing? He hoped not. At the very least, if, as the scholars insisted, Greene was referring to 'Shake-scene' as a playwright, the Bard was being accused of serious plagiarism. So how does evidence of plagiarism serve as proof of authorship? What sort of twisted logic was that? He put his pen down and pondered that for a time. As he read and studied further, it began to come together. Blodgett had told him that the 'Upstart Crow' was a reference to the famous Aesop fable in which a jackdaw (the European crow notorious for being a thief) "beautified" himself with the feathers of other birds, in hopes of becoming King of the Birds. While the feathers could be the costume reference he'd thought of earlier, it made even more sense that the 'feathers' would be the works of the writers of the time, presumably including Greene, and three others. Again, it seemed to him that this was a charge that Shakespeare was either a professional plagiarist or theatrical agent. How, he wondered, had scholars managed to convert that very clear meaning to 'rival playwright of superior talent?' Then it struck him that the 'feathers' of others, was also a pun for their writing quills.

***

So, Greene was warning the other writers based on his own experience dealing with Shakespeare, who, as a theater company partner, had hired him to write plays. After which Shake-scene felt justified, as a businessman, to claim 'ownership' of them? Jake stared off into the distance. Good grief. He thought. This wasn't about an agent at all. This sounded very much, to him, like the Elizabethan equivalent of an unscrupulous *producer*. The Bard wasn't selling plays to the studio, as today's agents would do. He was acquiring plays on behalf of his employers who later became his partners, which is what an ambitious producer, or even more precisely, a studio executive would do. He also knew, from interviews in the past, that very few of today's or yesterday's film producers could resist at least a pretense at writing. He also knew that in present day Hollywood, virtually all producers and executives that considered themselves as 'Players' were either business lawyers or had MBAs. They were businesspeople. Not creative people. And once acquired, a play was the producer's property. Hence scripts and books were referred to not as literature, but as *property*.

Shakespeare and Hollywood? He jotted down and paused to mull that over.

A mouse-like gray-haired man in a rumpled suit passed the carrel and gave Jake a hard look through the glass partition. Jake met his eye for just a moment, and, if looks could kill, he felt like he'd been shot with a poisoned dart. His instincts kicked into overdrive: once more he was being watched. He rose to his feet.

"Excuse me, can I help you?" But the man hurried away and disappeared into the stacks.

Jake thought about pursuing him and decided against it. After all, what had the man actually done, besides give him a look that may have creeped him out, but was hardly a crime? Besides, he didn't want to leave his notes and materials unguarded in the carrel. Reluctantly, he sat back down, and tried to refocus.

Now tense and watchful, he contemplated the descriptive terms and phrases he'd underlined in the Greene text, not one of which appeared synonymous, he thought, with 'Bard.'

One more passage caught his attention:

> *In this I might insert two more, that both have writ against*
> *these buckram Gentlemen: but lette their own workes*
> *serve to witnesse against their owne wickednesse,*
> *if they persevere to maintaine any more such peasants.*

Jake began to organize his notes, systematically. Who was 'wicked,' and why? For dealing with this guy? Who, in the theatrical world of the day that was of peasant stock? Wouldn't that describe Shakespeare's background, regardless of his postmortem royal coronation? Greene was warning his peers not to "maintain" any more such 'peasants.' 'Maintain' would mean support. Support a 'peasant,' such as an uneducated upstart country bumpkin who'd somehow worked his way into a position of power. Support how? By providing him with plays, for a remuneration that Greene obviously felt was inadequate, if not usurious? Or never got paid at all, which meant theft?

As he turned back to the biographies, he soon confirmed that very little was actually known about William Shakespeare's life; that in fact, most of it was conjecture. Or, as Mark Twain had put it, *surmise*. Again, something rang a bell in the back of his mind. He wracked his brain and tried to remember. Was it that strange conversation he'd had with Desmond Lewis in Florida? It was still mostly a blur. They'd shared more than a few bottles of excellent California wine that weekend. But he had a vague recollection of a reference to a cultural icon, something about *'A Thief for All Time.'* Had he mentioned that to Melissa at some point in time since then, and it had stuck in her mind? Anyway, all that supposition and speculation would most certainly never have held up in court, he knew, from his court reporter days. It was nothing but hearsay.

Next, he turned to the biographer Blodgett had recommended, John Aubrey, and as he was skimming through Aubrey's chronicle of *Brief Lives,* he came across something else that caught his attention. According to Aubrey, Shakespeare's godson, a man named William Davenant, had claimed that Shakespeare was the Elizabethan equivalent of a Hollywood theater car-park valet in his early days in London, holding and grooming patrons' horses during the plays, which continued until Henry Burbage was forced to move the Curtain Theater across the Thames to escape the current plague. After which London theatergoers apparently traveled by ferry. Jake made a note: for those who don't read Dick Francis or go to the races, a horse-handler was known as a groom. So here was the corroboration Blodgett had been hinting at for Greene's 'rude groomes'.

So, what about this Davenant? Jake set off in search of more on said Sir William. Sure enough, there was a biography by Victor Hugo, who had written:

> *SHAKESPEARE went from time to time to pass some days at New Place. Half-way upon the short journey he encountered Oxford, and at Oxford the Crown Inn, and at the inn the hostess, a beautiful, intelligent creature, wife of the worthy innkeeper, Davenant. In 1606, Mrs. Davenant was brought to bed of a son, whom they named William;*

and in 1644 Sir William Davenant, created knight by Charles I, wrote to Rochester: "Know this, which does honor to my mother,—I am the son of Shakespeare."

Could this be the 'Oxford' reference from the Lewis list, then? Assuming Melissa was right and 'Ox' stood for Oxford and not oxygen, ox tail, or oxen? He found that Aubrey referred to Davenant repeatedly. It was Aubrey, he discovered, whom Shakespeareans cited as "proof" that young Shakespeare, while apprenticing in the butcher's shop in Stratford, was already a young man of literary prowess. According to Aubrey, "when he kill'd a calf he would do it in a high style, and make a speech." Perhaps something pithy about 'Morrals teaching education?' Once again, he could see how a player, or actor, particularly a boastful one who imagined himself to be a 'poet extempore,' might have a tendency towards 'bombast.' Especially after quaffing an ale or two at Mrs. Davenant's Oxford inn. Jake jotted in his notepad: 'reciting doggerel or making speeches while chopping mutton does not necessarily a poet make.'

Meanwhile, this Davenant, he noted with interest, had made a name for himself as a poet, with a place in the Poet's Corner at Westminster to prove it. Despite the fact that his poetry, according to his own biographer Joseph Knight, was "insufferably dull." Like father, like son?

As he headed back to Denmark Street Jake's thoughts were spinning, and he failed to note that he was being followed again. This time The Watcher had a car: a black sedan and was speaking to someone on a cell phone. Someone else also watched his departure unobserved, from an alcove near the library entrance: a gray-haired man with throbbing temples and growing rage in his heart.

Jake entered his building, nodded at the doorman, and took the elevator up to his floor, thinking that if someone from within Academe's own ranks such as Desmond Lewis should dare to challenge common knowledge—that Shakespeare was unquestionably the genius and author as they had always taught and insisted—he or she might very well become a pariah. Was that enough to place him in physical danger? How powerful was this name, Shakespeare, in British thoughts, hearts, and institutions? Or even economy? Was there an American equivalent that none dare question or revisit, let alone vilify? Certainly not in literature, he thought. Should someone write a book denouncing Twain or Hawthorne, or John Grisham or Dan Brown for that matter, the public would hardly notice. Besides, the Bard had already been challenged by the proponents of Bacon and others. There must be something else.

As William Goldman had written for his Watergate screenplay *All the King's Men*: "follow the money." There was something more than academic reputations at stake here. He felt sure of it.

Chapter Nineteen

So Foul and Fair a Day

London, early November, 6:15 p.m

Melissa returned towards dinner time, still looking out of sorts. Jake decided on the direct approach and followed her into the kitchen while she rummaged through the cupboards and cabinets. "How'd it go?"

"Oh," she shrugged. "I made the rounds in the Theater District, but there aren't a lot of casting calls this time of year. Not that I'd have time to do a whole season, but still."

"Can we talk?"

"Do we have any food around here besides yogurt?" She inquired, grumpily.

"There's always rice cakes," he noted. She made a face. "I have to tell you, Melissa, Robert Greene makes a pretty good case that the author, whoever he was, could not have been Shakespeare. As does Mark Twain, if you'd been listening last night."

"Actually, I really couldn't care less who wrote the plays, because that's not my department. What I care is that I get to play Ophelia, and Desdemona and Juliet some day on the main stage and not just college, and that's all. Period. End of story." Her voice took on its familiar stubborn tone, yet also revealed a certain anger. Jake couldn't even recall the last time anything he had to say sparked such anger in his daughter.

He smiled. "Right. *'The play's the thing.'* But just in case an injustice has taken place, and I know you care about justice since I've seen you out there demonstrating more than once, you might at least re-read Greene," he suggested, mildly. In too deep to turn back, he told her about the keywords that scholars had either overlooked or ignored. He didn't dare mention his idea about Shakespeare being a producer, just yet. He wondered if Lewis had stumbled into that same notion as well. He wondered whether he should ask Balsavar.

She remained unmoved. "Just because Greene said those things about him doesn't make it true," she pointed out. "He had an axe to grind."

Maybe, he thought. On the other hand, what was being said, or had been said about him to refute these charges, back in 1592 when they were made? Robert Greene, he had found out, had not lived long after writing this tirade, and had died of food poisoning. Shakespeare's one critic had been silenced. Then what?

Once again, Melissa wouldn't talk about it, and went about trying to fix some sort of rice dish out of leftovers. She seemed unable to concentrate on the task at hand and wasn't making much progress.

The door buzzer rang. They exchanged worried glances. Jake called down on the intercom. "Who is it?"

"It's Sunir Balsavar. I hope you are not busy."

Ignoring Melissa's negative gestures and eye rolling, Jake pressed the buzzer to let him in.

Sunir arrived a minute later bearing gifts: a dinner of Chinese take-out from Tottenham Court Road. "I was in the neighborhood and thought you might be hungry. No MSG," he promised. This was almost, but not quite, enough to mollify Melissa, whose animosity towards him had not abated since the day before.

Jake thanked him. "So, what brings you to our humble borrowed abode?" he asked.

While Melissa took charge of the provisions, Balsavar took Jake aside and spoke to him in low, urgent tones. "I have made enemies, I'm afraid. It is more urgent than ever that I recover my and Dr. Lewis's work, it is too important to let die."

"Did you think I have it, after yesterday?" asked Jake, a little put off.

"No, I am asking your help. I fear something untoward has definitely happened to our friend," he said, pacing the foyer. "And we cannot wait any longer."

"Take a seat," Jake told him. "You're making me nervous." Balsavar obeyed, reluctantly. "So, tell me something. Exactly how do you and Lewis know each other?"

"We met at one of those faculty parties at the university, if you can believe it, which is odd because neither of us was much for parties as a rule. He asked me where I was from, my education in English, and one thing led to another, somehow the subject of the Bard came up, and that's when we found that we were comrades in arms, so to speak."

"So. A couple of Bolsheviks decide to clean out all the White Russians?" commented Melissa, from the kitchen. Oddly, as she spoke Jake recalled that her favorite movie role as a starry-eyed teenager had been Lara in *Dr. Zhivago*. "You're not the first, you know. Those de Vere people are all over the place, back in Berkeley."

"Who?" asked Jake, in confusion.

"Another pretender to the throne. He's totally bogus."

"I must apologize, that I seem to have offended your daughter," said the Asian to Jake, regretfully.

"Welcome to my world," said Jake, dryly. "But I agree that in regards to major weaknesses in the Shakespeare biography, Twain and Greene have made a strong case. But that leaves open a wide and gaping hole in the historical record. Nor does it explain why a contemporary author or authors should be in jeopardy."

"To say the least," said Melissa. "You still haven't told us who you and Dr. Lewis think actually wrote those plays, since you're so adamant it couldn't be Shakespeare. And puh-leeze, don't tell me it was Bacon. Or that Oxford guy, de Vere."

Jake looked up at her sharply. "Oxford guy?"

Her eyes widened. "Oh yeah. He was the Earl of Oxford. Why, you think that was the—"

Jake cut her off with a warning sign.

Balsavar, not noticing, let out a sigh. "No, as you say, those candidates were not new and have been widely refuted. I would like to tell you more. But that is what he refused to share with me. He said it was to be a surprise that would shock and astonish the world."

"Humph. I doubt it," scoffed Melissa.

"In any case, until we find out what has happened to Dr. Lewis, it would not be appropriate to disclose that, even if I knew. Besides, given what I know about the possibilities, until you have the opportunity to consider the evidence for yourselves, I doubt that you would believe it."

Melissa looked up from the table where she was setting out dishes and chopsticks. "Then why are you wasting my Dad's and my time with all this bullshit?"

"Melissa, there's still the matter of there being a missing person," Jake reminded her. "Also, you might consider at least a modicum of common courtesy towards someone who brought you dinner."

She blushed, then nodded. "Yeah, right. Sorry. Thank you, Sunir for the no MSG. But your friend has been missing a week already. What do you think we—Dad can do?"

"She has a point," said Jake. "Time is our enemy, here."

"Maybe not the only one," said Sunir, once again pacing the floor. "It's very delicate. You know, others have tried to speak out before, but were always silenced, such as Sir George Greenwood back in the early 1900s."

"Do you ever have time for physics?" Melissa asked with a teasing smile, setting out the plates.

"Of course. But physics can be rather tiresome, wouldn't you say?"

"Don't let Steven Hawking hear you say that," she quipped, enjoying her new role as flirtatious skeptic—the kind of role her patron saint Katherine Hepburn made her specialty.

Jake sat down, opened the box of mu shu pork, and popped a Cool Mint.

"You should try yogurt with that. It is very healthy," suggested the Pakistani. With that he took his leave, saying he had a class to teach in the morning.

"I still don't trust him," said Melissa, with her mouth full of noodles.

The next morning Jake was up at 9, and after coffee and the remaining dregs of the Chinese takeout (which Melissa had apparently rediscovered in the wee hours), he was too impatient to wait any longer. He wrote Melissa a note: "Be back later," and left the flat, locking the door behind him. Fred the doorman was busy with a delivery, and he was about to step out onto the street when something made him hesitate, the hair on the back of his neck bristling its ancient, primordial warning. A black sedan with tinted windows was parked in a no parking zone across from the apartment building. Jake didn't like its looks. There was little need for tinted windows in a daylight-deprived northern climate zone such as Great Britain.

Unless one had something to hide.

Stepping back quickly into the lobby, he turned and looked for another way out. There was an emergency exit sign at the rear, above the door leading to the service area, and he headed that way. It led to an alley occupied by a row of dumpsters and an ill-clad, ill-mannered homeless man, who greeted him with a bizarre combination of insults and demands for "resitution." Jake ignored him and hurried to the end of the alley, which brought him almost directly behind the bookstore on Charing Cross Road.

As he entered through the front Blodgett greeted him with an odd combination of good cheer and resignation. "So, back so soon?"

"Can't seem to stay away," said Jake. "I read Twain's essay, and it was as you said. Very interesting stuff."

"No word from our friend Dr. Lewis?"

" 'Fraid not."

"Me either. I'm starting to fear you are right."

Jake nodded, slowly. "How about the tax bureau? Have they called back?"

Blodgett shook his head. "Not a word. It was all bluff and bluster, I'm sure. So, what'll it be today?"

Jake decided it was time to show him the list of Desmond Lewis.

Blodgett accepted it eagerly and looked it over with a magnifying glass. "Hmm. Mmm hmm. 'Ox' sounds like Oxford, of course. Possibly de Vere, although . . . 'Lamb.' As in led to slaughter, perhaps? Could be Lambeth Palace, of course. Wonder why? Perhaps the library? Hmm. Crow. Greene, as you say. Hoff." That stopped him. "Hoffman, maybe?"

"Whoa, could you back up a second? What was that about Lambeth Palace?"

"Right. It's just across the river from Westminster."

"Anything special about it I should know about?"

"Just the library and archives. It's the London residence of the Archbishop of Canterbury, last I knew."

"Really." Jake wrote down 'Lambeth Palace' and 'library,' and drew a large circle around them.

Meanwhile, Blodgett was moving right along. "Huh. LWT is the Will, no doubt, hm hmm hmmm. V.A. rings a bell. Apoc. Apocalypse . . . apocryphal? Don't know . . ."

"OK, you were saying about Hoffman. Does it mean anything to you?"

"No, but let's have a look."

Blodgett was not up to snuff on computers, unfortunately, and had to resort to wading through a cumbersome stack of publishers' directories and his old *Thompson's Books in Print*. "Hoffman, Hoffman," he muttered, thumbing away. "Alice Hoffman, Mary Hoffman, Susanna Hoffman, George Hoffman . . . Dustin Hoffman? Sorry nothing jumps out at me."

"How about a title?"

"Well, there's *Tales of Hoffman*, I suppose."

"What's that about?"

"It's very Germanic. Doesn't sound like our lad." Blodgett looked up. "You know, I do seem to recall some sort of scholarly or historical flap years ago involving a journalist like yourself, by that name. I think he'd written a book, if I can just recall." Distracted, he tore himself away from the list, glanced up, then tapped on one of the entries. "Getting back to this 'Ox' item. Yes. The more I think about it, this is probably just an abbreviation for Oxford University. It was Dr. Lewis's alma mater, among other things."

"I noticed he has degrees from there. Does he still have any connection with Oxford? Faculty friends, research contacts, anything like that?"

The bookseller thought for a moment. "Well, nothing lately. I think he had some kind of falling out, there. But that was some time ago."

"What kind of falling out?"

"I'm not sure. He very rarely spoke of it, I'm afraid."

"What was that you said about a de Vere?"

"Well, I suppose he could also be referring to Edward de Vere, of course. But—"

"My daughter Melissa also mentioned something about this de Vere. I keep hearing that name. Who is that?"

Blodgett took on a conspiratorial look. "Wait a moment," he said, rising to his feet and starting towards the back. "I happen to have something that I took in trade a few years back and have been saddled with ever since." Once again he bumped and coaxed his ladder to a particularly perilous section of the high wall of books and began to climb, to Jake's growing dismay: "But I promise you, if you're looking for a smoking gun as it were, you won't find it here—Ah, here we are." He reached out a full arm's length and then some, teetered precariously, and once more somehow managed to acquire, then secure, then brandish a large, somewhat tattered volume. In triumph, he climbed wheezily back down, his old bones croaking and groaning like a building about to collapse in an earthquake, causing Jake's own nerves considerable wear and tear, finally alighting safely on the floor once more.

"Here you go," he said. "*The Man Who Was Shakespeare*, by a gent named Charleton Ogburn. You're welcome to give it a read. The author's American."

"What does this have to do with Oxford?"

Blodgett pursed his lips in distaste. "Well, the premise here is that William Shakespeare was actually that fool, Edward de Vere, the seventeenth Earl of Oxford. There are newer books on this as well."

So. The first entry on Lewis's list might refer to a Shakespeare rival, or pretender. He should have made that connection a long time ago, Jake realized. He picked the book up off the counter and examined it, as if for clues. "Do you think Dr. Lewis believed that it was this Oxford who wrote the plays, then?"

"I'd find that chestnut a bit hard to swallow. But perhaps you should judge for yourself."

Jake eyed the book warily. It was large and heavy, for one thing.

"No relation to the university, mind you," sniffed Blodgett, in his what Jake now recognized as an Edinburgh accent. "Just an inherited title. He had some silly coat of arms involving someone allegedly shaking a spear, and that's all it took for that lot to go gallivanting off like you Yanks to a gold rush. 'Shake spear,' get it? Hmph. De Vere, indeed." He looked ready to spit. "How would they know it was shaking, anyway? It's a mailed fist, holding a spear. Maybe it was being thrown, or brandished. There's no proof that it was 'shaking.' Even if it was, this Osborne chap quotes Gabriel Harvey's 1578 address to the Queen in which he exhorts the Earl, a dabbler in verse and prose, that he should—here he put on a pompous theatrical face, then continued in a new voice entirely—" 'throw away the insignificant pen,' because 'thy countenance shakes a spear.' "

Jake had to laugh. As if embarrassed by his performance, Blodgett quickly resumed his own bespectacled bookish countenance. For a moment though, Jake could picture him shaking a spear or two himself, in his zeal.

Blodgett wasn't finished. "In the first place," he went on, "that was not an original expression coined by Harvey for this purpose. It was a common phrase in Elizabethan times. And in any case, all Harvey was saying was that this de Vere, being apparently a better soldier than he was writer, should quit dabbling and start soldiering. Hardly a ringing prognostication of literary greatness then or to come, wouldn't you say?"

"Good point. But who was Gabriel Harvey?"

"A minor poet and preacher. I have a volume of his verses around here somewhere, in fair condition, if you—"

"That's all right," said Jake, quickly. "I have enough reading to do as it is. How much for this de Vere one?"

Blodgett sighed. "I'd be embarrassed to take money for something like that," he said. "But you're welcome to give it a read."

Jake was beginning to wonder how the man managed to make a living but knew better by now than to argue.

He was on his way back to Denmark Street when he passed by a newsstand, and a lower left headline stopped him cold: *Missing Professor Found Dead.* He grabbed the paper, dropped some coins on the counter, and rushed back to Blodgett's, but the door was locked, the old bookseller apparently having adjourned early for lunch. Quickly Jake returned to the flat, scanning the article as he went. His heart sank as he absorbed the details, his dismay intensified by the fact that once again an anonymous rival at Reuters had scooped him. It was Lewis, all right. His badly burned remains had been found floating in the San

Francisco Bay estuary, about fifteen miles northeast of the Richmond bridge. While charred beyond recognition, dental forensics had confirmed it was him.

As he approached the building, Jake checked the street ahead and behind him. There was no sign of followers, and the black car was gone, to his momentary relief.

Fred the doorman stepped out of the shadows to greet him, a look of concern on his face.

"Mr. Fleming?"

Jake looked up from the paper, startled. "Yes, Fred. What is it?"

"Sorry, I didn't see you when you went out. When I came in this morning someone had left a note for you." He felt into his pocket and produced a business sized envelope. Jake recognized it right away: it was identical to the envelope with the warning to Balsavar at the Globe. Now he wished he'd kept that piece of evidence. He thanked Fred and went up to the flat without opening it. It was probably useless for fingerprints, but just in case, he was careful to handle only the edges.

Melissa was up and about. "Your editor called again," she said from the kitchen, where she was putting away a new supply of groceries. She looked up as he entered and saw from his expression that something was very wrong. "What?" she asked. "You OK, Dad?"

"Take a look," he said, dropping the newspaper on the table.

She read the first paragraph, then the second, and looked up at him sharply. "They are claiming suicide. Didn't you say someone ransacked his apartment?"

"And his office. I'll call Sunir." He sat down grimly, and dialed Sunir's number from his reporter's notepad, still crammed with random notes, Post-its, tattered business cards (including Sunir's) and a few actually alphabetized handwritten phone numbers. Balsavar answered after several rings, sounding harried. "Hello, what is it?"

"Sunir, it's Jake Fleming. You hear the news?"

"Yes, I read the papers and was just going to call you."

"Do you buy the suicide theory?"

Sunir hesitated for the briefest of moments, and Jake sensed fear creeping back into his voice. “No, I do not. In fact, I spoke to the medical examiner in California.”

“You called the Marin County Medical Examiner?”

“I explained that I was a colleague and friend, trying to arrange his affairs. I was the only one who’d called, so they took me at my word. He was in very bad shape from the fire and water, nor could they explain how he’d been burned. But they told me something they hadn’t told the media. Apparently, they found traces of poison. A very potent organic compound called Hebenon. Also known as Taxis Baccata.”

“Never heard of it.”

“I have. It is made from the bark of the yew tree. It dates back to Shakespeare’s time, in fact.”

“Oh really?” Jake wondered what to make of that. “So that’s their basis for suicide?”

“That and what the California police people have been saying, about that depression nonsense.” Sunir sounded ready to spit. “It sounds like an Elizabethan execution to me.”

“Good lord,” said Jake.

“How about you? Did you find out anything?”

“Not yet.”

“I hope you can get to the bottom of it. It’s quite worrying.”

Jake called his office and bullied his way through to a senior editor, Pat Wilson, at the crime desk. “Nice work on that Lewis story,” he conceded. “Who called it in?”

“We picked it up from the A.P. last night,” he was told, “and put the pieces together.”

“Good work. So, did you know about the poison?”

“What poison?”

“I’m all the way over here in London and I have to tell you?”

“C’mon, out with it. What poison?”

So, Jake told Wilson what Sunir had told him.

“Wow. Flannigan’s gonna love this. I gather they didn’t find the source?”

"You'd better check with the M.E. on that yourself."

"And I heard there was no note."

So in other words, the suicide theory was just that, and on the flimsiest of premises: that according to both the American police, as confirmed by their counterparts at Scotland Yard, Lewis was "depressed," due to job insecurity.

"Yeah, right," snorted Melissa, when Jake told her. "So, he went out and got himself some exotic poison to do himself in, then set himself on fire. What a crock."

On a related subject, Jake placed one more call, to Gloria Peckham at Lewis's office.

She was sniffling and blowing her nose when he reached her. "Yes, Gloria, I heard. I'm very sorry. And I agree, I doubt it was a suicide. But tell me, can you think of anyone who might want to do him harm?"

"Only everyone in the department," she sniffled.

"Right. OK. And that gray-haired man who visited you the week before. Anything more about him you can think of? Anything that could lead us to him?"

"No. The Inspector already asked me that. He also asked about you, I might add."

"What did you tell him?"

"That you were a journalist working on the story. He said you should call him."

Jake took the inspector's name and number. "OK, call me if you think of anything," he said, ringing off.

Melissa called out from the foyer: "What's this letter?"

"Oh, that came this morning. I almost forgot, with all this other crap. Don't touch it."

"Why?"

"Prints." Gingerly, he picked up the envelope, carefully carried it to the kitchen, and using paper towels to hold it and a knife, slit it open. The message inside was written in a neat script, identical to that used on the message given to Sunir at the Globe Theater. It read:

How far your eyes may pierce I cannot tell:
Striving to better, oft we mar what's well.

This was getting a little too close to home, he thought. Melissa read it over his shoulder and caught her breath.

"Do you recognize the quote?" he asked her.

"It's from *King Lear*. It's when he's feeling betrayed by everyone around him."

"Really."

"Dad, I think you'd better call the police."

"I was about to anyway, about this so-called suicide." Jake doubted it would do much good. But now at least he had a story to write. He picked up the phone and dialed London Metropolitan Police and asked for the name Gloria had given him, a Detective Donald Jenkins.

About an hour later, Jenkins, a thin, harried man in his late thirties with sandy hair and better things to do, he made it clear, stopped by, duly took a report, had some questions of his own, and put the note in a plastic bag. "Don't expect much, sir. This is rather ambiguous, and probably untraceable. But we'll do our best."

"We're also being followed, possibly by more than one person." Melissa chipped in. "You may as well put that in your report as well." Jenkins frowned, but took Jake's description and dutifully wrote it down.

After Inspector Jenkins departed, Jake made a note to ask the doorman Fred to redouble his vigilance. The death of Desmond Lewis would now kick his investigation into a whole new gear. He sat down to finally email his editor in San Francisco: *Tom, I need a few more days. Definitely onto something here. Suicide my ass. More later, Jake.* He knew Flannigan hated cryptic messages like that. But it would also spark his curiosity and buy him a little time. At least he hoped so.

He then placed an overseas call to the Medical Examiner in Marin County, California, to confirm the poison in his system. It was as Sunir had reported it.

Melissa received a text message a short while later and seemed agitated. "Dad, I have to go out for a while."

"I really wish you wouldn't go anywhere, just now."

"It's about my job. I can't just stop living."

He wanted to retort: Yes, you can. Lewis just did. But managed to bite his tongue. "Well please be careful." He tried to make a joke of it. "Don't take any candy from strangers."

She let out a terse laugh as she headed out the door. "I never do. Will you be OK?"

"I'll be fine. Do what you have to do. Will I see you for dinner?"

"Yes, I should be back before then." She gave him a quick kiss, which surprised him, and was out the door.

Trying to take his mind off his daughter and the latest developments, he spent the remainder of the morning and noon hour plodding through the Ogburn book about Edward de Vere. It was heavy going.

Chapter Twenty

Whether 'tis Nobler in the Mind

Jake had difficulty focusing on the material, but soon decided that Blodgett was right about the 17th Earl of Oxford. If this man was what Lewis' was referring to on his List, it begged the question, why? What was so interesting about him? What secret lay in this man's life or works, if not that he was Shakespeare? And even more to the point, why underline 'Ox' three times? The problem was that the earl, clearly an upper-crust dilettante, had much too much time and money on his hands and nothing in the way of a work ethic. He also seemed to have an inflated ego: not unheard of for the spoiled inheritors of wealth and power, he thought. He could certainly think of some recent examples of that sort. Was that the point? And given such an ego, what could possibly motivate him to labor so mightily to produce such Works under an assumed name?

His supporters seemed to believe that this was on orders from the Queen. But why? Sir Phillip Sydney was under no such restraints, nor his niece Mary. Besides, from what he already knew, de Vere had never been one to obey orders from anyone, including his Queen.

And as with Shakespeare, why had no one witnessed him doing this prodigious writing or made that connection in his lifetime? He just wasn't interesting enough to be so mysterious or warrant so much attention. Still, curled up on the sofa, Jake slogged on into the day. He ordered coffee and two ham sandwiches from the deli down the street, and asked Fred the doorman if he'd ever heard of Edward de Vere.

"I think so. Wasn't he a famous impostor, or some'n like that?"

"Something like that." He didn't mention the letter, and Fred was discreet enough not to ask.

Jake made one more attempt after lunch to wade through Ogburn's arguments in favor of his earl, before finally tossing it aside and checking his watch.

Melissa was due back. It was nearly dinner time. He tried her cell phone, and it rang through.

"Hi, Dad?" came her familiar voice, blurred with static.

"Melissa? Are you all right? Where are you?"

"Um, down at the West End. They're doing *Love Never Dies* at the Adelphi and I'm trying to get a reading for a standby part. What's up? You finally get some sleep?"

"Yes, of course," he fibbed. "Listen, I think I've identified another one of Lewis's list of clues."

"Oh, really? That's exciting." But she didn't sound very excited, he noted.

Melissa glanced up from her cell phone at the thin gray-haired man sitting opposite her in the hotel bar he'd insisted upon for their meeting. He nodded curtly for her to continue.

"What did you find out?" She asked, over the phone.

"I'm pretty sure 'Ox' was an abbreviation referring to Edward de Vere, the Earl of Oxford. I think you mentioned him?"

She rolled her eyes. "Yes, Dad. But this isn't a good time. Can we talk later?"

"Sure, but are you—"

"Ciao for now."

With that, she pressed the "end" button on her phone before her father could utter whatever expletive might come to mind.

"What's he on about?" The man sitting with her demanded to know, his tone petulant.

"The Earl of Oxford," she said. She'd already shown him the list, and he, rather than thanking her, had flown into a rage, which annoyed her more than a little. He should be grateful to her, she thought, for keeping him so well informed. She was beginning to think her loyalties had been misplaced. She was beginning to wonder if she had been more than a little naïve about her relationship with this man. "I'll see him later and scope him out, don't worry about it."

"Scope? As in microscope? This is one of your sophomoric collegiate idioms?"

"It means I'll ask him, all right? What is it with you? Excuse me for saying so, but sometimes you act like Shakespeare is Jehova himself, and you're Moses."

"I have a lot of years and work invested in this subject, and don't take it lightly. And one thing I will not brook is betrayal. *I could a tale unfold whose lightest word would harrow up thy soul.*"

"Lear? No wait, of course. Hamlet. His father's ghost. Right?"

"Yes," he nodded, thoughtfully. "And I know whereof he speaks."

"So, what is this tale you could tell?"

He looked away. "Nothing that need concern you." He looked back at her, thoughtfully. "Perhaps it's just as well your father wastes his time with de Vere. Maybe you should encourage him."

She studied him a moment, her feeling of disenchantment growing. Something about her employer had changed, and she couldn't quite put her finger on it. It was as though he was two different people at times: one outgoing and charming, the other paranoid and belligerent. And the latter characteristics had become more and more evident as of late. For example, just now he'd left the bar tab on the table as though he expected her to pick it up. Well maybe she would, just to show him what an independent American woman was really like.

"Maybe you should tell me one more time what the issues really are, at hand," she said. "The other day you spoke of a conspiracy to discredit The Name. Where is it? All I've seen is some dated references and a bunch of theories. Although I have to admit, some of them are starting to make a certain degree of sense. For example, what was Robert Greene so angry about, anyway? And have you read what Mark Twain wrote on the subject?"

The thin man's face darkened. He stared into his empty whiskey glass and then back at his erstwhile assistant. Was she so blinded by her own childish play-acting ambition she could not understand what was in the balance? He thought he'd made that clear, by now. Could he have been that mistaken about her? What could be wrong? He'd stopped that traitor Lewis in his tracks, and surely the man could not have gotten to her. Could the journalist be that good, to have uncovered his trail so quickly? Impossible. And yet, and yet, he could feel she would soon be slipping away from his grasp. If only he could separate her from Jake Fleming. But how? Otherwise, he feared, her ultimate defection from his cause might be inevitable, unthinkable as it was. Which would call for even more drastic action.

Well, so be it. But he couldn't let her go just yet. He had one more task for her first. Hopefully she would cooperate. His hold on her should suffice for that, at least, he thought. And if not . . .

"I brought you a ham sandwich," Jake told his daughter when she walked into the flat half an hour later, dripping with new rain and a troubled look about her that both puzzled and worried him.

She hardly touched the food he placed before her and her look remained distant.

"All right. Out with it. What's up?" he demanded, finally.

"Nothing," she said, looking away. "Just a little under the weather. So, tell me your great discoveries about the Seventeenth Earl. You think he wrote the Plays?"

Jake walked to the window and gazed out at the oddly quiet city, now glittering with early evening light. "How much do you know about this Edward de Vere?"

She shrugged. "Enough to know he wasn't the author. What do you want to know?"

He turned back. "Well, as you said yourself, he seems to have a considerable following. A lot of people think he was Shakespeare. What I'm trying to figure out is if Desmond Lewis was one of them."

She shook her head furiously and took an experimental bite of the ham sandwich.

"First of all," she said, "nobody with Lewis's stature would buy it. Why would somebody with that degree of vanity and privilege have to use a front man or foil? It sounds phony to me. He'd want to take extra credit, if anything. Not the reverse." Preferring to focus on her food, she declined further discussion. But that had been Jake's own conclusion, as well. On this issue, at least, believer and skeptic had found common ground.

Just then Melissa's phone beeped. It was the shorter ring tone reserved for text messages. With a frown, she turned aside and clicked on the message. It was, like most text messages, brief and simple. It read:

London Eye. Now. Else all is lost.

She quickly deleted it.

"Something wrong?" Jake asked. At that moment the house phone rang, and both of them froze.

Finally, Melissa reached for it, her expression tense. "Hello?" She listened a moment and handed Jake the receiver. "It's Dr. Balsavar," she said with an irritated shrug.

"Call me Sunir, please," insisted the voice on the other end.

Jake took the receiver. "Yes, Sunir. What's up?"

"Jake, the police were here this afternoon."

"They were here as well. Don't worry about it. They're just doing their job."

"But that's not all. I just got a message on my cell phone. It said 'London Eye or die. You and the Americans. Now!' Did you get a message like that? I don't know what to make of it."

Jake frowned, and turned to his daughter. "Melissa, what was that text message just now? Did it say something about the London Eye?"

"Dad, I wouldn't take it seriously. It's just somebody messing with us."

"Well Sunir just got the same message. Basically, it was a death threat."

She paled. "Oh God. I don't believe this."

Jake turned back to the phone. "Sunir, meet me at Trafalgar Square and we'll take the footbridge. Whoever this nutcase is won't be looking for us to come that way."

"Do you think that's a good idea?" the Pakistani asked, worriedly.

"Look, all I know is, if this is the person who killed Dr. Lewis, he has to be taken very seriously. And very carefully. He'll be watching the taxi stands, and there's a chance we may be able to take him from behind."

"Shouldn't we call the police? They will know what to do."

"No, don't call them. One sign of the cops and our man will be long gone."

"But that would be for the best, would it not?"

"No, it wouldn't. He'll then be even more dangerous, as well as on guard, and after us when we least expect it. He has all the advantages of knowing us while we don't know him. My sense is he has a message to deliver. Maybe he wants something. How quickly can you get to the Square? I'll be at the Nelson fountain."

"Give me fifteen minutes."

"Make it ten." Jake hung up and looked at his daughter. She was clearly shaken, but also angry.

"Dad, you don't think I'm going to just sit here by myself while you go out there to meet up with this nut case, do you?"

"That's exactly what I think. It's just too dangerous for you to go."

"No way," she said, reaching for her coat. "We're in this together, remember?"

"That was your idea, not mine. I've been in these situations before, Melissa. You haven't. You need to stay. I just wish I knew how this jerk got your cell number."

"Look, I *need* to go. That message was for me, remember?"

He stared at her. "I get the feeling there's a lot you haven't been telling me. Don't you realize we may be dealing with a killer?"

"No. I don't think so. I think it's a bluff. Anyway, I'm going. So, let's go," she said with finality, heading for the door.

As usual, he gave in. As they rode the elevator down, his mind raced in a hundred directions, seeking a way out of this increasingly perilous situation. He bitterly regretted allowing his daughter to come to London. But then, when had she ever listened to him?

"You haven't been exactly supportive of my investigation, Melissa," Jake commented, as they reached the lobby, now empty, with no doorman in sight.

To his surprise, her anger seemed to vanish abruptly, and there were tears in her eyes. "I'm sorry, Dad," she said. "You're right. I think I just wasn't ready to deal with it."

Jake hesitated, then took her arm. "Let's go out the back way," he insisted "I have a bad feeling about this."

She didn't resist, other than to mutter: "Whew!" at the stench in the alley, as they slipped out the rear service door.

"I have no vested interest in this controversy, you know," Jake reminded her. "Other than find out what happened to Desmond Lewis, and why. But it seems like you do. Can you tell me what's up with that?"

She shook her head, and quickened her pace, anxious to get out of that alley.

Balsavar was already there, pacing nervously, when they reached the Nelson monument. "Let's go," he said, leading the way towards the river.

They walked in silence towards the Strand, and the footbridge beyond. The London Eye gleamed like a malevolent orb of Mordor above the river, dead ahead.

Sunir tried to be conversational. "So, did you make any progress finding the book?"

"No. And I hate to say it, but with Lewis gone, it's a sure bet that book is gone with him."

Sunir digested that a moment. "That is bad. It means I must write it again, somehow, and I am not much of a writer. Nor do I know how it ends."

Jake was beginning to feel a pang of sympathy for the man. Maybe he would help him. He had to admit, at least to himself, that he, too, would like to know how it would end. "Did Dr. Lewis ever mention a book to you called *The Man Who was Shakespeare*? By a man named Ogburn?"

"Not that I can recall. What is it?"

"It's about Edward de Vere, the 17th Earl of Oxford?"

Melissa snorted. "Puh leeze. Spare me."

Balsavar laughed harshly. "Of course. Your daughter is right about him. I am quite confident it wasn't him."

"You're sure he wasn't the subject of Lewis's book, then?"

"Of that, yes, I am absolutely sure. Why would such a self-centered and shallow person write mediocre poems under his own name, then claim the need for a nom de plume to write great ones?"

"I agree, that makes no sense. So, can you think of anything he might have told you that might lead us in the right direction? To what happened to Lewis? To who might be responsible for his death? Or to the book itself?"

“So, are you going to tell him about the List?” commented Melissa, walking to his left.

He shook his head. “Not yet,” he mouthed.

Balsavar seemed not to hear, lost in thought as they sidestepped a pile of spilled garbage straddling the sidewalk. “He did say one thing, some months ago.”

“Go on.”

“He said ‘the key is in the Sonnets.’ ”

Jake looked at him in puzzlement. “ ‘The key is in the Sonnets’ ?”

Melissa looked up sharply, from where she was watching her step. “Did you say ‘Sonnets’? That was my senior thesis topic. I *love* the Sonnets.”

Balsavar gazed at the nearing blackened river and frowned. “He quoted a popular television show from your country. He said ‘the truth is out there.’ ”

‘ “The truth is out there.’ ” Jake shook his head. “And the key is in the Sonnets.”

Melissa laughed, in spite of herself. “What, now we’re entering *X Files* country?”

“Why not,” smiled her father, anxious to ease the tension. “Wouldn’t you love to be the next Agent Scully?”

“You have a point,” she grinned.

Chapter Twenty-One

Sweet Silent Thought

London, early November, 7:30 p.m.

They crossed the Strand against the light and hurried towards Hungerford Bridge, oblivious to the night sights, leaning into the cold November wind while Melissa, a California girl, shivered in her thin jacket and much to her credit did not complain. It was her father who was thinking that maybe this wasn't such a great idea.

"All right, Dr. Balsavar," she spoke up as they hurried their pace. "Out with it. What's the great secret in the Sonnets?"

"All I can tell you is what Dr. Lewis told me. But did you ever wonder about the huge disconnect between what was known about the author and the content of those poems?"

She shrugged and tightened her collar. "What do you mean?"

"Did you never wonder that they were so full of enigma?"

"Sometimes. But all great art contains enigma."

By this time, they had reached the stairs to the bridge, and the skyline ahead was dominated by the giant wheel across the river, revolving slowly like the gleaming gear of a stupendous clock.

As they mounted the footbridge, Sunir gazed down a moment at the murky river, seemed not to like what he saw, and nodded. "I do know this. That this enigma is particularly evident in the Sonnets. Your Shakespeare scholars have never been able to equate these beautiful, emotional poems to Shakespeare's conventional and mundane and loveless homebound life, and have been forced to resort to extraordinary lengths of inventiveness over the centuries to find meaning attributable to their alleged author, fabricating theoretical homosexual lovers, Dark Ladies and all sorts of other fantasies."

"My professors in Berkeley said he just had a great imagination, as all great poets do," said Melissa, with a shiver.

"I may be a physicist, but I do know that poets write about their own loves, and losses and lives, not make-believe characters living lives they know nothing about," responded Sunir. "There was nothing in the life of the man from Stratford even vaguely resembling that 'dark lady' or any of those images, or thoughts, or persons."

"So, whose life do you think it resembles?" she asked him.

"I don't know. But if you look, nearly every word, every line of the poems and sonnets resonates with the voice of a passionate man in exile, filled with imagery reflecting upon lost life, lost freedom, and personal guilt. It just doesn't sound like the man who was Shakespeare."

"What's that about exile?" interjected Jake.

"Dr. Lewis said the true author was someone living in exile, most likely in Italy, where so many of the plays were set."

Melissa frowned, but kept silent.

"Sounds pretty far-fetched," said Jake, trying to maintain an even keel. "Give me an example."

Sunir nodded. "All right. Begin with Sonnet 28," he said.

"When in disgrace with Fortune and men's eyes,
I all alone beweep my outcast state,
And trouble deaf heaven with my bootless cries,
And look upon myself and curse my fate,
Wishing me like to one more rich in hope,
Featur'd like him, like him with friends possess'd,
Desiring this man's art, and that man's scope,
With what I most enjoy contended least:
Yet in these thoughts myself almost despising,
Haply I think on thee, and then my state,
Like to the lark at break of day arising
From sullen earth, sings hymns at Heaven's gate,
For thy sweet love remember'd such wealth brings,
That then I scorn to change my state with kings."

Melissa shook her head. "A million studies have been made of that sonnet," she said. "It's an expression of man's condition, of his constant–"

"He's right," Jake interrupted her. "It's the voice of a man in exile. He clearly says so. Was Shakespeare ever in exile?"

Melissa didn't answer. Lost in thought, she turned away and continued across the bridge.

"The answer is no," said Sunir, hurrying to keep up. "This entire sonnet is about the plight of someone who has been rejected, declared non-gratis, banished from the land. In no possible way could that ever be Shakespeare."

"But why not?" asked Melissa, glancing back over her shoulder. "Since when can an author not see with his mind's eye?" But, Jake noted, her voice and expression were no longer hostile.

Sunir hurried after her. "This voice is in the first person. Listen to the words: *And look upon myself and curse my fate.* How could this possibly be Shakespeare, fat and happy and rich in Stratford from other people's labors? He was never an outcast. He had nothing to curse. This was definitely the lament of a man in exile."

She seemed temporarily taken aback. Then she wagged a finger at him almost playfully. "Michelangelo never saw God, or heaven, but he managed to paint the Sistine Ceiling quite well, thank you."

Jake had to grin at her comeback. Now it was Balsavar who seemed taken aback.

"I'm sorry, Miss. I cannot accept that explanation. Michelangelo was renowned as a great artist and people saw him at work, which was precisely why the Pope employed him for that assignment. And he was quite familiar with the subject as well as the works of his peers and predecessors. Never was Shakespeare so known in his lifetime."

Melissa shivered, with new doubt and wonder. Jake stared out over the river into unfathomable distances while he tried to make sense of this revelation. He had never heard or studied most of the Sonnets, and neither, he suspected, had most people other than college English majors.

"So, what about the Folio, which clearly names Shakespeare as the author of all those plays?" Jake reminded him.

"Ah yes. The Shakespeare 'Title page' conundrum. I am still troubled about how that happened. It remains the bulwark of academe's argument supporting Shakespeare."

"It's a strong argument," said Jake. "It's like 'possession is 9/10ths of the law.' "

"You've said it exactly," said Sunir. "It has always been impolitic to inquire as to how one acquired one's riches." They walked on in silence, absorbed in their own thoughts, or the view, until they had reached the far side of the river. "Here we are." Sunir led the way along the quay towards the entry gate. The wheel now loomed directly above them. He looked up. "What now?"

Jake glanced up and stopped cold. Just beyond the edge of the now rapidly dissipating crowd, he felt sure that he'd seen the large man up on the promenade. The Watcher was still with them, then. Could he be behind those messages just now? But if so, why not just confront them and be done with it? Easy there, he told himself. Keep a steady hand.

"What now?" asked Melissa, looking around. "Are we supposed to go up on that thing?"

"Beat's me," said Jake. "But keep moving. The Watcher is right over there."

For once she didn't look. "This is crazy," she muttered. Jake could hardly disagree.

Her cell phone bleeped. "Another message," she announced, flipping it open.

"Get on the next car," she was instructed. Britain's great rush of excitement for the Millennium Eye had long since dissipated, and this being off-season they got right on, alone in their car. It was nearly closing time.

"You're the last ones," the ticket taker told them. "Enjoy your ride."

They slowly began their ascent, which would soon take them hundreds of feet above the river in a giant arc. Jake took in the increasingly stunning views of everything from Bankside to St. Paul's to Westminster and Big Ben, his head miles away, pondering all that he'd heard and read these last few days. Melissa, for her part, pressed her nose against the glass and stared out at the night-lit city.

"So," said Sunir, nervously. "Now what?"

"We wait," said Jake. "He'll be in contact. He must know we are here."

"So," said Melissa, staring out through the glass. "Meanwhile, this is London, in all its glory."

"And all its history," added Sunir. He pointed to the northwest. "Speaking of history, do you see Parliament over there? And the large cathedral to the right? In Parliament there is a room called The Star Chamber. Ever hear of it?"

"Oh yeah," said Jake, somberly.

Melissa shivered. "I think the Star Chamber is where they invented judicial murder. They could just accuse someone and execute them without further legal recourse."

Sunir nodded, thoughtfully. "Dr. Lewis mentioned that more than once. He said that room is essential to what happened four centuries ago, and what drove him to write his book. And that cathedral is Westminster Abbey. It is the place where the kings and queens are interred, and also seat of the Poet's Corner. He said that until a scant few years ago, England's greatest poet was banned from that Corner. We must find out who he meant, and why."

They looked in silence. The city was beautiful at night, for all its dark secrets.

"And there's something else. Look straight ahead along the river, opposite Westminster. It's too dark to see clearly, but there is an old castle there, which contains a riddle that may be key to the entire—"

"Lambeth Palace," Jake breathed softly, scanning through the darkness.

At that moment the wheel suddenly lurched to a stop, the car swung sickeningly, and the entire structure shuddered and went dark.

"Oh shit," muttered Jake, as Melissa let out a cry of alarm.

"What is wrong?" asked Sunir, fearfully, hanging onto the handrail for dear life.

"Looks like the power went out," said Jake, peering down into the darkness. "You see an intercom or any kind of emergency device?"

"It's too dark to see," cried Melissa.

"Try your cell phone, see if you can call anyone and find out what the problem is."

They could hear voices shouting faintly down below, but the city noise and the distance was too much to make any of it out.

Melissa frantically punched numbers, only to be put on hold, then dismissed, or met with incredulity. It was apparent that emergencies pertaining to the London Eye were not in anyone's jurisdiction that she could find. She finally had to content herself with shouting at a police dispatcher, who was less than sympathetic. "Ma'am, the London Eye is closed now," she was informed.

It was clear to all three of them now that they had walked straight into a trap.

Five minutes went by, then ten, and still nothing. The nearest cars were empty, and there was no one within shouting distance. It began to get cold, as the night wind whistled around their car, which continued to swing unsteadily, as the temperature continued to drop.

Melissa thought she was going to be sick. Sunir already was, doubled over in the corner, and beginning to vomit. Jake tried to shout for help, but the windows—basically glassed-in walls to maximize the views—were sealed: for security, and against the weather. Five more minutes went by, and the lights along the quay winked out, as well.

"Jesus," said Jake. "They're shutting down. It's like they don't know we're up here."

"Somebody does," insisted Sunir. "Whoever sent us here." He doubled over and retched once again.

Melissa, meanwhile, was busy groping around the edges of the walls. "There should be some kind of intercom or emergency alarm, don't you think?"

"Be careful you don't open a door or something," Jake warned her. "It's over a hundred meters drop."

That stopped her.

His own thoughts raced furiously, spinning in circles of their own. He felt pretty confident that The Watcher had followed them here. Was he someone with enough clout, or savvy, to shut this thing down somehow, or maybe just shut down the power? Was it he, or someone else sending them another message? Or worse?

There was a tinny musical sound. Melissa fumbled for her bag. "It's my cell phone."

She looked at the glowing screen in the darkness and caught her breath.

"What is it?" asked Jake. Sunir was now gasping in the corner, where he had slumped to the floor in panic.

"Another text message," she replied, an odd strain in her voice.

Jake took it from her and stared at the screen: *"Enjoying your ride?"* it read.

"Oh my God," she wailed.

"Can you capture the number of who sent it? Don't cell phones have caller I.D., or something like that?"

"No, it's blocked, the same as the other calls. It just says 'out of area.' It could be anyone."

Another message followed quickly and chilled all of them even more than they were already chilled. It read: *"Thus worse begins and bad remains behind."*

"What's that supposed to mean?" demanded Jake.

"It's a reversal of a line from *Hamlet*," said Sunir, his voice quavering. "It's when—"

At that moment, the wheel suddenly broke free, and began to turn once more, but now it was accelerating, faster and faster, until they were in near free fall. Melissa and Sunir both screamed, and to Jake it was now just a question of whether someone was simply trying their damnedest to scare them to death or trying to kill them.

"Hang on." he shouted. "I don't think there's any way the car can break loose." At least he hoped not. Melissa was too busy hanging on, and Sunir too busy vomiting again, to respond. They reached the end of their sickening plunge and whooshed past the perigee, then started back up once again, then back down once more. They were almost to the bottom of the arc when the lights and power returned, and the brakes began to apply. The car finally slowed, and at last came to a stop.

A very apologetic and anxious-looking attendant yanked open the door and ushered the shaken threesome out. "We are so sorry," he apologized, profusely. "We don't know what happened. Someone got into the control room and shut off everything, then released the brake. Are you all right?"

"Could be worse," said Melissa. Sunir, grateful to find himself still among the living, nodded vigorously and clutched the side rail, gasping for air.

"We're OK," said Jake. "But I'd like a word with whoever's in charge."

Suddenly he heard Melissa let out a gasp and followed her stare to where the large man in a London Fog stood waiting by the exit gate casting dark glances in the direction of their car. The Watcher was no longer even trying to remain out of sight.

"Wait here," Jake said, grimly. "I'm going to have a little chat with that guy. If he had something to do with what just happened, I am seriously going to kick his ass from here to Denmark."

"Dad, don't." Melissa called after him in alarm.

Jake leaped off the dismount platform and headed straight for the big man, brawn be damned–he knew how to fight dirty.

The big man hesitated, then held his ground as Jake raced towards him, pushing his way through and around the gaping onlookers as fast as he could. "Excuse me," Jake had to apologize several times, elbowing past people. "Sorry."

"Dad, be careful!" Melissa called out after him.

As she watched, she could see the big man pivot in her direction at the sound of her voice, scan the area, and seem to change his mind just as Jake reached him. He braced himself for Jake's onslaught, which luckily did not include actual blows, and responded in kind, shaking his head and gesturing at the wheel. Jake shouted some more, then from out of nowhere, two men seized him by the arms and slammed him back against the nearby fence. Jake resisted, and then, as one of them showed him something, he seemed to give up, and raised his hands in surrender.

"Cops," exclaimed Sunir, watching breathlessly. "Those are cops."

"But what about the big guy?" exclaimed Melissa. "I'm sure as shit those messages weren't sent by any cops."

Meanwhile, the big man had vanished abruptly, and was no longer in sight.

The other two men, if indeed they were constables of police, questioned Jake for what seemed like an interminable amount of time, scrutinizing his I.D., and checking by phone with headquarters. But his rightful indignation at what had happened on the wheel seemed to weaken their resolve, and after a while, they let him go.

Jake hurried back to the wheel, searched around in a moment of alarm, then, in relief, spotted Melissa waving to him by the platform.

"Are you all right?" she called out.

"I'm fine," he replied, rejoining her, rubbing his shoulder, ruefully.

"You don't look so fine," she protested. "Were those the police?"

"Yeah. Those last two, anyway. Apparently, they've been watching us. They wanted to ask about Lewis. I told them it wasn't a good time."

"What about the big man?" she asked. "What did he say to you?"

Jake frowned. "That's the thing. He claimed to be our 'friend,' as he put it. That it was his job to keep us safe, and he wanted to apologize for what happened up there."

"Safe? I don't get it. If not safe from him, then safe from who? Or what?" Melissa wanted to know.

"So, you don't think he was behind what just happened?" asked Sunir, wide-eyed.

"Obviously someone was, but unfortunately I didn't get around to that question before the cops showed up. But it is certainly no coincidence that we were the last, and apparently only passengers left. We were sitting ducks up there."

"Bastards," muttered Melissa. "Whoever did this."

"But what was the point?" Sunir wanted to know.

"The point was to scare us off the Lewis case, and let us know they could do worse, I'm sure," said Jake, grimly. "And maybe that was that Watcher man's job as well. If I see him again, I intend to ask him."

When they reached the Waterloo Bridge, Melissa managed to flag a taxi and they rode in silence the whole way back, still too shaken to talk. The cabbie dropped Jake and Melissa off at Denmark Street and Sunir remained aboard, waving goodbye. "Regent's Park," he told the driver, but Jake had a distinct feeling that he wasn't staying in any one place. Possibly for security reasons?

As they took the elevator up to the flat, Melissa seemed withdrawn. Jake had to nudge her when the elevator reached their floor. "OK, we're here."

She looked at him, her eyes wide. "Dad. We need to talk."

He flopped onto the sofa, while she went to the window. "OK, so let's talk. What's been eating you lately?"

She turned to face him. “I think they believe you are stealing their National Treasure.”

“Me? Who thinks that? The people who sent you those messages?”

She shook her head. “I don’t know. Just people. English people. Theater people. Also, my employer’s colleague, Dr. Childers, if you must know.”

“Professor Childers of London University? You’ve been talking to him?”

“Yes,” she admitted. “It’s about the role of women in the Shakespearean theater. You know no women were allowed on stage for the first century or so? And yet all those great roles . . . God.”

He absorbed that for a moment. What had she gotten herself into? “It seems to me that woman department head might be a better choice,” he commented. “What was her name?”

“Professor Parker? She wouldn’t talk to me when she found out who I was,” she explained. “I mean, who you were.”

“Oh.” That, he could understand. “Could these friends of yours or could Dr. Childers have the chutzpah to shut down that wheel?”

“Oh no. No way, not them. That has to be some other entity. That big man has to be connected to something shady. Something or someone that has a vested interest.”

“What kind of vested interest are you thinking of?”

“I don’t know. The status quo. I don’t know! Something.”

“Follow the money,” murmured Jake.

“What?”

“Nothing. So, what about Desmond Lewis? Do these ‘people’ of yours think that he was stealing their ‘National Treasure’ as well?”

“But that’s what he was doing. And now you’re trying to dredge it all up again.”

“Are you saying he deserved what happened to him? And we both know it was murder at this point. Who have you been talking to, anyway? Is that Childers’ opinion?”

“I don’t mean that. My colleagues most certainly had nothing to do with any of that. It’s just–” she threw up her hands. “Forget it. Sorry. I’m just worried about you, that’s all.”

"Well I'll tell you this. You'd better think twice about who you keep company with. We could have been killed up there, tonight."

Just then the phone rang. It was Balsavar.

Jake picked up the extension. "Yes, Sunir, what's up?"

"Listen, I just got word there will be a funeral tomorrow for Desmond Lewis. They have flown his body back from the States, and I plan to attend. I hope you can join me."

"I wouldn't miss it for the world," said Jake. "Just tell me when and where."

"There is a train at eleven from Waterloo Station. Can you get there by then? And I do hope your daughter will accompany us."

Jake had to laugh at that. Obviously, the Pakistani professor was smitten by Melissa despite her initial rudeness, and who could blame him? "I'll tell her," he replied. "Train to where?"

"I'll tell you when we meet. But it has given me some food for thought. I think I may know where Professor Lewis was going with his book."

"I can't wait to hear." Jake had no idea what Melissa's reaction would be at this point to this invitation, but he would leave that up to her.

"Do you know how to get to Waterloo?" Sunir asked him.

"Yeah, no problem." One of the wonders of London was the plethora of train stations, each more archaic and grand than the next: Waterloo/Victoria/Charing Cross, King's Cross, Euston and St. Pancras, Paddington, and Liverpool Street. So many stations! So many trains! Emanating from London in all directions like the spokes of a giant wheel. So many destinations (and targets, as recent terrorist acts had proven). Yet so small a country.

Melissa nodded in silence when he told her about the funeral.

"You don't have to go if you don't want to."

"I'll go." With that, she went straight to her room. He noticed, however, that she had taken the Mark Twain biography with her.

In the morning, dressed as appropriately as they could on such short notice, they took a taxi to Waterloo Station. Balsavar, dressed like a businessman, had them spotted before they'd even gotten out of the cab, appearing before them like a sudden apparition, waving both arms. “There is little time. We must hurry!”

The Pakistani physicist wended his way through the color-splashed crowds like a soccer forward dribbling for a goal. Perhaps he learned that skill as a child in Islamabad, thought Jake, struggling to keep up. The singular individual determined to find his own way through–or against–the pressure of surging masses. Not that London was Islamabad. Melissa, of course, had no trouble keeping up at all and left a wake of turned heads as she hurried along, trim and spiff in her black pantsuit and wool overcoat. Jake had made do in his raincoat, tweed jacket and gray slacks.

Balsavar already had tickets, but still refused to say where they were going. They hurried to the designated platform, marked “London Southeast,” and boarded with two minutes to spare. Balsavar secured seats in a forward compartment and they settled back to recover their wind after their strenuous sprint for the train.

Jake dozed for a while despite the lurching and train noise, dreaming of spies and scoundrels, and woke up suddenly as the brakes squealed and the train began to slow down.

Melissa tugged on his sleeve. “Dad. We get off here.” He looked around groggily and saw Balsavar rising from his seat, beckoning for them to follow. Grumpily, he swallowed another antacid, arose and trailed behind his daughter to the exit door. As they emerged onto an elevated station platform, he glanced around the area and noted with relief that no one else had gotten off the train besides them. With Balsavar leading the way, they descended to the street below.

Chapter Twenty-Two

Cut is the Branch

He'd heard of the place. Vaguely, somewhere in the dust-clogged archives of his undergraduate memory: Deptford. Something had happened here once upon a time, and from the looks of it now–much of it a tawdry urban slum–it couldn't have been good.

He glanced at Melissa. She, too, had noticed the sign and from her faraway expression, he suspected that she had also heard of it. "You know this place?" he asked her. She just shook her head with a brief shudder and turned towards the stairs.

While the area looked and smelled of poverty and decay, the street, like many such city streets (and certainly in London) was teeming with commerce. All manner of commerce. There were rows of carts and kiosks, selling cheap clothing from Third World countries, bootleg CD's and DVD's were rampant; arts and crafts of all sorts, of the overpriced sweatshop mass-production variety; transactions in broad daylight suspiciously suggestive of drugs; dark faces, yellow faces, brown faces, and a few ruddy Anglo faces.

Jake felt a growing sense of trepidation.

"This was once the principal seaport, at the time of King Henry VII," Balsavar informed them. Henry VII? Jake pondered. Something dark and sinister was associated with that name, if he could just remember what. Father of Henry VIII? That couldn't be good. But it was something more . . . and worse.

"Isn't all of London a port city?" asked Melissa, scanning the area.

"Yes. But this was where the king headquartered his Royal Navy."

"Is that why the name Deptford rings a bell?" asked Jake. Yet there was clearly nothing noteworthy about the district now, other than its seediness.

Balsavar shook his head. "It's just ahead," he said. "Follow me."

"It's hard to believe Desmond Lewis would choose to be buried here," commented Jake, in increasing doubt.

Melissa remained silent. She had a wary look about her, though, as they walked.

Jake began to wonder, ungraciously, if their new Asian acquaintance had led them into some kind of trap. He gazed off to the left towards the container cranes, packet freighters, and various rusting river barges. They walked several blocks at Balsavar's usual breakneck pace and turned right, away from the roaring, clanking tumult of the docks fronting the Thames. Up ahead loomed an aging, modest-sized stone church with a short, square bell tower, surrounded by a brick-walled cemetery. "We are almost there," he told them, an odd look of determination on his face.

Melissa held back for a moment, as though the gravitas of what was about to happen was slowly sinking in.

They reached the church and an unseasonable chill swept over Jake. Perhaps it was the presence of death, he thought. Or was it the sense of being followed? The church and yard were ages old, built in the year 1120, Balsavar told them later, and were still well kept. "Welcome to St. Nicholas Church," a weathered sign declared, along with the announcement of the Desmond Lewis Funeral, and the current pastor's next intended efforts to save his churchgoers' clearly errant souls.

A line of cars and even several limousines were parked along the road, and a sizable crowd had gathered for the funeral services of Professor Desmond Lewis, late of the University of London.

Balsavar opened the wrought iron gate, and nodding at several black-clad ushers, beckoned them to follow. The ancient graveyard surrounded the entire church, a city block of crumbling stones and facades, memories of lives little mourned and long forgotten. He moved through its midst like a wraith. The Flemings followed reluctantly, Jake with ever-growing unease.

The wall completely surrounded the grounds, and as they approached the gathering at the back of the cemetery, at the furthest point from the church proper, Jake recognized some of the assembled mourners. Among them, he was startled to observe, was, as far as he could tell, the entire English Department faculty of London University, along with at least a dozen or so students, and several attractive and affluent looking young men and women, which made Jake immediately suspect that Desmond Lewis had had a social life after all. There were also several uniformed police, he noted.

Diana Parker, the Department Chair, was also there, looking startlingly elegant in black. She caught his eye, then looked away without a smile. Dr. Childers was there as well, on the opposite side of the open grave from Parker. They didn't seem friendly, Jake noticed. Childers did manage an odd smile for Melissa, which vanished at once when he spotted Jake.

Gloria Peckham, sniffling loudly, waved at them from graveside and blew her nose.

Jake made his way over to stand beside her, while Melissa instinctively hung back with the younger set. Sunir followed Jake's lead. "You've met Sunir Balsavar?" Jake murmured to Gloria.

She nodded, curtly.

Balsavar suddenly tensed up.

"What is it?" asked Jake.

The Pakistani nodded ahead and sweat appeared on his brow. On the far side of the gathering, at a discreet distance from the crowd, stood a large man in an overcoat. The Watcher was with them, once again.

Jake nodded. "I see. We have company, as usual. Relax, he won't do anything here."

The Watcher made no attempt to conceal his presence and eyed them with a terse half-smile, his body loose, almost relaxed. But Jake could detect something underneath, a distinct sense of danger. It was as if he was daring them to try something.

Jake saw a well-dressed elderly couple moving towards the grave site, the woman weeping discreetly, the man looking somber. "But I don't understand!" the woman was complaining. "Why in the world would he want to be buried here, in God-forsaken Deptford?"

The vicar overheard, but seemed resigned to his duties, and did not respond. But the woman, who was apparently Lewis's elderly mother, was not alone in her views. Embarrassed, but also wondering himself at who had chosen this spot and why, Jake listened in silence as the last rites were read and the coffin was lowered.

He murmured condolences to the parents, shook a few hands, and moved away.

Suddenly he felt someone grip his arm. It was Sunir. "Over here!" he whispered urgently.

Jake hadn't noticed it earlier because it was behind where he'd been standing. But nearly adjacent to the Desmond Lewis grave site, mounted on the wall not far below the top, was a small bronze plaque. On it was imprinted in barely legible letters: *Cut is the branch that might have grown full straight*. Above was a name: Christopher Marlowe.

Jake squinted at the plaque. "What does this mean? 'Cut is the branch'?"

Melissa stood silently, gazing at the plaque for a long moment. "It's a line from a play," she said. "It means someone died before their time."

"One of the greatest plays ever written prior to Shakespeare," said Balsavar, in reverent tones. "*Doctor Faustus*. By Christopher Marlowe."

"I've heard of it," said Jake.

"I was in it," said Melissa, in wonder. "In summer stock."

"This is it," Sunir breathed, in growing excitement. "This is what Lewis was onto. Why else would he choose to be buried here in such a place?"

"Marlowe?" asked Jake. "You think he was writing about Marlowe?"

"There is no body, you know," said Balsavar, after a while. "He was supposedly murdered nearby and buried here in 1593. But there is no grave. Someone mounted that plaque years after, allegedly his friend, Thomas Nashe, as a eulogy. There is no other marker in existence."

Melissa continued to stare at the plaque, in silence.

"This was Professor Lewis's final message to us," said Sunir, in hushed tones. "Perhaps he sensed what was coming, I don't know. But I think this was his way of making his play for immortality."

"Immortality? But how?" Jake shook his head in dismay at the surroundings. Melissa, in the meantime, had turned away once more, deep in thought.

"By bringing to light what I had long suspected, but he wouldn't tell me," Balsavar sighed. "But now that Dr. Lewis is dead, I feel it is up to us to finish the work that he began. We must find out what happened here, and let your readers, at least, know the truth."

"Truth about what?" Jake asked, in confusion. "You mean about his book?"

"Mr. Fleming, you are a journalist. You must put an end to the lies. For I am now convinced that what Desmond Lewis intended to tell the world is that Christopher Marlowe was the victim of the greatest theft of all time."

Jake stared at Balsavar, then at the plaque, and then at Lewis's new grave site. "You are saying that Marlowe wrote the Plays and Shakespeare stole them?"

"It must be so. Somewhere there is proof, and Lewis found it, that Marlowe's life's work was stolen from him, plundered by Shake-scene, his name slandered, and his memory buried here in this dismal graveyard, for all time. I am certain of it now."

Melissa spoke up. "You forget one thing. Christopher Marlowe was dismissed as a candidate for the Authorship ages ago, mostly on account of being dead before most of the plays were even written."

Balsavar shook his head. "Surely you remember what Mark Twain said about that?"

Mark Twain again, thought Jake in exasperation. "Something about 'rumors of my death have been greatly exaggerated'?" He was suddenly reminded of Twain's preface, about words from the grave.

"That's correct. It's in his autobiography."

"Mark Twain said that?" Melissa asked, in spite of herself.

"And the same goes for Kit Marlowe. He was only presumed dead. There is a difference. A very big difference."

By this time Melissa was shaking her head, with growing impatience. "I don't think so. Dead is dead. Marlowe was dead. Period. He wrote *Faustus*, and *Tamburlaine* and a few other pretty good plays for which he got full credit. Then he died. End of story."

"No," said Sunir. "I believe it is only the beginning." He glanced about the now nearly empty cemetery and moved closer to them, speaking with growing intensity. "You know he has been cast as a villain and a rogue and dismissed to the margins of literary history. Have you ever wondered why?"

"Maybe because he was a villain and a rogue?"

"Like the Knights Templar? Or the women in Salem? Or perhaps the Falun Gong in China, or the labor leaders in 19th Century England, or the Jews in Nazi Germany? They too were all once cast as villains and rogues."

Melissa just shook her head. "So now you're claiming that Marlowe lived after 1593 and somehow wrote all those plays Shakespeare got credit for, but he never spoke up? Why?"

"Because Marlowe could not claim them and also be officially dead."

"So, you're saying Marlowe was your poet in exile."

"Yes!"

"So what's your basis for this interesting new theory of yours?" asked Jake, dubiously.

"There is evidence. Evidence I am certain Dr. Lewis must have found." He looked up at them with his earnest brown eyes entreating them to believe him. "You already know that Shakespeare could not possibly have written anything, let alone those great plays and poems."

"Says you," grumbled Melissa.

"Well, I'm not ready to go that far, but I agree Twain and Greene make some pretty strong arguments to that effect," acknowledged Jake. "But why Marlowe?"

"And you agree it could not have been Oxford, am I right?"

"I'll go along with that, yes."

"He was also dead at the time, I might add," added Melissa.

"So, who is left? Bacon? Like Oxford he had no reason to hide. And I've studied his poetry. It is much too wordy, for one thing. And where would he have time? It was not Bacon. It was Marlowe. He fits the part in every way."

"Except for being dead," Melissa pointed out.

Sunir glanced over Jake's shoulder, and his eyes widened. "He's still here," he whispered. "Your Watcher. I think we should get out of here."

Jake agreed. The crowd was already dissipating. The other professors and students were trickling away, some of them eying the threesome with open hostility. Lewis's distraught parents were being led away to the nearest limousine, counseled by the vicar, and Jake decided not to interrupt. Lewis may have been his friend, but these people didn't know him from Adam.

They began to walk, searching for a taxi, but those were few and far between in this desolate part of the city.

"I think," said Jake, "It's time to pay another visit to my friend Mr. Blodgett."

"Blodgett's Books?" asked Sunir. "I've heard of him."

"Yes. I want to do some homework on this new discovery of yours, this Mr. Marlowe."

"I still say you're wasting your time," grumbled Melissa.

They had just reached the street in front of the church when Jake glanced to his left and noticed a black car moving slowly along towards them. He'd seen that car before. And it wasn't The Watcher, who was now walking away in the opposite direction, with a glance back and what Jake could swear was a faint wave. He looked around and spotted a gypsy cab that had stationed itself nearby, hoping for a fare from the funeral crowd. Jake waved him over.

"Go!" he said, as they clambered in the back. "And lose that black car behind us."

"Yes, of course," grinned the cabbie with a heavy accent. "No problem. I am expert of driving!" He looked to be African, or possibly Caribbean, and was probably well accustomed to such requests in these quarters. He stepped on the gas, and the threesome fell back in their seats.

"After you get rid of him, go to Denmark Street, Bloomsbury," Jake instructed the driver. He glanced at Sunir. "That OK?"

"Very good, sir, no worries," said the cabbie, with a cheerful grin.

Sunir nodded. They hung on for dear life as the taxi swerved, surged and lurched into traffic, ran a light, then another, spun in front of a bus, and cheerfully racked up enough violations to assure the happy driver deportation or worse.

As they hurtled through the city, Jake glanced at Melissa, wondering what she could be thinking now. She looked away. He looked past her, then, and saw something that turned him cold. It was a stone wall, with an ancient, tarnished bronze plaque in the wall. It read: Lambeth Palace.

It was time, he decided, to do some more reading.

The black car was nowhere in sight, but Jake was not appeased. If not being followed, they were certainly under what now seemed like constant surveillance.

"We should split up, just in case," said Sunir. "Driver, let me off at that Underground station just ahead. They can't follow me there. But as for you . . .?"

"Don't worry about it," said Jake. "They already know where we live."

He tried to avoid Melissa's look, but failed. Guilt set in. "Maybe it's time to send you back to Berkeley," he said, as Sunir jumped out at the corner and hurried into the station.

"Now," she declared, punching his arm, "you've made me mad."

When they got back to Denmark Street unmolested, the black car long gone, the driver seemed almost disappointed there wasn't at least going to be a shootout. But he was happy enough with the tip and sped away singing a Bob Marley tune. There was no one suspicious looking in the vicinity as they hurried into the building. Fred the doorman was nowhere in sight.

The game of cat and mouse, if that's what it was, would continue, thought Jake. He didn't like it, but there wasn't much he could do about it. The police had been informed and had told him exactly that.

Chapter Twenty-Three

Have More than Thou Showest

London, morning, early November

When Jake prepared to head over to Blodgett's Books, Melissa announced, to his surprise, that she was going with him.

"Do I detect a change of heart?" he asked.

"No, I just don't feel like staying home alone. Anyway, I've been wanting to see this bookstore of yours."

Going out the back way once more, they skirted the sleeping homeless man and reached the store unaccosted. Blodgett was gracious as always, and happy to welcome Jake's daughter into his humble emporium. "Charmed, I'm sure," he said, accepting Melissa's proffered hand. Jake was sure, too. "So, to what do I owe the honor of this unexpected visit by our future damsel of the stage?"

"In a word," said Jake, "Marlowe."

The white eyebrows shot skyward once more. "Ah. The great, unlamented Kit Marlowe." The brows slanted downwards again. "Are you thinking he may be our missing Bard?"

"Desmond Lewis may have thought so. At least that's what his partner thinks."

Blodgett frowned. "The elusive Pakistani chap?"

"Yes. His first line of reasoning is a pretty good one: Lewis elected to be buried right next to him."

Blodgett nodded. "I know. Actually, I was there."

Jake stared in surprise. "You were? I didn't see you. Why didn't you say hello?"

"You seemed preoccupied, and my wife wanted me home for lunch."

"Ah yes. And how is she?" asked Jake, forcing a smile. He still missed Beverly terribly.

"Fine, fine. Never better. If only she could cook."

"So, what can you tell us about Marlowe?" asked Jake, while Melissa poked about the store, keeping her opinions to herself.

Blodgett made himself as comfortable as possible on his desk chair, which was upholstered mostly with old paperbacks. "Very well. Let us review those facts about Marlowe that are irrefutable, or generally accepted by orthodox scholars."

"You studied Marlowe?"

"Oh yes. In my undergraduate days. Like Shakespeare, he was born in 1564."

"Interesting," remarked Jake. "So, they were the same age."

"Correct. They were also both of humble origins. Shakespeare, of course, was the son of a glover in Stratford. Marlowe was the son of a shoemaker in Canterbury."

Jake glanced at Melissa. "So, this isn't about class snobbery."

"Oh, no. But unlike Shakespeare, Kit won scholarships to the finest schools in England—the King's School in Canterbury, England's oldest school, then Cambridge University where he earned his Bachelors and Masters."

"Shakespeare may not have a fancy degree but that doesn't mean a thing," said Melissa, from over by the ladder, which she was eying dubiously.

"Tell that to the dons at Oxford and Harvard," said Blodgett. "They seem to value their own fancy degrees very highly indeed. Meanwhile," he went on, turning back to Jake, "Marlowe accomplished these proven things all the while working as a secret agent for Francis Walsingham and the Queen against religious plots brewing on the Continent."

"Sounds like a real-life James Bond," laughed Jake. That got Melissa's attention. Not, as she'd told him more than once, that she'd ever want to be a Bond girl. They tended to be one-role careers.

"Meanwhile," Blodgett continued, "while Shakespeare was busy learning primary school Latin and animal husbandry in Stratford, our intrepid Marlowe, in between missions for Walsingham and graduate studies at Cambridge, managed to translate four books of Greek and Latin poetry, including Ovid's Elegies."

"It was Shakespeare who studied Ovid," insisted Melissa.

Blodgett looked at her in surprise. "Really? But where? When? In second grade? That's nonsense. There is no evidence for that supposition at all; besides, it was all about sex!"

"You're kidding," said Jake, embarrassed.

Blodgett chuckled. "Indeed. Can you imagine a conservative rural farm school teaching their young children Latin sex poems? But we know Marlowe studied Latin at Cambridge and liked Ovid enough to translate him and write *Hero and Leander*, which is certainly an homage to the poet. The Shakespeareans can only surmise that their Bard 'must have' read him, or that his grade school Latin was perfectly adequate to translate Ovid."

"Go on," said Jake, increasingly intrigued.

Blodgett nodded, as if to gather his thoughts further, then went on: "It's astonishing, what even the scholars have said about him. They admit his influence is found throughout the Canon. There is a note of wonder that sometimes slips through, even from the most learned Shakespeare scholars. Like E. K. Chambers, who once wrote: 'Marlowe's death in 1593 probably puts him out of the question.' You notice he used that ubiquitous word 'probably,' which is the basis for most Shakespearean biography."

"Tell that to the Folger Library," snapped Melissa.

"Read Twain," Jake snapped back. "Go on," he said to Blodgett.

Blodgett threw Melissa a worried glance, and continued: "The first person to actually raise the question of Marlowe as true author of the plays was the Shakespeare biographer F.G. Fleay, who wrote in his 1876 *Shakespeare Manual* that he 'did not think it possible to separate Shakespeare's work from Marlowe.' I have a copy over here somewhere," he said, fumbling about.

"Really?" asked Jake in surprise. "A biographer wrote that in 1876?"

Blodgett gave up the search. "Yes. Then a writer named Wilbur Gleason Ziegler took it one step further in his 1895 novel, *It was Marlowe*. I sold a copy of that once, I think in 1957. Anyway that was dismissed as fiction, and after the silencing of Sir George Greenwood, the issue wasn't raised again until 1923, when an American chap from Harvard named Archie Webster wrote in the *National Review* that Christopher Marlowe was in fact the author of the entire Shakespeare Canon. Webster contended that Shakespeare, as one of 16 partners of the Blackfriars Theater company, began his usurping ways with the play *Richard II* and continued with others after that by putting his name on them. Webster was the first to make this charge openly. Since then most doubters have preferred to say Shakespeare was just a willing front man for someone, like Oxford. But I find that doubtful."

Melissa, staring out the store window, listened in uncharacteristic silence. Another customer entered: a middle aged woman, who gave Melissa a disapproving look, and proceeded to review the Agatha Christie collection.

"Marlowe wrote his first play, *Dido, Queen of Carthage*, while still at Cambridge," Blodgett went on. "Then he took London by storm directly upon graduation, with *Edward II, Massacre at Paris, Tamburlaine, The Jew of Malta,* and *Dr. Faustus*, the play mentioned on that plaque back there in Deptford. That was the source of the line that goes *"Was this the face that launched a thousand ships?' "*

"Wait, I know that!" exclaimed Melissa, in surprise. " *'And burnt the topless towers of Ilium!' "*

The new customer looked up and joined in, enthusiastically. "I know that poem! *'Sweet Helen, make me immortal with thy kiss,' "* she recited, with a smile.

" *'Her lips suck forth my soul; see where it flies.' "* Finished Blodgett, in amusement.

"I just adore that Shakespeare poetry," said the woman, poking among the ruins of the Victorian novels section.

Blodgett shook his head, sadly. "See what I mean? Yet Marlowe was a sensation from the start: every play a hit, one after another in quick succession. He was the first playwright to use blank verse. *Edward II* was the first history play, and the first to depict the oppression of gays. *Faustus* and *Jew of Malta* introduced the English tragedy. His poem *The Passionate Shepherd* is still widely quoted, including in Shakespeare."

"How so? Can you give me an example?" asked Jake.

" 'Come *live with me and be my love.' "*

"I've heard that."

" *'And we will all the pleasures prove' "* the woman customer chimed in.

" *'By shallow rivers to whose falls,'* " Blodgett rejoined.

" *'Melodious birds sing madrigals.'* " Melissa concluded. "Funny, I always thought that was Shakespeare."

"Of course it was, dear," said the woman.

By now Jake Fleming was ready to strangle all of them.

Blodgett coughed and quickly regained his composure as the woman customer moved on to the Anthony Trollope department. "Did you know that entire poem was plagiarized by the Bard in *The Passionate Pilgrim* and later on those same lines turn up in *The Merry Wives of Windsor*? And that *'the face that launched a thousand ships'* is recycled later in *Troilus and Cressida*? Put that in your pipe and smoke it."

Jake took out his pen to jot some notes in his reporter's shorthand.

Melissa spoke up. "Wait a minute, first you say Shakespeare didn't write anything, and then you say he's a plagiarist. Which is it?"

"Well, it must be one or the other," noted Blodgett, pointedly. "It is only after Marlowe is out of the picture–in fact not two weeks go by after his alleged death–that suddenly Shakespeare turns up out of nowhere."

"Tell us about this alleged death," said Jake, now intrigued.

"You need to read the Inquest. Then it will be as plain as day."

"Inquest?" Even Melissa stopped and took note of that. Jake scrambled for the Lewis List, and Blodgett nodded eagerly. "Yes, of course, why didn't I think of that? If *Inq* stands for Inquest, that would certainly fill the bill."

"What inquest?" asked Jake, no longer concealing his excitement.

"The official Inquest into the death of Christopher Marlowe. It is a patently fraudulent document, which you will see when you read it."

"Do you have it here?"

Blodgett looked around and frowned apologetically. "Yes, of course. The question, however, is where?" He scanned the shelves, scratching his head. "I know it's somewhere."

"Maybe you should try the library," said Melissa, stepping aside while the Trollope reader bought three used paperbacks for a total of one pound and stomped out of the store, with a haughty look back.

"Marlowe my left foot," Jake overheard her mutter.

"I hope we haven't cost you a customer," said Jake.

"Hardly. That's the first time she didn't demand change," chuckled the bookseller. "She'll be back." He flashed a smile to overmatch Melissa's continuing scowl. "So, will there be anything else?"

"What," said Jake, thinking hard, "can you tell us about the Star Chamber? Does that relate to Marlowe in any way?" He was thinking of that ride on the London Eye.

Up went the eyebrows. "Indeed it does. That's where he was indicted for heresy. A capital offense, I might add. The charges were very detailed. He was pretty much a goner after that."

Melissa was more than ready to leave. Determined to prove herself a better customer than her father, however, she cheerfully bought a brand new copy of *Name of the Rose*.

As Jake chatted with Blodgett by the register, she wandered towards the door, and glanced out into the street. Traffic on Charing Cross Road was busy as usual. She noticed a long black limousine parked across the way in a bus zone, while the uniformed driver, oddly enough, stood on the sidewalk conversing with a group of skinheads. They appeared, to her, to be in the midst of some kind of transaction. Nearby, a policeman seemed unconcerned, so either he was on the dole or it was nothing illegal, she decided. She also noted that there was no sign of their erstwhile 'Watcher.'

"Uh oh," said Melissa, looking out the window.

"What?" Jake hurried to join her.

"Company coming." She pointed. The limousine had departed. The skinheads, a group of at least five she could see, were in the process of cavorting and dodging through the traffic, middle fingers erect, jaywalking in their direction in plain sight of the still oblivious constable, across the road towards the bookstore.

Jake saw them too. "Henry," he said, urgently. "I think there's trouble."

As two of the group split off and started down the alley towards the back of the store, Blodgett turned to head them off. "I'd better check the locks." He hurried toward the back, leaving the Flemings to man the gates.

"I don't suppose there's much use calling the police?" asked Melissa, as the group strode straight towards them, leering expressions on their heavily pierced faces.

The leader, a much-tatooed and bejangled thug, kicked the door open and strode into the store, his two cohorts in tow, and knocked over the nearest bookcase with immense glee.

"Oooh, check out the stonker bird!" smirked the shortest of the group, confronting Melissa. "Maybe Dirk won't be out on the pull tonight, eh mate?"

The leader looked her over. "Thinks she's too posh for us, maybe?"

While quailing inside with deep revulsion, Melissa stood her ground.

Jake stepped forward. "What do you dipsticks want?"

The second skinhead sneered: "Mayhem, mate." With that the rampage began, as the first row of bookshelves was overturned, and the two minions tried to grab Melissa, who responded with a scream and a kick.

The rampage ended just as quickly, as a surprisingly loud voice behind them shouted: "Stop! That will do!"

The skinheads stopped and stared, ostensibly for good reason, as Henry Blodgett appeared before them from out of the rubble aiming a World War Two vintage military carbine straight at the leader's shiny head.

"Jesus muthah!" yelped Dirk, dashing for the door, the others close behind yelling with fear, their two outside buddies joining them in full flight.

Jake looked at the old bookseller in astonishment as he lowered the gun, strode to the door, closed, then locked it. Melissa stared at the weapon, still speechless.

Blodgett chuckled, and set the old carbine on the floor. "Always thought that would come in handy one day." He scratched his head. "I wonder if they sell bullets for these things?"

Jake and Melissa stared at him, then at each other, and in a moment of relief, all three burst into peals of laughter. Jake practically had to pick himself up off the floor, as sobriety set in once more. "Here, let me give you a hand with this," he said finally, picking up the first fallen bookcase.

Chapter Twenty-Four

The Good is Oft Interred

London, Sunday morning, early November

The weather had turned foul once more. Wipers slashing, the taxicab turned onto Whitehall Road towards Westminster. Jake watched the London city sights roll past, his mind in another century.

Melissa stared dolefully out the window as Westminster Abbey loomed directly ahead, with Big Ben and the London Eye staring back from across the river, where it jutted into the low flying clouds. It looked better at night, Jake decided.

"Stop at the next corner," Jake called out to the driver. The cabbie complied with disconcerting abruptness, deftly swooping into the long pullover area on Victoria Street intended for cabs and buses. He pulled smartly to a stop, somehow avoiding a large puddle of water, and awaited their next command. Melissa turned and looked at her father in consternation. "Are you really serious about this?"

"Sure. After yesterday's excitement it'll do you some good." Jake paid the fare and got out, opening an umbrella, which Melissa ignored.

"You're really going to drag me to a church service?" she asked, incredulously, following as he hurried towards the Abbey entrance. She knew perfectly well that her parents had been agnostics, and she'd taken little interest in religion herself other than from a historical perspective. But he'd been insistent, and she'd finally agreed if only to humor him. Like the Flemings, people were dressed up in their Sunday best, in Jake's case such as it was, namely a well-worn sports jacket and unpressed wool slacks. As for Melissa, she looked, as usual, just good enough to stop people in their tracks. Not that she felt like it. She would much rather have been elsewhere, but still, she'd admitted in the taxi, she'd always wanted to see the Poet's Corner. On the other hand, "This better be good," she warned him as they approached the archway.

But first things first: they would attend church service as the price of admission. It was that or join the daily throng and pay a stiff fee for a crowded, unwanted tour of the tombs of the kings and naves and chapels. They both hated tours, official or otherwise, but Jake had been given a tip (by none other than Fred the doorman) and attending church didn't seem like such a bad alternative.

The sound of organ music could be heard wafting from somewhere deep in the church's vast interior. Bach. Or was that Handel? He couldn't quite recall. Either one sounded good to him.

"This way," he called back to Melissa, where she was trying to step around the puddles in her dress shoes. He could tell she hated every moment of this but wasn't repentant. "Did you know this abbey was founded by Edward the Confessor, in 1066?" he asked her. He'd only just found that out online, but she needn't know that.

"No," she retorted, and made a face. She was clearly not into the role of dutiful churchgoing daughter. Sunday mornings were supposed to be for sleeping in!

"Then I bet you didn't know he was the son of Ethelred the Unready," he said, making a face back.

"You don't say?" She responded and stuck her tongue out at him.

"The Norse were the forebears of the Normans, who ruled for centuries here. This place was built by the Vikings."

"I knew that." Actually, she hadn't but wasn't about to admit it.

As the Flemings vanished into the great stone edifice, a gray-haired man, hunched under an umbrella, stepped out from behind a taxi stand. The thin man had followed them from their building, expecting any scenario but this. Were they religious people, these two? Somehow he doubted it. She wasn't the type, certainly. And an investigative journalist, trained to ask hard questions? Hard to fathom. So, what then? What else could have drawn them to the great cathedral of the tombs of Kings on a rainy Sunday morning, after that strange funeral in Deptford he'd of necessity so gladly avoided? Were they plotting, even now, against him?

For, though I am not splenitive and rash,

Yet have I something in me dangerous,
Which let thy wiseness fear: hold off thy hand, he thought, fretfully.

He closed his eyes, and felt the shadows drawing around him. Brushing at them like invisible flies, he shook his aching head in dismay, wishing he'd stayed in bed. Instead, he sensed a new threat, and new danger. More than ever, he felt the walls protecting his domain closing in, pushed ever inward by growing menace from without. Or even from within this cherished fortress of heritage and lore? He had struggled so hard and for so long to reach the pinnacle of success, only to be betrayed by that ingrate Lewis. Was it about to happen again?

Inside the chapel Jake and Melissa knelt, and stood, and sang, and listened as the Westminster Boy's Choir intoned traditional English hymns, unaware of a dark, clouded spirit not far away.

As the service progressed, both Flemings, through an exchange of glances, had to admit that the music alone was worth the visit. Finally, the Dean, in a long satin robe, offered a simple nonthreatening prayer written by St. Benedict, on the always-safe subject of the virtues of wisdom. Then the choir sang once more, and it was over.

As they followed the Sunday worshipers toward the gathering tour groups in the foyer, Jake grabbed Melissa's hand, pulled her aside, and ducked behind a column. The gray-haired lone parishioner in the back row nearly missed this movement, and followed suit just in time, drawing closer, like a dark shadow, amidst the pillars of history all around. After a few minutes, the crowd dissipated, and freed at last from what to her had been a religious charade, Melissa looked around with a feeling of awe. They were practically alone in the famed Westminster Abbey in all its splendor and glory, where kings and queens were coroneted and buried. High above knights and angels soared on gilded, frescoed ceilings, and danced for the ages on glorious stained glass windows.

"God, that's gorgeous," muttered Melissa, gazing upwards at the painted heavens.

At the far end, what seemed like a mile away, were the tombs of the kings. Pretty much all of them, Jake had read somewhere. Some of them were truly worthy souls, fitting of burial in a great church. Others, on the other hand, might well belong elsewhere.

As the Flemings moved toward the northern nave, the thin man drawing closer among the shadows, someone else was also trailing them: a large man who remained well to the rear of the building. His instructions remained as before: make no overt moves, until his quarry's true intentions were plainly known. That fiasco at the bookstore yesterday hadn't helped matters, he knew. And this new wrinkle only added to his growing doubts. What could these people possibly be doing in this place on Sunday? He felt certain that it had not been to worship.

And then he saw the gray-haired man. Well, well, well, he thought to himself. This is getting more interesting by the moment. Maybe it's time to kill three birds with one stone.

Not far away, the thin man, having detected The Watcher at last, was having much the same thought.

***

Jake finally saw it up ahead: a cordoned area with a cacophony of monuments and plaques arrayed seemingly at random on the floor, pillars, wall, and points in between. Melissa recognized it at the same moment. "There it is," she exclaimed, in a stage whisper. "The Poet's Corner!"

The famed Poet's Corner, from which Christopher Marlowe had been banned until only recently. Their mission was to find out why.

Melissa, in the meantime, began to feel edgy. "Something creeps me out about this place," she whispered. "It's like a weird combination of mysticism and malice, all at once." Jake could see her delving through her movie memory banks for a suitable role to play.

Jake found an Abbey tour guide and asked him point blank. "Where's Christopher Marlowe?"

The tour guide, a young man, seemed nonplussed by the question. "Marlowe?" he had to search among his evidently disorderly recollections. Certainly the name rang a bell somewhere, if not in a chapel. Meanwhile, Melissa wandered ahead to peruse the famed Corner, along with a group of Dutch tourists who had just arrived from the opposite direction. The tour guide finally told Jake, "Wait here, sir, and I'll ask the Dean's aide." He waved to a dark-haired slender man in a monogrammed blazer, who excused himself from a pair of Dutch women and came over.

"Christopher Marlowe?" The aide's face suddenly reddened, in recollection. "Ah, yes. You mean The Atheist."

"Is that what he's called?" Jake jotted it down while the aide stood by, fully immune to irony.

One of the Dutch tourists, a portly man in a beige sports jacket and gold-rimmed spectacles, overheard this dialogue and spoke up. "What about Shelley, then? Wasn't he the 'Eton Atheist?' " As the man spoke, Jake noticed a sizable monument nearby commemorating Percy Shelley.

The Dean's aide reddened even more. "I'm sure the Directors had their reasons," he said, stiffly. "We only maintain the exhibits, here. It is up to the scholars to decide who is deserving of acknowledgment and who is not, and in what manner."

God, thought Jake. Marlowe's fate remained at the mercy of a committee of Ecclesiastics. Even here. Poor Marlowe. The Dutch tourist wandered off to join his receding group.

"I understand that he is credited for five great plays and some of poetry's most famous lines," Jake mentioned to the aide, pointedly.

The aide blushed once again. "I wouldn't know, sir."

"I mean, from what I've read there's no question Marlowe was a much greater poet and playwright than most of these people, if not all. So, where is he? And why was he banned from here until now?"

"It's not for me to say, sir," said the Dean's aide, brusquely. "Perhaps it was because of his scurrilous reputation," he added, and turned away to greet a less querulous visitor.

Not far away, the eminent scholar seethed at this interchange, the demons in his head screaming warnings he could no longer ignore.

Further back in the cathedral, The Watcher strained to hear what was going on between the tour guides and Flemings but could not. The large man knew if he was seen, he'd be back where he started. But he felt an increasingly urgent need to be closer to the action. Moving as quickly as his bulk would allow, he edged along the far aisle, quickly joining the tour group, which seemed not to notice one more large man among many.

Jake wandered on into the Poet's Corner to find his daughter, while Melissa, feeling increasingly driven, had hurried on ahead. Jake proceeded at a more leisurely pace, studying the stone and bronzed markers and monuments arrayed on the chapel floor and walls. He paused briefly at Shakespeare's substantial effigy, then saw Melissa waving urgently for him to come over. She was standing below a tall stained glass window near the tomb of Chaucer. He hurried to join her.

"Did you find him?" he asked, pausing for a moment of homage to the first great English poet. Then he scanned the area around the Chaucer tomb for some sign of Marlowe's recently added presence.

"No, look up!" she said, pointing at the stained glass window directly above them. He followed her gaze, and finally saw it. The lower center area of the window consisted of six diamond-shaped panes of glass, etched with the names of six poets. Three he recognized: Alexander Pope, Oscar Wilde, and in the lower right, Christopher Marlowe. Then his heart skipped a beat. The window showed Marlowe's birth year 1564. But next to the year of death, shown as 1593, there was engraved a question mark.

He glanced at Melissa, who seemed not to have noticed. "What I want to know," she said, waving at the window in annoyance, "is who these Herrick, Houseman and Burney people are?" These lesser poets had been given equal importance, it seemed, to Christopher Marlowe. Or at least, equal window space in the three panels above.

"The Shakespeare people were very upset about that question mark, you know," said a voice behind them. It was the young tour guide again, whose appearance caused the thin man to draw back once more.

"Interesting," said Jake, gazing up. "Good question, Melissa." Supposedly Marlowe had been murdered in 1593, a year after Robert Greene's death. Clearly Desmond Lewis had been of the belief that Marlowe had not died at all that year. Had he somehow convinced the Deans of Westminster to add him at last? And what about that question mark?

And where was Shakespeare at that time? Too bad the library was closed. He needed to look at some dates.

The location of the Poet's Corner in Westminster Abbey, among the thrones and coffins of so many kings made Jake wonder about something else. When a powerful person wanted to get rid of someone, the best way was to establish grounds, legitimate or not. That was the basis of judicial murder, he'd learned online that morning. He'd also learned its origins: a charming innovation of one of the kings most gloriously interred here in the Abbey, and the original purpose for the Star Chamber, as Sunir had mentioned to them up on the Ferris wheel. That's what Jake had been trying to recall in Deptford. The Star Chamber had been established by Henry VII, victor at Bosworth Field over the hapless, alleged hunchback Richard III. It was this first Henry Tudor who had overthrown a legitimate king and founded the Tudor dynasty. And judicial murder had proved a convenient way to rid himself of enemies, witnesses, historians, and critics alike.

According to Blodgett, Christopher Marlowe had supposedly died while under indictment in that dreaded chamber for heresy: a certain death sentence. He needed to find out more about that indictment.

"Dad, let's get out of here," Melissa said, suddenly feeling a sense of urgency. "I have a bad feeling something is going to happen."

As the Flemings quickly left the building, sensing something wrong but still unaware of being followed, the thin man hesitated, not wanting to be spotted in the bright light of day outside. Seeing him hesitate, The Watcher made a call on his cell phone, using the tour guide's continuing narrative for cover. Then, as his new quarry made a decision and headed for the back exit, he was forced to make a decision. The Flemings he knew where to find. But this gray-haired man remained an open question mark. And if what he was starting to piece together was true, this man was a walking time bomb. Ending his call quickly, he moved to intercept the older man and have a closer look. But as he stepped out of the tour group and looked around, the thin man had vanished once again.

Bloody hell! Thought The Watcher, in frustration. He was getting bloody tired of this freak show. Maybe it was time to become a bit more proactive himself.

Outside on the portico, Jake gave his daughter a sidelong glance. "Melissa, I know you don't agree with this investigation, but I could use your help, if you'd set aside your doubts for a moment."

"What is it?" she asked warily, as, weaving to avoid the side splashes from passing taxis, they passed a line of policemen on the sidewalk, who appeared determined to protect their national heroes from terrorists and apostates alike. But these days more particularly terrorists.

From the way the Bobbies regarded them, Jake felt fairly certain that they weren't likely suspects for terrorism. As to Melissa—wet hair and all—she was being regarded, as usual, with an uncomfortable (for him) combination of lust and awe. But one fortunate result of all that police protection was that The Watcher had been forced to withdraw.

The thin man, on the other hand, was still unknown and unobserved, at least to Jake.

He lowered his voice. "It's apparent that Mr. Marlowe's reputation has been seriously sullied, in Merry Old England. Setting aside the authorship question, I'd like to find out exactly why. It's the kind of thing I think Des Lewis would have been drawn to. And these English keep records of everything. Somewhere in this city are copies of the charges presented in the Star Chamber."

"O-kay," she said, slowly, as though verbally mulling that over.

He nodded towards the Houses of Parliament, just across the way. "I read that technically, it was an off-the-record meeting of the Privy Council in a different room."

"Yes, I know: one that happened to have a starry fresco on the ceiling."

"Right." He told her about his research that morning. "Apparently the key difference is that the Star Chamber was presided over by the Archbishop of Canterbury instead of the Queen, so he governed the agenda. But it had to have a façade of legality. Before condemning people, they had to at least present charges and make the appearance of hearing them."

"Are you sure about that? The Archbishop of Canterbury?"

"We're not talking about Becket or Thomas More here. We're talking Spanish Inquisition, English-style."

"Then it's probably in the history books. Or a Marlowe biography, somewhere."

Jake continued to gaze thoughtfully across the grassy mall towards the nearby adjoining Courts of Westminster and Houses of Parliament.

She looked at him sideways. "I don't suppose I'm going to convince you to give up this wild goose chase, am I?"

He laughed, wryly. 'No, I don't suppose you are. I've made a commitment to find out what happened to Des Lewis and what he was trying to do. And if that has brought me here, to the long dead trail of Christopher Marlowe, so be it."

"That Sunir really got you hooked on this Marlowe quest, didn't he?"

"Maybe. I will admit I'm beginning to see what had Lewis so intrigued."

She paused. "Dad, you do know, don't you, that whatever happened to him, could happen to you. To us? That scared me yesterday. And the night before, up on that wheel."

He looked at her. "I know. I've been worried about that. I should never have dragged you into this mess."

"You didn't drag me, it was my idea, remember? And I'm not going to cut and run, especially with a theater dissertation ahead of me, and an opportunity to do something out of the ordinary."

"You didn't mention a dissertation."

"Yeah, well, it comes with the territory. I need it for my degree."

"Hmph. You're as bad as Desmond Lewis when it comes to keeping secrets. Are you going to tell me what you're going to do for this dissertation of yours?"

"Not yet. To tell you the truth, I've been under a lot of pressure about it, but I've decided to wait and see where all this leads to." She turned away for a moment, then turned back. "Look, I want you to listen to me a moment and promise not to yell or anything."

He ushered her to a reasonably dry bench in a bus shelter and they sat. "Come on. Out with it. You've been less than forthcoming about your 'English friends' for starters. What's going on? Is this still about National Treasures?"

She looked at the ground, kicked at a pebble, then back at him. "For you, this is just another caper, another chase after the bad guys and rescue the poor misbegotten or something. But for me, you're talking about a lifetime of believing one thing, and then seeing it all blow up in my face. You know, you don't just waltz into the Vatican and announce to the Cardinals that Jesus was gay, or Mary had twins or something."

"Did I do that?"

"I think that's what Desmond Lewis tried to do. And you might be thinking about it. I mean, come on. This isn't easy for me. We're talking about changing history, here. All that work for Dr. Scofield—who's a big fan of yours, by the way."

"I doubt it, but thanks. Anyway, I get your point. But as a responsible parent I also—"

"Hello? Dad, I'm an adult, remember?"

He threw up his hands. "So, what do you want to do? I just don't want to put you in any more of an uncompromising situation than you're already in, not to mention danger. I liked your original plan of seeing some plays and taking notes or whatever a lot better."

She stared at him. "You really don't know me, do you?"

He grinned, sheepishly. "So, I gather you don't want to go home?"

"Dad, I just got here. And I have news for you. I have a lot of respect for Marlowe and used to toy with the 'what ifs' about him, but never got past Deptford, I guess. Or more to the point, never got past my faculty advisers. And there are some things that do intrigue me, such as why he was excluded for so long from the Poet's Corner, as you say. That makes absolutely no sense. And I agree the Shakespeare biography is troubling. I read Mark Twain's essay last night, by the way. And while I'm not convinced Lewis and Sunir were right yet by any means, I guess what I'm trying to say is you've got me hooked on this thing, for better or worse. And God knows career-wise for me probably the worse, but I've made up my mind, and I want to see this through, wherever it leads. OK?"

"You know, even if they have to change the name on the titles and festivals or whatever, all those great plays and roles will remain the same, won't they?"

"I guess so. But it sure won't feel the same. Not that that's likely ever to happen anyway, I guess." She shrugged, in atypical indecision.

"But risks aside, how does this affect your relationship with Childers, and Scofield and so on?" He asked her.

"It doesn't. They don't need to know about it. At least not yet."

He scratched his nose. "I see. Well, OK then. Good luck on that score. Shall we get to work?"

She nodded, resolutely. "Absolutely. So. What next?"

"Um, The library, first thing tomorrow. Libraries are safe. So we'll be spending a lot of time in libraries. Maybe we'll sleep in the libraries," he laughed. Not that he felt very humorous.

"Libraries?" She looked disappointed. He suspected she had imagined them in a suspense movie, her as heroine, digging up treasures in dragon's pits or discovering lost manuscripts in pirate's caves and such. Then she looked at him thoughtfully. "Maybe we should try to get into the Lambeth Library," she said, getting to her feet and gazing past Big Ben across the river, through the now steady drizzle of rain. "I've read they have a lot of historical documents in there."

He followed her gaze. "Lambeth," he murmured, thoughtfully. He'd actually been creeped out the night before by the sight of that old castle. A creepy-looking place, with perhaps an equally creepy history? He remembered Blodgett's theory, that the Lewis List's 'Lamb' was very likely 'Lambeth' for short. He told her, and her eyes lit up.

"Dad, I think he's right! There's something there, I'm sure."

The possible second entry on the Lewis list was just visible above the mist-shrouded trees. It was a squat, homely brown castle of little note or distinction to the casual observer, set back from the river between two bridges, almost directly opposite the Houses of Parliament. As he studied it through the rain and fog, Jake couldn't help but wonder what secrets lay within those ancient walls and battlements, and how would they know where to look for them? And worse, what primordial horrors might lurk there, and how would they know how to avoid them? Lambeth Palace was the color, he thought, of dried blood.

"Henry Blodgett said that Lambeth Palace is the historic London residence of the Archbishop of Canterbury," he told her.

She stared. "Whoa. Really? Dad, you've been holding out on me. The Archbishop of Canterbury is the one who would have indicted Marlowe in the Star Chamber. If he was the presiding magistrate, then he had to give the order."

He whistled. His daughter the actress was also a scholar, it seemed.

Melissa was busy tapping on her Smartphone while he pondered his next move.

"We will have to find a way to get in over there, though. It's not open to the public," she said, as he flagged down a taxi. Her expression showed excitement as they got into the cab. He hoped she couldn't read his; he was feeling increasingly uneasy about her safety. As the cab pulled away from the curb, Jake asked her, in confusion: "Were you planning to go there now?"

She laughed. "No, it'll be closed Sunday. And we'll have to make a plan of attack, anyway."

He had to force himself not to stare at her in amazement. My how she's grown! He reflected. And somehow he'd missed the whole thing.

They were both in a reflective mood when they got back to the flat. As they got off the elevator and started down the hall, Jake drew to a halt.

Something was wrong. Melissa saw it at the same time. "Shit," she muttered.

The entry door was ajar.

Moving cautiously, Jake motioned for her to stay put, which she ignored, as he approached the door in silence. He stopped, listened, then, hearing nothing, threw the door open and stepped inside, flipping on the light switch.

"Dammit to hell," said Melissa, right behind him. The flat had been entered and searched, although with nowhere near the wanton intensity of Desmond

Lewis's office and apartment. To Melissa, as she inspected the damage, the rifling through of her personal items was a violation beyond the pale. But to Jake, it looked like a professional job.

"Dad." she wailed, in livid indignation. "They went through my *underwear.*"

"They also took our hard drive," Jake reported, a short while later. The good news, Jake thought, soberly, was that there was nothing essential on the computer that couldn't be reinstalled with CDs the newspaper had thoughtfully provided. Their notes and notepads had been in their possession. And those, as he told a skeptical cop an hour later, were what the burglars had been after. Nothing else was missing.

The doorman Fred was almost overly effusive with apologies.

"I'm sorry, Mr. Fleming. I jes' went to the loo for a minute; they musta come in then."

"It's all right, Fred. You're doing your best," Jake assured him.

Fred was mollified, but only somewhat so.

After the police had left, Melissa was grim, and seemed more than ready to do business.

"OK," he said, laying the Desmond Lewis list on the table. "Here's the deal. We are on the trail of a probable killer or killers. And the motive was almost certainly Dr. Lewis's missing book. And what we know about the book is on this list. So, all our personal prejudices and opinions aside, our job is to fill in the blanks, and figure out exactly what it was these killers didn't want the world to know about Shakespeare. And I don't care if it was Marlowe, Oxford, or the Archbishop of Paducah. What I do care about is the truth, who is trying to suppress it, and why. Agreed?"

She pursed her lips. "Partly."

"Partly?"

"OK, mostly." She nodded, grudgingly. "Anyway, I find out who went through my undies I'm going to slap him senseless, the friggin' pervert."

"Or, you could just call the cops," suggested Jake, mildly.

Jake had tried to call Sunir last night and gotten no answer. Now he wanted to warn him about the break-in, but there was still no answer. Hasn't this man heard of voice mail? He hung up in frustration.

Chapter Twenty-Five

Like the Baseless Fabric of This Vision

London, morning, early November

While Jake went out to get a new hard drive, Melissa tried a call to the Lambeth Library for an appointment, and as she feared, had gotten nowhere. They were going to need a referral, and that would take some thought. Henry Blodgett wasn't going to be good enough. It would have to come from within the ranks of Academe, where friends were in short supply, aside from Sunir.

If he was a friend. Melissa was still not so sure about that yet. She could always try Childers, she supposed, but then he would want to know why, and she wasn't ready to tell him she'd gone over to the enemy, as he would see it.

Meanwhile, there was always the British Library.

They made the trek without incident, watchful of surveillance and seeing none. As they entered through the lobby, Jake noted that it had not changed in his absence. Jake introduced a now-determined Melissa to the head librarian, who had, for some reason, either taken a shine to, or pity on him. "My daughter's a student at the University of California at Berkeley," he explained. She even had a student I.D. That was good enough for the librarian to issue a reader's pass.

"I'll look for the Inquest," he told Melissa. "Maybe you can find some clue to that 'Hoffman' entry. Then see what you can find out about those charges in the Star Chamber."

"Okey dokey, boss," she agreed, with a mock salute. Jake knew that as a long-time UC student back in Berkeley, she was accustomed to large libraries. She seemed right at home. He watched her with a mixture of pride and chagrin as she swept away and vanished among the stacks, turning heads as usual.

As Jake headed for the research room, he was stopped in his tracks by a glass case for all the world to see and ponder, housing the original copy of Shakespeare's Last Will and Testament. Sunir had belittled it so, as had Mark

Twain, that he now felt confident that Sunir was right, that Desmond Lewis had been referring to this document as the 'LWT' on his list.

Then, as he examined the three pages more closely, he noticed something striking. The signatures were not only an illiterate-looking scrawl, but each of the three was written and spelled differently. And if Shakespeare signed his wedding certificate with an "x" that would render the question of whether it was third grade Latin, Sixth grade Latin, or the latest claim, that it "must have been" eighth grade Latin, very moot indeed. He couldn't read the script very well, but there was a plain text version he could make a copy of.

Jake studied the will with growing astonishment. It was a profoundly damning document insofar as the case for Shakespeare the poet and playwright went. As Mark Twain had recognized, there was nothing in it that would even begin to suggest, in any way at all, that Will Shakspere (one of the three spellings) was anything other than an uneducated but successful businessman, who didn't much care for his wife. He couldn't believe it. But Twain had pretty much covered this material before, so why had Lewis put it on the list? He forced himself to read it through once more, when one small entry caught his eye. It was a description of one of daughter Judith's bequests: for a collection of "apparrell." Now why would an agrarian businessman collect apparel? He wondered, in growing excitement. But there it was, and he felt sure he'd found the answer. Robert Greene had charged Shake-scene with being a broker of 'playing apparel.' i.e. costumes. He had bragged of apparel worth 200 pounds, as early as 1592. His collection would have been substantial–and valuable–after twenty-six years. And probably a source of considerable income in the interim, renting it out for productions, especially to his own company, the Lord Chamberlain's Men, who managed the Globe Theater.

Jake continued to the stacks, where he began his search for the Marlowe Inquest. The library had a solid collection of Marlowe biographical material, several volumes of which contained copies of the Coroner's report. The Inquest was in two forms: a photocopy of a tattered yellow-brown parchment upon which had been inscribed the coroner's determination and recounting of the events, and a text "translation" in both English and Latin, which he found surprising. Why Latin, which was apparently the original version? Could that have been an effort to keep it from the public?

He went in search of a copy machine to make copies, and as he read it through, it was clear to him that the Inquest was even more damning—of the official story of Marlowe's death—than the will was of Shakespeare. Which gave him the germ of an idea. According to biographer Leslie Hotson, who had first discovered it, there was only one coroner present: the Queen's own, which was illegal. There were three witnesses including the supposed killer, who hadn't fled, and willingly turned himself in. Why not? He was pardoned within the month. Maybe he knew he would be.

This was confirmed by another similar document, alongside the first. It was the Queen's Pardon of Ingram Frizer, the man who allegedly killed Marlowe. The phrasing of "self-defense" was used twice. Even so, a pardon, for the murder of a popular playwright? From the Queen? Not even a trial? This was unheard of, it seemed to Jake. Clearly someone wanted this case to go away, and swiftly, without public comment or notice. Mostly the Pardon repeated the wording of the Inquest, ending with:

> *". . . And so that the said Ingram killed & slew Christopher Morley (Marlowe) aforesaid on the thirtieth day of last May aforesaid at Deptford Strande aforesaid in our said County of Kent within the verge in the room aforesaid within the verge in the manner & form aforesaid in the defence and saving of his own life against our peace our crown & dignity. As more fully appears by the tenor of the Record of the Inquisition aforesaid which we caused to come before us in our Chancery by virtue of our writ. We therefore moved by piety have pardoned the same Ingram ffrisar the breach of our peace which pertains to us against the said Ingram for the death above mentioned & grant to him our firm peace. Provided nevertheless that the right remain in our Court if anyone should wish to complain of him concerning the death above mentioned In testimony &c Witness the Queen at Kewe on the 28th day of June."*

Jake guessed no one complained. Apparently, no one even knew, for the next 400 years.

He decided to see what else he could learn about this Frizer and company. He found several references among the Elizabethan history sites. The three men had a bad reputation, it seemed. They were con artists, mercenaries, and veterans of overt and covert wars at home and abroad. To them a con or fraud of any sort was all in a day's work.

Next, he wanted to determine what was actually "known" about the death of Marlowe, by the general public. The first sketchy reports he could find were that he had died of the plague. It wasn't until three months after Deptford that preacher Gabriel Harvey–apparently no fan of Marlowe's–had unleashed a devastating broadside, denouncing the famed poet. Jake's heartbeat quickened. Was there a growing conspiracy here? He gathered his photocopies, and carefully folded and tucked them in his notepad with the other papers. His notepad was getting cluttered, so he digressed to the library bookstore and bought several spiral-bound notebooks, a valise to carry them in, with another for Melissa.

Melissa had asked more than once why he didn't use a tablet, but he simply preferred keeping notes the old fashioned way. He liked having a hard copy of his work. The break-in the night before was a good reason, and he'd experienced similar attacks before in his work abroad.

He found a pay phone and called Sunir, just catching him on the way to lunch. "You were right about the Will," he said, and told him about the apparel. "And I agree, it's looking a lot like Marlowe didn't die in Deptford." He told him about the Inquest.

Sunir listened with astonishment, then said: "Then you must read the Sonnets. Read Sonnet 74. Meanwhile, I must go. I'm following some leads myself." With that he rang off.

When Melissa caught up with Jake around midday, she grinned, and handed him a paper sack. "For you," she said. "I already had one."

Inside was a cup of yogurt. He made a face, but gladly spooned it down, much to the relief, he had to admit, of his stomach, which, he realized, had been much improved as of late due to her health-food ministrations, wanted or no.

She reported no luck so far on the elusive Hoffman book. "Maybe it's because it's not British," she decided. "If it even is a book."

Setting that aside, he told her the good news: that he'd found the Shakespeare Will as well as the Marlowe Inquest. She didn't seem surprised. She accepted the notebooks and case without looking at them and said, "So you read the part in the will about the second-best bed?"

"Yeah. But I found something even better than that."

"What? What? C'mon, I'm all tears."

He told her about the apparel, and Greene's charge that Shake-scene was a costume broker. "Did you ever notice that?"

She frowned and shook her head, but he could tell that she was intrigued. "You think he kept them all those years?"

"Why not? They were probably a money machine. He could rent them to the players again and again. Or the company. He could probably get a company seamstress to keep them in repair. Or his daughters, for that matter. Since he didn't bother educating them maybe he kept them housebound for just such chores."

"You aren't going to relent, are you?"

"What? It's free labor. Barefoot and illiterate so they don't know any better."

She sighed, and sat down, pursing her lips. "You know I read once, I think in college, that there was a plague in London around 1590, and all the theaters were shut down for a time. If that's relevant to anything."

He nodded. "Yes. Two things, actually. Apparently the first reports of Marlowe's death were that he'd died of the plague. But if the theater business was shut down and Shake-scene was already a money lender and broker, it makes perfect sense he'd go around buying up the costumes, probably for pennies to the pound, from all the unemployed actors or theater managers. He could then rent them back for exorbitant fees once the theaters were reopened. I want to look into that some more."

Melissa let out a sigh. "Incredible," was all she could say.

"If so, the man really was a genius. He innovated not only valet parking, but also costume rentals."

"Valet parking?" Melissa just shook her head in amazement when he told her about the horse grooming story. "That's pretty funny," she said.

"OK, so are you ready to hear about the Inquest?"

"I suppose. Ready as I'll ever be." She followed him to the nearest vacant alcove and sat down opposite him. "So, what was the deal? We never went into that in Comparative Literature. Everyone always just said he was murdered in a bar brawl."

"Put that down as a classic case of disinformation."

"So, what really happened?"

"Basically, the official story went that Marlowe, while out on bail awaiting his imminent death sentence from the Privy Council, chose to spend one of his last remaining days on earth in the even-then seedy dump of Deptford carousing with three low-life thugs, no doubt discussing religion and philosophy, arts and letters. Their names were Robert Poley, a known government agent; Nicholas Skeres, another government agent and known 'coney-catcher'–"

"Con-man," interjected Melissa. "Con comes from 'coney,' which means 'rabbit.' "

"Thank you–And the alleged killer, Ingram Frizer, another known 'rabbit-catcher' in the employ of none other than Marlowe's patron, Sir Thomas Walsingham, cousin of the spy-master."

"Wait a minute." She sprang to her feet. "Did you say Marlowe was out on bail when he was quote-unquote murdered?"

"That's right."

"My God." She sat down again, yanked one of her notebooks out of her valise and flipped it open. "That's impossible. Out on bail? From the Star Chamber? That makes no sense at all."

He'd only just read the details himself that morning. "Yes. But the trial had not yet taken place. Only a hearing, at which the charges were read."

"Even so I don't believe it. Out on bail for heresy? They burned people for that." She scribbled a note in an angry scrawl. "They never let anyone just walk out, like that. Never."

"I got hold of Sunir, by the way."

"What did he say?"

"He got all excited, then said to look at Sonnet 74." He thumbed through his notes, and found the text, he'd just written down that morning: Here we go:

But be contented when that fell arrest
Without all bail shall carry me away,
My life hath in this line some interest,
Which for memorial still with thee shall stay.
When thou reviewest this, thou dost review
The very part was consecrate to thee.
The earth can have but earth, which is his due;
My spirit is thine, the better part of me.
So then thou hast but lost the dregs of life,
The prey of worms, my body being dead,
The coward conquest of a wretch's knife,
Too base of thee to be remembered.
The worth is that which it contains,
And that is this, and this with thee remains.

"Melissa, this literally details the faked murder at Deptford, beginning with his 'arrest,' and 'bail.' "

"You think this could be Marlowe speaking from the grave?"

"Yes. That's why we need to see those charges. And also find out who posted bail. He was evidently free to move about London for two weeks after the hearing. Plenty of time to leave the country, for one thing. Whoever posted bail was someone of influence, and also willing to lose it."

"There's a neatly tied-up package. Is it true there was no body?"

"No. The witnesses swore upon some body or other, but Marlowe was a stranger to them: they were simply merchants and residents of Deptford. So, it could have been anyone. There's no real proof of identity, nor was it ever interred anywhere. The body the witnesses supposedly identified simply vanished. There is no record of burial. I'm not sure why the plaque was posted at that church in Deptford, but again, there was no grave."

Melissa frowned. "So, it could have been a drunken sailor, or some dead guy those guys picked up on the street. Or even a plague victim."

"Right. There was a plague in London at the time. Anyway, it was someone who wouldn't be missed."

Suddenly, he saw her undergo a change, as though she'd remembered some key insight from long ago. "John Penry." Melissa murmured, in hushed tones.

"What? Who's he?"

"Wait here, I'll be right back." Before he could even respond Melissa was on her feet again and rushing off in the direction of the nearest vacant library computer.

Melissa returned twenty minutes later looking somber, like one who has discovered some great truth she didn't want to know. Jake had tried to busy himself reviewing his notes, with minimal success. His daughter plunked herself back down at the table opposite him, the way she used to do when she'd won a race or a contest, at school. Or later, wowed an audience as Desdemona. "I thought so," she said.

Still a bit put off for being so suddenly abandoned, Jake grumbled in a displeased tone: "Thought what? Where did you go?"

"I checked the dates, it's all consistent." She gazed into the distance a moment, then refocused on her notebook. "Dad, there was an execution not far from Deptford the day before Marlowe's alleged death, on May 29th, 1593, and two days before the Inquest. It was another heretic, a Puritan martyr named John Penry, who was also a classmate of Marlowe's at Cambridge. I remember reading about him in Elizabethan Studies. Here's the thing: John Penry was hung, and his body disappeared that same day. So it might have been him that the Inquest jury saw on May 31rst, possibly mutilated to match the killers' statements. The jurors would not have known the difference."

Jake looked up from his notebook where he'd been trying to keep up with shorthand notes and frowned. "Wouldn't he be a bit ripe after two days?"

"This is England, not the Everglades. Besides, there was a plague and death was all over, and everybody probably smelled bad anyway, besides which, there was no such thing as forensic medicine back then."

He looked at his brilliant daughter with combined pride and skepticism. "Interesting," he said, which of course Melissa took as a put down. Too late to turn back, he plowed ahead. "Anyway, that is supposition, although a very intriguing one. But it fits perfectly with what I was trying to tell you–"

"You were trying to tell me what? Go on, do educate me."

"Sorry. Touche. Look, I'm glad you seem to be open-minded about this. I'm just saying I don't think Marlowe would have stayed around or even gone there to supervise this 'murder,' nor would Walsingham. From what I can see Marlowe was a gentleman, in the classical sense, and not given to hanging about in tough seaport taverns with thugs, despite any reputation to the contrary. So your Penry theory actually fits very well."

She seemed mollified. "Well, right or wrong, that reputation is probably why Westminster Abbey avoided recognizing him for so long," she noted, her perceived hurt quickly forgotten. "Like with that Watson incident."

"What was that?"

"I read about it in one of my lit classes, the one that covered Marlowe. He'd been challenged to a duel by this man named Bradley, who'd been harassing him. His close friend Thomas Watson, who was another poet, jumped into the fray and ended up killing Bradley. Both Watson and Marlowe got jailed, and ultimately exonerated, because it was clearly self-defense."

He leaned back in his chair and tapped his palm with his pen–a nervous tick dating back to his cub reporter days. "So that duel made him no more of a ruffian than, say, Alexander Hamilton."

"Good point. I also found what Gabriel Harvey had to say about Marlowe. This person was a real charmer."

"Wasn't he the one who said Oxford should 'go shake a spear'?"

"The very one." She opened her notebook. "Being a poet as well as a preacher, he wrote this triumphal poem rejoicing over Marlowe's death, full of loving and forgiving Christian phrases like: 'He and the plague contended for the game; The haughty man extolls his hideous thoughts,' and 'The grand disease disdained his toad conceit, And smiling at his Tamburlaine contempt, Sternly struck home the peremptory stroke.' "

"Whoa. Nice sentiments," said Jake.

"Yeah. The Puritans hated Marlowe almost as much as the Anglicans."

"Why do you suppose?"

"Because he was outspoken, skeptical, probably agnostic, and questioned authority. So, no big surprise they fell over each other celebrating his 'demise,' with references to 'the justice of God,' and so forth. Another cleric named Thomas Beard said he hoped that 'all atheists in this realm, and in all the world beside . . . in like manner come to destruction.' "

"Hmm. Seems like I've heard that theme recently. The more things change etcetera. But that lends a nice touch of irony to his friends using a Puritan's dead body to cover his escape."

"Dad, it's like everyone was against him. You have to wonder why."

"So, you think there's some possible merit to Lewis' theory?"

"I'm starting to. Give me some time, OK? This is pretty heady stuff."

"So, what do you think really happened back there in Deptford?"

"I don't know. But I'm starting to agree it wasn't what they said."

He pondered. "So, all anyone knows for certain is that three known thugs claimed they killed Marlowe in self-defense, the government accepted them at their word, or even facilitated the cover-up, and that was the end of it. No one even knew what had happened to Marlowe for centuries; it was all conjecture and speculation."

"Yeah, and all those nasty rumors and innuendo were enough to try and convict him in absentia in the Court of Public Opinion and ban him for four hundred years from the Poet's Corner." Melissa was actually starting to sound angry about that. "And why? Why?"

"To protect someone else. Someone with a growing following and vested interest?" He paused, reflectively. "Until Leslie Hotson found the Inquest. But what that did was throw everyone off the scent once again because they all took it at face value."

That gave him an idea, so he asked Melissa to wait before further discussion until Sunir was present. He wanted to try an experiment but didn't want to give it away just yet.

Meanwhile, Melissa continued poring over her own notes. "Still, I can't get over how Marlowe gets arrested for a capital offense, and all the Privy Council does is slap his wrist and let him out. I mean, doesn't that blow your mind?"

"That certainly sounds like an invitation to get out while he had the chance."

"Which supports the Queen's comments six years later, that she was his 'benefactor.' That could confirm what Sunir was saying: that Marlowe was long gone by then with her blessing, probably on a boat to France."

"On his way into exile." He whistled. "So you know what this means, don't you? Someone has to dig up that graveyard and find out exactly who is there, if anyone, by means of—"

"DNA. The technology is out there. Sally Hemming and Thomas Jefferson, remember?"

Jake remembered very well. He'd just missed out on the assignment of interviewing Ms. Hemming's descendant and the other relatives because of a missed flight from Jakarta on another story.

Melissa's eyes were beginning to glow with the excitement of a new role: the Quest. "Dad, I'll tell you this. If we can prove that Marlowe survived Deptford, the whole authorship is thrown wide open." She laughed in spite of herself. "My English professors will kill me, I'll say that."

He frowned, lost in thought. "First things first. About those charges made in the Star Chamber against Marlowe. Did you find anything on that?"

"Not yet. There were plenty of history texts with references to the Court of Star Chamber, but I couldn't find anything in those transcripts about the Marlowe indictment. I'll keep looking after lunch."

"For one thing, try to find out who made the complaint to begin with. Who was it that wanted him out of the picture so badly?"

"I don't know. But the Archbishop of Canterbury at the time was a real weasel by the name of John Whitgift, whose specialty was torturing Puritans and heretics."

"Hmm. A Protestant Torquemada or Richelieu."

"Maybe. In which case he'd really have it in for Marlowe, for *Tamburlaine* alone."

Suddenly she stopped cold, and her eyes widened. He looked at her. "What?"

"Dad. Maybe there never was an indictment."

"What?"

She stopped, suddenly, and snapped her fingers. "Wait a minute. I'll be right back." Before he could protest, she hurried away once more and once again vanished among the stacks.

Jake waited helplessly, with growing exasperation. Fifteen minutes went by and still no sign of her. He began to worry. They clearly had enemies out there. Pacing the little room, he leafed through his notes, trying to picture how a man would go about staging his own death. Still no sign of his daughter. Just when he was about to go looking for her, she finally reappeared, her face flushed in triumph, brandishing her new notebook.

"I found it. I was looking in the wrong place."

"Found what?" This time he didn't even try to conceal his annoyance.

"A letter to the Privy Council, from one Richard Baines."

"The Baines letter." Where had he read about that?

"Yeah. I made a copy. Do you want to see it?"

"Yes, of course. That may be the sum and total of the charges in any case."

She unfolded her copy and spread it out on the table. He read it through:

> *A note Containing the opinion of one Christopher Marly Concerning his Damnable Judgment of Religion, and scorn of gods word.*
>
> *That the Pakistanis and many Authors of antiquity haue assuredly writen aboue 16 thousand yeares agone wher as Adam is proued to haue lived within 6 thowsand yeares. ...*
>
> *That the first beginning of Religioun was only to keep men in awe...*
>
> *That all protestants are Hypocriticall asses.*

That if he were put to write a new Religion, he would
vndertake both a more Exellent and Admirable methode...
That the woman of Samaria & her sister were whores
& that Christ knew them dishonestly.
That St John the Evangelist was bedfellow to Christ
and leaned alwaies in his bosome, that he vsed him
as the sinners of Sodoma.
That all they that loue not Tobacco & Boies were fooles...
That he had as good Right to Coine as the Queene of
England...also that
almost into every Company he Cometh
he perswades men to Atheism
willing them not to be afeard of bugbeares and
hobgoblins, and vtterly scorning both god and his
ministers as I Richard Baines will Justify &
approue both by mine oth and the testimony
of many honest men, and... I think all men in
Cristianity ought to indevor that the mouth of
so dangerous a member may be stopped...
Richard Baines

The charges also included assertions that Marlowe would "name names," and included various additional aspersions on Christianity, Judaism, religion in general, and the Queen.

"Pretty ugly. So, this is where they got that 'loves tobacco and boys' business you always hear," he said, thoughtfully.

Melissa nodded. "Apart from gay bashing, it looks to me like a lot of these charges amount to a shopping list of all the worst offenses a man could commit in Elizabethan times short of murder, in order to get him condemned and executed. And some of it was clearly stuff put in there to provoke the authorities, like saying the Papists were better," she pointed out. "But he did include some points that could be valid. Such as that Moses wanted to get rid of the doubters and reinforce superstition."

"Or that he could have done a better job writing the scriptures?"

"Definitely."

"Some of those ideas are pretty modern," he noted. "So, he may have said them."

"I know. But I doubt Baines would have known the difference between truth and slander."

"In any case," said Jake, "this confirms that slander for political purposes has been a time-honored legal expedient since the dawn of history. Just look at the elections back home in the States." Maybe he could use that as an angle for a story.

"I know." Melissa had been looking over her father's shoulder while he read. "It's character assassination. This Baines person was trying to brand Kit as a gay pederast as well as an atheist, at a time when either one was grounds for execution."

"Presumably on behalf of Archbishop Whitgift. Let's find out if there is any other source for these charges, or anything like it in Kit's own works they could use to pin on him."

"Roger," she nodded. "But can we get lunch first?"

He laughed. "I thought you'd never ask."

The library restaurant had a line, so he cheerfully followed her as she led the way out onto the street and turned south towards Euston Road.

Neither of them spotted The Watcher this time, who'd been observing the library from a car parked opposite and awaiting their reappearance.

"Do you know where you're going?"

"We'll find something." Melissa wasn't finished with Baines. "You know, being an atheist in those days was as good as being a heretic. Or as bad, I should say." He hurried to keep within earshot as she turned in to a nearby lunch counter. "Yet," she went on, scanning the room for two empty seats, "Kit Marlowe was the same man who wrote:

'Thinkst thou that I who saw the face of God,
And tasted the eternal joys of Heaven,
Am not tormented with ten thousand hells,

In being deprived of everlasting bliss?' "

"Marlowe wrote that?"

"Yep. From *Dr. Faustus*."

Jake was astounded. "How many Marlowe lines have you memorized, anyway?"

"Dad, Faustus is basic reading for the classics."

He found a table and waved to the server, a young man, probably a student trying to make ends meet in this very expensive city. Both of them ordered "today's special" sight unseen. Taking out his notebook, Jake leafed through it, leaned back, and pondered the paint peeling on the ceiling.

"Cut is the branch," he murmured.

"Yes. *'And burned is Apollo's laurel bough, that sometime grew within this learned man.'* That play alone should have put Kit in Poet's Corner on a pedestal three hundred years ago."

He remained silent, momentarily awe-stricken both by his daughter's literary acumen and by the words themselves. The words in the graveyard in Deptford. He knew now they'd have to go back there. He wasn't looking forward to that.

"Well, I suppose they could have still been upset over Ovid. Or *Tamburlaine*."

Melissa nodded, still recalling lines from Faustus. "Maybe the church fathers didn't like it when he wrote this, also in Faustus:

'Hell hath no limits, nor is circumscribed
In one self place, for wherever we are is hell,
And where hell is, there must we ever be.' "

"Sounds like the beginnings of secularism," he said. Her ability to memorize poetry was something she had in common with Sunir, he realized.

Two plates of something vaguely resembling tuna salad arrived. He glowered at it a moment, took a dubious bite, then gestured for her to eat.

Melissa wasn't through with Faustus. She wolfed down a forkful, barely taking time to swallow before rushing on: "But then he wrote, in the same play:

'The Devil will come, and Faustus must be damned.
O, I'll leap up to my God. Who pulls me down?
See, see where Christ's blood streams in the firmament.
One drop would save my soul—half a drop;
Aaah, my Christ!'

Jake put down his fork. The words chilled him like a dip in the North Sea.

"Dad, Marlowe invented the deathbed conversion with that line. He was a Christian. No one could write that with such fervor otherwise."

"Poor Faustus. And Marlowe. Those are powerful words. I agree, it's hard to imagine an atheist could have written that. We'd better call Sunir."

Melissa dialed and handed him her phone.

Sunir answered at the second ring. "Sunir? Jake here. I wonder if you could round up a colleague, preferably someone from the English department. I want to run an experiment."

"What kind of experiment?"

"I'll tell you later. Could you ask around for someone, please?"

Sunir sighed. "Very well. But you should know the English Department faculty are unified in their opposition to what we are doing."

"Yeah, no doubt. How much do they actually know about your and Dr. Lewis's book?"

"I made the mistake of approaching Dr. Childers and one or two others a few years ago when I first stumbled across the Greene invective. Some of them actually agreed that we might be right, but they were adamant that the subject of Shakespeare's biography and authorship was simply not open to review."

"Interesting. Maybe they have something to be afraid of."

"They do. Their reputations, primarily."

"So, can you get someone else? Maybe a grad student who hasn't been indoctrinated yet?"

"I'll do my best, but remember, they still have to answer to their professors if they want their degrees, which is a key reason the Shakespeare mythos persists."

"Maybe it's time someone shook their foundation a little."

Sunir chuckled wryly. "Well, I'll see what I can do, but as you know, I'm an outsider."

"Four o'clock still good?"

"Let's make it five. At the St. Francis Hotel, lobby bar?"

"Got it." Jake jotted down the appointment and returned Melissa's phone. She seemed lost in thought, ignoring her food.

"So, do you think it's a cover-up?" she asked him, after a while.

"Marlowe? Or Lewis?"

She blinked. "Both. But I'm thinking Marlowe, right now." Melissa twirled a strand of silky blond hair, absently. "You know, if Kit actually did say any of those things in the Baines letter, like about Moses? It was just youthful contrariness, letting off steam in a religiously oppressive world. It was a rhetorical exercise. Those 'quotes,' if they were even real, were taken while he was at Walter Raleigh's with all those skeptics and Renaissance Men from his 'School of Night.' You know about them, right?"

He looked at her sharply. "Lewis wrote a book about that. It was in his office."

"There, you see? And Baines also referred to Raleigh's men."

"So, who were they?"

"They were a covert gathering of all the intellectuals and Renaissance people, not just of England, but of Europe. That's how he knew Giordano Bruno. I'm sure they talked about all kinds of wild ideas in that setting."

Jake nodded. "Like moot court," he said, with his mouth full of faux tuna.

"Or a debate club."

"Can I assume Shakespeare wasn't one of them?"

She made a face. "Yeah, that's a safe assumption."

"Anyway, Baines must have infiltrated them somehow."

Suddenly, her eyes flew wide open. "Oh shit." she exclaimed.

"What? What?" Heads pivoted in their direction. Jake felt uneasy about attracting attention. Melissa attracted enough attention as it was, on her own.

"The Templars." she was beside herself. "Those charges of Baines? I knew they sounded familiar. Now I remember why. They are almost the exact same charges Pope Clement used to condemn the Knights Templar to death in 1307."

He stared at her, then glanced at his watch. "Hold that thought, and please don't go careening off somewhere," he pleaded. "We still have work to do. Eat your lunch."

Before returning to the library, Jake made one more call, to Gloria Peckham. He wanted to ask her if Lewis had ever mentioned the Templars. An operator's voice came on the line: "The number you are calling is no longer in service," he was informed.

"That's not good," he muttered, pressing the 'off' button.

"What?"

"Lewis's assistant. Her phone's been disconnected."

"Office or home?"

"Office."

"They've probably closed it now. With him gone and all, she's probably out of a job."

"Good point." He looked up her home number from his note pad and tried that. It rang through. He waited for ten rings, looked at Melissa, and shook his head. "No answer."

"Can we go now?" she asked, itching to get back to the stacks.

As they walked back and passed the car with the tinted windows, The Watcher in the front seat noted the time and placed a call.

Chapter Twenty-Six

Speak Less Than Thou Knowest

Gloria Peckham, home on indefinite leave, stared in dread at the once-again ringing telephone, hands on her ears, until it finally stopped. It had been tormenting her for days, until it had finally become her mortal enemy and she was too frightened to touch it. Indeed, had she any courage left she would have simply torn it from its wires. But like a huge spider on the wall, it sat, a black thing of pure menace, and dared her to come nearer. She wasn't up to the dare.

Her fear now was palpable. She had stood by while the police took over her workplace, then her life. Now this. She had to get out of here, now. She had packed her bag, paid her bills, and emptied her accounts. Then she had written one last letter, and posted it that morning to Mr. Jacob Fleming, c/o *The San Francisco Tribune*. Perhaps her recent accidental discovery might yet be useful. Meanwhile, a stay in Majorca for a time until the dust settled, she thought. She had a cousin who'd moved there and had been badgering her for years to come visit. Surely it would be safe in Majorca!

She checked her flat one last time to make sure all was in order. She was realistic enough to sense, at some level, that she might not come back. But still, this was home. And where else could she return to, in the end? She watered the plants one last time and made sure the lights were out and the heat was turned down. It was time to go. With a pang of regret, she put on her coat, gave one last wistful glance around what had been her home and haven for the past six years, picked up her bag, slid back the bolt, and opened the door.

Someone was standing there. Her worst nightmare was about to come true.

London, evening, early November

Sunir was waiting for the Flemings in the lobby of the St. Francis Hotel when they arrived at a few minutes past five and insisted on ordering drinks. Melissa selected an Australian Shiraz, and Jake settled for a beer: this time an appropriate-sounding Hook Norton Haymaker.

Jake brought Sunir up to speed with what they'd learned about the Marlowe Inquest and charges, and Melissa's insights regarding John Penry and the Knights Templar. It was then that he noticed the admittedly dapper Asian regarding his daughter in an entirely different way, which he didn't quite like.

"She's right," Sunir said, nodding in agreement. "By 1590 those charges were very much standard for getting rid of heretics and anyone who might cause dissent or stir up trouble."

"So, they mean nothing, in terms of what Kit actually might have done or said?"

"That's the point," said Melissa. "They used various tailored versions of those charges for witches, Catholics, Jews, you name it. So, Marlowe would have had plenty of previous company on those gallows," she added.

"Yes," agreed Sunir. "You mentioned John Penry. But even he wasn't the first."

They both looked at him. "First to what?"

"First to be arrested and tortured for heresy for those very charges you have there," he said, tapping the copy of the Baines letter Melissa had made.

"What do you mean?" asked Jake, quickly.

"Like you, I've been doing some reading. Do either of you remember a writer named Thomas Kyd?"

Jake shook his head. Melissa nodded. "Of course. One of the University Wits."

"Quite right." He threw her another glance, which Jake would have gladly intercepted and stuffed in a waste bin, it was so amative. Sunir's smile could have spanned the Thames. "He was one of the known playwrights of the London circuit back then. He was tortured and died from it, which is as good as an execution."

"Or worse," said Melissa, with a shudder. "Tortured to a slow death? Good god."

"Kyd was actually Marlowe's roommate, for a time. Maybe they were an item, who knows?"

"Or just a couple of young artists trying to make it in London, like today," pointed out Melissa.

"Right. Anyway, suddenly he gets arrested–by Whitgift, by the way–and lo and behold, the authorities 'discover' a very damning document in his possession, which, upon torture, he attributes to his pal Marlowe, hence Marlowe's arrest."

"So, his friend ratted him out," said Melissa. "Under torture."

"Or it could have been a setup," Sunir pointed out. "Perhaps an attempt to frame Marlowe."

"Yeah, but Kyd dies on the rack, and Marlowe gets out on bail, for basically the same offense," observed Jake.

"Maybe because he wrote better plays," said Sunir, half joking. No one laughed.

"So what was this damning document?" asked Melissa, to get back on subject.

"It was a passage denying the divinity of Christ."

"In other words, more of the same," said Jake.

"Yes, if it even existed. In any case, by then Marlowe had moved out and was staying at Chiselhurst, the estate of his patron Thomas Walsingham, cousin of Frances. That's where he was arrested."

"So, he'd moved up in the world," Melissa breathed out slowly, thinking hard.

"Well, he'd worked for Francis, as well as Burghley even at Cambridge. But yes. He was the toast of London by then. So he was staying with Walsingham, probably strategizing the storm he knew was imminent."

"Excuse me, who was Burghley?" asked Jake, checking his notes.

"He was head of the Queen's Privy Council," said Melissa. "They were the equivalent of the Cabinet, in the States. He was a heavyweight, like the Queen's top adviser."

"So, who posted bail, then?"

"Walsingham, of course. He was one who fancied himself a man of the theater, and certainly a patron of the arts. He was the backer, along with Pembroke, in financing the Marlowe productions at the Curtain and elsewhere. So he had a vested interest in seeing his friend and protege survive what was coming."

They were interrupted by the waiter, bringing drinks. As Jake reached in his pocket to pay, he was distracted by a motion at the far end of the bar. A large gentleman in a gray tweed jacket sat in earnest conversation with a slender, dark-haired woman who had her back to them. He recognized the man, however. Their friend, The Watcher again. Jake felt his face grow hot. He nudged Sunir. "We've got company."

Sunir followed his gaze and reacted in dismay. "Bloody hell," he muttered.

"What? What's up?" asked Melissa.

"It's that man who's been following us," said Sunir, grimly.

"Oh, him. Who's the woman?"

Just then the woman turned, cast a quick glance in their direction, and turned away.

Jake's pulse quickened. "I know her."

"What?" Sunir looked at him in alarm.

"You know her? From where?" Melissa's voice had an odd edge to it. The woman Jake now recognized was Diana Parker, the English Department chair, who'd given him the brush off the week before and had avoided them at the funeral.

"Wait here. I've had enough of this crap." Jake slid off the bar stool and headed towards the far end of the bar. Parker saw him coming and nudged the big man, who stood, or rather sat his ground. Jake walked up to them. "I see you get around, Professor Parker," he said to the woman, and turned to the big man, who raised his hands in a conciliatory gesture.

"All right, pal," said Jake. "What do you want now?"

"Easy, Mate. We're just havin' a drink here."

"You know what I'm talking about. You've been following my daughter and me for days now, and I want an explanation."

"I think I'll be going now," said Parker, who got up and knocked her drink over in the process. "Sorry," she said to the bartender. Embarrassed, she departed abruptly, tartan skirt swishing angrily around her slender woolen leggings, momentarily leaving both men looking after her. There was a mended tear in one of the leggings. Once again Jake felt the discomfort of a strong attraction he didn't want or need, just now.

The Watcher seemed unfazed. He turned back to his own drink, with only a dismissive glance in Jake's direction. "You interrupted a private conversation," he remarked.

Jake watched his hands, ready for anything. "That's your problem. What's your game, anyway? And please, spare me the bullshit."

This time the big man turned and faced him squarely. "Do you always assail people who might just be looking after your best interests, Mr. Fleming?" he asked. And now, for the first time, Jake saw something in his eyes, a flash of both power and menace, that stopped him cold. He was about to rethink his bravura, when the big man arose from his seat, tossing a ten-pound note on the bar. "Now, if you'll excuse me," he said, "I have places to go and people to see even more important than you." With that, he picked up his coat and headed for the door.

"Hold it." declared Jake, angrily, going after him. "What the hell do you mean 'best interests?' " But he was delayed by a passing waiter with a tray of drinks, and by the time he could resume his pursuit The Watcher was through the revolving door and into a waiting black Bentley before Jake could catch up to him. And because a taxi darted in between him and the departing vehicle, he was unable to get a license number.

Jake rejoined the others feeling sheepish, frustrated and short of breath. "Sooner or later he's going to make a mistake," he growled. "And then he's going to be in for a world of pain." He glanced at his daughter to apologize. He hadn't meant to frighten her. But she didn't look frightened. She looked like she was spoiling for a fight.

"I'm not afraid of that guy," she assured him.

He sat back down, not sure how to respond to that.

"So, who was the woman?" Melissa repeated.

"Diana Parker. She's Chairwoman of the English Department at the University," he replied, glaring out through the window in the general direction of her swift departure.

"Chair*person*," corrected Melissa.

"Whatever. Maybe you know her?" he glanced at Sunir.

"Yes. I've spoken to her, now that you remind me. She is not on our side. This development is not good."

Jake glanced at his daughter, who looked away.

"Maybe it's just as well you didn't cause a scene," said Sunir. "Until we have some idea whom we are dealing with. That man could be an executioner, for all we know." That was not a comforting thought. "I wonder what they were talking about."

"He gives me the creeps," said Melissa. "Whoever he is." Then her brows knitted darkly. "So does she. But they don't scare me."

Sunir stared at the painting on the wall behind them. It was a typical British Imperial huntsman tableau, a reprint from the Kipling era. He frowned, darkly. "Dr. Lewis did not want to go public with any of our findings until he had sufficient proof. But now with his death they are going to try to bury it all once again, along with him. We can't let that happen." He sighed. "Meanwhile, it seems I've run into a bit of difficulty with my own Department."

Jake looked at him, confused. "Which department?"

"The Physics Department. Apparently, they have been talking to the English Department, or vice versa. Probably Dr. Childers, who, I gather, is the so-called 'enforcer.' "

Jake's eyes narrowed. " 'Enforcer'?" he glanced at Melissa, who paled, slightly.

"Just an expression. He's the one who enforces the various department policies, protocol, and so on."

"I see." He looked at Melissa. "Didn't you say you've been talking to Childers?"

She looked defensive. "Yes. About my dissertation, remember? But if you think I'm in a position to march in and cross examine him about who shot Desmond Lewis or who's censuring Dr. Balsavar, you have got to be kidding."

He nodded. "OK, so we need to talk to Professor Parker. Maybe she can shed some light on why we're being followed, and she can sure as hell tell us who Big Brother there is."

"Good luck on that scoring," said Sunir. "She's very, how do you say? Private, from what I can gather."

"Maybe I can find something out," said Melissa, determinedly.

"In any case," said Sunir, with a shrug, "meanwhile I have been censured by my colleagues, for 'intellectual adventurism' and 'straying from my discipline.' Can you believe it?"

Melissa said she could, only too well, having been recently censured by her own colleagues for ditching in mid-term. Not to mention taking up with insurgents. But she still seemed put off about Parker.

"So, what happened today, exactly?" Jake asked Sunir.

Sunir raised his hands, palms up, with a glimmer of reproach. "I was attempting to recruit a graduate student from the English Department for your experiment, and may have said more than I should have, I'm afraid."

"You told them you were researching Marlowe?"

"I must have mentioned it." He brightened. "But the good news is, I found someone, and my recruit is available tomorrow between seven and nine p.m., if that is acceptable."

"Good work." Jake laughed. "I thought you were going to tell us you'd been banished from the land."

"Well, not yet, at least. I must say my borrowed graduate assistant—his name is Christopher, appropriately enough—is more than a little curious as to what we are up to."

"All the better. That's all I am going to say for now."

"I assume you will be needing a meeting place?"

"Yes. Can you help with that?"

"I'll do my best."

Jake gave him a list of specifics. "Ready to go?" He asked, turning to Melissa.

The police detective who sat down at their table a moment later had a different agenda.

"Mr.Fleming," he said, presenting his I.D. "Donald Jenkins, London Metropolitan P.D. Remember me?"

"Yes, you came to our flat after the break-in. Did you find who did it?"

"Sorry sir, no luck there. But perhaps you'd be so kind as to tell us about your connection with Professor Desmond Lewis."

Jake had been waiting for that, and, after presenting his newspaper credentials, grudgingly told Jenkins a stripped-down version of his interview with Gloria Peckham, and search for the missing manuscript. "Which I gather has still not been found?"

Jenkins shook his head. "Not a high priority, I'm afraid, sir. Not on a suicide."

"You still claim this is a suicide. Even though his office and apartment were violently trashed, and his body was burned to a crisp?"

Jenkins looked flustered, momentarily. "That's correct, sir."

"Then why ask me questions about my visits to the office?"

"Just routine, Mr. Fleming. Now, how long have you known Dr. Lewis?"

Jake finally told him how they'd met in Florida at a seminar. They'd talked by the hotel pool, where some redneck drunks from a business conference on offshore oil development had started to badger the dapper Brit, mocking his accent and calling him a "fag," among other things. Jake had come to his defense, and had been hit with a bottle, which had knocked him simultaneously unconscious, and into the swimming pool. He would have drowned, had Lewis not fought off the oil men long enough to get him out. The rest was a blur.

As he finished recounting his story, he noticed Melissa staring at him. "What?" he said.

"Dad, you never told me any of this before. I had no idea. It explains a lot."

"How do you mean?"

"I mean, like, you owed him. Like, basically, your life?"

He shrugged. "I had no reason to bring it up, I guess."

With an odd blush of embarrassment, he went on to explain to a now-intrigued Jenkins how it had been a moral victory of sorts, won at the price of a few bruises and a broken pair of glasses. Still, they'd become friends, and dropped each other an occasional note or email. But they hadn't seen each other since that weekend until that call ten days ago in Berkeley. And now, as a reporter, he was trying to get to the bottom of what had happened to his friend. As Melissa had just pointed out, he owed him. End of story.

The detective nodded and wrote that down in a cumbersome longhand. He didn't seem to believe it. "Right then. We'll be in touch," he said, then got up and left.

Chapter Twenty-Seven

A Great Reckoning in a Small Room

London, 6:50 p.m. early November

Sunir Balsavar, it turned out, had a sense of humor, and also a sense of drama. He'd figured out Jake's intentions, and had found the perfect staging place for his experiment: a private room upstairs in a restored waterfront tavern in Bankside. Oddly patronized primarily by Pakistanis, the place was called The Widow Bull, actually named, wittingly or no, for the original boarding house in Deptford where Marlowe had supposedly met his alleged demise.

Dr. Balsavar and his young recruit arrived at the bar a few minutes after seven, watchful for followers. Melissa had already gone upstairs to inspect the location, also having some suspicion as to what was afoot. Jake shook hands with the grad student: a tall, muscular ebony black West Indian with a shaved head. "Chris Braithwaite," the young man introduced himself, his accent liltingly Jamaican. "So, what's this all about?"

"You'll find out," Sunir assured him.

"Anyone care for a drink or anything, before we get started?" asked Jake, momentarily amused by the diversity of his team.

"Tea is cool," said Chris. "Make it green."

Sunir nodded. "Same here is good."

The innkeeper, an appropriately buxom middle-aged Pakistani woman, scowled, perhaps not all that happy about the "foreigners," as she'd describe them later to her husband, Ravi. Nevertheless, she dutifully filled three Styrofoam cups from the hot water spigot behind the bar and slapped each with a tea bag. "Make that four, please," said Jake, withstanding a withering glower from the barkeeper.

Melissa was waiting for them when they went upstairs. "I checked out that Dr. Parker," she said. "She's a major authority on Shakespeare. Not like Scofield, but she has written a number of books and articles."

"So, did you talk to her?" Jake asked. "About the guy she was speaking with?"

"Yeah. Matter of fact I did." She paused, with a frown.

"And?"

"She said she couldn't discuss it and hung up."

"Nice," he muttered. Women. Why were the attractive ones always the most difficult? Take Melissa, for example, presently sticking her tongue out at him like she'd read his mind.

Jake made a wry face and scanned the room. The space was small, about fourteen by eighteen feet, but the immigrant owner had authoritatively assured them it was typical of the Elizabethan era. What the hell, figured Jake. Close enough.

"So," said Chris, looking around. "What's the deal, mon?" He was clearly one who didn't waste time or mince words. He didn't much care for the room, Jake could see, but the presence of Melissa more than made up for it.

"All right," Jake began. "What we are going to do is a little bit of staging, of what supposedly happened four hundred years ago in a room similar to this." The room was equipped with a few basic furnishings: a six foot wooden tea table on one side, a large wooden dining table in the center, and a single bench on the interior side. There was also a blackened, aged mirror on the wall opposite the bench, behind the table.

Chris spoke up, tearing his eyes willfully away from Melissa, who for her own part was doing a good job of seemingly ignoring him completely. "Excuse me, but will this take long? I have something at nine."

"No, it shouldn't. Here's the setup." Jake gestured at a photocopy of a document that was on the table. "This is a copy of the official British government Christopher Marlowe murder inquest." He gestured at the room. "What we are going to do is restage the events that occurred on May 30th, 1593 when the alleged killing took place, according to the Inquest."

There was an appropriate silence in the room. Then the grad student let out a low whistle.

Jake proceeded. "The setting is Deptford Strand, Kent. Pretend we are situated in a small room in the tavern of one Widow Bull."

"Is this going to be a 'great reckoning'?" asked Chris, with a note of sarcasm in his voice.

Jake frowned. Where had he heard that expression before? "You might say that," he shrugged. "And our job is to recreate that reckoning exactly as described by the witnesses who were present."

"Cool." said Chris, with a shrug. Melissa, who hadn't been able to get her father to reveal his plans, merely scowled. Sunir appeared bemused.

The others looked at Jake expectantly. "Okay," he began. "Now, imagine that we are the four people who were allegedly in Widow Bull's room that day."

Chris raised his hand quickly. "Can I be Marlowe?"

"Sure. You be Kit Marlowe." Jake turned to the other two. "We'll be Frizer, Poley and Skeres. All right?"

"I'll be Frizer," said Melissa with a sly grin. "I always wanted to get away with murder."

"Okay, Ingram Frizer you are. Sunir, shall we flip a coin as to who gets to be Poley, and who Skeres?"

"It hardly matters," noted Sunir.

"All right. I'm Robert Poley, you can be the 'coney catcher,' Nicholas Skeres." He picked up the Inquisition document. "Let us begin." He began to read out loud: "It is 'about the tenth hour before noon' and 'the aforesaid gentlemen met together in a room in the house of a certain Eleanor Bull, widow; & there passed the time together and dined and after dinner were in quiet sort together there and walked in the garden belonging to the said house until the sixth hour after noon of the same day and then returned from the said garden to the room aforesaid and there together and in company supped.' "

Sunir couldn't resist interrupting. "The only possible reason Marlowe would spend a day with three low-lifes would be to hatch a plot, to stage a death. I am sure he was long gone, but if he was there, and if they were walking in the garden, that would be the perfect opportunity for Kit to slip away and be replaced later by whoever was actually in that room when the coroner came."

"Can we continue please?" asked Melissa.

"You're saying somebody volunteered to stand in for Marlowe and be murdered in his place?" asked Chris, an edge of scorn in his voice.

"Not at all. They could have sneaked a dead body in from the garden," said Melissa. "And I think I know who it was." Jake gestured for her to wait.

"Or found a live victim, maybe a drunk or something, and brought him up to the room. From what I read, those men were killers," noted Sunir.

Jake resumed reading: " 'and after supper the said Ingram and Christopher Morley—' "

"That's Marlowe's original name. That or Marley," Melissa explained to Chris.

"I know. *'A rose by any other name.'* "

"So." Jake continued:

> *" 'Ingram and Morley were in speech and uttered one to the other diverse malicious words for the reason that they could not be at one nor agree about the payment of the sum of pence, that is, the reckoning, there; and the said Christopher Morley then lying upon a bed in the room where they supped, and moved with anger against the said Ingram Frysar upon the words aforesaid spoken between them...' "*

Was that the 'reckoning' Chris was referring to? He stopped for breath and pointed at the tea table. "All right. Chris, you're over there on the bed muttering epithets about the 'reckoning,' which was supposedly the bar tab."

"I know that. Mutter mutter," mumbled Chris, moving into position and getting into the spirit of the thing right away.

"Same to you. Mutter mutter," Melissa-as-Frizer muttered back, looking fierce.

Jake continued reading:

> *'and the said Ingram then and there sitting in the room aforesaid with his back towards the bed where the said Christopher Morley was then lying, sitting near the bed, that is, nere the bed, and'—"*

"Wait a minute," interrupted Melissa. "If Frizer was sitting near the bed, the bed had to be near the table. We have to move it, then."

Jake nodded to Chris, who got up and dragged the tea table over towards the dining table. "How near?" he asked.

Jake frowned and scanned the document. "Hmm. Nowhere does it say that Morley got up off the bed. Lying on the bed, it specifically says. So, he had to have been within reach of the bench, from a reclining position."

"That's awfully close," noted Sunir.

Chris shrugged, and shoved the tea table a foot or so closer to the bench.

"How small were those rooms anyway?" Melissa wondered.

"Keep reading," said Sunir.

"Okay, Frizer is sitting near the bed *'with the front part of his body towards the table,'* in other words, facing the table, with his back to the bed."

Melissa as Frizer sat down on the bench, accordingly.

"—and the aforesaid Nicholas Skeres and Robert Poley sitting on either side of the said Ingram' "–Jake continued. Melissa slid to the middle of the bench, and Jake and Sunir sat next to her on either side.

"Why isn't someone sitting on the other side of the table. There'd be a bench there also, wouldn't there?" asked Chris.

"You'd think," said Melissa.

"I'm reading it exactly as it supposedly happened," said Jake. "The Inquest is very specific. All three are sitting on the same side, with their backs to Marlowe."

"Wait a sec," interrupted Melissa again. "Why does Frizer have his back to Marlowe during this alleged argument?"

"That's what it says." He showed her the passage.

She shook her head. "How many arguments have you had with people who have their backs to you?"

"Sometimes they turn or walk away, and you shout after them," suggested Sunir.

"Was Frizer turning or walking away?"

Jake tapped the paper, impatiently. "No, he was sitting, like we are," he said.

"Was Marlowe?"

"No, he was lying on the bed."

"Keep reading," said Sunir.

Chris reclaimed his place on the "bed" and the others turned back to face away from him.

"This is weird," said Chris.

"All right. So: *'and the aforesaid Nicholas Skeres and Robert Poley sitting on either side of the said Ingram'—"* he nodded to Melissa, wedged next to him in the middle of the bench, and she nodded back. " *'In such a manner,'* " he continued reading, *'that the same Ingram Fryser could in no wise take flight:'* Melissa wiggled and squirmed, but it was clear she was firmly wedged between the two men.

"Okay, no wise can I take flight," she confirmed.

Jake continued:

> *" 'It so befell that the said Christopher Morley on a sudden and of his malice towards the said Ingram aforethought, then and there maliciously drew the dagger of the said Ingram which was at his back,'—"*

"Hold on, we need a dagger," insisted Melissa. She could not move, which didn't help.

"I'll get something," said Chris, getting up.

"Ask the bartender. Maybe there's a wooden spoon or something."

Chris was already out the door. The other three sat waiting, wedged together. Melissa, pinned in the middle, squirmed uncomfortably. A minute went by, then another.

"I wish he'd hurry up," she complained, edgily.

Chris returned a minute later with a bartender's whisk. "Sorry. This is the closest thing she had. Where do you want it?"

Jake consulted the Inquest. "It says the knife was 'at his back.' How odd. Maybe because he was eating?"

"But didn't people use their daggers to eat with in those days?" noted Melissa, looking at the whisk, doubtfully.

"That is correct," said Sunir.

"Whatever," said Chris, and tucked it in her jeans' waistband behind her back. "Maybe he was a vegan." He resumed his lounging position. "I'm still lying down, right?"

"Right. Okay, let's see, where were we: *'drew the dagger at his back'—"* The others resumed their positions. Chris reached over from his lounging position and could just reach the whisk, which he yanked back out of Melissa's waistband. "Good," said Jake, watching him in the wall mirror. *'And with the same dagger the said Christopher Morley then and there maliciously gave the aforesaid Ingram two wounds on his head'—"*

"On his head?" exclaimed Melissa. "That's ridiculous. You don't stab somebody on the head. Especially with their back turned to you. You go for the back, as in 'stabbed in the back.' "

"What kind of wounds?" Chris demanded to know.

"Silence." Jake commanded them. *"—'two wounds on the head of the length of two inches and of the depth of a quarter of an inch;' —"*

"Like this?" Chris sat up and feigned whacking Melissa on top of the head twice.

"You are still lying down," Sunir reminded him. "According to the Inquest."

"That's impossible." complained Chris. "How am I supposed to stab her on the top of her head when I'm lying down? And like she said, why would I even try?"

"Point well taken," noted Jake. "But do as it says."

They watched in the wall mirror as Chris slumped back down, then reached awkwardly over from his lying down position and attempted to whack Melissa on top of the head, once again. They all burst into laughter the effort was so preposterous. Her head was well out of reach.

"Maybe Frizer was a dwarf?" suggested Chris, happy for the comic relief.

"Go on." urged Melissa. "Keep reading."

"All right: *'whereupon the said Ingram, in fear of being slain, and sitting in the manner aforesaid between the said Nicholas Skeres and Robert Poley so that he could not in any wise get away, in his own defense and for the saving of his life, then and there struggled with the said Christopher Morley to get back from him his dagger aforesaid;' "* —Melissa tried again to get out of her seat but she remained firmly wedged in place by the men on either side. "Hey," she complained. "I have to get my dagger."

Chris also interrupted. "Am I supposed to be struggling with you while you're sitting like that and I'm still lying down?"

Melissa and Sunir looked at Jake, who shrugged. "Don't look at me, I'm just reading what the witnesses said at the Inquest," he said.

"And I still have my back to him because I am wedged in here between you guys, right?" asked Melissa, looking at them in the mirror. Jake nodded. Gamely she attempted to twist around, but the two men wedged next to her kept her firmly pinned in place.

"Let me get this straight," said Melissa. "So, Chris is lying down while supposedly stabbing me, and I am wedged in here with my back to him, but somehow I'm supposed to reach behind me to struggle with him to get my dagger back? I can't even move, let alone try to do all that."

"Just try."

They attempted that maneuver, again with no success. She did manage to get her right arm past Sunir and behind her, but that was as far as she got. She couldn't lift it any further up than the small of her back. "This is impossible," she complained.

"Come on," mocked Chris, waving the 'dagger' around. "You're supposed to take it away from me and kill me."

Melissa tried a different tack, reaching backwards up over her shoulder. She could just reach his wrist, but only after he held it still within six inches or so of the back of her neck, and allowed her to grasp his wrist with one hand, then held still so she could reach back over her other shoulder with her other hand to pry the whisk away from him.

Sunir just shook his head. "Do you think the coroner managed a straight face while recording this?"

"People. Please. Let me continue," said Jake.

"Hurry up," said Melissa, her right arm behind her, now holding the stirring whisk poised. "I'm getting tired."

"Where were we? Oh yes, *'struggled with the said Christopher Morley to get back from him his dagger aforesaid,'* " Jake continued, " *'in which affray the same Ingram could not get away from the said Christopher Morley'* "—

"At least they got that part right." Melissa gamely wiggled some more in a futile effort to get up from where she remained wedged.

"— 'and so it befell in that affray that the said Ingram, in defense of his life, with the dagger aforesaid to the value of 12d gave the said Christopher then and there a mortal wound over his right eye of the depth of two inches and the width of one inch; of which mortal wound the aforesaid Christopher Morley then and there instantly died."

"Hell of a way to go," said Melissa.

"Of what possible importance is the value of the dagger?" muttered Chris, while Melissa made a weak jabbing motion backwards over her shoulder with the 'dagger,' the way the superstitious throw salt.

"Did I get you?" she asked.

"Can I sit up yet, since we are presumably now in a death struggle and if I'm lying here my eye is about three feet out of reach?"

"Well, it doesn't say you did, and this is very detailed, but we'll go with that," said Jake.

Chris sat up and leaned towards her, holding his hands up to ward off any possible random blow that might actually come in the vicinity of his eye. Melissa managed another feeble swipe over her shoulder. "Now did I get you?"

"This is ridiculous," said Chris, throwing up his hands. "It's not possible."

"All right. I think we've seen and done enough," said Jake. "Let's call it a night."

"I couldn't agree more," said Sunir.

Melissa gave up, and Sunir, watching in the mirror, informed her that she had been able to raise her 'weapon' no higher than Chris's mid-section. Never mind that she had to try it blind and backwards, given there was no room to turn around.

"So maybe Marlowe was lying down on the job," she said with a grimace.

"I'll be right back," said Chris. "I have to return this." He took the whisk and departed, whistling cheerfully.

"Can I get up now?" asked Melissa.

Suddenly the room went dark.

"Shit," muttered Jake. "Not again."

Sunir struggled to turn, but his feet were still stuck under the bench. The room door groaned open behind them, and Sunir called out, anxiously, "Chris, can you put on the light?"

There was no answer.

"I don't like this," complained Melissa, struggling to move. "Chris, stop messing around." She tried to turn but was too tightly wedged in to move. That's when she glanced up and saw the dark shape looming above her in the mirror. It was a black wraith wearing the white mask of death, and brandishing a butcher's knife, high over his head.

"Dad!" she screamed, as the knife flashed for a moment in the dim light of the window and plunged towards them.

At that moment, Jake, also seeing what was coming in the mirror, shoved Melissa hard to the left against Sunir, dumping him onto the floor and her onto her side, and just as the knife drove downwards he knocked it aside, where it landed with a sickening thud onto the wooden table top. At the same time, he rolled off the bench backwards and kicked out at the dark figure as it turned to flee. Just then a voice called out from the hallway:

"Sorry, mon, I had to visit the—hey!" Chris, coming back into the room, was nearly toppled by the fleeing dark shadow, who dashed past him into the hallway, and away.

"Chris, stop him!" shouted Jake, but it was too late. As Chris stared, transfixed by the nightmare vision that flashed before his eyes, their assailant was gone.

Chris fumbled for and found the light switch, which was just outside in the hallway, and as the others struggled to recover their wits and composure, he apologized profusely for leaving them so exposed. "I thought it was just part of the show," he explained, woefully. "I mean, that was right out of Halloween. Or *Hamlet*."

"Forget it, you couldn't have known," said Jake, pretty shaken himself, as he picked himself up and brushed himself off.

"Did anyone actually see him?" asked Melissa, trembling at the sight of the knife, still wobbling on the tabletop. Jake picked it up. It was a large, lethal dagger.

"I think," said Jake, struggling to sound reasonable, "that was just meant to frighten us."

"You think?" snapped Melissa, acerbically. "If so, he fucking well succeeded."

"I'm really sorry," said Chris, again. "I had to go to the loo."

"Well, in a way whoever it was proved my point," said Jake. "None of us were exactly in a position to defend ourselves, let alone disarm and kill the guy."

"Shouldn't we at least telephone the police?" complained Sunir. "Get finger marks and such?"

"And tell them what? We were performing a play when this guy in a costume entered stage right with a giant knife?" retorted Melissa. "Anyway, he was wearing gloves."

"Everyone wait here," said Jake. "I'm going downstairs to talk to the owner."

"I will go with you," said Chris.

"No, you stay here with them. I don't want a repeat performance."

"Dad, we'll be fine," said Melissa.

Jake relented, as usual. "At least lock the door when we go out," he insisted.

Jake and Chris went downstairs and confronted the tavern owner. "Did you see someone go upstairs just now, dressed in a costume?" Jake asked the woman.

She shook her head. "No one go upstairs except him," she said, pointing at Chris.

"Do you have a back stairway?"

"Not for customers," she said, with finality. Jake knew she was lying, but with a dozen hostile Pakistani regulars eying them, some looking more than ready for a fight, he saw no point in pressing the issue. He and Chris retreated back upstairs, where Sunir and Melissa waited. Sunir looked more apprehensive than ever.

“Perhaps we should call it an evening,” he said, wiping his brow. “I think I could have use for a stronger beverage.”

“Well, I think we have now not once, but twice demonstrated,” said Jake, finally, “that this ‘murder’ in ‘self-defense,’ as so described, is impossible to accomplish, absurd in its entirety and therefore not to be believed.”

“So much for the Queen’s coroner,” said Sunir. “Let’s get out of here. My nerves are quite shattered.”

They adjourned downstairs to the bar, and Jake paid the room tab, suddenly double what he’d been quoted before. He chose not to argue, as by now the hostility in the place was conspicuous.

They hastily departed the Widow Bull tavern and walked together back to the underground station, several blocks away. Chris chatted earnestly with Melissa while Jake and Sunir fell behind a few paces, walking in silence. Finally, Jake turned to Sunir and spoke in a low voice. “Do you trust this guy?”

“Chris? Yes. I can trust him. But he’s a born skeptic. He knows all about the authorship controversy and has his own opinions.”

“Which are?”

“He won’t say, but I suspect he would have spoken up if he supported Marlowe.”

“Maybe this re-enactment will give him something to think about,” said Jake, thoughtfully.

“Perhaps. I hope so.”

“Aren’t you concerned that he’ll stir up the department even more than they seem to be stirred already?” asked Jake.

“Let him. I’m not afraid of those old bluenoses.”

Some of whom weren’t that old, Jake thought.

“Something still bothers me about the Coroner’s Inquest,” said Melissa, dropping back to join them. They looked at her expectantly. “Why would these three witnesses make up such an asinine story? Why not at least come up with something plausible?”

“These guys weren’t rocket scientists,” Jake pointed out. “Or playwrights.”

“Even so, it has to make sense. It has to at least be within the realm of physical possibility, never mind plausibility. And this was neither.”

"I agree those three characters were not deep thinkers," noted Sunir, as they reached the underground station. "Perhaps, in their hurry to get this unpleasantness over with, they too-hastily improvised their account, and then had to adhere to their story."

"I'll buy that," said Melissa. "Anyway, no one was there to question it."

"Or," suggested Jake, thoughtfully, "maybe the Coroner, or even the Queen, was trying to send a message to Marlowe's supporters, to the effect that this Inquest was not to be believed."

"Do you think so?" pondered Sunir, in wonder.

"That's pretty subtle," noted Melissa, as Chris rejoined them.

"Maybe. Maybe not. But let's not forget motive here," Jake interjected, as he purchased underground tickets for the group. "What were the motives of everyone involved?"

"To establish that Marlowe was officially dead, first of all," Sunir replied, now having to shout over the din of the Underground, as they took the escalator down. "Then, to prove self-defense, so as to avoid imprisonment of the co-conspirators."

"Which was duly accomplished. They needed a dead body. Any dead body, and this John Penry was apparently available," Jake nodded to Melissa.

A train was just pulling in as they reached the platform, and as the train pulled up, all talk ended until they had all clambered on. The car was nearly full, and they had to squeeze into a section in the rear.

"Who is this John Penry?" Chris inquired, clearly desirous of rejoining the conversation, which was clearly more welcomed by his daughter than Jake preferred.

"I'll explain later," Melissa assured him. Which Chris seemed to like a good deal more than Jake Fleming did.

Chris and Melissa fell back for a quick conversation of their own, which involved a rapid exchange of information of some sort. Jake could pretty well guess what sort and didn't like it.

Nor did he like his own feelings about it. Was he being paternally possessive? Jealous, even? Or—no, he was sure this couldn't be so, but . . . even racist?

He had risked his life to live among people of color on many occasions, often in the company of NGO's of a benevolent nature, so surely . . .?

He forced his attention back to the topic at hand. "Sorry, Sunir, you were saying?"

Melissa rejoined them a moment later, as Chris got off at the next stop, for his appointment, whatever it was.

Sunir resumed, having patiently awaited the opportunity once they were rolling again. "Then of course the supposed killers needed an alibi."

"Right. Right!" Exclaimed Jake. "And they probably got overly creative, as you suggested. In any case, it worked, on both counts. Frizer was pardoned within the month and the other two resumed their employment with Walsingham straightaway."

"Which also means that Thomas Walsingham also got his bail bond refunded," noted Melissa.

"So, everyone wins," said Jake, leaning back and closing his eyes a moment. "Or so it must have seemed, at the time. Marlowe is Scott free in Europe, the perps get off, Shakespeare gets to be rich and famous, the Queen gets to continue to enjoy her favorite plays, and Walsingham gets to keep an active interest in the theater business. Which by then was becoming a clearly lucrative enterprise."

"And Archbishop Whitgift?"

"Whitgift and Harvey and their friends get to think their nemesis has met a violent death, and get to celebrate at his expense," said Jake.

"Which they did," noted Sunir. "In spades, as you say."

Jake shook his head in dismay. He was too tired to think. Furthermore, Melissa's mention of the Archbishop had reminded him of the still unexplained 'Lamb' entry on Desmond Lewis's cryptic list. He looked at Sunir as the train lurched into motion.

"By the way, do you have any idea why Desmond Lewis would be interested in the Lambeth Palace?"

Sunir looked startled. "Where did you get that information?"

Jake and Melissa exchanged glances. She nodded, slightly. "I think the time has come to show you something," said Jake. "We found a list of words and abbreviations in Dr. Lewis' pocket. You might want to take a look." Digging into his notebook, he produced the list.

Sunir studied it with growing excitement. "Yes, yes, these were main talking points," he shouted, above the growing din of the train. "I can't answer about Lambeth yet. I have to check something first. But I promise you'll have an answer within two days. And V.A. is on the tip of my tongue. What was it? I may have an idea about that third entry, too."

" 'Herb'?" asked Melissa, looking at the notepad.

"Yes indeed. That may be the most astonishing revelation of all, if what I think happened bears out."

"Why not tell us now?" demanded Melissa, petulantly.

"Not until I am certain," he said, and would speak no more on the subject.

The train stopped at Waterloo Station, and they all got out, to go their different directions. As they inserted their tickets and exited the turnstile, Sunir stopped.

"I must go my own way," he said. "I will transfer here. We'll be in touch."

Melissa waved absently as the Pakistani left, momentarily distracted by a jingling sound in her purse, like wind chimes wrapped in foam.

"That's mine. A text message." Melissa fished out her cell phone, glanced at it, and flushed red. The message was cryptic, but she understood its meaning at once: *"Beware the undiscovered country."* She was getting more than a little tired of this harassment. What she didn't know yet, was what to do about it.

"Everything OK?" Jake asked her, as they reached the escalator.

"Fine. No problem." She closed the phone with a snap and stared around the station, angrily. This was crazy. It had to be whoever had set them up on the London Eye, then attacked her in the room back there. But who? And how did he get her number? No way anyone she knew would send something like this. Had Desmond Lewis unwittingly run afoul of the same person or persons? She glanced at her father. Should she tell him about it? No, she decided. No point in alarming him further, after what had happened earlier. But the more she thought about it, the less certain she was about her so-called friends and advisers in this increasingly unwelcoming city. This new message was nothing less than a death threat.

Chapter Twenty-Eight

For Jesus' Sake Forbear

London, 9:15 p.m. early November

Melissa and Jake rode the escalator up to the street, now lively with the sounds of revelry all around them as the evening crowds began to gather around the famed Trafalgar Square and Nelson statue. Melissa felt an anxious need for some respite from the harrowing events of earlier that evening. "Dad, I don't know about you, but I could use an actual drink, after that scene. Can we find a pub or something?"

"Weren't we just in one?" teased her father, with a wry grimace.

"Come on, you know what I mean. I mean one where we can have a beer and not get mugged at the same time."

"Touche. Actually," he admitted, "I was thinking the same thing. Anything special in mind?"

"Well, this is England, and I've always wanted to visit one of those authentic English Public Houses I always read about in Dickens and Arthur Conan Doyle?"

"Well, 'tis true, 'tis sad, I have yet to set foot in a real pub, this trip."

"You're kidding. The whole time? Really?"

"I know. Here I am in a city of ten thousand pubs, and a stranger to every one."

"You've been in London over a week and you haven't been to a pub? What is *wrong* with you?" she laughed. "What were you thinking?"

"Well, it was on my list."

"On your list? With what else? Tea with the Queen? We have some catching up to do."

"I don't know, maybe we should just–"

"Come on," she said. "We are going to remedy that oversight right now. You are coming with me." She seized his arm and practically dragged him down the street.

It was cold and damp, and the wetness of the night penetrated through coat, jacket, sweater, to the skin, and then deeper to the very bone. They were both shivering by the time they agreed upon a pub: one of Bloomsbury's busier establishments. It was called The Jeremy Bentham and was decked out complete with a Tudor facade and twelve-light 'olde English' windows. It reeked of authenticity, but then appearances can be deceptive, thought Jake. Like that damned Folio. Which still needed to be addressed. He wished he could recall what Lewis had told him, that night. But he had definitely said something about the Folio.

The pub was popular with the university crowd, a refreshing change from the usual London tourist scene. "I think we've come to the right place," said Melissa, eying the gathering of multi-pierced, black and denim-clad young people, intermingling with a good representation of tweedy professorial types.

"Yep. We should fit right in," quipped Jake, ordering a Black Sheep Ale, to suit his mood.

Melissa ordered a Titanic White Star. "Here's to loose lips sinking ships," she declared, proposing a toast. With a wry face Jake clinked her glass, finished off his ale and ordered another, which led to another. Melissa was doing an alarmingly good job of keeping up with him, perhaps in her zeal to forget about their earlier nightmare. Soon, however, things took a decided turn for the worst when Melissa, her ship rapidly sinking under a Titanic plethora of suds, spotted a Shakespearean quote above the bar: *Do as adversaries do in law; strive mightily, but eat and drink as friends*. Followed by: William Shakespeare, *The Taming of the Shrew*, I, ii, 281. This newly offensive proclamation pushed her over the edge, and she threw open the lid to Pandora's Box.

Or at least, that was how her father saw it at the time.

Finishing off her third pint, which to a slender sleep-impaired woman might as well have been her sixth, Melissa slammed her tankard down on the bartop, turned towards the crowd, and shouted to the group of male undergraduates who had been attempting to flirt with her. She was oblivious to flirting. "Okay, you guys are so smart," she blurted, "I'm gonna give you a quote." Shouting above the barroom din she delivered the epitaph from Shakespeare's grave:

"Good friend for Jesus sake forbear,
To dig the dust enclosed here:
Blest be the man that spares these stones
Curst be he that moves these bones."

"Okay, so who wrote those immortal words?" she demanded, looking around.

There was a brief silence in the room, then an abundance of shrugs and shaking heads.

"Who cares?" was the consensus.

"Jeremy Bentham?" suggested one wag.

"George W. Bush?" proposed another, to hearty laughter.

"It doesn't even rhyme," pointed out a third. " 'forbear,' and 'here?' "

"Right. Should be 'for beer' and 'here.' "

"Hear hear," shouted a freshman, as the room became raucous. "More beer."

Jake threw Melissa a look of warning, eyes like a shaken spear, but she turned away pretending she didn't know him.

"Who then?" demanded a sophomore.

"William Shakespeare, the Bard of Avon," she retorted, pointing at the inscription above the bar. "It's his gravestone epitaph."

Amid the ensuing headshaking and muttering, she found another quote, and shouted once more over the din:

"All right, oh for one. Now tell me who wrote this one:

It lies not in our power to love or hate,
For will in us is overruled by fate.
When two are stripped, long ere the course begin,
We wish that one should love, the other win,
And one especially o we affect
Of two gold ingots, like in each respect.
The reason no man knows; let it suffice
What we behold is censured by our eyes.

Where both deliberate, the love is slight."

"Shakespeare?" queried one hapless sophomore.

A female voice interrupted in a calm, educated accent and finished:

"Who ever loved, that loved not at first sight? Christopher Marlowe."

"Right. So who wrote this: *'Oh, thou art fairer than the evening air—' "*

" 'Clad in the beauty of a thousand stars,' " the other women finished, for her. "Christopher Marlowe."

Melissa, without bothering with more than a cursory glance and nod to the speaker, was gracious in defeat. "Very good, Madam," she said. "You win the gold star."

Jake glanced over at who'd spoken, a casually dressed thirty-something woman with short black hair, dark eyes, and dressed in a short woolen skirt, leggings, and a loose rumpled sweater. It took him a moment to recognize her in the dim lighting.

"Hello, Professor Parker. Small world."

She glanced at him, sideways. "Oh. You, again. I forgot your name."

"Jake Fleming. *San Francisco Tribune*. We had a discussion about literature."

"Yes. How could I forget? Then you interrupted us at the St. Francis yesterday. The American inquisitor seeking to overthrow Academia."

Melissa took one look at her, one at her father, and decided, in her sobriety-challenged state, that he was a goner. "Uh oh," she said.

"Melissa, this is Professor Parker," he said, pointedly.

"Yeah. We've spoken." Melissa eyed Parker like a child taking her medicine.

Jake tried to make the best of it. "So, you know your Marlowe."

Parker sniffed. "Of course. He was a great writer. He might have been almost as good as Shakespeare. Had he lived."

"That's big of you. He'd already invented blank verse and the history play and wrote half of Henry VI, according to your own authorities, before Shakespeare could even spell his name."

"What authorities?"

"Robinson, among others. Anyway, what if he did live?" Melissa persisted.

"Excuse me?" Parker blinked, not sure she'd heard correctly.

"What if he survived Deptford?"

Parker frowned and sipped her red wine. "That's absurd. Also, irrelevant. He didn't."

"Maybe you're wrong. Maybe he did."

"Then he would have written more plays, wouldn't he," the professor sniffed, ready to end the conversation.

"That's my whole point. Maybe he did write more plays," Melissa pressed on.

Parker looked at her, then at Jake. "Is she drunk?"

"She's drunk and I'm working on it. How about you? Buy you another?"

She looked him up and down and shrugged. Jake nodded to the bartender, who poured her a red wine refill. She turned back to Melissa. "So why all this interest in Marlowe, all of a sudden?"

Just then, Jake glanced across the room and spotted another familiar face, seated at a booth with two other members of the college faculty. It was Melissa's apparent new mentor, Dr. Childers, eying both of them balefully. Jake held his breath and nodded a warning. Instead, this seemed to push Melissa over a precipice like a novice on a hang glider, and from this point forward, there was no turning back. Melissa cleared her thoughts, jumbled and beer soaked as they were, clearly unnerved by the sudden presence of the voices of authority. Now, more than ever, she was determined to hold her own. She turned slowly and regarded her new rival haughtily. "Because maybe," she sniffed, "he wrote the plays."

Parker frowned. "What do you mean? Of course, he wrote *Tamburlaine*, and—"

"I mean the thirty-six plays in the so-called Shakespeare Canon."

The room—or at least the part of it within earshot—caught its collective breath. Across the room Childers could be seen asking a colleague what had been said, then shaking his head in angry disapproval. Parker, however, merely retorted: "That is patent nonsense, as anyone with a smidgen of education knows," and the fight was on.

Melissa, seemingly having made her decision to switch allegiances on the spur of the moment, was nevertheless well prepared. She launched a broadside with a full recitation of the charges of Robert Greene, Parker rebuffed it with the standard defense of jealousy, and all of the known arguments back and forth regarding the authorship, until the barroom audience was dizzy with all the head turning and hopes were escalating, especially among the male patrons, for an all out fur-flying cat fight, until Jake finally intervened.

"OK," said Jake, hoping to wrap things up. "Nobody's going to convince anybody of anything, obviously, at least not in this setting. So, what say we drink up and call it a night?"

Both women glared at him, the crowd booed, and the arguments escalated. After shaking her head through Sidney Lee and all the "it is well known" arguments, Melissa put down her empty tankard, folded her arms and pursed her lips. "What about the Quiney letter?" she asked.

"What was that?" asked Jake, in a quick aside. This was new to him.

"The only letter ever found addressed to Shakeshpeare." declared Melissa, rolling her eyes at him as if speaking to an ignorant child.

Diana shrugged dismissively. "It means nothing."

Melissa turned to her father. "The one letter ever found in Shakespeare's poshession, dated 1597, was some schmuck ashking for a loan. Hic." She began to hiccup, much to Jake's mortification. The college boys loved it.

Diana was beginning to weary of the fight. "All that means is that it's the only *surviving* letter to Shakespeare."

"Really?" asked Jake, in growing interest. Melissa was certainly full of surprises, not to mention beer. "A letter about a loan?"

"So what?" snapped Diana. "What's your point?"

"Well," he noted. "I'd have to say it's certainly a shame, if so, that the only letter he bothered to save was the one about a loan." Shakespeare the userer, he was thinking.

"Yeah. Not advice on a sonnet he was writing, or an opinion about his latest play. A loan," Melissa sniffed, as though she'd been a staunch Marlovian her whole life long. Which, in her heart, she perhaps might have been, before that notion had been violently snuffed in the classrooms of Berkeley.

"Well," Diana pointed out, "it proves that Shakespeare could read and write, I should think, since you seem so doubtful even on that score. Quiney would hardly have written to him if he couldn't read, and Quiney also would have expected a reply. In writing."

"That's a pretty weak argument for literacy," noted Jake. "Let alone genius."

Melissa spoke up quickly. "Wasn't this Quiney person the father of his despised son-in-law, Judith's husband Thomas? A convicted felon and fornicator?"

Diana was taken aback. "I hardly see the relevance to–"

"It proves he was a low life loan shark who hung out with other low lifes, that 'shwhat." Melissa practically shouted. "You can't tell me he was the same person who wrote: *Neither a borrower nor a lender be, for loan oft loses both itself and friend, and borrowing dulls the edge of husbandry.*"

That got a laugh. Diana glared around the room, and then countered: "Well, since you seem so fond of Marlowe, you might recall it was Marlowe who said, *'While money doesn't buy love, it puts you in a great bargaining position.'* "

Jake couldn't resist a chuckle, which cost him two glares.

"You're the one who called him 'Willy the Shake,' " Melissa reminded him.

Childers got up and left. Diana glowered back and forth from one to the other in growing indignation–the same kind of indignation, Jake remembered, that his daughter had shown not long ago. "Shakespeare was a very busy and successful man, and such people are often approached for money, Mr.–what's your name again?"

"Fleming. Jake Fleming."

Diana looked at him again. "You've obviously bought into Desmond Lewis' twisted line of thinking, Jake Fleming."

That brought him up sharply. “So, you do know what Lewis was working on?”

Sensing the trap, she tried to backtrack. “Not really. There were rumors. That’s all.”

“I see.”

Quickly, she took the offensive. “So, you have decided, Mr. Journalist, to put our Shakespeare on trial?”

“Not me. Although to be honest, it strikes me that possibly it should have been done four centuries ago.”

“What all of this shows,” Melissà pressed on, “is to underline what the biographers have consishtently ignored: that Shakespeare was a businessman, and nothing more, busy in Stratford making deals when he was shupposed to be in London writing plays, whether or not he could read.”

Another ripple of murmurs swept around the room.

“So, you are saying it’s not possible to be an astute businessman and also a literary genius?”

“Name one other case,” Melissa demanded.

“T. S. Elliot,” came the instant response.

“Touche,” said Jake, with a wry scowl.

Melissa shrugged, indifferently. “He was the excepshun that rules the proof.” she persisted, unsteadily. “Busineshmen and poets are simply not of the same mind set. Yes, of course, shome businessmen may have excellent literary skills, I admit. Which they apply to the writing of informative, frequently witty books and articles. About business. And some even wrote a few poems. Good (hic) for them.”

Jake, in addition to the wry awareness that his daughter was displaying the typical zeal of the newly converted, felt also a guilty tinge of pride that his daughter was still on her feet despite her present handicap. “Isn’t it fair to say that as a rule, businessmen are motivated by making money, not art?”

“Not at all,” said Diana. “I’ve already named Elliot. How about Wallace Stevens? Or Paul Gauguin? They were all bankers.”

Melissa shook her head. “I bet at least Gauguin could spell his own name.” she snapped. This brought a chortle from several of the younger patrons. “Ditto

Elliot. In fact, I heard that thoshe guys actually wrote letters. I bet they even owned a book. Maybe two."

Diana turned livid. Clearly, she didn't know where to begin to counter that outburst.

Melissa seemed to be enjoying herself in her new role as traitor to the cause. Jake noticed that a fair number of male collegial types were enjoying her, as well, especially the still-flirting barflies. He could suddenly relate to those Muslims who covered their women from head to toe. How dare these young punks stare at his daughter with such open lust? On the other hand, he was doing a pretty good job of staring at their attractive new rival, himself. Diana seemed on the verge of tears. She dropped her wallet. He picked it up.

"Look, Dr. Parker," he said. "All my daughter is saying is that artists and writers take years to achieve a certain level of aptitude. By the same token businessmen have to dedicate themselves to mastering a trade and making a profit, in order to succeed. It's the way of the world. I do have trouble seeing how Shakespeare could possibly have done both, especially with no significant schooling on either score. They are two entirely different mindsets."

Diana gave him a look of dubious appraisal. "She is your daughter?"

"Yes," Jake replied. "I think."

"The bottom line is profit, not art, and businish people will be the first to tell you so," said Melissa, ignoring the jibe. She turned to her father and chose her syllables with exaggerated care. "Tell her," she said, setting her jaw. "About the producers."

Diana looked at him, expectantly. "Yes, do tell, Mr. Fleming. About the producers."

"Maybe my daughter's said enough."

"Will Shaksper was, like, the P.T. Barnum of his time," Melissa went on, sipping her beer.

That created a stir around the room. Jake looked at Melissa in growing appreciation. "P.T. Barnum? Where did you come up with that one?" She made a face at him.

"All right. I've had enough of this gibberish," Diana sighed. "First you started this nonsensical harangue quoting Marlowe. Then this long diatribe against Shakespeare. Do you actually think anyone will take you seriously with all this?"

"Desmond Lewis thought so, and obviously someone did," noted Jake.

"Not the way I heard it. My understanding is that he succumbed to his own despair. No doubt due to his failures, which were numerous."

Oh really? Thought Jake. "By the way," he said, changing the subject. "Maybe you could tell us who the man was you were talking to at the hotel bar last night."

She froze for a moment, and gave him a long, hard look, finally reaching a decision not in his favor. "I don't think so," she said. "Have a nice life."

The bar patrons snickered, then expressed their approval, at least in part, Jake suspected, of the elegant, slender legs she kicked into the air in her dismount from her bar stool. She looked magnificent in her very unprofessorial short skirt as she stalked out of the pub. Even though it was on crooked.

"That went well," remarked Melissa, finishing her beer.

Chapter Twenty-Nine

Thou Canst Not Then be False

London, 11:00 p.m., early November

Still shaken and unsettled by the events of earlier that evening, Jake decided to work into the night hours to appease his increasingly impatient editor Tom ("Fleming, what the hell's going on over there?") Flannigan. His next dispatch would deal with the personalities and contentiousness apparent on the academic scene, regarding a possible issue of historical verity. He would keep it to the bare bones, still, in regard to the Shakespeare/Marlowe rivalry now emerging on his watch (and in which, although he was trying his best to remain detached from it all, he was becoming a player). The readers should at least be treated to the melodrama of the "attack" at the Widow Bull, and also the skinheads' raid on the bookstore, he decided. That would sell papers.

He was distracted by the ringing of Melissa's cell phone from the bedroom. She answered and poked her head out, already pulling on her sweater.

"Dad, I'm going out for a while. I'll call you later." Apparently, in some mysterious transaction Jake had entirely missed, she'd made a date with the Jamaican grad student. At eleven o'clock at night. Jake was appalled.

"At this hour? Kiddo, there may be people out there you do not want to run into."

"Don't worry, Chris will protect me, he's very big and strong, remember?"

Big and strong wasn't much help against, say, a butcher's knife or handgun, he thought.

"Melissa, I know you're a grown woman. But I'm serious, it may be dangerous for you to go out there right now. Please, tell him another time." Like, next decade?

"Dad, this isn't about him being black, I hope?" She was goading him, he knew, but the words rankled anyway.

"I don't think that was called for," he said. "You saw what happened at that pub."

"Yes, and as Chris pointed out, very correctly, that was a carefully staged ploy to scare us off, and I, for one, don't scare that easily."

He'd had difficulty coping with her dating ever since puberty had kicked in and he became her "enemy keeper," as she put it. They were friends now. Or at least civil. He hoped it would last. She was an adult. He saw little use in standing in her way at this stage and ruining their new relationship and collaboration. On the other hand, part of him very much wished he could. In any other situation he'd have to admit that a beautiful twenty-three year old American girl at large in London by night would probably own the crown jewels before dawn. But her going out now was truly reckless, he felt. At least her companion was a sober, serious, preoccupied graduate student. From Jamaica. Things could be worse. Couldn't they?

Jamaica. The land of Rasta and ganja. His head spun. She wasn't even sober yet. Was she?

"Don't worry, I'll be careful," she promised, and with a jaunty wave she was out the door.

He sighed and went to the fridge. Didn't she say there was some yogurt in there somewhere?

Outside, the London night life was going full bore. Melissa couldn't believe the intensity of the foot traffic, mostly young people hurrying to and fro, as if desperate that they might miss out on the next glass of beer, or dance, or tub of fries, or music set. Or in her case, plate of jerk chicken. She crossed Charing Cross and caught a red double decker bus to Picadilly. This was going to be fun. She needed to get Shakespeare and Marlowe out of her mind for a while and clear her head from all that ale. And, for all her bravado, the specter of that attack in the Widow Bull still haunted her, and would for some time to come, she knew.

She didn't notice the gray-haired man get on behind her, until he sat down next to her.

"Hello," he said.

She looked up with a start. "Oh." she exclaimed, when she recognized him. "Small world! Sorry, you scared me."

He smiled, thinly. “Well, we wouldn’t want that, would we?”

Only then did it strike her as wrong, that he should suddenly appear like this. Had he been following her? Masking her sudden fear, she cast him a sidelong glance.

He smiled back, for all the world like a Cheshire cat, eying a favorite rodent.

After Melissa left the flat Jake filed his story, then returned to the ‘real’ task at hand.

If somebody had died in that tavern in the shabby town of Deptford on May 30th, 1593, the absurdity of the Inquest, the swift forgiveness of the alleged killer, the Queen’s later testimony about being the playwright’s ‘benefactor’, the interests of the Walsinghams, all added up to one thing: whoever it was buried there in Deptford—if anyone—it was not likely Christopher Marlowe.

The next thing he wanted to check for was possible career overlaps between Shakespeare and Marlowe. There were none. The only other reference to Shakespeare’s name other than Greene’s invective and the various title pages in his lifetime was a brief notation by a clergyman named Frances Meres who, in a 1598 book called *Palladis Tamia*, listed Shakespeare among the Elizabethan playwrights on page 281. While complimentary of the plays themselves, further digging revealed that Meres was a man of muddled and inaccurate learning, of no judgment, and of no critical power, a sort of Elizabethan Boswell without Boswell’s virtues, according to one leading scholar. He had no access to the theater and no clue as to who wrote what beyond what he was told. He was merely publishing a list based on the names printed on the Quartos. Meres did have something to say about Marlowe, however. In his *Wit’s Treasury* (also 1598) Frances Meres declared that “Christopher Marlowe was stabbed to death by a certain bawdy Serving-man, a rival in his lewd love.” In other words, thought Jake, Mere’s sources for Marlowe were about on a par with his sources for Shakespeare.

And so the pattern of character assassination and slander continued, of someone in no position to defend himself. The next item he found that bore any semblance to the eventually accepted official story of Marlowe’s death was from a book titled *Golden Grove* by William Vaughn (1600), who was the first to mention Deptford and the stabbing in a tavern by "one named Ingram."

The death certificate at the Church of St. Nicholas, Deptford, stated: *First of June, 1593, Christopher Marlowe, slain by Francis Archer.* Again, he noted, the actual coroner's report was not discovered until 1925 by biographer Leslie Hotson. It had been hidden all those years in the archives of the London Public Record Office, but no one knew, or had bothered to look. This document thoroughly contradicted many of the previous assumptions, but not the "fact" of Marlowe's death or the unsavory setting in which it supposedly occurred. And so the official story, once revealed, was all but set in stone.

Around 2:00 a.m. Jake checked his watch, fretted about Melissa's whereabouts, and went back online.

He was again struck by the strange disconnect between Marlowe's life and writings and this entire heresy-murder thing. What no one in the Star Chamber had taken the trouble to examine (and doing so was probably not in their interests anyway) was the evidence of Marlowe's genuine religious and philosophical beliefs, as revealed in the known early plays themselves, as Melissa had so eloquently pointed out. As further evidence, he'd found a study by a professor of English at Indiana University named Roy Battenhouse, of the religious content in Marlowe's writing. Battenhouse vigorously supported what Jake and Melissa had both concluded: that Kit could not have been an atheist at all. As Battenhouse put it: "The blasphemous and desperate character pictured in those testimonies (of Baines and Kyd) is most difficult to reconcile with the Marlowe who studied Divinity at Cambridge and whose loyalty to her Majesty's religion was vouched for by the Privy Council." Trying to cut him with both sides of the same sword, Baines had accused Kit of being pro-Catholic–a rehashing of the charges wrongfully leveled against him at Cambridge. Battenhouse wrote that if Marlowe ever made statements contrary to the interests of either England or the church, they were made in the context of his role as a spy. As Battenhouse noted: "If Marlowe was in real life an actor in the disguise drama of Elizabethan underground politics, then words reported of him–

particularly when reported by witnesses themselves politically suspect–must be regarded as dramatic talk."

In other words, bullshit.

Melissa, he remembered, had said almost the same thing. Battenhouse also quoted another British scholar named U.M. Ellis-Fermor, who remarked on Marlowe's modernism: *"Marlowe appears to have been on the verge of formulating the idea that the spirit and 'desire' of man are neither more nor less than God in man . . . The conception . . . is startlingly modern, or at least startlingly independent of his contemporaries."* But the Court of the Star Chamber had ears only for Marlowe's accusers (or at least Archbishop Whitgift did), and Marlowe, like Cordelia in *King Lear*, was too proud, or perhaps stubborn, to defend himself. With a sigh, Jake ran a quick search on Baines, to see if there was something he might have missed.

He noted with interest that Baines had known Marlowe as a divinity student at Cambridge. Or at least had attended there at the same time. Could they have had a falling out back then? Or been on opposing sides on cultural or religious issues like the 1960s American campus wars between the pro-war frat rats and the anti-war stoner hippies? One point he hadn't noticed earlier was that, to further assure the success of his purpose–the complete destruction of Christopher Marlowe–Baines had thrown in a whole new capital offense especially intended to enrage Marlowe's greatest patron, the Queen, because it involved money–namely counterfeiting. Counterfeiting alone was punishable by death. Furthermore, several cross references to law texts confirmed there was no such thing as acquittal by the Star Chamber. Once they had their "evidence" (an accusation would do, Baines needn't have gone to so much trouble), the case was as good as closed. There were no F. Lee Baileys or last-minute pardons in Elizabethan England. Once handed over to the Privy Council it was only a matter of whether the accused would be hanged, burned, drawn and quartered, or beheaded. Richard Baines, unopposed by counsel and simply listing what Archbishop Whitgift wanted to hear, had been given a free hand to write a death sentence for Christopher Marlowe. It occurred to Jake that Richard Baines would probably have made a successful American talk radio personality or political operative, if he lived today. Or radical Imam. He jotted a note to find a way to include that in his next article, which was already beginning to take form in his mind.

As he searched further, he found confirmation for what Melissa had been saying about the charges being so similar to those leveled against the Knights Templar. Almost line by line many of those additional charges were drawn from a liturgical treatise of the time titled *Fall of the Latter Arian*, essentially a textbook of blasphemies to which Marlowe had once referred while researching Dr. Faustus. The implication here was that because Marlowe had read it for his research (which he admitted) he therefore "must have" believed and condoned it. Sounded just like the Patriot Act, thought Jake, grimly. Or that because Shakespeare had a play on his desk, he "must have" written it. It also occurred to him that the publishers of the Folio itself could have made that same assumption, for much the same reason.

And so, by late May of 1593, Christopher Marlowe's "death" was all but inevitable.

But what about the cause of death itself? That hadn't looked right either, in the Inquest. Sure enough, as he delved deeper, he discovered, among the online biographies, that even those medical details described in the Inquest could not be believed. He found a link to a book by a Dr. Samuel A. Tannenbaum, *The Assassination of Christopher Marlowe*, written in1928. Tannenbaum had gathered the opinions of several top neurosurgeons of his time, all of whom had agreed that such a knife wound as Frizer allegedly inflicted on Marlowe could not be fatal. The Queen's coroner had claimed that this wound had caused "instant death." Yet there was little or no blood at the scene, which meant either no artery was severed (hence the blow could not have been fatal) or the body had been brought into the room already dead, as Melissa had suggested.

It struck Jake then that if those three men had been better storytellers, the truth would have been forever lost. Which reinforced his earlier notion that the ludicrous Inquest had been a deliberate falsehood, intended as a message, that things are not what they seem.

In any case there it was. Kit Marlowe, with the help of others with a vested interest in his survival, did what he had to do. Merely to flee the country–which he'd been given every opportunity to do simply by being out on bail–would be folly: he would be tracked by agents of the church to the ends of the earth and killed–possibly by those same three men. That would be a good twist for a story, he thought. To be murdered twice, by the same people! *But if Marlowe was officially dead, he could carry on writing in exile without living in constant fear of discovery.* It was the best solution, and the only solution. He was the poet in exile, then, who wrote those Sonnets. Not surprising that the Stratfordians cling to the official story of Marlowe's death with the determination of a baby clutching his bottle, with good reason. Because as Melissa herself had said, if Marlowe lives, the case for Shakespeare is mortally wounded. Why else would the idea that a man who invented special effects to stage the mighty *Tamburlaine*, who literally lived by theatrics, could fake his own death be so difficult to accept? Why else would a scholar like Desmond Lewis and his partner become such targets?

The Coroner's report had been signed by the Honorable William Danby, Gentleman Coroner to the Queen. Which, as Jake began to suspect, meant nothing at all other than at some point in time, someone placed it before Danby on his desk to sign. Like so much else in question now, it didn't prove he wrote it. Or even read it. Let alone verify its contents. It didn't prove he was even at the hearing in Deptford. Why would he bother to go to that dreary place? The document was so full of holes and inconsistencies he would probably have never signed it if he had read it unless directed to do so by the Queen herself. A reasonably good lawyer would have had it thrown out as inadmissible, with a couple of pointed bon mots worthy of Gerry Spence. So, if anything, since Danby was a reputedly honest man, either he was part of a conspiracy to cover Marlowe's escape, or he didn't read it. Since it was such a risible document, he would have questioned it. Which meant he was under orders to rubber stamp it. The real question was why had the Queen ordered her own coroner to handle a routine matter not even in his jurisdiction? The answer had to be exactly as Sunir had implied: that she had reasons of her own to execute a cover-up and maintain silence on the matter, which might also explain how the report so swiftly vanished from sight, along with the "body." Especially if her own government had quietly spirited her favorite playwright and gifted foreign agent out of harm's way, in order to be put to better purpose abroad than any death warrant could serve at home.

As the hours waned into the cold stillness before dawn, and his worries about Melissa intensified, one other thought kept rolling through Jake's mind over and over again: if the inquest was a fabrication, which it was, who, if anyone, was in that unmarked grave at St. Nicholas Church in Deptford? Was it John Penry? Some poor, unlucky wandering drunk or plague victim? Or no one at all? Then it dawned on him: *there was no grave.*

Chapter Thirty

Thou Art the Mars of Malcontents

London, morning, early November

Melissa dragged herself in just after dawn, exhausted and hung over after a long night of eating, drinking, talking and thinking, with her she-had-to-admit stimulating and intriguing new friend Chris.

She had decided not to mention what had happened earlier that evening on the bus to either Chris or her father. She knew a lot of people, even at Berkeley, who believed there was no such thing as coincidence, and that everything happened for a purpose. Some called it fate, others cited such theories as six degrees of separation. Either way, the fact that she'd run into her old mentor in the middle of a city of ten million had to mean something.

And it had proven useful. He had given her a name, a lead, despite his negative views about her burgeoning interest in Marlowe, and her father's pursuit of the trail left by Desmond Lewis. When she'd asked him why, he'd patted her knee, and said, "You know I truly do admire that fiery actor's spirit of yours. Maybe it's just my way of saying *'tis an unweeded garden, that grows to seed.'* "

"*Hamlet*, Act I, Scene II Page 5," she'd responded.

"Very good, my girl," he'd said, patting her knee again.

"Dad?" She came over to the sofa and shook him.

"Awright, awright, I'm awake," he grumbled, not pleased about being awakened, but nonetheless greatly relieved by her safe return. He'd been asleep at most for an hour when she came in, having finally nodded off not long before. He must have resembled some red-eyed demon from *The Decameron*, because even though she too was obviously fatigued, she found great amusement in his unkempt condition. She, of course, still looked as fresh as a Dove ad, as always.

"What's up? You OK?" he asked her.

"I'm fine. Listen, what do you know about The Shakespeare Foundation?"

"Not much. Why?"

"I ran into someone who told me they have been known to take strong measures to protect The Name. Did you ever find out who trashed Dr. Lewis's office and apartment?"

"Same people who broke in here, is my guess. Why? You think it might be this Foundation?"

She peeled off her sweater and hung it on a hanger. "I don't know, but it's possible. Maybe you should check it out." She went into the bathroom and turned on the shower.

Half an hour later Melissa was dead to the world, and Jake was wide awake. He was starting to relate to Macbeth regarding sleep: *Balm of hurt minds, great nature's second course, Chief nourisher in life's feast.* Alas, it seemed that sleep was a feast not in the offing for him, just now. He decided that before he went any further into what had happened to Kit Marlowe back in 1593, he needed to get a firmer grasp on what Will Shakespeare was doing, or had actually done, in the meantime.

Reinforced with fresh coffee, shirt half tucked and collar askew, Jake was back on the doorstep when the British Library opened at 9:30, and deep in the archives shortly thereafter.

First, he wanted to confirm something that Sunir had told him, what seemed like eons ago. After quickly browsing the first of many Shakespeare compendiums in the stacks, he found what he was looking for. Sure enough, the first appearance of William Shakespeare as sole author of a written work came less than two weeks after the "death" of Christopher Marlowe, in June of 1593. It came with the publication of the long poem that had been registered anonymously with the Company of Stationers in April, when Marlowe was still alive and well. That poem, *Venus and Adonis*, was first published anonymously in mid-June. But then, on a dedication page that was added two months later, the alleged author was named as William Shakespeare, who claimed in his dedication that "this was the first heir of my invention."

Venus and Adonis. He dug into his valise and found the List. 'V.A.' "Bingo," he murmured to himself.

He called Sunir in hopes of catching him between classes and lucked out. "Sunir, its Jake Fleming. Got a minute?"

"I suppose. Mostly. What is up?"

"Tell me about *Venus and Adonis*."

"Yes, of course! That was the item I was trying to recall from your list. The 'heir' to the Bard's invention. My colleagues over in the English Department claim, of course, that this was an overt statement by Shakespeare that this poem was his first written work. Even though the *Henry VI* plays had already been put into production, a discrepancy they cannot explain. Likewise, *Titus Andronicus*, I might add."

"That's an important discrepancy. They can't have it both ways."

"Yet Shakespeare made that claim himself."

"So that's why the scholars grudgingly acknowledge that Marlowe had a hand in those plays?"

"As you said, they shouldn't have it both ways. Yet they've gotten away with just that for centuries, actually. It's another reason I am sure Dr. Lewis was onto Marlowe."

"So, let me be sure I've got this right," said Jake, checking over his notes. "All three *Henry VI* plays are in the 1623 Folio under Shakespeare's name, claiming he wrote them. Yet all of them as well as *Titus Andronicus* were produced prior to 1593 and the publication of this poem, right?"

"Which of course belies the claim of 'first invention.' "

This was incredible, thought Jake. How do they get away with this? It couldn't be right. By 1593 the previously unknown extraordinarily late-blooming Will Shakespeare was nearly thirty and not been heard from or about in any capacity other than all that glowing praise from Robert Greene. So here suddenly appears his 'first invention' all instantly polished, which begged an important question: what was he doing up until then, aside from grooming horses, acting, and selling grain or brokering costumes and plays, to become so instantly literate, not to mention successful?

"Sunir, how do they explain this discrepancy?"

"As with all the other discrepancies, they brush it aside like so much chaff."

"I see. So how would you explain it?"

“Well, considering the Bard’s known propensities and Greene’s invective, Shakespeare simply got his hands on the Venus manuscript, learned that the author was ‘dead,’ and, also knowing the printer Richard Field—who happened to hail from Stratford, by the way and may have even given it to him—he helped himself. According to Shakespeare’s first biographer Nicholas Rowe, this is the quote ‘only Piece of his Poetry that he ever published himself,’ end quote.”

“Interesting. But in any case, given that Marlowe was already ‘dead,’ and most likely already in exile, he had to have had it published anonymously, right?”

“Yes. Look, I have to run, I have a class already starting without me. Let’s meet later, shall we? We need to talk about Lambeth.”

Jake wished later that he had set a time.

The poem itself was long and flowery, but quite lovely. Jake read it through, then turned back to the title page. It seemed to him that its rather fawning dedication, fraught with farmer’s imagery, far more similarly approached the literacy of the Shakespeare Will than the poem itself. Which certainly supported Sunir’s opinion that Shakespeare simply stole the poem, put his name on it, and then wrote (or dictated) the dedication later. But as he studied the page, he saw something else that made his pulse quicken. Above the title on the title page was written a motto in Latin: *Vilia miretur vulgus: mihi flauus Apollo Pocula Castalia plena ministret aqua*. Those lines looked familiar. He returned to the Research Desk and asked the librarian, on a whim. She looked at the page and raised her eyebrows, regarding him with a look that suggested that *amore*, in general, was sorely lacking in her life: a lack this American patron before her could easily remedy.

“These lines are from Ovid’s *Amores*,” she said, throatily. “It’s funny, I never noticed that was there before.”

Ovid again. The same Ovid that had landed Marlowe in the Star Chamber.

He thanked her and returned to his carrel. Searching through his notes, he found what he was looking for: Ovid’s *Amores* had indeed first been translated from Latin by Christopher Marlowe, while at Cambridge. The lines translated as: *‘Let base-conceited wits admire vile things, Fair Phoebus lead me to the*

Muses' springs.' If anything, it was a mockery of Shakespeare himself. He had already proven himself a "base-conceited wit," according to Robert Greene. Marlowe, whom Greene had been warning, might well have felt the same way, and was taunting him from his new place in exile. As to his admiration of "vile things," one can only guess. But Greene's list of charges certainly could be summed up as being "vile." As for 'the Muse's springs,' it was Marlowe, not Shakespeare, that Thomas Peele had affectionately called "The Muse's Darling." Furthermore, he discovered, the Earl of Southampton, to whom the poem had been dedicated, had been a schoolmate of Marlowe's at Cambridge, with no known connection to Shakespeare. All of which put the concept of 'invention' in a different light altogether.

My God! Thought Jake. It would be a marvelous and terrible irony indeed, were the thief to have been completely unaware that he was naming the true author, and at the same time mocking himself, front and center! And yet, even more ironic, if so, he (Shakespeare) got away with it.

A short while later, no sooner had Jake returned to the stacks when he discovered something else so extraordinary, he was tempted to ring Sunir back. There, discreetly buried among the many compilations of the Bard's alleged "works," was a list of plays to which Shakespeare had attached his name, yet which Shakespearean scholars had rejected from the Canon: the so-called 'Apocrypha.' He didn't need to check the Lewis List to recognize the abbreviation 'Apoc'. Here it was, clear as crystal. Lewis hadn't meant 'apocalypse' at all. Quickly, he jotted down the titles and notations:

Locrine (by the very angry Robert Greene? Others thought the tortured Thomas Kyd) . . . "Newly set form overseen and corrected by W.S." (compare to *Love's Labor's Lost*, 1598, title paged: "Newly corrected and augmented by W. Shakespeare.")

Sir John Oldcastle..."Written by William Shakespeare."

The True Chronicled History of Thomas Lord Cromwell..."Written by W.S."

The London Prodigal..."by William Shakespeare."

The Puritan..."Written by W.S."

A Yorkshire Tragedy..."Written by W. Shakespeare."

Pericles, Prince of Tyre (the Shakespeareans later reclaimed this one)

The Troublesome Reign of King John…"Written by W. Sh."

Jake checked his notes. Sir Edmond Chambers, Shakespeare's most eminent scholar, had acknowledged this last one to be "probably" Marlowe's play. So, what did Chambers have to say about 'Sh.' stamping his name on it? In addition to these were several more he'd never heard of:

Arden of Feversham
The Birth of Merlin
Fair Em
The Merry Devil of Edmonton
Mucedorus

Quickly he packed up and caught a bus to Charing Cross. He wanted to talk to Blodgett about this.

When Jake hurried in, Blodgett was in a bad temper. "Ah, the itinerant scholar," he remarked, glumly. "Better late than never, one can only suppose."

There was an acrid smell in the air, and a pall of smoke. "What happened?" asked Jake, looking around. Then he saw for himself. There had been a fire.

Blodgett was hunched over a stack of soaked, charred manuscripts in the back of the shop. "Luckily I came in early and it had only just started, so I caught it before any great damage was done." He gestured at a spent fire extinguisher, on the floor nearby.

"Looks like damage enough, to me." Jake had a bad thought. One that involved skinheads. "Any indication of the cause?"

"The fire lieutenant says it was probably the wiring. But I noticed one of the window locks was broken." He sniffed the air. "And there was a faint smell of kerosene earlier."

Jake was reminded of the suicide theory. "Coincidence, no doubt?"

"No doubt."

"So how much did you lose?"

"Not much. Some files, mostly. Tax files, ironically enough. And a few arcane books and manuscripts. Mostly odds and ends, and things I couldn't sell. Or wouldn't."

"I'm very sorry," said Jake.

"No matter. I have insurance. The wife has been urging me to sell the place and retire for years. Maybe it's time." He looked around wistfully. "I would miss it, though. Yes, indeed."

"Can I get you some tea or something?"

"Well, I had a hot plate on the file cabinet there, but it seems to have been confiscated. Suspect number one, or something. Even though it was the newest thing in the place. My wife bought it for me for Christmas just last century, in fact." He grinned. "Ah well." He dropped the papers he was holding on the ash-coated desk. "What can I do for you, this otherwise fine morning?"

"If you don't mind a distraction, maybe I could invite you out for lunch or something? I'd like to talk to you about the Apocrypha."

"Ah, yes, indeed. The mysterious Apocrypha. I knew there was something else from that list that rang a bell. 'Apoc.' Ah well. Quaint name, that, wouldn't you say? Can't recall who came up with it. Fleay, I think. Yes, indeed." He looked around, once again. "Frankly, I'm a bit chary about leaving the scene of the crime just now. If you can abide the added ambiance, the touch of aromatic essence of burnt bibles and whatnot, would you mind staying here? Besides, we might need a reference or two, if I can find it."

Blodgett rolled his desk chair away from the fire area and found another chair in the back for Jake. "Hope you don't mind a few ashes, to go with the soot," he chuckled.

"Not at all." Jake was too restless to sit, in any case, and perched on the edge of the desk, with his notebook open on his lap. "Have you ever thought it strange that the scholars could reject all these bad plays with Shakespeare's name on them, just because they were, what, no good?"

Blodgett snorted. "No good? Bloody awful, most of them."

"Yet later on these same scholars, or their successors, should we say? Insisted on crediting him with 'good' plays to which he had no previously known connection, like *Pericles, Edward III* and *St. Thomas More*."

"Even though that one had always been considered the work of Sir Anthony Munday."

"So, what this means is, Shakespeare's name on a playbook means nothing at all."

"You said it, not I. But I'd have to agree with you. There's a definite double standard there."

"So why should anyone put any faith in the Quartos or that Folio?"

"Because it's there. And because it's what we've always been told. For the same reason True Believers take the Bible so literally or bow towards Mecca. There's no accounting for faith, you know."

"Do you think Shakespeare is a religion?"

"Well, I wouldn't go that far. He certainly has his blind faithful, though. I'll say that."

"But why is that name alone, never mind the merits, such grounds for faith?"

"Perhaps because Shakespeare represents the dream of Everyman?"

"Everyman's dream." Jake noted that. "But you know, the more I think about it, Shakespeare has all the earmarks of a Brand Name."

Blodgett looked startled. "A brand name? There was no such thing, in those days."

"Then what was Robert Greene so bent out of shape about? He accused him of stealing, right? And then his name turns up on *Venus and Adonis*, then the Quartos. And now comes the lynchpin to the whole case: this Apocrypha. It's the only explanation."

Blodgett pursed his lips. "Dr. Lewis and I used to chat about this. He always felt that there were only two possible rationales for the Folio: either he was a flagrant plagiarist who lifted someone else's material right and left for his entire career, or he was a thief who stole the entire Works."

"Either way he got away with it."

"So, you are saying that there is a third possibility: that he simply bought them and put his name on them, as a product? And then convinced the world they were his?"

"Shakespeare, Incorporated," said Jake, mostly to himself.

Blodgett shook his head in disbelief. "A Thief for All Time?"

Jake laughed. "Good one. That's what Melissa said. I'm writing that down." Which he did. "In any case it's crystal clear from the 'crow' analogy. It just reminds me of Hollywood. The studios or producers buy scripts and call them their own. The writer, especially the original writer, is dismissed, replaced, forgotten, and out of the picture, literally. Especially in the early days."

Blodgett studied him, thoughtfully. "That is a very radical idea."

"But it happened in Hollywood. Why not Bankside? And it makes sense."

"Well, it's true that in those days there was no such thing as copyright laws or author's rights. It was in the interests of the company to keep their plays in-house at all times, to avoid piracy. So no doubt it was standard business to acquire plays in the company name."

"William Shakespeare. A name you can trust," chuckled Jake, shaking his head.

"So," said Blodgett, getting up and stretching. "How're we doing with the rest of that list of yours?"

Jake laid the List on the table, and they pondered it together. The Inquest was no longer in doubt, and Blodgett agreed about 'V.A.' being Venus and Adonis. "So, we're down to these last three items. There's something in Lambeth Palace. And that other possible item you were looking for, remember? Something or someone named Hoffman?"

"Yes, thank you for reminding me. I actually did locate something." The bookseller fumbled among the ashen debris, found a ledger, blew off the soot, and flipped it open.

"Yes, it's here somewhere. Quite a rarity, mind you. And wouldn't you know, the author's one of your lot."

"My lot?"

Blodgett found the entry he was looking for and stamped it with a blackened thumb. "Here we are. I found it on one of the auction lists, actually, because it's been out of print for half a century." Jake leaned closer, trying to see. "*Murder of the Man Who Was Shakespeare*, by Calvin Hoffman." He looked up, triumphantly. "Bloody close to that Ogburn title, actually."

"Did you find anything more about it?"

Blodgett's eyes twinkled, mysteriously. "Matter of fact I did. It seems this Hoffman chap was an American journalist, like yourself. Some magazine in New York. He got onto this subject and made quite a sensation. Then disappeared. Rather odd, really."

"So, what was the subject?"

Blodgett smiled, hugely. "That the author of the Plays and Sonnets, alleged to be William Shakespeare, was none other than our friend, Mr. Christopher Marlowe."

"That has to be it!" exclaimed Jake, excitedly. "Can we get a copy?"

"Well, I did find one, but it was rather pricey, I'm afraid."

"So where is it?" demanded Jake, eagerly.

Blodgett's expression turned sly. "I sold it. Just this morning, in fact."

"You have got to be kidding."

Blodgett's expression turned triumphant. "To a very attractive, rather insistent young woman with flaxen hair. In fact, in a remarkable coincidence, you share the same—"

"Melissa? She's been here?" He shook his head with a grin. "Why that crafty little devil."

"Well, I had no idea when you were coming back. It's been several days, you know, and I'm afraid your card has gone up in smoke, literally speaking."

"Never mind," said Jake, handing him another one. "Are you going to be around tomorrow? I'll let you know what it says."

"Lord willing, as they say."

Jake had just pulled on his coat and stepped out into the cold when something caught his eye: a car with dark tinted windows parked across the road in a no parking zone. He'd seen that car before, more than once. Throwing caution to the November winds, he headed straight for it, dodging through traffic to get to it. Rushing up to the driver's side door, he banged on the window.

"All right, open up!" he shouted, angrily.

There was no response. Finally, he kicked the door, and the window slid down. "What the hell do you bloody well think you're doing?" a fuming round-faced man he'd never seen before demanded to know.

"Sorry, my mistake," said Jake, reddening in embarrassment. He turned and hurried away feeling like an idiot, hoping Blodgett hadn't witnessed that foolishness.

Inside the car, the round-faced man punched a number on his cell phone. He spoke in terse tones. "He's left the store, but I'm afraid he's made me. Do you want me to follow him?"

"No," replied The Watcher, grabbing a quick bite in a nearby restaurant. "He's heading home. He misses his daughter."

Jake picked up a sandwich at the deli on Denmark Street and returned to the flat in a black mood. Melissa was nowhere around, and he wanted to see that book. To occupy himself he went online to see how many plays Shakespeare had actually claimed in his heyday. The Quartos, he now knew, canceled themselves out with the Apocrypha. No wonder his friend Des Lewis had been so excited, he thought.

It all came down, then, to the First Folio. This was the keystone, in fact the whole case, for Shakespeare. Not so much because his fellow players Heminge and Condell had named him. They might not know where their old partner had gotten the plays from and simply took him at his word. Much more critical was the fact that Ben Jonson had given his endorsement to the publishing scheme and the naming of Shakespeare as author. And yet there was evidence even at the outset that something wasn't quite right with that picture either. Literally.

Deep in the bowels of the Internet, Jake found an article proving that the famed Droushout engraving, the "portrait" published along with the Folio, was a fraud. To him, it looked like a generic theatrical mask. In an article in the April, 1996 issue of *Scientific American* researcher Lillian Schwartz had demonstrated that this engraving was actually a copy of a popular portrait of Queen Elizabeth, with a few masculine touchups and a costume change.

In any case, nobody aside from his old actor colleagues really knew or cared what the old player-factotum actually looked like because, at least in the role of Bard he, like his image, was a fraud. Hence the various fanciful busts and portraits to follow, all of them rendered long after the death of the alleged poet.

Jake began to write an assemblage of his thoughts. The First Folio was published in 1623, seven years after Shakespeare's death. It included those 36 plays, only nine of which had born the name Shakespeare (in various spellings) in the First Quartos published in his lifetime. Seven had appeared anonymously, and the remaining twenty appeared in the Folio for the first time ever, anywhere: among them *Macbeth, The Taming of the Shrew*, and *The Comedy of Errors*.

He tried to visualize the businesslike Will Shakspere as he brought the plays to the stage floor each day. And what had become of all those pages, all those manuscripts? If he was copying them, later publishing them, the originals–in the hand of another or others—would serve no further purpose, might lead to piracy, and could be used as evidence against him. So, of course, he'd destroy them. In any case, those six crude signatures on business documents were the only proven examples of his writing in existence.

His eyes were beginning to fail him. His stomach had begun to act up again. He glanced at his watch. It was nearly six o'clock. Where had the day gone? And where was Melissa? He was dying to see that book she'd picked up.

The telephone rang. He snapped out of his daze and snatched up the receiver just as the answering machine kicked in. "Hello?"

"Is this Mr. Fleming?" The voice was male, he guessed roughly his own age, and the accent was northern England, perhaps Yorkshire?

"Yes, speaking."

"Mr. Fleming, there are persons and interests in the UK and elsewhere who are rather concerned about the activities you and your daughter have been pursuing, as of late."

He felt a sudden coldness in his chest. "What activities would those be?"

"You are delving into matters that do not concern you. We ask that you stop. We are making the same recommendation to your friend Dr. Balsavar. We leave it up to you to dissuade your daughter, Melissa, again for her own well-being as well as yours."

"You leave her out of this!" shouted Jake.

"We would happily do so, if she would simply resume her acting career and studies back in California and drop this ill-advised quest of hers and yours."

"I see. Well, I got your other message already, so you needn't have bothered calling."

"I beg your pardon?"

"Didn't you send me a note recently? With a quote from *Hamlet*?"

There was a pause, however brief. "I wouldn't know what you mean, sir. Just take this request seriously, if you value your best interests."

That was disturbing. "Is this some sort of threat?"

"Not at all. Please just consider it a recommendation."

"Oh really? What about that guy in a demon suit with a knife the other night? What would you recommend we do about that?"

But the caller had already hung up.

Jake gripped the phone receiver tightly and stood frozen for several moments until the beeping signal switched on, alerting him that the phone was off the hook. He hung up, which took two tries because he was livid with rage. And once again he felt abandoned by his daughter. What was she up to, anyway?

But what he mostly felt, was dread. Dread of what she'd gotten herself into. And dread for her safety.

Chapter Thirty-One

Sharper Than the Sword

London, evening, November

Melissa came in around six thirty with two bags of groceries.

"Where were you, anyway?" demanded Jake, testily. His thoughts were churning with so much news and data he hardly knew where to begin.

"Hey, sorry, I was at the university library. Why? Is something wrong?"

He shook his head. "No, there's a lot to talk about and I was worried, that's all. You usually leave a note."

"Sorry, I forgot. You could have called me, you know."

"I tried and got no answer."

"Oh, sorry." She fumbled for her coat. "It was in my coat pocket. I guess I didn't hear it."

"Well, anyway I needed to talk to you in person. What were you doing?"

"Research. I'm having a hard time convincing Dr. Childers I'm not ready yet."

She went into the kitchen to put away the groceries. "He's really cool, you know," she said, putting a dozen new flavors of yogurt into the fridge.

"Childers?" he asked, doubtfully, still struggling with whether or not to tell her about the call.

"Hardly."

"The doorman, Fred?" he suggested, trying to calm himself with humor.

"You silly man."

"Sunir? The exotic albeit reticent Asian?"

"Yes, but I don't mean him."

"Chris Whomever?"

She laughed. "Yes, he's pretty cool, too, once you get past the Rasta act. But I meant Marlowe. I found a description of him, he's sounds breathtaking. And I saw his portrait." She dug into her newly adapted oversized valise-handbag and pulled out a notebook. Inside she'd tucked another Xeroxed document.

"Look, I found a picture of him:"

"Nice looking guy, I'll grant you."

" *'Nice looking?'* Give me a break! Did you know that Christopher Marlowe was, in the words of critic John Ingram, *'this youthful ringleader of free thought, this champion of revolutionary upheaval against countless centuries of mental oppression?' "*

He followed her back to the living room. "It's funny you should mention that, because I found something about that too–"

"And listen to this description I found by another friend, Thomas Nashe, at age 26:

'His status was of middle length, Well jointed of a good strength, Silken writs report to us Was that Trojan, Troilus.' Oooh, he must have been hot."

"Interesting, the comparison to Troilus. But we have to—"

"Shhh." She continued reading:

"For he was of comely visage,
And his manners of courteous usage
His hair in curled locks hung down,
And well I wot, the color was nut-brown,
And yet it was full bright and sheen.
Such wore Paris, I ween,

When he sailed to Grecia To fetch the fair Helena.'

Come on, is that cool, or what?" She went on:

"His eyes were luminous, Crystalline and beauteous,
Gray and sparkling like the stars, When the day her light up spars.'

And so on, it's all in verse."

He sighed and sat down. "I noticed. The Marlowe portrait certainly corresponds with Nashe's description of the "the gentleman." Small wonder the gays want to claim him as one of their own. Sounds like Nashe had a crush on him."

He looked at the picture she'd found. Jake's daughter, it was plain, had fallen in love. Except not with the sullen young grad student or ardent professor, but with the late, great, evidently sexy, possibly gay, or more probably bisexual Christopher Marlowe. *The Muse's Darling*, and now hers too, it seemed. He had to laugh. "That definitely does not sound like somebody who'd hang out in a tough seaport like Deptford," he acknowledged.

"Yeah, really."

"But listen, we have to talk."

Melissa, however, was still too absorbed in her own thoughts to listen. "So, do you think Nashe and Peele were the two other writers Greene was warning in Groatsworth?"

"I don't know. Probably. Or maybe Kyd." But right now, he wanted to talk to her about the Apocrypha. And, at the very least, put her on alert. That phone call just now had really scared him. There were people out there determined to stop him in his tracks. People who had stopped Desmond Lewis in his tracks permanently. People who knew his daughter's name and occupation. And the caller's evident puzzlement to Jake's reference to the cloak and dagger incident or the threats implied in those Shakepearean quotations (or should he now insist on referring to them only as Marlovian quotations?), suggested that danger was closing in on them on multiple fronts. Had he in fact, by pursuing the quest begun by Desmond Lewis, stirred up a nest of possibly lethal hornets? Or was it all bluff? And what had The Watcher meant by his comments about 'looking after your best interests'? Plus, he wanted to see the Hoffman book, and discuss *Venus and Adonis*. He hardly knew where to begin.

Meanwhile, his daughter's enthusiasm knew no bounds. "And I'm not the only one who thinks he was cool," she went on. "For example: he comes back to Cambridge from France having done all this dangerous praiseworthy spying for his Queen, and the university dons decide that he must be a traitor because he's been fraternizing with Catholics, which is exactly what he was sent there to do. So, they refuse to award him his Masters degree. So get this: the Privy Council sends a blistering letter to the university deans and orders them to get Marlowe reinstated and his degree granted. I found the letter, Dad." She showed him the copy, sat down, and read it out loud:

> *"Whereas it was reported that Christopher Marlowe was determined to have gone beyond the seas to Rheims and there remain, their Lordships thought good to certify that he behaved himself orderly and discreetly whereby he had done her Majesty good service, and deserved to be rewarded for his faithful dealing. Their Lordships request that the rumour thereof should be allayed by all possible means and that he should be furthered in the degree he was to take this next Commencement; because it was not her Majesty's pleasure that anyone employed as he had been in matters touching the benefit of his country should be defamed by those ignorant in the affairs he went about."*

"This document was in the minutes of the Privy Council headed by Lord Burghley."

"Where did you find it?"

"In the British Public Records Office, right in plain sight."

He whistled. "Good work. But I have some news too."

"It gets better. By the way, have you talked to Sunir?"

"That's what I was trying to tell you." He told her about his conversation about the 'first invention.' "But that's not all. I assume you are familiar with the 'Apocrypha'?"

"Yes, the 'bad plays.' I wanted to talk to you about those, I think that has to be the 'Apoc.' on the List."

"I think so too," he acknowledged, disappointed at losing his thunder.

"But Dad, you'll never guess what else I found."

He feigned innocence. "The Hoffman book?" Now they were even.

She glared and made a face. "Dammit! You ruined my surprise! I was all set to tell you about how that old nebbish Henry Blodgett on Charing Cross Road had it and he'd been looking for it for some customer who never came back, so he let me have it."

"He told me, actually. I was there this afternoon, I don't think he would appreciate being called an old nebbish, though."

"Dad I was joking."

She dug once again into her valise. "Check it out. It has his picture on the cover." She triumphantly produced a tattered paperback book with a faded cover, showing the familiar Drushout drawing of the Shakespeare mask superimposed over a larger image of what he recognized as the Marlowe portrait in Cambridge, which he'd seen in several biographies and Melissa had now fallen in love with.

"*Murder of the Man Who Was Shakespeare*. By Calvin Hoffman." He confirmed. "Way to go." All was forgiven. "How much was it?"

"You won't believe it, Dad. Twenty pounds for an old paperback? Obviously, this book has all but disappeared. Yet it was supposed to be a bestseller, from what I've heard."

"I'll reimburse you," he promised. "Or the paper will. Let's have a look."

"Your paper is flat broke, but never mind." She extended the treasure to him like it was the original Ten Commandments.

"So," he said brightly, looking it over. "What's it about?"

She badgered him until he agreed to let her read it first, on condition that she listen to his progress from his online research the night before and at the British Library this morning.

"Well, so much for six years of scholarship," she said, when he finished. She promptly disappeared into the bedroom, Hoffman's well-traveled book in hand.

By this time, he had decided against telling her about the strange phone call. It wouldn't change anything and would certainly spoil her good mood.

At dawn she woke him up, looking triumphant and thoughtful at the same time. "You know, it's kind of a travesty, what happened to this guy."

"Marlowe?"

"Hoffman. They really made a fool of him."

"Who?"

"The press. Everybody. I checked online. Yet it's plain as Nebraska that he was right."

He was too tired to read it now. "Tell me about it," he said, rubbing his eyes, and moving to the sofa.

She made herself comfortable in the armchair while he leaned back, eyes closed but listening.

"A lot of it is what Hoffman called 'parallelisms.' Those are companion pieces showing that having done an early developmental work on a theme close to his heart, the author then reworked and redeveloped it again, later, as his writing matured. Also, he repeated favorite lines of dialogue or text, which would serve the dual purpose of leaving signals or markers that he still lives."

"For example?"

She leafed quickly through the book, which was now, he noticed, cluttered with Post-its.

"Like *The Jew of Malta* and *The Merchant of Venice*; *The Massacre at Paris* and *Love's Labor's Lost*, both dealing with the French Huguenot holocaust; *Dido, Queen of Carthage* and *Antony and Cleopatra*, Dido being an early portrait of Cleopatra; *Dr. Faustus* and *Macbeth*, in which both protagonists invoke supernatural forces that lead to catastrophe and tragedy. And Kit's epic poem *Hero and Leander* is an obvious sequel to *Venus and Adonis*."

He told her about the quote from Ovid that Marlowe had translated and later appeared on the title page of *Venus and Adonis*, in which Ovid refers to 'sad lover's heads.'

"Well guess what?" she said, brandishing the book. "That quote perfectly matches the description of *Hero and Leander*, which was the masterpiece Marlowe was writing when he got arrested."

Jake stretched out on the sofa, while she went on: "There's forensic evidence too, about who wrote the plays. Hoffman talks about this study done in 1902 by a professor in Ohio named Mendenhall who had developed a scientific method of graphing the writing styles of specific authors. He would chart the unconscious habits of word usage, sentence construction, numbers of words in sentences, word length, and vocabulary, kind of like a precursor to what word processors and computers can do now. Mendenhall had been hired by a believer in Sir Francis Bacon, who wanted proof that Bacon wrote the Works."

"Yeah, Mark Twain thought it was Bacon, too. Speaking of bacon . . ." Jake dragged himself to the kitchen to look for some semblance of a breakfast. He found some cottage cheese, much to his distaste. But his stomach was expressing more than usual displeasure. He slapped some into a bowl. "Want some?" he asked.

She shook her head. "He didn't know Marlowe could have lived. Anyway, while comparing Bacon's writings to Shakespeare's, Mendenhall included the works of twenty other famous writers as well, basically for control purposes. Then he compared like 20,000 words from each author for word-length, vocabulary, cadence, and sentence length."

"Let me guess–one of them was Marlowe?"

"Hey. Let me tell it. So, he compared all these writers including Byron, Shelley, Keats, Thackeray, and Christopher Marlowe. Bacon's word lengths were way longer than anybody else's. So, instead of confirming his client's thesis, Mendenhall discovered–to his astonishment–that it was Marlowe who matched Shakespeare, identically. Dad, he proved they were the same author."

"All this was done back in 1902?" Jake shook his head, in dismay.

"Well, the Inquest hadn't been found yet, so they must have thought 'no, it can't be.' Anyway, Hoffman published his book in 1955, so it isn't like there hasn't been evidence for a long time out there if people had been willing to look."

Which made him wonder what good their efforts were going to do, however right she might be. Especially given the fate of Desmond Lewis. But he didn't want to say anything that would frighten or discourage her, now that she had a new mission in life.

"There's also a ton of what Hoffman calls 'internal evidence.' Like in *Hamlet*, the Prince of Denmark is a man forced into exile across the sea. And there's a direct tribute to Marlowe's early play *Dido, Queen of Carthage*, when Hamlet first greets the players."

He pushed aside his now empty bowl of cottage cheese. "Really? What players?"

"The ones he hired to expose the crimes of Gertrude and Claudius." She found the page, and read:

Hamlet, Act II, Scene 2 (436):

HAMLET: *I heard thee speak me a speech once, but it was never acted, or if it was, not above once; for the play, I remember, pleased not the million.*

"In this scene, the author is praising an obscure play, as *'Caviare to the general . . . an excellent play . . . well digested in the scenes'* and so on. This is about Marlowe's student play at Cambridge, which shocked its audience so much it was never performed again in his 'lifetime.' So Shakespeare could never have even seen it. And there is no doubt about which play it was—and whose—'cause check out the next line:

One speech I chiefly loved, 'twas Anaeus' tale to Dido, and thereabout of it especially where he speaks of Priam's slaughter.

"Then he goes on to quote almost directly from the Marlowe play:

> *'Pyrrhus at Priam drives, in rage strikes wide; But with the whiff and wind of his fell sword Th' unnerved father falls.'* Compare this to Dido when he wrote: *Disdaining, whiskt his sword about And with the wind thereof the King fell down."*

"Hmm. I do see a similarity. Do we have any coffee?"

She stared at him in disbelief. "Similarity? Where else did you ever hear of a guy getting knocked down by the wind from a sword? And in *Hamlet* it's more poetic. He's reusing his own material and improving it. He's progressing, as a writer."

"Go on." He got up and went into the kitchen to make some coffee. She followed him to make sure he was paying attention. He was. In between measuring spoonfuls of instant and filling the kettle.

"You know he invented those words, 'whisk' and 'whiff' and a lot of others. Then again in *Dr. Faustus* it was Faustus, in his opening soliloquy, who first delivered Hamlet's most famous line: *'to be or not to be.'* Except that Faustus said it in Greek: *on cai me on*."

He blinked. "Really?"

She went on: "The Stratfordians make a big deal out of how Shakespeare 'must have' read Ovid. But Marlowe not only translated Ovid's *Amores* and *Elegies* but also the first book of Lucan's *Pharsalia* from Latin."

Jake reminded her that he had discovered that same fact just that morning.

"That's my point. But check out the rest of it:

> *'About my head be quivering myrtle wound, And in sad lovers' heads let me be found. The living, not the dead, can envy bite, For after death all men receive their right. Then though death rakes my bones in funereal fire, I'll live, and as he pulls me down mount higher.' "*

She practically threw the book down. "He's talking about living on after you're dead. Two weeks after his so-called murder."

Jake set two cups on the counter and stirred some milk into his. It was low fat. He hated low fat. She ignored hers, pacing the room like a lawyer in court.

"Dad, there is a powerful message in *As You Like It*, that Marlowe is aware of his usurper, and names him. Out of more than thirty-six plays and close to a thousand characters, there is only one character named 'William.' Which, let's face it, is a pretty common name in Britain. And this character is a buffoon, who appears in Act V, Scene I, in an encounter with the prophetic clown, Touchstone. William is stupid, ignorant, and inarticulate. Touchstone derides him accordingly." She read:

> *"For all your writers do consent that ipse is he; now, you are not ipse, for I am he."*

She looked up at him. "This line comes out of nowhere, and it's dripping with significance. 'Ipse' is Latin for 'I, myself.' Marlowe is saying, 'you, William, are not the writer. It is I, *ipse*, who am the writer.' "

Jake nodded, sipped his coffee, resisted the temptation to spit it out, and surreptitiously unwrapped a chocolate bar he'd sequestered in the back of a drawer. "Go on."

"And Hoffman found another clue, again from *As You Like It*, spoken by Touchstone to Audrey:

> *'When a man's verses cannot be understood, nor a man's good wit seconded with the forward child, Understanding, it strikes a man more dead than a great reckoning in a little room.' "*

She looked up at him sharply. "That's about Deptford."

He whistled. "So that's what that grad student Chris was alluding to. He'd read how the Shakespeare scholars dismissed this as the Bard taking a back-handed potshot at his literary predecessor, whom he in no other way ever acknowledged. But for Marlowe to address his own 'demise' it lent an element of ominous subterfuge, subtext, and ever-so-slight mockery of his would-be destroyers." He wrote that thought down in shorthand.

"Dad, *'a great reckoning in a little room'* is about something only Marlowe, Walsingham, and Walsingham's hired guns Poley, Skeres and Frizer could possibly have known about. The details about Deptford were never known to the public, or anyone, until 1925. How would Shakespeare know about the little room? He couldn't."

He thought a moment. "And the same would be true of Edward de Vere. Danby's inquest was buried in the public record 48 hours after the killing, not to be seen again for three hundred years. So, you're right. There was no way Shakespeare could have known about what happened in the tavern at Deptford."

"But the playwright knew because he planned it. *'Ipse. I am he.'* " she spoke with near-reverence. "Hoffman also talks about the parallelism of *Hero and Leander* and *As You Like It*—like, *'Dead shepherd. Now I find thy saw of might, Who ever loved that loved not at first sight?'* 'Cause not only is that an exact repetition of two entire lines of Marlowe's, the second line is placed in quotes. Hoffman was convinced that this was another message from the dead, of Marlowe explicitly quoting himself as a signal to his play's readers that he lives on in his work."

"It could still be Shakespeare, putting Marlowe in quotes." Jake caught himself. Had they suddenly reversed roles?

She shook her head and flipped through the pages again. "He doesn't do it anywhere else in the Canon. Here. Check out some of these other 'Parallelisms.'

> 'MARLOWE: (In Jew of Malta): *These arms of mine shall be thy Sepulchre.*
> SHAKESPEARE: (in Henry VI part II) *These arms of mine shall be thy winding sheet; My heart, sweet boy, shall be thy Sephulchre.*
> MARLOWE: (in *Elegies*, his translation of Ovid): *The moon sleeps with Endymion every day.*
> SHAKESPEARE: (In ***Merchant of Venice***): *Peace ho. The Moon sleeps with Endymion.*
> MARLOWE: (in ***Tamburlaine***): *Holla, ye pampered jades of Asia. What, can ye draw but twenty miles a day?*
> SHAKESPEARE: (in **Henry IV, Part II**): *And hollow pampered jades of Asia, Which cannot go but thirty miles a day.'*

"And so on. There are hundreds of these."

"Hmm," said Jake. "So, he's either recycling his own material or it's blatant plagiarism."

"Or a literal message from the grave. Like Mark Twain!"

So, she had listened to him after all. Either that or gone back and read the Twain essay herself.

His stomach grumbled a gentle dissent over his recent regression to junk food. In penance, he went to the fridge and took out a banana-flavored yogurt. "This yogurt is good. Have you tried this?"

"Only about a thousand times since I was twelve. Unlike you." She shook her head. "I guess Hoffman was just trying to be politic. All of Marlowe's credited works predate Shakespeare's 'first invention,' remember? So, there's no way Marlowe could've plagiarized Shakespeare."

He nodded, slurped a spoonful of yogurt, and looked through his notes.

"I also noticed this morning that after he read 'Shakespeare's' *Richard II* and Marlowe's *Edward II,* Shakespeare scholar J. M. Robertson was so stunned by their similarities, he wrote that Shakespeare must be a quote 'fumbling plagiarist' unquote, if he was supposed to have written this. He said that 'Such absolute duplication of another man's ideas would prove, if anything, that Shakespeare felt himself unequal to the invention of new ones.' "

She looked at him in wonder. "Dad, Hoffman said the same thing. It's all been chronicled."

"And nobody listened."

After eating, Melissa, seeming a bit preoccupied, slipped into the bedroom and made a phone call, keeping her voice low so that Jake, now back on the Internet, wouldn't overhear and worry.

"Hello?" she whispered, "it's me."

"Long time no hear," came the aging voice over the line. "Did you get my message?"

"Yes," she said. "And I have a question for you, sir."

"Go on."

"Can you explain to me why Shakespeare's name is on The Apocrypha?"

There was a moment of silence. "It's as I feared. You are keeping bad company."

"You're saying my father is bad company? Frankly, I'm starting to wonder about you."

"Me? And why, pray tell, this sudden apostasy?"

"Tell me something else, then. Why did Shakespeare plagiarize so much material from Marlowe, and you never felt the need to mention it?"

The line went dead.

Melissa was too tired to think straight, and casting aside a growing unease, she finally succumbed to fatigue and dragged herself to her bed for a long overdue rest.

Jake, who'd already had a little sleep, began his turn reading Hoffman.

He'd just finished the preface when the phone rang. Wary of unexpected calls, he shouted out, "I got it," and grabbed the receiver. "Hello?"

"Mr. Fleming? Henry Blodgett. Are you busy?"

"Not at all. What can I do for you, Henry?"

"Well, now, here's the thing. I plumb forgot about it with the fire and funeral and all, so I neglected to tell you. But the last time Dr. Lewis was in the shop, he gave me a letter, and asked me to open it only if something should happen to him."

Jake sat up. "Really."

"I kept it at my flat for safekeeping, you see, so it wasn't burnt up in the fire. It is pertinent to you, and thought I should read it to you before calling the police."

"I'd appreciate that." He fumbled for his notepad and pen.

"Are you ready?"

"Go ahead."

> *" 'Dear Mr. Blodgett. Thank you for all the help you've given me with my research. However, I must confess to you that there may be someone who has a vested interest in opposing the book I am about to publish, whom I would just as soon avoid. Unfortunately, that may not be*

> *possible, because out of basic courtesy I made the mistake of offering to let him comment on the contents prior to publication, and he took it rather poorly, I'm afraid. And he may be stalking me.' "*

"And you have no idea who this person could be?"

"Afraid not, I'm sorry to say."

Jake took a deep breath. "Is that it?"

"No, there's more. He continues:

> *'Due to my unfamiliarity with matters of security and libel, I dare not say anything more than that at this time but will explain further as to the situation at Oxford when I next see you. Best wishes, Desmond Lewis.' "*

Jake was silent a moment. "And you don't have any idea as to what he means by 'the situation at Oxford?' "

"Sorry. As I said before, Mr. Fleming . . ."

"Right. Thanks for letting me know, Henry. Take care."

Melissa, awakened by the phone, came out of the bedroom rubbing her eyes. "What's up?"

He read her the letter, which he'd copied down in shorthand. Her reaction was startling. Her jaw dropped, then closed again, but he could see that she was troubled.

"What is it?" he asked her. "Do you know something about this?"

She shook her head. But he could tell that she was holding something back, and she seemed disturbed. Finally, Jake suggested they take a break and get some Pakistani food, after trying and failing to reach Sunir once more to tell him the Hoffman book had been located.

"It's pretty clear de Vere was a dead end, maybe even a smokescreen. There must be something else about Oxford," he said, as they put on their coats to go out. "And he did underline it three times."

"One to win, two to show, and three to place," she murmured.

"What?"

"Nothing."

"Just a minute." As they rode the elevator down, he checked his notes, and after a quick flip through the pages, found what he was looking for. He looked up at her.

"Did you ever hear of a William Davenant?"

She pursed her lips. "Vaguely."

"Apparently he claimed to be Shakespeare's illegitimate son."

"Oh, him." She shook her head. "What about him?"

"I don't know. Just that he was also from Oxford, is all. Davenant was the source of the stories about Shakespeare being a horse groom. There may be something more there. He keeps popping up unexpectedly. Also, Dr. Lewis got his degrees there, and Miss Peckham did tell me something about a 'falling out.' Maybe we'd better go up there and take a look."

"But look for what?" From her reaction he sensed she was worried. About something. Or someone? Something or someone related in some way to her work back in Berkeley? Was this Scofield the problem?

He decided to do some homework, as soon as possible.

As they ate a late lunch, Jake fiddled with his chicken curry, lost in thought. The waiter stopped by to see how everything was. Jake assured him the food looked fine. He might even try some, after a while. "You have any yogurt?" he asked.

Melissa glanced up from the book. As she did so, she noticed a well-dressed man with white hair and a jaunty handlebar mustache seated in a darkened booth in the corner behind Jake. Although he appeared engrossed in his meal, she had a strange feeling he'd been watching her. Aside from the mustache, the man bore a striking resemblance to Bob Hoskins.

The man made a discreet call with a cell phone and spoke softly, turning away as he did so. He listened, frowned, and gave the Flemings a look of cautious appraisal. He put his phone away and signaled to the waiter, speaking to him in low tones.

The Flemings finished their meal and walked back to the flat, still in animated conversation about Hoffman's parallelisms. Jake was just unlocking the door when, to his ever-further amazement, Melissa turned to him and touched his forearm. “I’m proud of you, Dad, for being open minded.”

He had to laugh.

London, early afternoon, November

Close by–very close– in a small, elegant flat on Russell Square, the thin man stood in a French window on a private balcony, and stared balefully through the fading light towards the west, past the unseen Elgin Marbles and Rosetta Stone and the British Museum, in the direction of Denmark Street. What is he telling her? He fretted. What mad theory of the late, unlamented Desmond Lewis might he have discovered? Has she gone over to his side? Her recent messages were too cryptic to tell. Had he killed one fiend only to create two, like a Hydra? Then what? And what is this many-headed monster in his own head that won’t let him sleep?

We are not ourselves, he thought,
When nature, being oppress’d,
commands the mind
To suffer with the body.

And what excruciating pain this was, that tormented his mind. How unfair to be so afflicted, then moreover twice betrayed, in a cause so righteous as his. What kind of world was this, that such things could be so? Yet endure he must, and would, until the moment was right.

Let Hercules himself do what he may, the cat will mew and dog will have his day.

Chapter Thirty-Two

The Muse's Springs

London, November

A chill, persistent rain began late that night, driven on a stiff easterly wind from off the North Sea, bringing a cold morning dampness to Jake's spirits, as well as to every cranny and corner of London. People huddled under umbrellas in the sodden glistening streets below, scurrying to and fro with typical British resignation, dodging puddles and impatient taxis, muttering and cursing their respective fates. Jake wrote feverishly, filled the first notebook, and started on the second. Occasionally he paced up and down, reasoning out this point, or that one.

Sunir had been gone for two days now, and he wanted to talk to him about Oxford. Like Hamlet, he felt torn between a sense of compulsion—even obligation—to do something; and the gnawing awareness that he was clueless as to what to do. He didn't want to go rushing off half-cocked, as it were, like the proverbial fool where angels feared to tread. Especially with Melissa to consider, although there was an angel that feared nothing, it seemed.

But Desmond Lewis's letter gnawed at his conscience like sharks on a dying whale.

Melissa slept until late in the afternoon, and once up and about she seemed as edgy as he was. "Why doesn't Sunir at least call?" she fretted.

He'd finished Hoffman and had done enough reading and writing for one day. "Tell you what. Why don't we take the night off and go see a film or something."

"You? A film? Last time we went to a film together I think was Harry Potter."

"Hey, that was good. Maybe there's a sequel."

She laughed and poked his arm. "Maybe just some takeout would do."

Glad to see that he'd apparently cheered her up, at least a little, he nodded happily."Deal."

As Jake placed the order, Melissa had a question. "Dad, at this point what do you really think? About Shakespeare, and Dr. Lewis's quest, and all?"

"I have to admit I'm troubled by the lack of documentation for anything but shady dealings by and for this man. Things like the altered bust in Stratford, changing him from a grain merchant to a scribe, a hundred years after his death. How did they get away with that? And all that Apocrypha, or his lawsuit against one of his borrowers for a few shillings."

"Plus, he was a tax-evader," added Melissa. "You do know about that, right?"

He looked at her sharply. "Shakespeare was a tax evader?"

"You didn't know?"

He shook his head. "I'd remember that."

"I found it in the library. He fled from London back to Stratford to avoid paying taxes on his theater profits. I forget the year. 1598, I think. Just after he started publishing Quartos."

He thought about that. "A tax evader. Huh." He shook his head. "It sure as hell doesn't sound like the sort of thing someone who writes *what a piece of work is man* would do."

"But it does sound a lot like the sort of thing someone who writes *cursed be he that moves my bones* might do."

"Hm. So what about Ben Jonson? All those academics insist that Ben Jonson's eulogy in the First Folio more than settles the fact of Shakespeare as the author. And there it is, all that glowing praise, all those testimonials."

"Yeah, I know. It really bugged Sunir, I could tell."

He stared wistfully into the depths of his empty coffee cup, as if willing it to top itself off. "So, I don't get it. From what I've been reading, wasn't Jonson the man who ridiculed Shakespeare for his entire career, and said that Shakespeare—like his epitaph—'wanted or lacked art'?"

"I don't know. Obviously, we're still missing something here."

"Give me that." Jake commandeered the Hoffman book and they settled into reading.

At about eleven p.m. that evening the phone rang. Both of them stirred uneasily from their respective chairs.

"Should I answer it?" asked Melissa.

Jake hesitated, then before he could respond, Melissa took matters into her own hands, answered, and listened a moment. She motioned quickly to Jake. "It's Dr. Balsavar."

"About time." Jake ran to the bedroom and snatched up the extension. "Sunir!" he exclaimed. "We were worried about you. Are you all right?"

Balsavar's voice sounded weak, and tired. "Yes. I am on a wireless, actually, and the battery is low so I can't talk for long. I have found something. I need you to meet me in one hour at the Lambeth Palace Library. Bring Melissa, but no one else, please."

So, thought Jake. Another piece of the puzzle is about to fall into place. The idea of a clandestine midnight meeting at the ancient London residence of the Archbishop of Canterbury was rather unsettling, to say the least. He hoped Sunir hadn't run afoul of John Whitgift's ghost. That would be a nasty piece of work.

"Isn't it closed now?" he asked, checking his watch, then realizing the absurdity of even wondering.

"Yes, but I am still inside. Come to the river entrance and knock twice. I must go now."

"Sunir, wait–" cried Melissa, but the line crackled, then went dead.

Chapter Thirty-Three

Perdition Catch My Soul

London, 11:30 p.m., November

"Stop here." Melissa ordered the driver, as the taxi reached the south end of the Lambeth Bridge. The ancient Archbishop's bastion loomed against the night sky up ahead, just east of Waterloo Station. Jake quickly paid, and they clambered out onto the roadway, much to the displeasure of the driver.

"He probably thinks we're going to jump in the river," whispered Melissa.

Following her instinctive sense of direction, she led the way through the gloom along Lambeth Palace Road and cut across the grounds of the darkened Museum of Garden History towards the adjacent castle, which lay black and menacing before them. The giddy London Eye leered at them from the distance, a half mile or so east along the river. It had closed down for the night.

Jake wondered if the current Archbishop was in residence. He wondered what the esteemed churchman would think of a pair of Yankees trespassing in his palace. He didn't dare think about what the friars, or whoever was in charge, would make of Sunir if they caught him. Get a grip, Jake, he scolded himself.

Melissa found the door. There was a weak 60-watt bulb above it, and the path was overgrown with weeds. A cold wind came slicing across the river like a sushi knife, making his bones ache. He reached up to knock.

"Two times," Melissa reminded him.

"You sure it wasn't three?"

She sighed, impatiently. He obeyed. The sound echoed into the depths. Nothing.

"Let me," she said, edging him aside. She reached up and pounded the door with her fist. Jake winced, fearing the entire Metropolitan London Police force–out in strength just across the river around Whitehall and Parliament on terror patrol–would hear them and come charging.

They heard a shuffling sound on the other side of the heavy door, then the bolt slid back. The latch eased up with a sharp click, and the ancient portal creaked slowly ajar.

"Sunir?" She asked, in a low voice. A short, dark, erect figure stood in the doorway, profiled against the dim light in the entryway behind him.

"Come in, come in, quickly." Sunir whispered impatiently. They hustled inside and he closed the door, as quietly as possible. Beckoning furtively, he ushered them to a steep, narrow flight of stairs that led down into what Jake assumed was the castle keep. He wondered if the Church of England had church police, like the Vatican. He hoped not. Those Swiss guys might be tougher than they looked, what with those blunderbusses and all.

Melissa seemed taken aback by Sunir's chilly greeting, and a quick glance at her made Jake wonder if she feared he was leading them to a dungeon or a torture chamber. He had fewer such qualms, although some of those archbishops–John Whitgift, for example–were pretty Augean characters, he knew. Still, this was the 21rst Century. Wasn't it? From the environs you couldn't tell.

Sunir looked and sounded to Jake like he was nearing collapse.

"Have you been here the whole time since I saw you last?" Melissa asked him. Sunir didn't respond.

"We should've brought him some food," she muttered, to her father.

At the bottom of what Jake counted as two flights of steps, Sunir led them along a stone corridor to a large, dark oaken door, reinforced with melanized bronze bracing. He pressed his ear against it for a moment, listening carefully. He rapped on it: two times. The door opened.

A dour-looking brown robed monk stood before them. "Come in, come in," he said, furtively. He ushered them into a large, dimly lit room entirely filled with row upon row of book stacks, boxes, piles of manuscripts, and several microfiche machines.

"Brother Michael, meet my friends Jake Fleming, and his daughter Melissa."

The monk nodded distractedly, barely restraining a certain degree of disapproval.

"This is the Archive Room, actually," Sunir told them. "Basically, a storage space. But this is where I found them, thanks to Brother Michael."

"Found what?" asked Melissa, looking around in apprehension.

"The Anthony Bacon Papers." Sunir spoke in an awed tone, which didn't reassure Jake at all.

Brother Michael turned and silently led the way among the racks and stacks to a battered, ancient wooden table with a banker's lamp, illuminating a substantial collection of ancient leather-bound volumes, yellowed manuscripts, and scattered documents.

"What are those?" asked Melissa, echoing Sunir's low voice.

"Evidence," he exclaimed softly. He gestured towards an antique footlocker-sized brass-bound wooden trunk, on the floor next to the table. The trunk alone was probably worth a bundle, thought Jake.

"They were kept in this trunk, which was first opened two hundred and fifty years ago, then but twice since. Brother Michael has been in charge of the archives, and I convinced him to let me have a look at the possessions of Monsieur Le Doux. I had read of them years ago, but no one paid much attention, so I had to see for myself."

Melissa stared at the erudite-looking collection before them, with a wary look.

"Monsieur Le Who?" she asked, testily.

Sunir was clearly approaching his limits of endurance. Jake began to suspect that he had been in this room for the entire time—other than to come to their apartment yesterday morning—since their reenactment of the Marlowe "killing" on Friday night two days and nights ago. He settled onto a rickety wooden chair that Brother Michael resignedly provided. Melissa perched onto another, and the Pakistani professor began to explain.

"Let me start at the beginning. In 1592, Anthony Bacon, who was younger brother of Sir Francis Bacon and one of Lord Burghley's nephews, returned to England from many years of foreign service as a master spy on behalf of Francis Walsingham and the Queen. Walsingham, as you know, was long the protector of the Queen and director of her intelligence service until he died in 1590, and a capable replacement was urgently needed. So, Bacon took the job and aligned himself in 1593 with Robert Devereaux, the 2nd Earl of Essex, who was on the rise at the time."

"Memorable year, that one," mumbled Melissa.

"Is this the same Essex that the people of Stratford were urging to do something about Shakespeare and the Maltsters for illegal hoarding?" asked Melissa, once again surprising her father.

"Illegal hoarding?" Jake stared at her.

"Later," she hissed.

"The very one," continued Sunir. "And also the same man who got in trouble with the Queen by staging *Richard II*, during the Irish Rebellion."

"Wasn't *Richard II* the play that Chambers said bore an uncanny resemblance to Marlowe's *Edward II*?" asked Jake.

"Yes, that is correct." Sunir continued: "Since Christopher Marlowe had also served the Queen under Francis Walsingham at Rheims, it was natural that Marlowe and Bacon should meet and work together." He looked around. "They met in this castle, possibly in this very room."

Brother Michael shrugged, as though everyone knew that.

"Was this before or after his death?" Asked Melissa, ironically. Jake looked at her sharply, wondering if Sunir somehow brought out the contrarian in her. He had seemed rather detached.

Sunir ignored her, fully focused on the subject at hand. "Marlowe, once forced into exile, would have desperate need for a cover of his own, to maintain contact with his English friends and colleagues, and more importantly, the London theater. Anthony Bacon, his own health failing, was still embroiled in desperate intrigue throughout the Continent, and would have great need of a multilingual operative of Marlowe's experience and caliber. Bacon had no reason to support the charges against Marlowe put forth by a reactionary like Archbishop Whitgift. Sorry, Brother Michael," he said, with an apologetic glance at the clergyman.

Brother Michael shrugged. "It doesn't matter," he said. "Its bygones, rest his soul."

"Furthermore," continued Sunir, "Bacon was connected to the Walsinghams. In 1590 Essex had just married Francis Walsingham's sister, who was also the widow of Marlowe's idol, Sir Philip Sidney, the great poet nobleman."

"Brother of Mary, Countess of Pembroke," Melissa exclaimed, her interest piqued.

"Right. So, in the 1750s a scholar named Thomas Birch came across this extraordinary cache of documents–the papers of Sir Anthony Bacon. These papers revealed a fascinating operative, an intelligence agent by the name of Monsieur Le Doux."

Melissa let out a sharp laugh. "Another real life James Bond?"

"Exactly. This agent, who had no first name, was supposedly 'a French gentleman,' yet he had all the earmarks of an Englishman. Take a look at this 'French gentleman.' " He glanced around as if expecting a ghost to appear at any moment. Then, when none did, he gingerly picked up a folio of bound documents. "He obviously had some powerful backers. For one thing he seems to have had the full support and authority of Essex, who issued an extraordinary passport in January of 1595 with the following commandment and I quote: *'to All Mayors, Sheriffs, Bailiffs, Constables, Headboroughs, also to all Customers, Comptrollers, Searchers and other of Her Majesty's officers to whom it may appertain and to every one of them.' "*

He turned to the friar. "Brother Michael, could we see that passport, please?"

Very carefully, Brother Michael extracted a yellowed parchment in a clear plastic cover from the folio and held it up for a moment before laying it flat on the table. Sunir leaned over it, almost protectively. He began to read:

"Whereas the bearer of proof Monsr Le Doux a French gentleman being repaired into England for the dispatch of some necessary business intending now presently to return into Germany by the low Countries: These are to will and require you and every one of you to whom it may appertain that you permit and suffer him quietly to pass and to embark himself with his servant in any of Her Majesty's port(s) without any of your lette, stay, molestation or hindrance whereof you

must not fail. And this shall be your sufficient warrant in that behalf. At London the 10 of February 1595. Essex."

The room was silent. Jake could almost hear the earth shifting.

"This means that Essex, who was now the most powerful man in England, had given Le Doux carte blanche to enter and leave the country at will, with specific orders not to be stopped or questioned, at the height of a period of maximum international suspicion, crisis and intrigue."

Jake, in all his years as a foreign correspondent and investigative journalist, had never heard of such a thing. Like so much else in the Lewis files, as he was calling them, it was unprecedented. "Did Lewis know about this?" he asked, suddenly.

"I don't know. I assume so."

Melissa's jaw dropped. "Are you saying that this Le Doux was Christopher Marlowe?"

"Yes. And you will note the date was 1595. Two years after Deptford." Sunir was visibly savoring the moment despite his fatigue. "It was the perfect setup: Marlowe could continue to serve his benefactors with the relative safety of a secret identity, while at the same time being allowed to continue with his play writing. Or he could die on the rack. Which would you choose?"

"Let me think," said Jake.

"Remember this: having fled the country into exile, Marlowe would have had no use for British credentials or anything revealing his true identity. In fact, any such I.D. would be fatal. But as Monsieur Le Doux, he had the perfect means to get access to his homeland, maintain his contacts with the Walsinghams, and continue producing the greatest plays London had ever seen."

"Essex was tight with the Walsinghams," admitted Melissa, grudgingly.

"But what makes you so sure Le Doux was Marlowe?" asked Jake.

"For one thing, Le Doux is a Huguenot name, found in England only in Canterbury. There were no surviving Le Douxes in France by that time."

"Are you sure?" asked Jake. "That's pretty circumstantial, even so."

"He's saying this goes back to the Huguenot immigrants that came to Canterbury after the St. Bartholomew massacres," noted Melissa.

"That's the point. The assuming of that name was anything but a coincidence. Le Doux was an avid reader and scholar. He traveled with a personal library of fifty-six books. A literal treasure trove." He gestured at the trunk. "Monsieur Le Doux, it seems, clearly had a much greater love for literature than our itinerant Bard, even though he had no visible means of support, no apparent home in which to keep his possessions, and had to carry them with him in that trunk as he traveled. Some of these he would have needed as an espionage agent. But his collection went far beyond that. Now listen to some of the titles:

Junius' Lexicon of 7 languages
Nomenclature of four languages
Italian/French dictionary
Tuscan and Castillian vocabularies
Rules of grammar (Spanish)
Giambullari's language of Florence

"Interesting, but I don't get it," said Jake.

But Melissa caught her breath. "Dad." she whispered, in awe. "A French dictionary, but not an English one. Why would a 'French' spy, working for the English, need a French dictionary, instead of an English one?"

"Exactly!" exclaimed Sunir. "He was a highly literate Englishman, entering England with French documents. The seven languages in the Lexicon were Latin, Greek, German, Dutch, French, Italian and Spanish. Monsieur Le Doux was therefore a serious scholar of all the major European languages except English. Which he obviously already knew, since as Melissa said, he didn't need an English dictionary. He worked for an English employer and was taking pains to learn all those other languages." Sunir looked solemn and continued: "Most of England's spies were little more than thugs, like Poley and Frizer. There was only one who fit the bill for the highly literate Le Doux, and that was Marlowe."

"Apart from the alphabet book, what's the significance of the rest of them?" Jake wanted to know, still skeptical.

"The listing of the Giambullari book indicates he spent time in Florence. This is within easy reach of Venice, Padua, and Verona."

"The settings for the Italian plays," exclaimed Melissa, a little too loudly. Brother Michael scowled and put his finger to his lips, like the librarian he was.

"Exactly. These books were from and about Italy. Shakespeare never ventured out of England. But the true author wrote seven plays strongly influenced by the environs and writers of Northern Italy."

Melissa cut in, and counted them off: *"Romeo and Juliet, The Merchant of Venice, Measure for Measure, All's Well that Ends Well, Othello, Twelfth Night,* and, um, *Much Ado About Nothing."*

"Right. And there are four other plays reflecting personal knowledge of the life, geography and customs of that same region: *The Taming of the Shrew, As You Like It, The Winter's Tale*, and *Cymbeline*."

"OK, I see your point," conceded Jake. "But an author doesn't need to spend a lot of time in Italy to know some of the details. I've never been to Tuscany, but I'd recognize it in a heartbeat."

"Maybe. From books. Or films. But Shake-scene had no way of knowing about Italy. Kit Marlowe was known to have traveled in Europe. He had a proven mastery of Latin and showed a fascination for Roman history in his early plays. Where else would a true Renaissance Man be drawn to more than Italy? He knew Giordano Bruno from Raleigh's School of Night. He knew the Duke of Orsino, who may have been his protector."

"He was in *The Twelfth Night*," commented Melissa, barely constraining her excitement.

"Yes. Among Le Doux's other possessions are an English bible and an assortment of religious books. Again, note: an English bible, not a French one. This is particularly ironic, since Marlowe was condemned for being an atheist, despite having been a divinity student at Cambridge."

"Yes, we were wondering about that too," said Melissa.

"Exactly," nodded Sunir. "Even according to *The Encyclopedia Brittanica*, Christopher Marlowe was 'astonishingly learned for a man who died at 29,' who 'could understand that a Muslim could honor Christ' as in *Tamburlaine*, and that a man could take 'the whole universe into his compass' like in *Dr. Faustus*. Then the Brittanica editors went on to say, 'his understanding of theology is masterly.' Which deserves one more recollection of Shakespeare's Will. He who did not own a book, also did not own a bible."

Sunir gestured at the stack of books on the table. "Now here's the clincher. Almost every one of the books in the possession of Monsieur Le Doux was a key reference or basis for one of the plays in the Shakespeare Canon." As Sunir named them, Brother Michael indicated each volume, but did not touch them. "Start with this: Plautus. According to the Shakespeare Encyclopedia: 'The plays of Shakespeare show Plautine elements down to the very end of his literary activity. The plot for *The Comedy of Errors* as well as some plot elements of *The Merchant of Venice, Twelfth Night* and *The Merry Wives of Windsor* all indicate knowledge of the works of Plautus.'

"Next comes Terence. *Twelfth Night* and *A Midsummer Night's Dream* each owes plot lines to Terence's *Andria*. Right there," he pointed. "Poet John Davies once addressed Shakespeare as 'Our English Terence.' "

Brother Michael nodded, in agreement.

"There's more. *The History of Ethiopia* was research for *Othello*. *Caesar's Commentaries* were well known to anyone who spoke Latin. *Henry VI, Part II*, was full of references to Marlowe's homeland district, Kent. And Caesar himself wrote about it: *'Kent, in the Commentaries Caesar writ, Is term'd the civil'st place of all this isle.'* That's in Act IV scene 7 lines 59-60. Yet there is no mention, anywhere in the Canon, of either Stratford-Upon-Avon or Shake-scene's home county of Warwickshire."

Again, a knowing nod from Brother Michael.

"Monsieur Le Doux had all these resource materials on a pack animal, while Shakespeare had none at all in his large house. It goes on and on. All of it is here: Tasso, Montaigne, Wecker, these are the reference materials and the bases for the Shakespeare Canon."

Jake was beginning to feel more like a juror than a journalist, feeling overwhelmed by the preponderance of evidence. "So, it was Le Doux who wrote the Plays," he said, half-jokingly.

"Which would mean," said Melissa, "that Kit could easily have lived on in Italy another thirty years or more."

“Can you get copies of these? We will need documentation of these items, at least.”

“Yes. I will do that.”

They sat in silent contemplation for a moment. Jake glanced at his watch. It was close to one a.m. “Meanwhile, maybe,” he said, “we should get you home, my friend, and–”

Suddenly there was a thumping noise somewhere above, followed by the sound of fast, heavy footsteps, rapidly approaching. Brother Michael sprang to his feet.

“It’s as I feared,” he exclaimed.

“What is it?” Jake demanded. Melissa looked up at the ceiling in alarm.

“We have been detected, somehow. Perhaps your entry tripped a silent alarm I did not know about. You must leave at once.”

Not about to argue, they grabbed their notes and rushed for the door, turning towards the stairs. But whoever was coming was coming from that direction. “Damn.” shouted Jake. “We’re cut off.”

“This way,” cried Brother Michael. “There’s another way out.”

They followed him at a run, having no other choice. Sunir began to lag. Obviously weakened from his two-day bender among the archives, his exhaustion was taking its toll at last. Finally, he stopped and doubled over, gasping.

“You go on,” he panted. “I’ll catch up.”

“No way.” cried Melissa, seizing his arm. “We’ll help you.”

“Don’t!” he shouted, pushing her away. “You go. There is no time.”

Brother Michael stopped at a doorway at the end of the corridor, looking increasingly alarmed. “Hurry!” he cried.

The heavy footfalls stormed down the last flight of stairs at the far end of the hall, from where they’d just come. Jake ran back and grabbed Melissa with one hand and pulled Sunir up by the arm with the other. “Come on,” he said. “You can make it.”

Melissa tugged with all her strength, but Sunir wasn’t helping. He started dragging his feet and pulled back. “No.” He cried out. “It’s no use. You go on and tell the others.”

“What others?” asked Jake, in exasperation.

"Whoever will listen." He gasped. "I'll catch up later. I promise."

They were interrupted by an authoritative shout from behind them. "You! Stop!"

Brother Michael ducked low, hurried back to them, seized Melissa's hand in a powerful grip, and literally dragged the threesome towards the room at the far end of the hall.

A sharp sound reverberated through the stone corridor that Jake had not heard from close range since his days in Beirut. It was a sound he had never hoped to hear again: a gunshot, followed swiftly by two more.

"Stop it!" Jake shouted at their pursuers, in outrage. "What the hell are you doing? I'm an American journalist, God damn it!" He reached for his credentials. More shots rang out.

"Dad, they don't believe you! Maybe they think we're terrorists."

"They're the ones shooting!" More shots, as if in confirmation. That was enough. "Let's go! Run!"

Another shot rang out, and Jake felt Sunir jerk, then slump under his arm like dead weight. It happened so suddenly he lost his grip on the Asian, who collapsed hard onto the cold stone floor. A pool of dark red ebbed from beneath his jacket.

"Sunir." Melissa cried out. She tried to go back for him, but Brother Michael was pulling on one arm while Jake held on to her other one.

"I've been hit," gasped Sunir. "Leave me. You must go on. Hurry."

Brother Michael crossed himself and obeyed. Melissa hesitated a long, anguished moment, then raced after him, followed reluctantly by Jake. The monk led them to a heavy door at the end of the corridor, hurried them inside, and slammed the heavy metal bolt home behind them. "That'll hold them," he said, grimly. "At least for a while."

"Now what do we do?" Melissa asked in bewilderment, looking around. They were in some kind of service area, that led to a loading platform at the rear basement of the palace. The police were already pounding hard on the door. Their friend was down. They were being hunted and shot at like terrorists. It was almost too much to believe, what was happening. Yet it was.

Brother Michael maintained his remarkable calm, however, and quickly led them to an unmarked lorry–evidently the palace delivery truck–backed up to the platform. No police were in sight.

"Quick, get in the back!" Ordered the monk. As they scrambled onto the ramp into the back of the truck, he closed the overhead door, jumped down and ran around to the driver's cab. Moments later they felt a shift in weight, heard the cab door open and slam shut, then the sound of the motor starting up. The truck vibrated noisily, then lurched forward with a clattering of metal sounds. As they tore out onto Lambeth Palace Road past a startled palace guard, Brother Michael deftly merged into the southbound traffic and sped across Kensington Road towards the Imperial War Museum.

"Melissa," Jake called out. "Are you all right?"

"I'm good," she shouted back. "Except I can't see. And it stinks in here."

"Irrefutable proof that monks are human. Hang on, your eyes will adjust in a moment."

He reached out and felt racks of robes on heavy hangers, judging from their aroma fully ripe and bound for the cleaners.

"I hope Sunir is all right," said Melissa, nearby, trying not to breathe.

His pulse returned gradually to normal and he calmed down after they had put several blocks between themselves and the palace.

"Dad, if he's hurt bad–"

"Don't go there. He'll be all right. It was probably only a flesh wound. They'll take him to the hospital. They have to. He's committed no crime."

"We know of," she mumbled, almost to herself.

"You know, there's something *deja vu* about this." Jake couldn't quite place it, but it was there, just out of reach in the back of his mind. Luckily, he still had his notebooks in his coat pocket.

"Not to me there isn't."

"Melissa," he said. "There is no turning back. We are committed now to see this thing through."

"But when, how, what, to where?" She demanded, tearfully. "Maybe that creep in the mask was just bluffing. But now it's pretty clear they want to kill us."

"Stop it. We still don't know that for sure. Maybe someone had bad information, the cops thought we were escaping artifact thieves or something like that. Those trunks, those books, that collection was extremely valuable, I'm sure. That could be all it was. They thought we were going to steal the Bacon Papers, or some art treasure."

"I don't think so," said Melissa with a sigh. "Do you really believe that?"

Jake reached out and touched her shoulder–all he could do at the moment–as they lurched along Westminster Bridge Road. "I don't know," he admitted. The truck made a sudden turn, and they nearly fell over into a pile of robes. It made another turn, then slowed, brakes squealing, and came to a stop. The rear gate of the truck swung open, and Brother Michael stood below staring up at them, his face a mask of inscrutability.

"End of the line," he said. "Everybody out."

"Thank you so much," breathed Melissa, with a gasp and a quick hug. "You are amazing."

"No worries," he said, with a dour expression. "I have been aware for many years that a great injustice occurred in Elizabeth's time. And it is not too late, in the eyes of God, to make things right. Sunir said Dr. Lewis had tried, and now perhaps you will try. Kit Marlowe was not always a man of virtue, perhaps, but his name does deserve restoration. I will do what I can."

Jake shook his hand and glanced back over his shoulder. They could hear sirens in the distance, heading their way. There was a sudden rumbling noise and Jake looked up towards the source. Brother Michael had brought them to an elevated underground station. A train was just entering the platform overhead. "Go!" The friar urged them on. "Hurry, it's the last train." They ran. He watched them for a moment, then turned away and disappeared from view as they reached the platform. They had to jump the turnstile; there was no time to buy tickets.

" 'Ay, you!" a cockney voice shouted after them. Hell, thought Jake as they ran. We're already fugitives anyway, we might as well be scofflaws too.

Father and daughter pushed their way through the meager crowd on the platform and managed to lose the furious station attendant by wedging their way past the few exiting passengers and onto the train. The doors closed. They were safe.

For now, thought Jake.

Melissa leaned against her father and looked up at him with angry eyes. “Dad,” she said, sounding like a lawyer-turned-warrior. “They can’t get away with this.” She’d found a new role and was ready to play it.

“They already have gotten away with it for four centuries. You’d be amazed what people get away with. Just read the papers.”

“So, what are we going to do?”

“Fight back,” he said.

Chapter Thirty-Four

An Improbable Fiction

London, 2:26 a.m.

Ever watchful for pursuit, the Flemings got off at the next stop—Waterloo Station—and caught the last connecting train to Trafalgar, unimpeded except by renewed rainfall. From there they edged through the late-night revelers and slogged wearily back towards Denmark Street, soaked, exhausted, heartsick and apprehensive.

"I don't think anyone followed us," Melissa said, looking back. "They didn't know who we were, and I don't think Sunir will tell them, assuming he's all right."

"That's a big assumption." Sunir hadn't looked all right to Jake, but he didn't want to worry her even more. "And chances are they have already staked out our building, if we are really subjects of interest."

She stopped. "So, what should we do?"

"Go home and get some sleep." No one challenged them along the way, and they made it safely back to the flat, where Melissa collapsed on the sofa and pulled a pillow over her head. Meanwhile, Jake began to call the area hospitals listed in the phone book to see if a Sunir Balsavar had been admitted. He had to be in one of them. On the other hand, there were dozens of hospitals in London, and he quickly realized he wouldn't get that kind of information anyway, at least not this soon.

Calling the police wasn't an option either. For one thing, they could hardly own up to having been witnesses to a shooting while trespassing at Lambeth Palace in the middle of the night. For another thing, Jake had a new worry: their flat might be bugged already, and even if not, he didn't want to risk being traced. If the London Metropolitan Police had in fact been called upon to silence a latter-day cultural and economic subversive, as Balsavar might well be considered to be, it was just a matter of time before they would come looking for him, instead. And now Melissa, as well. It was all his fault, as she would surely remind him before it was over.

They both resisted the urge to collapse back in their respective beds and sleep, at least in Melissa's case in the faint hope that this would all turn out to be a nightmare. But there was no fighting the fatigue they both felt. In any case, there was little to be done until morning.

"I'm afraid to sit down," said Melissa, wearily, a princess once more. "I'm afraid I'll fall instantly asleep for a hundred years and miss the prince and the end of the world and everything."

"You wouldn't want to miss that." Jake fought to stay awake, but it was a losing cause. He struggled with increasingly declining energy and finally gave in and collapsed on the sofa, while Melissa stumbled off to the bedroom. His eyes closed and all became darkness and peace.

London, morning, November

"Dad?" he heard her voice, faintly, a thousand miles away. It was morning; a harsh, cold sunlight slanting in between the closed blinds. The phone was ringing, shattering his repose. Melissa was already up and picked up the receiver. "Hello?" Jake sat up and looked at her, askance. "Yes, I'm fine." She listened a moment. "Hang on a sec'." She pressed the mute button. "It's Chris Braithwaite. Sunir missed class this morning and he wonders if we've seen him. What should I tell him?"

Jake sat upright. "What?"

"Dad, you've been asleep for like, a week. It's Monday morning."

It all came rushing back, and he scrambled to his feet. "Jesus, why didn't you wake me? Don't mention Lambeth or the shooting. Just tell him we don't know anything."

She nodded and pressed the button. "Sorry, Chris. I'll let you know if we hear anything, OK?" She hung up.

Jake struggled to get his bearings.

"So, there's been no news in my absence amongst the Morpheans?"

She shook her head. "Nothing."

"I hate to say this," said Jake, checking the time, "but it's been long enough they should know. Maybe we'd better call the morgue."

Her eyes widened. "Oh God. Dad."

Jake opened the fridge and winced at the scant offerings. "Well, it is the one place they would take him if he, er,—"

She glared. "If he's dead, you mean?"

"Let's hope not. But much as I hate to say so, he looked pretty bad." He re-closed the fridge, avoiding her accusing look.

"Dad! My God, the morgue?"

"Some government offices might be open now," he insisted, as he looked up the number in the directory, and placed the call. "It's almost 8:30."

Weaving his way through the maze of telephone bureaucracy to find an actual person in the coroner's office who might actually know something was predictably frustrating. "I'm looking for a missing person and was wondering if you have someone by that name, or who might fit the description," he said, when someone finally came on the line. He was put on hold, then another, crisper, older female voice came on. She asked his business, and he told her he was an American reporter, checking on a report that someone may have been shot at Lambeth Palace. He didn't mention the police.

"We'll need more information, sir," he was brusquely informed.

"Yes, of course. He's an Asian male, Pakistani to be exact, around mid-forties. The name is Sunir Balsavar, and he is a professor of physics at London University. It would've been around one a.m. this morning."

"One moment, sir, I'll check the logs." She put him on hold for what seemed like an hour, during which he put on water for instant coffee, all there was left. The water was already boiling when she finally returned. "Hello, sir? May I ask who's calling?"

He hung up the phone immediately, fearing it was already too late. He'd been on hold long enough that if they were in collusion with the police–and why wouldn't they be?–they would have had enough time to trace his call and send a police car to intercept them.

"Melissa." he called, urgently. "Get your things. We have to leave, now."

"Why? What happened?"

"I'll tell you on the way, let's go, now."

He thought he heard a distant siren; but then, sirens were commonplace in the city–any city. Quickly turning off the stove, he grabbed his wallet, valise, notebooks, coat, and keys, and hustled Melissa out the door still clutching her coat and valise as they ran towards the elevator. She got there first and reached for the button, but at that moment the elevator emitted a ding and the lights indicated it was about to stop at their floor.

"This way. Take the stairs." They spun and raced for the emergency stairwell.

"Wait." gasped Melissa, as they pounded down the stairs. "What's going on?"

"They may have traced the call. My fault."

"Shit."

When they reached ground level, Jake checked the lobby entry for the sound of voices or activity. He opened the door cautiously. Fred the doorman was out on the sidewalk talking to someone in a black car at the curb. He couldn't see who because whoever it was, was blocked by the door frame.

"Take the back way," he said, keeping his voice low. "They may be waiting for us out front."

She looked alarmed but didn't argue. After all, this had become practically routine.

They slipped out through the service entrance into the alleyway, which was now familiar territory, and broke into a run, nearly toppling the weaving homeless drunk who occupied the alley entrance.

The drunk shouted threats and epithets after them as they emerged onto Charing Cross Road and were swept up into the morning traffic. They ducked into the nearest coffee shop and took the last remaining table, near the back. Watching the door, Melissa ordered a full English Breakfast of eggs, ham, bacon, and biscuits. Jake just wanted coffee. He'd been running on empty for days and had no appetite. But Melissa insisted he eat something, "preferably something non-acidic, for God's sake, Dad."

The coffee shop didn't have yogurt. He compromised and ordered oatmeal, which never tasted better, and coffee, which never tasted worse, but no matter.

Melissa was in a mood to talk. "Dad, do you remember I mentioned the Shakespeare Foundation might be behind all this?"

"Behind what?"

"Dr. Lewis disappearing. Us being followed. And now Sunir . . ."

"You mentioned it. But you didn't say why, or where you got that little tidbit, so I haven't given it much thought."

She poked at her eggs. "Maybe you should."

He sipped his coffee, winced, and put it down. "Look, despite what you might think, I'm not much of a conspiracy theorist. If the Lambeth security cops thought we were thieves, I can see them calling the police. Maybe they were just trigger happy, like back home."

She shook her head. "I don't think so. Besides, aren't the English police prohibited from carrying guns?"

"Good point." Melissa had still not told Jake about her contact in London, much less the latest warning message, and was thinking maybe the time had come. She wasn't sure she could trust the man anymore; besides which, she was beginning to harbor suspicions that he might know more than he was saying about Desmond Lewis.

Jake stirred his coffee, lost in thought for a time, then something dawned on him. "We need to pay someone a visit."

She looked alarmed. "Who?"

"Diana Parker. Chair*person* of the English Department at London University," he said. "I think she owes us some answers."

Melissa nodded, thoughtfully. "She may also know something about The Foundation. If there is a vested interest trying to stop us, maybe it's the same ones who stopped Dr. Lewis." At least that's what her contact had told her.

Jake was skeptical. "OK, we'll ask her about that as well," he conceded. They finished their coffee, paid the bill, and walked to the campus.

They were in luck. Diana Parker was in her office and more than a little surprised to see the two bedraggled Americans come barging in.

"Well, hello there," she said, nearly spilling her tea. "If it isn't the American journalist and his daughter, the wayward actor and scholar. Been out on another bender?"

Jake ignored the barb. “You do know that your professor Desmond Lewis was murdered?” he said, bluntly.

Diana’s firm glare faltered, then she shook her head virulently. “The police said it was a suicide.”

“Did they tell you about the break-ins and ransacking of Lewis’s office and apartment?”

Her eyes widened. “No one told me about that,” she admitted. “I knew they’d sealed off his office, but they said it was routine.”

“Yeah, right,” muttered Melissa.

“So, what am I expected to do or say about this?” asked Diana, defensively.

Jake told her about the meeting with Dr. Balsavar, without going into detail about the Bacon Papers or purpose of the meeting. Melissa picked up the baton and told her about the cops, the escape, and the shooting.

Diana looked dubious. “That just does not sound like the London Police. Your Miami police or L. A. police, maybe. But not ours.”

Jake tilted his head. “What are you saying? That it didn’t happen?”

“I didn’t say that. What I’m saying is I don’t think it happened the way you describe it.”

“Excuse me, but I know what I saw,” said Melissa. “They were police, in uniform, and they shot our friend. Your colleague. We were there.”

“Are you absolutely sure they weren’t private security? Or possibly even impostors?”

“Impostors?” Jake was incredulous. “Are you serious?”

“Just a moment.” Diana made a phone call, spoke in low tones for a minute, then listened. They fidgeted impatiently. Finally, she hung up and turned back to them. “I just called the Library Dean at Lambeth Palace. He and I were colleagues back in graduate school. He denied any shootings took place there, or any other incident. Although,” and here she paused, momentarily, “he did acknowledge that there was some sort of ruckus in the vicinity last night.”

“Ruckus?” repeated Jake, incredulously.

“ ‘In the vicinity?’ ” Melissa’s outrage was palpable. “We were inside the building.”

Jake motioned for her to calm down and shook his head. "Maybe they were rent-a-cops. They have less training and fewer constraints than public servants. They use them all over, in the States. They're privatizing everything, these days."

"But if so, wouldn't the Palace Guard know about them?" Melissa pointed out.

"And why would they deny that anything happened?" Diana wanted to know.

"You tell us," said Jake.

"What about emergency medical? Wouldn't they have called them?" Diana asked.

"They said nothing happened, ergo why would they call EMS?" Jake pointed out.

"Shit," Melissa muttered.

Jake glared at Diana. "Unless you can make a case that Sunir worked for Al Quaeda and got shot as a spy, I don't think–"

"That isn't impossible, you know," Diana interrupted him.

"I really doubt that," said Jake. "Besides, the man is Hindu, not Muslim."

"All right," Diana acknowledged. "But not everyone can tell the difference. How much do you know about him, anyway?"

Jake had to stop and think about that. "Not much," he admitted. "He seems to be something of a loner."

"Which does fit the terrorist profile," Diana pointed out.

"Well I'll tell you this," said Jake, forcefully. "Even if your hypothesis that Dr. Balsavar was a Hindu terrorist—a first, I might add—Desmond Lewis was no terrorist. And whoever killed him has the same reasons to be a threat to Sunir Balsavar. Furthermore, this is starting to sound a lot like a case of 'blame the victim.' "

"I beg your pardon?" Diana looked stung.

"The point is, instead of looking for terrorists under every cobblestone, I think it's time to take a closer look at your Shakespeare establishment, no offense. They are the ones he was a threat to."

"My Shakespeare establishment?" Her eyes were blazing. "How was he a threat to me? I have a tenured professor's chair at a major university. I have published four books on the applications of blank verse in Shakespeare and on the accuracy of the historical plays–"

"Such as *Richard the Third*?" Melissa asked, pointedly. "Ask her about the Foundation."

Way to pour gasoline on a fire, thought Jake, in exasperation.

"You can blame Thomas More for that," said Diana, blistering. "I have several chapters in my second book addressing that issue, as to Richard being framed. There are plausible arguments on both sides. And yes, I believe he was slandered by the Tudors, and yes, I read *The Daughter of Time.*"

Jake hadn't. "Daughter of Time?" he looked at Melissa, blankly.

"A fifties novel that exonerated Richard. It cited evidence that proved Henry VII murdered Richard in order to seize the throne. Then he killed the boys in the tower and blamed Richard, who had no motive and couldn't defend himself," Melissa explained. "Being dead."

"Like Marlowe?"

"I can't believe you two, I really can't," said Diana.

"All right, sorry," said Jake. "The point is, who would have a motive to silence Dr. Lewis and Dr. Balsavar, if not vested interests in Shakespeare or Stratford?"

"Ask her about the Foundation," repeated Melissa, in a quick aside.

Diana scowled, and shook her head. "Certainly no one from academe, that's too preposterous. And as I was saying, my interests are in the plays themselves, not who wrote them. And I think that can be said for most of my colleagues."

"What about financial interests? Didn't I read that the combined Shakespeare sites are the number two tourist attraction in the UK?"

She shrugged. "You mean the Globe and Stratford? I wouldn't know. But I'd believe it."

Melissa elbowed him, sharply. "All right, all right." He turned back to Diana. "What do you know," he asked her, "about the Shakespeare Foundation?"

Her jaw dropped. "You are talking about the protectors of The Canon," she said. "Are you implying–"

"I'm not implying anything. I'm telling you. Someone invaded our apartment two days ago. And we have received threats, and also got attacked by a mime with a knife."

She gave him a look of disbelief. "A who with a what?"

"Please don't make me repeat it."

"Fine. And when did this supposed attack take place?"

"Last week. And Melissa here seems to have some reason to suspect some possible involvement by this Foundation."

Diana turned to her. "That's quite absurd."

Melissa faced her defiantly. "I was led to believe otherwise. What I hear is they are the literary equivalent to the PETA."

"And what is this PETA?"

"People for the Ethical Treatment of Animals. Forget it. Jesus," she said, resentfully. "Sorry I mentioned it."

Jake gave his daughter a quizzical look. "Well there is something going on," he went on. "Someone also made overt threats to Dr. Balsavar and has been following him. And there's that man who interviewed you. He was following us, too. Maybe it's time to own up and tell us who that guy was and what you know about him."

Diana looked flustered and dropped her notebook. Jake picked it up. "All right," she sighed. "He was canvassing the department." She glanced at Jake and glanced away. "Same as you were. Looking for information about Des Lewis. I talked to him for maybe five minutes before you came in the bar and told him the same thing I told you."

"And he didn't say who he was? Give you a name? Or a card?"

"Yes, he did. But I threw it away without looking at it. I'm sorry."

Melissa didn't believe a word of it.

Jake hesitated, then decided it was time. "Someone also left a note at our apartment and called me two days ago telling me to back off."

Melissa stared at him. "Dad, were you gonna tell me about this?"

"I didn't want to worry you. Besides, I'm not the only one harboring secrets," he added, pointedly. He showed Diana the note. Then Melissa, with an accusing glare at her father, grabbed it and read it for herself. She flushed darkly as she read.

Diana looked bewildered. "Where did all this happen?"

"At the Globe Theater a week ago," he said. "And since then. We've even tried to confront the man like you saw, but he was too quick." He looked her in the eye once more, and noticed, for the first time, a tiny flaw in the corner of one iris. Jake had a terrible weakness for faintly flawed women. It brought out the rescuer in him, as Melissa had once put it in her rebellious teen years. Beverly, too, had been flawed. Flawed enough to die of breast cancer. "Listen, all I know is that as of last night somebody may have considered Dr. Balsavar a serious enough threat to kill him." He heard Melissa gasp at that and quickly appended: "Or try to."

Diana was still having none of it. "I'd buy the spy thing first. The man is a physicist."

"Well what atomic secrets would he have, anyway?" Melissa demanded to know. "Pakistan already has the bomb, so does India, and probably Iran. And North Korea, for that matter. And like I said, I can't believe he would support radical Islam, it's literally against his religion. Besides," she added, "that would not explain Dr. Lewis's disappearance. Or the threats to us. Or his list. Or what he'd want from us."

"What list?"

Father and daughter exchanged glances. Melissa shrugged and let out an audible sigh. Jake reached into his pocket for his small notepad. "Desmond Lewis left a list of keywords or terms pertaining to his missing book. Most, if not all of it points to Shakespeare."

"Let me see this list."

Reluctantly, Jake showed it to her, and she looked it over, dubiously. "Ox as in Oxford, as in de Vere, yes, yes, I see. Herb? Got me. Crow, what's that? Oh yes, Greene, I suppose. M.T., Mark Twain, LWT, Last Will and Testament, we've been over that, Inq?"

"We think it means 'inquest.' Specifically, the official Inquest into the Marlowe murder. It proves he survived Deptford, by the way. Or at least that he couldn't have died there."

"What?"

Jake filled her in, and she shook her head in disbelief. Nor was he surprised when she dismissed the *Venus and Adonis* and Apocrypha entries, as he suspected she would. "Lamb, short for Lambeth, I suppose you're telling me? Although what for I'd love to know. And what's this 'Hoff' item supposed to mean?"

Now it was Melissa's turn to act reluctant, but she dug into her valise and forked over the tattered paperback, *Murder of the Man Who Was Shakespeare*. Diana glanced over it and tossed it aside. "Pop fiction," she said, dismissively. "What's this third one, 'Herb,' supposed to mean?" But even as she spoke, Jake spotted a change in her expression indicating that she did, indeed, have some idea of what it might mean.

"We don't know," said Jake, noting that brief moment of revelation in her eyes. "And I suppose if you did, you wouldn't tell us, would you."

"Thank you so much. I have nothing to hide from you or anyone. But I must say, I have no idea what Dr. Lewis was trying to prove, when all has been hashed and rehashed for so many centuries." Still, Jake could tell that she knew more than she was saying.

"Then why kill him? Because I have no doubt at this point that the reason is right here on this list." She shook her head. Suddenly he remembered something.

"Getting back to Oxford, for a second." He glanced at Melissa. "We're not so sure this was about Edward de Vere."

"What do you mean?" she asked.

"Lewis left a letter before he disappeared. Apparently, he was worried about someone who might be after him, with some kind of connection to Oxford."

Diana frowned. "Well, he studied there, way back when. But more than that I don't know."

"Can you check his CV? It must be on file, right?"

"I suppose, but that's in storage by now, he'd been here a decade. Have you searched online?"

Melissa, in the meantime, had turned pale.

"Meanwhile somebody else working on the same subject has also vanished. I think you're beloved Shakespeare is questionable, Ms. Professor, and maybe you need to take a look at that."

Diana's distress was evident. She seemed at a loss. "They could be two separate cases," she insisted, in a tone that lacked conviction.

"Let me put it another way," said Jake. "If Desmond Lewis, or Sunir Balsavar for that matter, were about to prove that only Christopher Marlowe could have written the Canon, who would have the most to lose?"

"You can never prove that, it's impossible."

"Just for the sake of the argument, please."

She glowered, then thought about it. "We can always revise our books, I suppose, and write new biographies and what have you, so I think Academia would recover, at least in the long run, although certain major egos and careers would certainly suffer hugely. Especially one or two I can think of. Actually, there'd be whole a rash of new books, I'm sure. Which leaves–"

"Stratford," breathed Melissa, softly. "And the Globe."

"The Bard's own company," noted Jake.

"Wouldn't that be ironic," said Melissa, softly.

"That is too absurd for words," insisted Diana. "What do you mean, 'his own company' ?"

"Well, wasn't he a partner in the company?"

"Tell her about the way he got paid three times," said Melissa.

"Not now." He turned back to Diana. "Again, for the sake of the argument. How much money is the Shakespeare name worth, in England? I mean for everything? Tourism, performances, publishing, scholastics, bobble heads, the works. How much are we talking about here?"

She sighed. "I suppose when you add up all those institutions, the theaters, tours, hotels, the restaurants, the museums, the publishers, ancillary products, not to mention certain reputations and people's lecture fees and honorariums, I suppose we are talking about billions of pounds per annum. Not counting the comparable numbers in the U.S., Canada, Australia and so on."

"So, isn't it possible, if not probable, that certain such interests might resort to murder, in order to protect their assets and income?" persisted Jake. "I mean, people have been murdered for their shoes."

Diana gave him a wary look. "Wasn't it Pontius Pilate who said: *'what is truth?'* "

"Truth," murmured Melissa, now deep in thought, *"is the daughter of time."*

"So now we're quoting Bacon?" said Diana, irritably.

"You OK?" Jake asked his own daughter, as they left the department chair's office minutes later. She looked distracted. She forced a smile, shrugged and said, "Fine. I was just thinking about a friend of mine. Where to?"

Chapter Thirty-Five

From Me My Good Name

London, Monday 3:00 p.m., November

By mid-afternoon, after checking the building from the rear and seeing no sign of police or surveillance, they decided to risk a return to Denmark Street, at least for the time being.

For one thing, Jake was anxious to file a new story, and hurried to log in to his secure *Tribune* account. He kept it short and to the point: *Second London Professor Shot*. With the subtext: *Is there a connection?* He kept to the facts as he knew them, while adding the element of intrigue: *"Dr. Sunir Balsavar, a noted physicist, was gunned down early Monday morning in London while doing research at the famed Lambeth Palace Library near Waterloo Station. According to several sources, Lambeth Palace, residence of the Archbishop of Canterbury, had been the subject of a previous still undisclosed investigation by another London University professor, Dr. Desmond Lewis, who was found dead in the Bay Area last week with a single gunshot wound to the head. Lewis had been declared missing after failing to appear for a lecture at the University of California the week before. Dr. Lewis, whose death is still being described as a suicide by the Marin County Sheriff's Office, had authored a number of controversial books in the past and was reportedly about to publish another, which has disappeared. As an added twist, London authorities, as of this writing, deny that any shooting at Lambeth Palace took place, as did a spokesman for the Archbishop. However, several witnesses to the event insist that at least four London policemen took part in a raid at the palace, during which Dr. Balsavar was alleged to have been hit by gunfire at least once and taken into custody. An investigation is continuing."* Just to be sure, he called Reuters to see if they had any comments to report from the police, since he didn't dare call them himself, just now.

"Comments about what?" had been the response.

Late that afternoon, while Melissa was resting, Jake risked an excursion out to the nearest newsstand to buy the evening newspapers. Taking the back way, the homeless drunk recognized and greeted him this time like an old friend and proved himself useful.

"Got your back, Mate," he declared. "They're too bleedin' finicky to come back here. You're comin's and goins' are safe with me."

Jake gave him a pound for his trouble. He also wanted to see Henry Blodgett and tell him what had happened and to be especially careful now.

As he cautiously emerged from the alley onto Charing Cross Road and the front of the bookstore, his heart sank. The storefront was padlocked with an iron gate. Even more ominously, the windows had been painted black, and a sign on the door read, simply: "Closed." Jake felt sick. He considered the possibilities. Blodgett had either had enough, or the skinheads—or someone—had run him out at last. Or worse. He knew he could try to track the man down, but if Blodgett had any sense, which he certainly did, he was in hiding. He hoped so. Probably back in Edinburgh with his wife. Or overseas. Like Marlowe. Jake was going to miss him, he realized.

Fighting back an insidious, creeping sensation of sorrow and foreboding, he hurried to the newsstand, bought the evening papers, and scanned the front sections on his way back to the flat.

"Blodgett's gone," he informed his daughter. He told her about the closed-up bookshop.

"That sucks. I liked him. I hope he's safe on a beach in Tahiti or somewhere."

"On a bookseller's budget? I doubt that." He handed her a newspaper to get started. "Here. Check the second section for anything about a shooting."

"You think it would be in the papers, even though they denied it happened?"

"Reporters have a way of digging under the pavement," he pointed out. "People call them. They get tips. It's worth a shot." He realized his bad pun. "So to speak."

She threw him a look, but nodded, and began scanning the pages.

She found it right away. "Here it is." She held up a story in the B section of *The Evening Sentinel*. " 'Mysterious Gunshots Reported at Lambeth Palace over

Weekend.' So Dr. Parker was right. There's no mention of the police or anyone being shot."

He snatched the paper and scanned the article. According to the story, the palace guard had called the police early Sunday morning to report gunfire "in the vicinity," but they had found nothing. 'In the vicinity' were the exact words Diana had used. And the story also contradicted what the Dean had told her.

Something was very wrong, there was no doubt about it. There was no trace of Sunir Balsavar whatsoever. It was as if the man had never existed. Is that what had happened to Kit Marlowe for the last 400 years? Or Desmond Lewis, for that matter, until the San Francisco Bay gave him up?

Melissa looked stricken. "Jesus. What if he really is dead?"

He winced. "Well, let's not write the man's obituary just yet, all right?"

"But what if they really killed him? We could be next."

Jake looked at her. She was shivering. "Don't go there, Melissa. Not until we know more."

Melissa gazed out the window, and he could almost see one of her inspirations forming in her mind. She would get this faraway look, then frown, and her face would look slightly flushed. Then her eyes would focus sharply, usually on him (or whoever was present) with a look implying that it was all his fault for her not having thought of whatever it was sooner.

"What did you say just now, about an obituary?"

"Just that it's a bit premature to–"

"When Marlowe was presumed dead, even though he had a lot of enemies, everyone had something to say about him, right?"

"What are you getting at?"

"Dad, do you remember, from all the biographical material you've read about Shakespeare, what was said or written about him, when he died?"

Jake raised his eyebrows, seeing where she was going. "You mean in terms of elegy?"

"Elegy, eulogy, obits, remembrances, memorials, what was there besides that stupid grave marker he wrote for himself?"

Elegy. Where was the elegy for William Shakespeare? It was one of those moments when he realized something so obvious, he wanted to slap himself for not having seen it sooner. "Of course." he exclaimed. "Right under our noses." They raced each other to the computer and Melissa, who won, quickly logged on to Google. Shakespeare biographies, she entered, and a long list popped up. She entered 'elegy,' and they watched in fascination as the numbers dropped off sharply.

Elegy was the most common method of tribute and recognition in Elizabethan times, as now, they both knew. They adjourned for supper–a quick sandwich of leftovers from the fridge–then continued on into the evening. Occasionally one would comment on a section or paragraph, or ask the other to stop, or backtrack. Finally, around midnight, Melissa turned away from the keyboard in disgust.

"Anything?" he asked her from the sofa, where he'd retreated to rest for a while.

"Nothing. For seven years after his death and prior to the Folio not a word of mention. Zip. Nada. Zilch."

Again, this sounded impossible, to both of them. So, Melissa's hunch had been right. For Shakespeare's passing there was not one word of recognition. No eulogy. No elegy. No obituary. None at all. Nothing for The Bard of Avon, supposedly the greatest writer in English history, until years after his death. Not a word, even from his alleged friend Ben Jonson. And then only by way of the Folio.

"Why would no one, not one person, acknowledge him in some way, with some tribute, however slight?" Melissa wanted to know. "How could it be that no one would lament or even note the passing of such a great man?"

Jake nodded in mystification and checked his notes. "The only mention at all of his death in 1616 was by his son-in-law, John Hall, who wrote in his journal: 'My father-in-law died on Thursday.' "

"That's it?"

"That's it."

She turned away. "Christ. You can almost hear the yawns of ennui across the centuries." She set her jaw. "This confirms everything else we know, now. Hall said nothing about his father-in-law being the famed poet and playwright Shakespeare, the great author, the beloved Bard of Avon. Nor did anyone else, because there was nothing to say. Dad, *there was no Bard of Avon.* That's what Desmond Lewis was trying to tell everyone."

Jake couldn't quite bring himself to accept that just yet, despite all their findings, and Sunir's certainty. Yet this lack of remembrance didn't make sense at all. There must be some mistake, he thought. On the other hand, why had Ben Jonson failed to mention Shakespeare either, during his lifetime? Or at least upon his passing? "Let's talk about Ben Jonson a minute," he said, pacing the floor. "What about that famous eulogy for William Shakespeare in the Folio?"

"Yeah. The friggin' Folio again. But not when he died. Jonson's flowery praise was only written seven years after his death. Why didn't he say or write something in 1616 when his great alleged colleague and friend died? He knew him from the Globe. Allegedly they were peers. Yet he said nothing." She went back over to the computer. "Hang on, I want to check something."

She logged back on and ran a search for Ben Jonson. Clicking quickly through the links and articles, she found what she was looking for. She read it in silence, then reread it once more to make certain, and hit the 'print' button. "Dad." she called out, at last. "I found the answer."

He'd been poring through the Hoffman book again. "Answer to what?"

"Why Ben Jonson didn't eulogize Shakespeare in 1616 when he died."

"Why didn't he?"

"Because he didn't know him."

He stared. "What? How can that be?"

"In 1619 Ben Jonson made a list of all the famous and important people he had ever known and met. He was a classic name dropper. And *Shakespeare was not on that list.* Jesus. Ben Jonson never knew William Shakespeare, or he would have said so."

"You're kidding. How could he not know him?"

"Why else would he not put him on the list? Unless . . ." she snapped her fingers.

He beat her to it. "Unless he knew him only as a player and producer or business associate and not worthy of mention."

"Right. The plays were all famous, the nine that were produced or published, anyway. So, if Johnson knew Shakespeare was the author when he was alive, he'd have said so. Dad, this proves all that hypocritical bullshit in the First Folio was just that. Bullshit."

"You're sure of that? Shakespeare wasn't on the list?" He hurried over to look at the source: a paper from a professor in Birmingham, footnoted with a dozen biographical references.

"Correctamundo. No Shakspur, or Shakspere for that matter."

"That's incredible."

"You should call that Professor Parker and stuff that up her snooty little nose. At least when Marlowe died, he was remembered."

"Yeah. But when Shakespeare died, he ordered a gravestone that said *'Curst be he that moves my bones.'* That's gotta count for something. Whereas Marlowe has no grave at all."

"Your point being?"

"Shakespeare wins."

This set both of them into a new flurry of digging. A short while later it was Jake's turn to uncover pay dirt. "Kiddo, check this out. Did you know that Stratford-Upon-Avon's own historian Camden didn't mention him in the history he published of the town in 1605? Shake-scene didn't even make the Who's Who of Stratford while he was still alive, supposedly famous, and living there fat and happy. Who is Jonson kidding?"

"So, what was Jonson's *'man for all time'* bullshit all about?"

"Maybe he was being ironic."

"I don't think so. Or he would have acknowledged him in some way when he was alive. Or at least when he died."

"Maybe he was jealous."

"Then why the Folio eulogy?"

"Maybe he changed his mind later."

"What would change his mind? *'Time heals all things?'* I don't think so."

"Maybe Shakespeare had him bamboozled the whole time, unveiling his 'latest work' each time it came across the transom from Europe or wherever."

"But then he'd remember him as being somebody, right?"

"True. You would think so."

"You know what this means, don't you? William Shakespeare wasn't acknowledged because there was nothing to acknowledge. He was a front, and everybody knew it."

"Which leaves one remaining possibility: they had made a deal."

"A deal? You mean Jonson and the Globe partners?"

"Yes. It was all about business. The Folio was a business plan. The making of a brand name."

Jake's thoughts raced. Even the English skeptics had all treated the glove-maker's son with kid gloves, making excuses for him, afraid to take on the vast Shakespearean institutional establishment and tourist trade. Now, given Sunir's disappearance on top of Desmond Lewis, they had good reason to be concerned. Because if the skeptics were right, there was a strong possibility that crimes were committed, history was deliberately twisted, distorted, and falsified to benefit Shakespeare and Company, and fortunes were made because of it. Including Shakespeare's own. He didn't have to recap that for his daughter. He could tell that she was thinking the same thing.

A loud chirping sound like a hundred birds in an aviary broke their silence. "What's that?" Jake sat upright, startled. He was getting jittery.

Melissa flipped open her cell phone. "Yes? Hello?" Her brow furrowed. "Who's calling?" She listened and caught her breath. "Just a minute, please." She looked at her father, wide-eyed. "It's somebody from the Shakespeare Foundation. He asked to speak to you."

With a mixture of anger and trepidation, he took the phone. "Yes, this is Jake Fleming."

The voice was familiar, and Jake recognized at once the same Oxford accent of the previous caller. "Mr. Fleming, we spoke earlier. My name is Harold Sherwood, Executive Director of the Shakespeare Foundation. Just to cut through the formalities, we want to make it very clear at the outset that the Foundation had nothing whatsoever to do with the shooting of your colleague."

This was one of those moments when Jake wished he'd had a recording device. "Then how do you even know about it? It wasn't in the papers or on the news. And by the way, how did you get this number?"

"We have our ways, sir. More to the point, we would like to reach an accord with you and your daughter–an exemplary talent and scholar, by the way, by all accounts. Her professors speak highly of her."

"Really. What else do you know about my daughter, and what right do you have prying into people's privacy?" He glanced at Melissa, who had turned livid.

"Dad," she hissed. "Tell him to go fuck himself."

"Sir, this is hardly a private matter."

"I see. So, what do you want?"

"The same thing we have been asking all along. That you let sleeping dogs lie, as it were."

"Lie, as in prevaricate?" Sherwood, if that was his name, didn't laugh.

"How about a meeting? You can name the time and place. We are a reputable institution, sir. We promise there will be no possibility of harm or deception."

Jake whispered to Melissa: "They want a meeting."

She shook her head vehemently. He turned back to the phone. "How about inside the British Library? Somewhere public."

"As you wish. In the lobby?"

"Let's make it at the desk. I assume you can get in?"

The caller laughed. "I'll manage, sir. What time?"

Jake glanced at Melissa, who was still red with rage. "How about 10:30 tomorrow?"

"Very well. I'll be wearing a black suit and bowler hat. I will know you. Are you bringing Melissa?"

Jake glanced at her. "Um, I don't think she wants to—"

She cut him off with a glare. "Hey. I'm part of this. Don't even think of going without me."

He sighed. "Apparently she's coming. But I want you to know that should anything happen to either of us, there will be a full account of our research and findings, together with a letter describing all our communications and the events here the past week, registered and in the hands of my editors in San Francisco. Is that clear?"

"Yes, of course. But you have no cause for worry. As I said, we are a respected institution with considerable support in the academic and business communities. Good day, sir, I'll see you in the morning." He rang off.

Melissa glared at her father. "Listen, I'm going along for one reason only, and that is the express purpose of kicking his ass. What else do they know about me?"

"They know you're doing graduate studies and apparently some of your professors. That's all they mentioned."

She frowned. "Christ. That reminds me. I need to start doing some work on that." She banged her fist on the desk. "You know we haven't had time to write up all this information. What if this guy calls your bluff?"

"Well before we put our faith in the good graces of The Shakespeare Foundation, I think we should run a little background check, don't you agree?"

She beat him to the punch. Seated together, Melissa led the web search through the various engines and sites, enough to give them a pretty good overview. It seemed legitimate enough, a stylish and substantial-looking headquarters in Stratford complete with virtual tour (which they declined); a list of supported projects, including ongoing regional theaters and educational outreach activities, a small press featuring extracts and individual plays, "kind of like mini-quartos," noted Melissa; and the sponsorship of several chairs at various colleges and universities. Including one at London University. "Currently held by Vice Dean Dr. Donald Childers," noted Jake, with a glance at Melissa. She bit her lip and read on. Other links included corporate and private sponsors and donors, on which an impressive list of major businesses came up, including several big names in both the UK and USA. One name Jake remembered having seen somewhere recently: *Avena Global Partners*. Where was that? Probably at the Globe, he thought. Another link displayed a list of staff, and sure enough, there at the top was Harold Sherwood, Executive Director, with an undated photo reminiscent of a younger Bob Hoskins with a mustache. Clicking on his link led to an impressive biography including degrees from Birmingham, Cambridge and Yale Law School.

"I've seen that guy," said Melissa.

"Well, if there's a Shakespeare lobby, this seems to be it," said Jake.

"So, we're going to the meeting?"

"Yes. But just in case, I'm going to see if I can recruit some backup."

"Who? Chris?"

"No, I was thinking of someone closer to the mark." Actually, he was thinking of the librarian at the British Library, whose number he happened to have. She had flirted with him more than once during his visits and given him her card. He even remembered her name: Evelyn Armwood.

He dialed the number on the house phone. It rang. A harried female voice answered in crisp British tones.

"Hello? Ms. Armwood? This is Jake Fleming, the American journalist doing research there at the library? Yes. Fine thank you. And you? Good, good. Listen, my daughter and I are going to be meeting someone there in the morning, and I need to ask you a favor." He lowered his voice and explained his plan.

She hemmed and hawed, and finally agreed. He decided that he had touched her inner Miss Marple, and this might be the most exciting thing that had ever happened in her mundane life. Either that or he'd touched her inner Jane Austen.

London, Tuesday, 10:10 a.m. November

The white-haired mustachioed man in the bowler hat seemed to have put on weight and years since his website photo, which if anything enhanced his resemblance to Bob Hoskins. He entered clutching a briefcase. He was alone, which they had carefully determined by monitoring the entryway both inside and out and watching his approach. Ms. Armwood, the librarian, was literally tickled pink with her new assignment and gave Jake a broad wink, which he was grateful the man didn't see. He walked up to them and extended his hand, which Jake reluctantly accepted.

"Good day, Mr. Fleming. Ms. Fleming. Harold Sherwood, Shakespeare Foundation." Sherwood handed each of them a business card and looked around. "Could we sit down?"

There was only one table within view of the desk, which was essential to Jake's plan. Unfortunately, it was presently occupied by a disheveled looking grad student who appeared as though he was on the last lap of an all-nighter.

Ms. Armwood earned her stripes right away. She walked over and in polite but firm tones asked the student to move, explaining that the table had been reserved. He departed, grumbling.

They sat on opposite sides and regarded one another with mutual distaste, tempered by a tinge of curiosity. Melissa had insisted on stopping at Starbucks for a coffee, which she now sipped cautiously, in violation of library rules. Sherwood got right to the point.

"Mr. and er, Ms. Fleming. In recognition of your efforts and accomplishments in furthering the base of knowledge about our William and other lesser poets, we would like to make you a proposition."

"Lesser poets?" responded Melissa, hotly.

"Go on," Jake said, nudging her under the table.

Melissa narrowed her eyes and stirred her coffee. She'd added too much nutmeg.

Sherwood glanced at her, warily. "Right then. We've been in touch with your employers in San Francisco, Mr. Fleming, and—"

"You've talked to *The Tribune*?"

"Right. And your editor, Mr. Flannigan, seems to be a very reasonable man. Some of our sponsors are heavy advertisers there, and we all agree it's in the best interests of everyone to leave well enough alone. Mr. Flannigan asked me to tell you to call him, and I am confident he'll confirm what I am telling you. Oh, and I think they'll be needing that flat you've been using."

Jake's outrage was such that he was ready to leap across the table and strangle the man. Melissa held his arm. Evelyn Armwood was eying him in growing alarm from her desk, ready to pounce on the emergency alarm button.

Finally, Jake recovered his voice. "And what if we refuse?" he asked. "Are you going to shoot us?"

"I can only assume you are being humorous," said Sherwood, with a scowl.

"Just one question, Mr. Sherwood, if you don't mind."

Sherwood paused. "And that would be?"

"Did you make this offer to Dr. Desmond Lewis before he was abducted and murdered?"

Sherwood's face darkened. "I see. So that's how it is." With that, he reached for his inner jacket pocket, which was enough for Jake. He quickly gave Armwood the pre-arranged nod, and, with a look of both fear and excitement combined, she pressed the button on her desk, just as Jake realized too late that Sherwood had merely been reaching for his cell phone. Meanwhile, there was a brief moment of silence, while unseen sentinels gathered their wits, and presumably weapons. Suddenly he heard it: the distinct sound of an alarm, somewhere in the depths of the building.

Sherwood heard it as well. With a frown, he hesitated, put his cell phone back in his pocket, closed his briefcase and rose quickly to his feet. "Well, sir and Miss. It seems I have wasted my time. I wish you good day." With that he abruptly turned and hurried out of the library.

Jake took Melissa by the arm. "Let's go," he said, urgently. "We can't stay here."

"Why?"

"They're not through with us by a long shot." Taking a resisting Melissa by the arm, he hustled her to the door, stopping just long enough to hand a ten spot to Evelyn Armwood. "Thanks Evelyn. Good job. We'll be in touch." She blushed. Money wasn't what she'd had in mind.

"Wait!" she called after them. "Let me show you the back way out."

Thanks to the librarian Jake and Melissa were able to leave the library by a staff entrance unobserved, onto a back street. Melissa hailed a cruising taxi, amid the roar of traffic and shriek of alarms. They climbed in, and Melissa leaned back, closing her eyes. "Dad, did that man just try to threaten us?"

"I'm not sure, but I'm not taking any chances. Let's not talk about it right now," he cautioned her, nodding towards the driver, who, fortunately, sat on the other side of a sound-proof barrier. He put his arm over her shoulder, and she shuddered a moment. Then she laughed.

"And you said libraries would be safe."

"What was I thinking? I'm sorry. I never should have gotten you into this."

"You already said that."

"I did?"

“And my answer is the same. I’m staying. But at least for now, we definitely can’t go back to Denmark Street, even if we haven’t been evicted like he was implying. Too many people know where to find us, including Sherwood.”

“Where to?” the driver wanted to know, through the speaker phone.

“A train station. King’s Cross or St. Pancras will do.”

“We’re practically there,” the driver pointed out.

As they pulled up to the hulking station Melissa stared out the window. She’d calmed down by now and seemed fully in control once again. He marveled at her stamina. He wasn’t so sure about his own. His stomach was beginning to assert signs of distress, once again. And he’d stopped carrying Mylanta.

Meanwhile, they had to make a decision.

“So where do we go now?” Melissa wanted to know.

The obvious answer was Oxford. But they were still no closer to what to do there, or who they would see. Instead, they took another road entirely.

Chapter Thirty-Six

And All Our Yesterdays

Mid-November, Tuesday, late afternoon

In the end, their choice was easy. Jake had felt for days now that he wanted to see Kent: the fabled countryside Marlowe had come from and written so much about. He wanted to see Kit's home, and the place of his formative schooling. He wanted to see Canterbury. Melissa was in full agreement and anxious to be anywhere besides London at that moment. But first things first.

"The train isn't for an hour," said Jake, checking the clock. "I need to find a pay phone and call my editor."

"You can use my cell phone. It's a U.S. service, remember?" She pulled it out and extended it to him.

He hesitated. "Better not," he said. "It may not be secure."

She stared at it in horror, like it might explode. "Now you tell me."

Jake found a bank of phones in the station and punched in his calling card numbers. "C'mon, c'mon, answer, Tom," he muttered. It was still early in California, but Flannigan was an early bird, usually prone to a habit of reading four or five morning papers with his usual copious quantities of coffees and carbs.

He answered on the first ring. "Yeth, what ith it?" His mouth was full as usual, probably Krispy Kremes knowing him, thought Jake.

"It's Jake Fleming. Listen, I may not have much time, Tom. But I need to know. Did somebody, anybody, try to pressure you into pulling me off the Desmond Lewis story?"

There was a brief hesitation. "Well, I wouldn't put it that way exthactly," said Flannigan, defensively. "The Managing Editor did call down last night, though, and gently suggested you need to get back here. We've reserved the London flat for Gerri Shapiro, who is on her way to cover the Prince's world tour, and—"

"To cover what?" shouted Jake. "Are you fucking shitting me?"

"Easy, now, down boy," said Flannigan, swallowing some coffee. "We do have people to answer to. They are very appreciative, in fact I am very appreciative of the great work you do and have been doing. That story about the professors was good, although we could not find any connection between either one of them and that burning barge in Sausalito, just so you know. But the police are satisfied with the suicide verdict, and there is no reason to think—"

Jake didn't hear what else Flannigan had to say on the subject. He had already hung up. "Let's go," he said, tersely. "I think I saw a lunch counter back there."

They had just ordered a sandwich when Melissa's cell phone rang. She froze.

"Let it ring." he said, quickly.

She hesitated, then shook her head. "This might be important." Visibly steeling herself, she pressed the button to answer. "Hello?"

Jake watched in concern as she listened, then turned away and spoke in low tones he couldn't hear. When he saw her apprehension transform into interest, his irritation was diluted by relief, at least momentarily. She listened again for a moment, then looked at her father.

"It's Chris Braithwaite. He wants to speak to you. He knows about the shooting."

Jake reluctantly put his bag down and took the phone. "Hey, Chris," he said. "What's up?"

"Melissa says you are going to Canterbury?" the graduate student inquired.

Jake felt like reprimanding her for giving out that information, but what was done was done. "Yes," he said. "And please keep that close to your vest, we may be followed."

"I don't wear a vest. But don't worry. I am on your side. Dr. Balsavar was a friend, and I knew Dr. Lewis. I want the people responsible for these actions caught, and you seem to be the only ones willing to do something."

Jake wasn't at all sure just what they were willing to do but thanked him for his support and asked what he wanted.

"There is someone there you should see. At the King's School where Marlowe attended as a boy. I also attended there, also on scholarship."

"Oh really?" No wonder he'd been so interested in their little project.

"I think my friend may have some interesting information for you. I can't say more on the phone." He sounded nervous.

"Well, can you say his name?" asked Jake, in exasperation.

"Samuel Poulson. Dr. Poulson. He's curator of the archives there and a good man. And while you are there, you should visit the cathedral where Thomas Becket was murdered. It's right on the edge of the campus." Suddenly his voice dropped. "I have to go," he said, and hung up abruptly.

Canterbury, England, early Wednesday, mid-November

After spending the night in a dismal hotel near the bus station, Jake and Melissa ventured out into the walled city of Canterbury for coffee and sustenance (although to Jake, they were one and the same). Both agreed the city was an odd mixture of ancient and modern. Built by the Romans in the first century A.D., its combination of Roman and medieval fortifications, the magnificent towering cathedral, authentic Tudor and Elizabethan architecture, and the old King's School had all been almost perfectly preserved. Except for the city center. According to the Fodor's Jake had picked up at the London station, the Nazis had bombed the heart out of the old city during their relentless aerial assault on Britain during World War II, and what had been rebuilt since was garish. Still, Melissa was enthralled with what remained of the historic center. And for whatever reasons, the ancient Cathedral and King's School had been spared in the bombings.

Melissa gazed around the ivy-covered stone architecture in awe, once they were permitted entry to the campus. Dr. Poulson had left what amounted to a campus pass at the gate. "This school is *two thousand years old*?"

"Does that make it Old School?" asked Jake, getting an elbow for his trouble.

The King's School grounds were in themselves a walled compound within the walled city. The buildings, like the walls that enclosed them, were of stone, gray and stately, with steep tile roofs and rectangular ivy-covered towers. Here, surely, was the original archetype for the Cambridge, Oxford and Ivy League college campuses. The fresh-faced sport coat-and-tie wearing male student population, chatting earnestly as they hurried to and from their classes, clearly represented some of Britain's first and finest families.

The Flemings almost missed the bronze plaque overlooking the charmingly named Mint Yard near the school entrance, opposite the Admissions Office. About the size of the small plaque in the St. Nicholas churchyard, it briefly commemorated Christopher Marlowe's attendance at the school from 1579 to 1580, when he matriculated to Cambridge University at the age of sixteen.

Dr. Samuel Poulson was well into his seventies, but still energetic and gregarious, of short, rotund stature with a crown of red hair surrounding a bald pate, who evidently lived for those rare opportunities to welcome guests. It seemed that he seldom emerged from the library basement where the archives were kept (formerly a church, he told them) except for special occasions. The arrival of the delegation from America was such an occasion. Poulson remembered his West Pakistani protege well and was well-aware of the maverick opinions of Desmond Lewis. "I heard about his passing," he said, sadly. "Terrible. Terrible. Can't imagine why he'd do such a thing, I must say."

"Maybe he didn't," said Jake.

"Beg pardon?" Poulson blinked. "Didn't what?"

"Commit suicide. That's the official story isn't it? Or was, last I heard."

"It was, it was. Shot himself over a book review, or some such. Horrible, horrible."

"Book review?" Melissa blinked, and glanced at her father. "That's a new one."

"Well, not much we can do now, I'm afraid," said Poulson, with a sigh. "Can I get you a cup of tea?"

In short order, he whisked together three cups of excellent Earl Grey on a small apartment stove in his office area, and it was clear he was delighted to have company. "I am given to understand you are interested in Kit Marlowe?" he asked cautiously, after a while.

Jake acknowledged that they were. "How did you know that?"

Poulson chuckled. "Word gets around." He contemplated his tea leaves for a moment, then put his cup down. "If you have a chance to look around the town, you will find precious little in the way of acknowledgment of Mr. Marlowe, despite his being a native son."

"What? That's an outrage!" Melissa shouted. "Sounds like Poet's Corner all over again. But this is his hometown!"

Poulson sighed. "For the same reason he's little regarded at Cambridge or in London, for that matter. He's still considered a pariah in literary circles, even though Swinburne called him 'The Father of English tragedy and the creator of English blank verse.' In Canterbury, you'll find the plaque at the school, another in a kiosk in the market center where his family's house once stood, and a recompense statue in a trash-strewn corner of a plaza near the local theater. Actually, it depicts not Marlowe, but a classical Muse. The inscription mentions 'The Muse's Darling' and other quotes and duly cites him as a renowned poet, but the area is sadly neglected. At least someone had the courtesy to name the theater itself for Marlowe, which I suppose is some consolation. But I can't recommend you bother going there."

It sounded dreary enough to make Jake feel depressed. Melissa, he noted, was already depressed and had been for a while.

He was thinking it was time for that detective work he'd been postponing about John Scofield.

"Are you familiar with the works of a Professor John Scofield?"

"Dad," said Melissa, with a warning tone and an angry glare. But he sensed doubt beneath that glare and chose to ignore it.

"Scofield. Scofield. I think we may have a book or two of his in the library upstairs." He pointed unnecessarily at the ceiling. "Oxford chap, as I recall."

"Oxford?" He looked at his daughter. She shook her head vehemently and mouthed "not now!"

They settled more comfortably in their seats and sipped their tea, while Poulson lit a pipe. He didn't ask if it would bother them, and they didn't object, although back in the States Melissa, at least, certainly would have. They both sat bolt upright at what he said next.

"Have either of you ever heard of an American journalist named Calvin Hoffman?"

"Yes! *Murder of the Man Who Was Shakespeare*. We both just read it." Melissa dug in her bag and produced the tattered paperback copy.

Poulson reacted with astonishment and delight. "Yes. Very good! Where did you find that? It's been out of print for years."

"It wasn't easy," said Jake, pointedly.

"Indeed. Well, I actually met Mr. Hoffman many years ago when, like you, he came here seeking the truth about Marlowe. I was an undergraduate in London at the time, but his 'parallelisms' intrigued me so much I accompanied him here, and then to Cambridge. He's the one who discovered the portrait, you know. It was about to be discarded and burned. Burned! Can you imagine?" He showed them a full-sized reproduction he proudly kept on the floor behind his desk, where no one would ever see it unless invited to do so.

"Maybe we should go to Cambridge next," said Melissa, after a moment.

She definitely has a crush, thinks Jake.

"I wouldn't bother. Lovely place, I first went up there to listen to Pink Floyd in the clubs, before they went famous. But they won't discuss Marlowe, up there, not even his heroics for our Queen nor will they let you see the picture."

"You listened to Pink Floyd in a club?" Melissa was stunned.

"Do you think Hoffman was right?" Jake asked him, notepad ready.

Poulson took a draw on his pipe and leaned back. "Much of it, yes, although not all. You remember his reference to the Mendenhall word study way back when?"

Jake remembered Melissa mentioning it. Melissa nodded.

"Not many people know this, but Hoffman had two subsequent word and scriptural analyses of Shakespeare and Marlowe's writings done at his own expense—one by the F.B.I., and the other by IBM. In each case Marlowe was proven author of both samples."

"Really," said Jake, writing that down. That was more than a little interesting, he thought, with a glance at Melissa.

"I do question some of Hoffman's interpretations of the Sonnets, however, especially his theory about one of the most puzzling enigmas in all of literary lore: the identity of that confoundingly mysterious 'W.H.' in the dedication. Do you know what I'm referring to?"

Melissa nodded vigorously. Jake did, vaguely. Hadn't Sunir been about to tell them something about that? Poulson produced a copy of *The Sonnets of William Shakespeare* from a nearby shelf with the Shakespeare name irreverently crossed out, and handed it to him. Melissa moved her chair so she could see better.

"So, what about Hoffman's theory?" asked Jake.

"Open it to the dedication page," Poulson instructed them. Jake did so. It read as follows:

TO THE ONLIE BEGETTER OF
THESE ENSUING SONNETS
MR. W.H. ALL HAPPINESSE
AND THAT ETERNITIE
PROMISED
BY
OUR EVER-LIVING POET
WISHETH
THE WELL-WISHING
ADVENTURER IN
SETTING FORTH

Poulson took another draught on his pipe, while they read it.

" 'Ever-living poet,' " said Melissa. "It's like, he had to point that out."

"Calvin Hoffman was convinced, mostly based on the affectionate intimations in the sonnets and the fact that they were dedicated to 'Mr. W.H.,' that Marlowe was involved in a homosexual relationship with Thomas Walsingham, his patron. W. H. for 'Walsing-Ham,' get it?"

Melissa shook her head dismissively. "I don't buy it."

Jake was inclined to agree with her. It was too much of a reach. He looked up at Poulson. "Who do the Stratford people think this is?" he asked.

"They are clueless. Absolutely clueless. All sorts of theories have been postulated, none very plausible. Biographer A. L. Rouse tried to turn things around in typical Stratfordian style, insisting the 'W.H.' is really 'H.W.' supposedly standing for Henry Wriothesley, the Earl of Southampton. This is the Earl to whom Shakespeare dedicated *Venus and Adonis*, if you recall, then a year later on *The Rape of Lucrece*. Interestingly, no one has ever been able to connect those two, but what can you do?"

"Yeah, that's no better than 'Walsing Ham,' " said Jake. "Sounds like some kind of lunch meat." Which, of course, reminded him of the List.

"I've read there are even people now trying to accredit the whole Canon to this character. It's Oxford all over again."

Melissa eyed him quizzically. "Who do you think it was, Dr. Poulson?"

"I wish I knew," he said, wistfully. "But if you've got time, which I never did, you're welcome to delve through Hoffman's research files. He left them with me when he passed away." He gestured. "They're in the back, I'll find them for you."

Melissa raised her hand like an eager undergrad. "I'd love to take a look at those files back there."

"Help yourself, Miss," said Poulson with a smile, then added: "If it's all right with you, sir. Dr. Lewis came here last year with the same idea in mind."

"Is that right?" Jake asked, with a warning glance to Melissa. "You have any idea what he came up with?"

"No, he left in a rush, and I was tied up with school business at the time."

"Dad, let me take a look," said Melissa, meaningfully. "I have an idea."

"Sure. Meanwhile I'll stroll into town and see about lodgings for a few days."

Poulson raised his hands and shook his head. "That won't be necessary. You are more than welcome at my house. My wife passed away six years ago, and the children are long gone. It's just me and the dog, and we would welcome company. Plus," he added, with a courtly bow to Melissa, "your lovely daughter would do much to brighten my sadly dreary home."

"Well, she is an actress," noted Jake.

"Actor," corrected Melissa. "In training," she added.

"Are you sure?" Jake asked Poulson. "There is such a thing as too much of a good thing." Earning himself another elbow bruise, albeit a mild one.

"Of course, I'm sure. In fact, I insist. Please make yourself at home, I'll be right back." With that he led Melissa into the depths of the archives, which gave Jake a very unpleasant *deja vu* of Lambeth Palace. He returned a short while later. "She's all set. Why don't you get your car and I'll show you the way."

"Actually, we came by train."

Jake was nervous about leaving Melissa, but she called out from the back room sounding actually cheerful. "I'm fine. You go ahead, I'll meet you later."

Poulson drove Jake around the town for a quick look at the Marlowe sites, then to his home: an ancient stone farmhouse with a tiled roof, on a tidy village square at the outskirts of the city. Jake was entranced. "How old is this place?"

Poulson chuckled. "Well, there's a story that Edward the Black Prince used to keep a mistress here around 1350. But then, there are many stories like that in these parts."

Edward the Black Prince. Jake could almost feel his presence in the dark, empty rooms, and the echoes of ancient booted footfalls on the time-blackened wooden floors. He knew Melissa would be thrilled to even hear about let alone stay in this brush with history, legend or not.

Poulson led the way to the guest quarters upstairs. "Did you know he was also the father of Richard II?"

Jake felt like a thunderbolt had struck inside the room. " *'I am Richard II,'* said the Queen," he murmured. Just then a black Labrador Retriever trotted into the parlor, and warmly greeted the visitor in typical Lab fashion. His name, Poulson said with a grin, was Prince.

"Richard was the boy king, against whom we of Kent led a rebellion over taxes, rather like you Yanks and, er, Tea Drinkers, which is what Elizabeth feared the play would inspire anew. He was eventually deposed, then murdered."

"Small wonder she censored the play." It was all falling together as if a video image of a collapsed house of cards was running backwards.

The telephone rang. It was the old fashioned kind, similar to Blodgett's: the kind with actual bells and wires attached. Poulson hurried into the foyer to answer it, and Jake busied himself washing up in the guest lav. He could hear his host speaking downstairs, and something about the rising tone in his voice made him pause to listen.

"Are you sure about that?" Poulson was saying. "I hardly see what you hope to—yes, very well, I see." There was a pause. "I see. Well, if you say so, you're certainly welcome. All right, we'll see you then," he said, and hung up.

Jake, close to exhaustion, napped that afternoon, cheerfully supervised then guarded by the watchful, patient Prince.

When he awoke, Melissa was seated in an armchair across the sitting room, where Poulson had left him to nap. A fire was crackling cheerfully in a fireplace Jake had failed to even notice, earlier, but welcomed now.

Prince, the black Lab, was stretched out on an oval throw rug right in front of the fire, looking very content.

Almost envying him, Jake sat up and turned towards his daughter.

"Finally!" She exclaimed. But there was a teasing note in her voice. "Dad! Did you know that Edward the Black Prince kept a girlfriend here! In 1350? In this building?"

"Well, there's a rumor to that effect," said Poulson, poking his head in from the kitchen area. "Drinks, anyone?"

Much refreshed from his nap, Jake was ready for a drink. Especially after a day like this one had been, and their literal flight from London.

"Would you care for a Scotch? I have a very decent Windsor XR blend. Of course, if—

"That sounds great. Thanks," Jake assured him.

"Do you have any Chardonnay?" asked Melissa, with her most winsome smile—a smile she only reserved for special people. Jake supposed this mentor of Hoffman, proponent of Marlowe, guardian of his legacy, even, merited her favor.

"I do indeed. That was Eleanor's favorite wine, in fact."

"His late wife," explained Jake.

Poulson handed Jake what he recognized to be a very expensive faceted crystal whiskey glass.

"Nice glass," said Jake, admiringly, holding it up to the firelight.

"Thank you. Waterford, I believe."

"I've heard of them," said Melissa.

"For you, my dear, for your Chardonnay—just a moment, I have one chilling. Eleanor always loved her white wine glasses chilled, along with the wine." He vanished into the kitchen.

"Works for me!" Melissa called after him, with a 'try to stop me' grin at her dad.

Meanwhile, Jake has sipped his Scotch.

"Oh," he said. Then another sip. "Wow."

Melissa tilted her head at him. "Wow?"

"How about *yowsa?*"

"Yowsa?"

"But with three exclamation marks."

"Oh, well in that case . . . so it's that good, huh?"

Jake took another sip and nodded vigorously.

"Can I try a sip? Since it's supposed to be so good?"

He handed her the glass. "Careful," he said.

She stuck her tongue out, then stuck it in the glass. One sip and she nearly gagged and thrust it back at him.

"Um, was it me, or do you just not like Scotch?"

She gasped, then tossed a guilty glance in the direction of the kitchen. "Sorry. I just—it's just—"

"Methinks the young lady simply does not care for the whiskey of my Scottish ancestors," said Poulson, re-entering the sitting room with a small silver tray upon which were balanced an ice bucket containing a wine bottle, and a crystal wine glass with a hint of mist around the rim.

"It's—it just kind of startled me, I think. Kind of a sharp taste?" Then, with a guilty expression, she adds, "I never tried Scotch before. Sorry. So sue me?" That was for Jake. For Poulson, she had her best, top category Oscar-winning smile.

"That won't be necessary," Poulson assured her, handing her the wine glass. "I hope you will find this Russian River Valley Chardonnay palatable. A *Benovia,* I think." He checked the label. "Yes. Just from last year, actually, but I hope you'll find it satisfactory."

He presented her with the misty glass and filled it to the proper level.

Jake and Melissa raised their glasses towards him. "To Christopher Marlowe!"

"And maybe his legacy be restored," added Jake, as they all clinked about $200 worth of crystal (calculated Jake).

"Hear, hear," nodded Poulson, they clinked again and drank. Jake restraining the urge to toss it down in a single luxurious gulp and instead savored one more sip, only to see his host toss his down and go for a refill.

Deciding on valor over discretion, Jake went to join him.

Melissa, in the meantime, took a careful sip of her Chardonnay. Swished it around in her mouth like a true sommelier and swallowed it.

"Yowsa?" Asked Jake, with a grin.

She nodded, vigorously, and took another sip.

"Pardon?" asked Poulson, confused by that exchange.

"An old Yankee expression," explained Jake. It means, really, really, really good.

"An old Yankee expression? What, from the Civil War?" Melissa demanded to know.

"Well, I am delighted to see that your father is savoring his Scotch quite nicely. Am I right, Mr. Fleming?"

"Oh, you are so right, Mr. Poulson. I have never tasted a Scotch of this quality before. And please, call me Jake."

"Well, er, Jake, it's mostly been gathering dust in the sidebar over there. I don't drink much—not at all, actually, other than when I have company. It was a gift from an old friend, actually." He glanced at the fourth place setting on the table, and his guests who were present glanced at each other.

Poulson poured himself another glass, retook a seat, and turned to the fire. "Now then." Poulson raised his own glass and announced a toast. "To Christopher Marlowe!"

"I think we did that one already," said Melissa.

"Oh, we did, didn't we. Oh dear."

"Never mind. To Christopher Marlowe." She raised her glass.

"And may his legacy be restored," repeated Jake.

They all clinked and drank.

"And on that note," announced Poulson, "it's time for dinner."

He vanished into the kitchen once more, and they could hear him crashing around.

"Let me help!" Melissa called after him, tossing down the rest of her Chardonnay and jumping to her feet, following him in, and quickly joining the clash and clatter.

Left to his own devices, Jake pondered the empty place setting on the dining room table (why hadn't he noticed that before?), then sat down and fished into his valise for his tablet, which he seldom used, if there was a desktop available. He hadn't had the chance to ask Poulson about it.

Logging on, he Googled John Scofield. Then added PhD, then after a moment added Oxford University, on a whim.

The tablet blinked, coughed, blinked some more, then the name appeared on numerous lists, including Oxford (tenured professor), the University of California at Berkeley (visiting professor) and several books, including three pertaining to Shakespeare.

Then he noticed something that caught his eye: Richard Scofield was currently back in England for a book tour, for his newest book: *The Sonnets of Shakespeare, Revisited.* He was just checking the schedule when Melissa and Poulson re-emerged from the kitchen, both now wearing aprons and carrying platters.

They set down the dishes and took their seats, at Poulson's insistence.

"We're having venison," he informed them.

"Venison? Really?" Jake couldn't even remember the last time he'd had venison. On assignment in Norway, possibly? That was over twenty years ago.

"It's excellent with Chardonnay, in fact," Poulson assured them, uncorking a fresh bottle and setting it in the ice bucket, now on the table. "Chardonnay or Cabernet. Would anyone prefer a red wine?"

"Not me," said Melissa, sipping her Chardonnay with open pleasure.

"I'm good," said Jake, as Poulson filled his glass to the proper level.

Once again Jake couldn't help but take note of the fourth place setting opposite Poulson's. Melissa had noticed it too, and they exchanged glances, but neither felt it appropriate to ask about. For all Melissa knew, Dr. Poulson had set it as a memorial to his late wife, or for that matter The Black Prince's mistress's ghost. But Jake, having overheard part of that earlier conversation, thought otherwise.

"Well, I suppose we'd better start," said Poulson, checking his watch.

Jake never knew English country fare could look so scrumptious: oven-roasted venison, fresh green beans in white wine and butter sauce, and new potatoes and all set out in a historic dining room that would have shamed the most trendy Bed and Breakfast anywhere.

Melissa seemed on edge, anxious to tell them something. She'd brought a stack of materials with her to the table.

As he served the food and poured the wine, Poulson seemed a little distracted and kept glancing in the direction of the front hall. Jake, noticing, wondered about it. Obviously the fourth place setting was not just a memorial setting. Clearly, he was expecting someone. But who?

After several bites of Pollack's ambrosial cooking, washed down by a generous swig of wine, Jake turned to Melissa. "Okay, what's going on? You look like you won the lottery."

She did appear stunned, like a young astronomer who's just discovered a new galaxy. Or an actress who's just won the lead role. "I don't know about that, but I have found the last entry on the list."

Poulson looked up from his plate, quizzically. "List?" he asked.

Jake quickly filled their host in on the List of Desmond Lewis. Poulson looked astonished. "Don't tell me you've identified the Dark Lady as well," he exclaimed, half joking.

Melissa looked at him and didn't smile. "As a matter of fact, I believe I have." She glanced at their host. "This venison is awesome, by the way."

"Thank you, my dear. It's from the forests of Kent, so they tell me."

Jake sat forward, intently and focused his gaze on his daughter. "So, you found our mysterious spicy 'Herb' entre?" Even Prince, laying on the floor at Poulson's feet awaiting leftovers, perked up his ears.

"Yes. And spicy is right, but it isn't 'herb.' It was capitalized, right?"

"Yes, but—"

"Dad. Dr. Poulson. Lewis's 'Herb' stands for a name. Not Herb as in Herbie, but a family name: Herbert. It's a love story. And not a gay one either, in any sense of the word."

"Herbert. That rings a bell," said Poulson, glancing once more at the door. For some reason Jake could only guess at, he seemed tense.

Taking her cue, perhaps, from her host, Melissa refused to be rushed. "Ironically, it was one of the leading Shakespeare biographers—Edmund Chambers—who first recognized the identity of the 'pretty boy' in the sonnets. And, as so often is the case with truth, the answer was right under everyone's noses the whole time."

"Do tell," said Poulson. Jake listened in astonished silence, surreptitiously digging into his venison, while Poulson lit his pipe and blew smoke rings towards the blackened rafters, adding to the centuries of tar that coated them already.

"Chambers believed that 'W.H.' was William Herbert, the 3rd Earl of Pembroke, who was named on the dedication page of the First Folio. He had in fact become Lord Chamberlain for a time, but nobody could find any personal connection between Shakespeare and the Pembrokes, so why the dedication to him?"

Poulson nodded in agreement. "Right. 'Tis a puzzlement," he said.

"Well now I am convinced that Chambers was right all along, except for different reasons. The second Earl William Herbert was the husband of Mary Sidney, for starters."

Jake drew a blank, but Paulson's eyes lit up immediately.

"Mary Sidney, Countess of Pembroke," breathed their aging host, in wonder.

"I don't get it," said Jake.

"The 2nd Earl of Pembroke founded the Pembroke Players in 1592 primarily for the purpose of producing the plays of Christopher Marlowe. Among the plays this company produced was *Edward II*, naming the author as 'Christopher

Marlowe, gentleman.' That in itself is an important point, because it confirms a direct relationship between these two."

Poulson tapped his pipe on the ash tray, thoughtfully. "Quite. It's true that no production company advertised Shakespeare as the author that way for their productions until much later. And despite rumors to the contrary, our Marlowe was a gentleman, not a street brawler prone to attacking armed thugs over bar tabs, like the historians have labeled and libeled him. He had to've been so, in order to be welcomed into the Court, or the great houses, and the company of countesses and Earls like the Sidneys, as he was."

"So, a nobleman such as de Vere might get away with boorishness in those quarters, but never a commoner," noted Jake, taking notes as usual.

"Absolutely," said Poulson.

Jake managed another mouthful of potato while Melissa continued, her excitement mounting: "It was the 2nd Earl of Pembroke who became Lord Chamberlain and tried to stop the further publication of unauthorized Quartos. This was done to protect Marlowe's work and keep his identity and the fact that he was still alive from discovery by the church."

Jake's dinner was getting cold, and it was hard to chew and listen at the same time. "But why would this guy be named on the Sonnets?"

"It wasn't him." Melissa took a sip of wine, just to emphasize her point, then continued: "Okay. Here it is: the reason the true author of the sonnets loved 'W.H.' so much was that the 3rd Earl of Pembroke was the author's own son."

Jake almost spilled his wine. Poulson remained speechless.

"That's what the Sonnets are about. That's what Sunir was leading up to, that night at the London Eye."

Jake put down his fork, almost forgetting all about the venison. "Please explain."

"I've been interested in Mary Sidney for a long time, actually. She was younger sister of Sir Phillip Sidney. She was a noted poet—a lot better than Oxford, I might add. There are a lot of people in Berkeley who think she was actually the author of the plays."

"And do you?" asked Poulson.

"I considered it. I am convinced that she was an influence on Marlowe. Her brother Philip was the first courtly poet of major literary stature. And Mary was one of the most celebrated women of her time: educated, erudite, and literate. My kind of woman," she added, with a smile.

"OK, I'll drink to that," agreed Jake, raising his glass. Poulson hesitated momentarily, then followed suit.

Melissa picked up her pace. "Mary Sidney was only three years older than Kit Marlowe. The Sidneys lived in Kent not far from here, in fact. Before Marlowe first came here to the King's School, Philip Sidney had been traveling extensively in France and was there at the time of the Massacre of St. Bartholomew's. The British Ambassador to France at the time was Mary's grandfather, Francis Walsingham. Remember, Marlowe knew and wrote all sorts of details about that event which he included in his play *Massacre at Paris*, and the histories hadn't been written yet."

"Remind me again," said Jake, his head spinning to keep up. "Exactly what happened in Paris back then?"

Poulson answered that one. "The beginning of a holocaust that rivals the Nazis. In one day as many as 70,000 French Protestant Huguenots were slaughtered at the instigation of the Catholic Medicis. Almost half the population of France was eventually exterminated, and the few survivors fled either here to Canterbury or to America."

Melissa went on, excitedly. "This ties in perfectly with Kit's early recruitment into espionage while he was still at Cambridge. He was trying to prevent the same thing happening in England with the restoration of Mary, Queen of Scots."

"She's right," said Poulson. "He knew the territory, as you Yanks would say." He glanced towards the door as he spoke, which Jake again noticed and wondered about.

Melissa continued eagerly: "So Mary Sidney's grandfather Francis Walsingham became Marlowe's employer in the Secret Service. As a known lover of poets and the theater, Mary was close to her father's cousin Thomas as well, who would become Marlowe's patron. See how it all fits?"

"But what's the Pembroke connection?" asked Jake.

"I'm getting to that. Mary was known to be an alluring beauty. So, no surprise Henry Herbert, the 2nd Earl of Pembroke wanted to snatch her up as his third wife. So," she checked her notes again, "on April 21, 1577, at the age of fifteen, Mary Sidney became the Countess of Pembroke." Here she glared at both men with feminist ire. "The Count was 43."

" 'Tis true, old earls married young girls," said Poulson, with a wry grimace.

"His first two wives were twelve and fifteen. Give me a break." The men nodded in hasty acquiescence, and she continued: "Mary was the subject of her brother Philip's poem *The Countess of Pembroke's Arcadia.* She was also the living inspiration for Kit Marlowe's second most famous line: *'Whoever loved that loved not at first sight?'* from *Faustus*. So, Mary gets pregnant and has her first child in 1581 at the age of twenty, a son, named William Herbert. But get this: up till then the Earl had been childless in his two prior marriages and a bunch of affairs. And don't tell me both of those prior teenage wives were barren, please. Which he claimed, by the way."

"Maybe they took the pill?"

"Dad."

Poulson frowned, blew smoke rings and checked his watch once more.

"Meanwhile, Marlowe remained closely involved with the Pembroke family, and after five years with the Chamberlain's Men he went on to become resident playwright to Pembroke's Players in 1592, wearing the Countess's livery in his forays about London. I have proof that shows they were close for years, not just a teenage flingy thing."

"And the proof?" Jake urged her on.

"Right here." She held up an old leather-bound volume. "I found in this dedication he addressed directly to her on behalf of his deceased friend Thomas Watson. It was published in 1593. This dedication was originally written in Latin, by the way. It absolutely sizzles with personal and intimately sensual knowledge of Mary Pembroke, the boy Herbert's mother." She opened the book to a well-marked page. "Listen to this:

'To the most noble and renowned lady, endowed with every gift of mind and body, Mary, the Countess of Pembroke: Thou, Delia, of the laurel-crowned race, sister of Sidney the bard of Apollo, patroness of letters, to whose pure embrace virtue flies from the slings of barbarism and ignorance, as Philomela from the Tyrant of Thrace, thou Muse of the age for poets and all aspiring wits, daughter of the gods, able to inspire a rude pen with such feelings of lofty rapture that even my poor self, it seems, might write above the wonted pitch of my unripe talent. Deign to accept this posthumous Amyntas as you would an adopted son, the rather that the dying father humbly bequeathed its care to thee. And, granted that thy illustrious name is blazoned so far abroad, not only among us but among other nations, as ever to be lost to the rusting years of time, or even to be increased by the praise of mortals (how, indeed, could anything be more infinite), crowned by the songs of as many as Ariadne by a diadem of stars, spurn not this pure priest of Phoebus bestowing yet another star upon thy crown but, with that openness of mind which Jupiter, the sower of men and of gods, graced your noble family, receive and protect him.

So we, whose slender wealth is but the Seabank myrtle of Venus and Daphne's evergreen laurel garland, shall on the very first page of a poem call on thee, Mistress of the Muses, for aid. And finally, thy virtue, which shall outlast virtue itself, shall outlast even eternity. Most desirous to do thee honor. C.M.' "

They were silent.

"I wish someone would write me a letter like that," sighed Melissa. "This was in the public record. The dedication to Watson is almost in passing. It also shows considerable religious sensitivity, which once again belies Whitgift's charge of atheism, don't you think? You should read it, Dad."

Poulson finally spoke up. "It certainly sounds like a love letter," he acknowledged. "And it plays on a lot of the same themes as the Sonnets, with all those double entendres, like *'mind and body, even to be increased*', which also means have children, and *'to whose pure embrace, or feelings of lofty rapture.' "*

"And how about the line *'Deign to accept this posthumous Amyntas as you would an adopted son, the rather that the dying father humbly bequeathed its care to thee,' "* exclaimed Melissa. "That's Kit talking about himself, their son, and what's going to happen to them!"

Paulson nodded, excitedly. "Then he ends with *'desirous to do thee honor'* which has all sorts of double meanings. Oh my."

"And this is the language of the Sonnets," she added. "Christopher Marlowe would have kept the secret of William Herbert's illegitimacy to his actual dying day, to protect the boy's inheritance as well as Mary Pembroke's reputation. And its right there in black in white."

Jake was thinking about how that dedication compared to the one attributed to Shakespeare in *Venus and Adonis*. It was like diamonds to coal. Maybe Shake-scene did write that V.A. dedication, he thought, when he decided to claim the purloined poem. Or he dictated it to some errant scribe.

Jake took the page from her, scanned it, then looked up at the others. "And you say this was published the year of Marlowe's alleged death?"

Melissa nodded. "He is asking her for aid. That would be significant whether before or after Deptford."

"That's right. There's a story that Mary protected Marlowe and kept him in hiding at Wilton House after Deptford. I've been meaning to check that out," said Poulson. "Wilton House is the ancestral home of the Herbert family. It's down near Stonehenge, in Salisbury."

"Amazing," said Jake. "You did all this in one afternoon?"

Melissa noticed there was food on her plate for the first time. Without further comment she put down her books and papers and ate some cold venison. "Good," she said, mouth full.

Poulson poured the last of the wine. With one final glance in the direction of the foyer, he let out a sigh, and his shoulders, Jake noted, seemed to slump a little. He had evidently given up on whoever he was waiting for.

"You say there's more evidence of Marlowe's parentage of William Herbert in the Sonnets?" Poulson spoke up, tapping out the ashes and refilling his pipe.

Melissa beamed. "I know it. I was getting to that." She glanced at her father, significantly. *' "The truth is in the Sonnets.' "*

"Here, let me reheat that for you," said Poulson, rising and reaching for her plate.

It was the last thing he would ever say. Just as he stood up there was a crash of shattering glass, followed by a strange whooshing sound.

Melissa let out a scream, as she spotted the projectile—a medieval feathered bolt, wobbling in the side of the pheasant. Poulson looked at it in bewilderment, turned toward the window, and a moment later a second bolt tore through the hole in glass and lodged in his chest. He stared down at it in surprise, reached to pull it out, then collapsed onto the dinner platter, the dark gravy commingling with a spreading pool of bright red blood.

Melissa screamed once again. Prince, the dog, sniffed at his dead master, understood at once, and began to howl: a frightful sound—an almost human Lear-like cry at this sudden, certain, unfathomable, calamitous turn of events.

"Melissa. Get down!" shouted Jake as he dove across the table, threw the light switch off, and dragged her to the floor. "That was from a crossbow," he muttered in disbelief.

They listened, frozen, for any sound of movement, or other threatening noise. Jake could hear heavy footsteps, running. Then nothing but the whistling of the November wind, pouring through the shattered window opening.

Showing what Jake now recognized as typical presence of mind, Melissa was already calling the operator on her cell phone, speaking in a low urgent whisper. "Someone's been shot!" she cried. "With some kind of arrow. Send an ambulance." She raised her voice. "I don't know the address, dammit. We are guests here." She thought a moment. "It's the Black Prince cottage. Something like that. Dr. Poulson, Samuel Poulson."

In a moment of reckless foolhardiness, Jake crept to the window and peered out. For a moment he could have sworn he saw a large, dark running figure in a trench coat profiled against a distant streetlight. But he couldn't be sure of anything in the darkness and confusion. He heard a car motor start somewhere nearby, but again, that could have been anyone in the neighborhood. Still, for one chilling moment he felt certain he had seen The Watcher again.

"Dad, stay down." Melissa admonished him from her new position behind the nearest connecting wall leading to the parlor.

"I need to check Dr. Poulson," he said. He felt his pulse, then checked for breath. There was none. No Deptford deception, this. He felt sick. "He's dead," he exclaimed, angrily. "I don't get it. It didn't even puncture any vital—oh God."

"What?" she asked, staring.

"Poison. I bet anything it turns out to be the same kind that killed Lewis."

"Hebanon? Like from Shakespeare?"

"Or Marlowe."

He bade a silent farewell to Poulson, along with an apology since he was positive he had been the target, not Poulson. Dropping to the floor, he crawled across the dining room to rejoin his daughter in the next room. Prince stayed behind by his master's side and continued to howl.

"What do we do now?" she asked. She looked pale in the dim light. Pale, he thought, as Desdemona.

In the distance, they could hear the whee-up, whee-up of police sirens shrieking towards them in urgent reproach, an eerie counterpoint to the frantic dog. They had to make a decision and fast: stay and cope with the police and authorities, face further peril, or leave the scene of a shooting for the second time in four days, right now. And still risk further peril.

"Grab your stuff and go." Jake shouted, and scrambled to do the same. The notebooks and documents were first and foremost, and devil take the hindmost. Luckily neither of them had taken time to unpack. They had just retrieved their bags from the foyer when Melissa's cell phone shattered the silence.

"Don't answer it." Jake commanded.

"Hello?" she answered it, rebel that she was. She listened a moment, then she gaped at him, incredulously. "It's Professor Parker," she said. "She's in a car. She's just a block away."

They'd find out how and why later. Meanwhile they ran for it, grateful for the deliverance, however unexpected. Charging through the front door, they crouched as they went, lugging their books and bags. A vintage silver Jaguar 3.8 salon of indeterminate age swept around the corner and pulled up at the curb like a taxi. The window slid down and Diana called out: "Hello, there."

Melissa dove in the back, Jake threw the bags in after her, opened the front passenger door and slid in beside the startled Diana. "Go!" he shouted.

She stared at him, confused. "What? I just got here. I know I'm late, but the traffic on the motorway was horrendous." She looked at the house. "Where's Samuel?"

"He's been shot!" screamed Melissa. "He's dead."

Her jaw dropped. "Oh dear Lord. What happened? Did you call the police?"

"Just go. We could be next!"

Diana bit her lip, shifted into gear and hit the gas. The old Jag was, as they say, in good nick. She accelerated down the block, spun left scraping the curb, and tore around the next corner heading west just as the ambulance, followed by two police cars, came tearing around the bend from the opposite direction.

The learned thin man fled on foot, the usual demons dancing and screeching in his head, his stolen crossbow forgotten in the grass. What folly. What horror, what unfairness was this, that he should be deprived of justice when it had been so close at hand? His luck had gone sour yet again when the fool Poulson had stood up so suddenly like that. Even after mistakenly shooting the wrong man through the window, he'd had the Yankee Rosencrantz dead in his sights. Then the bloody big man had appeared out of nowhere racing toward him and he'd had to run, in a mad scramble through the bushes. And then the woman in the Jaguar had come out of nowhere. And what of the big man, who had been dogging him for a week now, he felt certain? Whose relentless pursuit had forced him to kill once again. Who was he? And what did he want?

Seething with rage that his thirst for revenge had once again been so abruptly frustrated, the thin man slipped away into the street behind the house where he'd parked his rented Passat, and barely got out of there in time, driving frantically to overtake the big black Jaguar up ahead. Never had he felt so vexed or frustrated by a woman.

Make that two women.

If nothing else, his car would now be his weapon.

Be thou as chaste as ice, as pure as snow, he thought, acidly, *Thou shalt not escape calumny!*

Chapter Thirty-Seven

Of Hair-Breadth Escapes

Kent County, England,
Wednesday night,
November, 9:10 p.m.

Diana drove her antique Jaguar like a London cabbie, careening around corners, swerving around bends, doubling back, then hurtling towards the motorway at upwards of 150 kph, sustaining more than a few dings and scratches along the way, making Jake feel even more guilty.

Melissa watched their back the whole time, expecting to see the flashing lights of a chase vehicle at any moment.

"All right you two." Diana shouted over the roar of the engine, visibly torn between fear, anger, and wonder. "What the hell happened? You say Sam is dead? I don't understand."

"Did you see anyone leaving the area just before you called?" Jake asked tersely, looking back.

"I almost hit some big hulking man in the middle of the road just before I got there. Why? What did he do?"

"The Watcher," said Melissa, bitterly.

"Who?"

"I'll bet pounds to pennies that was the same guy who interviewed you in London."

"Oh, good heavens. I thought he looked familiar."

Jake called back to Melissa. "Are we being followed?"

"I can't tell. I don't think so." She craned her neck for a better look through the narrow rear windscreen.

As they reached the motorway, Jake took a long, deep breath and let it out slowly, grateful for every cubic centimeter of available air along with his good fortune at still being able to breathe it. "First Dr. Lewis. Then Dr. Balsavar.

Now Dr. Poulson. All of them professors, and either friends, or colleagues of yours, Dr. Parker. No offense."

"Please start making sense. Are you accusing me of having something to do with this?"

"No, no, not at all," insisted Jake, apologetically.

"Then why is all this happening?"

"We already told you," shouted Melissa.

"Don't tell me all this is about Shakespeare. That's just lunacy."

"Maybe. How do—did you know him, anyway? Dr. Poulson?" asked Jake. "And what are you doing here, by the way?"

"We're old friends from our Cambridge days when he was a professor and I a student. I've known about his Marlowe proclivities for a long time, so the late Desmond Lewis wasn't the first, Jake Fleming."

"I see. So, I gather you were the expected mystery guest for dinner this evening?"

"I spoke to Chris Braithwaite and pried out of him that you were in Canterbury, so I called Sam this afternoon. The police came looking for you right after you left yesterday. I wanted to warn you."

He looked at her askance. "You came all the way to Canterbury to do that?" He found that more than a little difficult to believe.

"And there's something else." Her tone sounded grim, and Jake braced himself.

"What?"

"Dr. Lewis's administrative assistant, Gloria Peckham was found dead this morning. Apparently, someone cut her to shreds with an antique dagger, right out of *Macbeth*. Obviously, whoever did it wished to make a statement, because the weapon was left at the scene."

"Jesus."

"They want to talk to you about that as well."

"Oh my God," gasped Melissa.

Jake stared morosely out into the darkness. "Did Poulson know about all this?"

"No. I saw no reason to alarm him. I just told him I wanted to surprise you."

"Why all the secrecy?"

"To be honest, because I felt it was imperative that I talk to you before whatever dynamite Des Lewis has gone and concocted blows up in your faces. And now Sam is dead because of it. It's gone too far. You need to turn back, and let the authorities handle it."

Melissa called out impatiently from the back: "Dad, just tell her what happened."

Two of a kind, he thought. He looked at Diana. Her jaw was set firm, although her upper front teeth, so pearly white in the moonlight outside, still bit hard on her lower lip, which, he noticed, had a small blister, perhaps from previous such abuse. Her beautiful-flawed eyes remained fixed on the road, her lovely imperfect brows narrow and determined, her firm breasts rising as she—he managed to stop himself there.

"So yes, do tell. What happened?" she asked.

"Someone shot him through a window with a crossbow. I think they were aiming for us."

Diana let out a long sigh. "Poor Sam. He didn't deserve this." She gave him a hard look. "You I'm not so sure about."

Jake didn't know how close she'd been to the man, but he knew the news had to have hurt her, and again he felt guilty.

"It happened while we were having dinner and talking," he explained. "He had just gotten up to get Melissa's plate and was hit in the chest. I'm sure it was poisoned, since he died so quickly."

"That's horrible. But who–?"

"We don't know. Whoever poisoned Dr. Lewis. Whoever stabbed Ms. Peckham. And shot Dr. Balsavar. Whoever's been threatening us. Whoever that big pal of yours is."

She drove on, her face stony. "He is not my pal," she said, angrily.

"By the way, you're not the only one asking us to cease and desist. We had a meeting with a representative of The Shakespeare Foundation this morning at the British Library."

"You're joking. What did they want?"

"To scare us off," said Melissa, matter-of-factly.

"I can't believe it. That is insane."

"Tell that to Peckham. And Poulson and Lewis."

"Oh, dear Lord." Diana just shook her head.

"And now the same man who's been following us for days shows up again," Jake added.

"So, you think he shot Sam?"

"It certainly looks that way. We don't know."

"But why all these Shakespearean weapons? What is the point of all that added melodrama? Someone is trying to make a statement and using all of us like props and actors! And for what?" She shook her head. "This makes no sense. The Shakespeare Foundation? They are a Foundation, for God's sake. Not a Cosa Nostra. This sounds like–like Mexican drugs or something."

Drugs or Shakespeare, what if it is just about money, at the end of the day? Jake pondered. It was a disturbing thought.

Diana's expression darkened. "But then who was the other one?"

"What other one?" Jake stared at her.

"The older man. I noticed him bent over under the porch light behind the house, just as I pulled up. Kind of the opposite of the other. Very thin, he looked to me."

Melissa let out a short gasp in the back, then bit her lip.

"What the hell—?" pondered Jake. "You've got me there."

"I don't understand it," Diana said, her distress evident on her face. "I don't understand why someone would do this, over a question of history."

"They're still shooting each other in the Middle East," noted Jake. "That's about history, isn't it?"

"Well I absolutely refuse to believe it was anyone having anything to do with the university," said Diana. "And that goes for The Shakespeare Foundation as well, whatever they said to you."

"Then who?"

"God only knows. Some nut case."

Diana pulled into the passing lane, straining to see in the darkness. It was getting foggier by the minute.

Melissa, who had been silent for several minutes, spoke up from the back. "So, excuse me for asking, but where are you taking us?"

Diana considered the question for a moment. Then she said, in a matter-of-fact tone: "To the airport. Gatwick, I should think, it's closest."

Since the break-in, they'd had the foresight to make a habit of keeping their essential documents with them, including passports. But Jake was not in the mood for ultimatums.

"So, whose errand lady are you, really? The Shakespeare Taliban? Scotland Yard? The London Police? Who's asking you to get us out of the country?"

Diana slammed on the brakes, almost throwing all of them into the dash and partition, despite the seat belts. She pulled over to the shoulder and turned to face them.

"Look, I didn't have to come and rescue you two miscreants from probably well-deserved detention and maybe a good thrashing by British authorities. Nor do I have to take you one step further, and if you don't like it, you can bloody well get out and exercise your right to walk!"

A quarter mile back, another car, discerning their movements just in time, had also pulled to the shoulder: a white Passat. The learned driver quickly switched off his lights.

"Uh, Dad, she has a point. She's the one holding all the cards at the moment, it appears to me."

"This is no bloody game," Diana snapped. "This is life and death. A very close friend of mine is dead, and a member of my faculty, and a valued staffer, and perhaps this physicist you've been cavorting with as well. And much as I deplore what Desmond Lewis was trying to do, and while I don't question his right to do it, there are limits. You are dragging my department, and by association my university, and quite possibly my career, into the mud. So, yes. I want you out of the country, before any more damage is done. And believe me or not, I am doing you an immense favor. Those policemen who came by yesterday and again this morning were not interested in having tea. You, sir, are now a prime suspect in murder. Possibly more than one."

"So, the suicide theory was bunk all along?" asked Melissa, from the back seat.

"Do you actually think I had something to do with that?" demanded Jake.

"I don't know. No, I doubt it. I think you're what you say you are, a nosy meddling journalist, and the police are just fishing. But that doesn't lessen your danger. Or mine."

"She's right," allowed Melissa, grudgingly.

"So, what's it going to be?" asked Diana, glancing at her rear view mirror in growing concern. "There's somebody back there."

Melissa turned and scanned the rear view. "I don't see anyone. Are you sure?"

Jake looked at Diana, trying hard to ignore the fact that she was so damned attractive. "You mentioned your job, just now. Do you mind if I ask you a question?"

"Go ahead but make it fast. You are rapidly running out of time."

"Tell me this: what, exactly, is your job?"

"As you should know by now, I am Department Chair of the English—"

"No, I know all that. I mean, what is your *job*? What do you do, in that chair of yours? Issue edicts? *Fatwas*? 'Thou shalt not question Shakespeare or thy father, or the holy—' "

"Stop it. My job is to oversee and advise the department staff and faculty, occasionally hire and fire as needed and tenure allows, arrange and approve curricula, and so on."

"Does learning fit in there anywhere?"

Diana looked at her watch. "That was a bit snide. I'll give you one more minute."

"That would be the curricula, Dad," observed Melissa, helpfully.

"Well it seems to me that a university is supposed to be a place where learning takes place. Not just memorizing names or numbers, like one of those *madrassas*—I've seen them, by the way. Or at least a provision for the possibility of new knowledge, or new understanding? Isn't that what research is supposed to be all about?"

"I don't think you get the—"

"Do you think Princeton hired Einstein just so he could lecture students about the latest conventional wisdom in math?"

"So what are you saying? That my faculty and I are just purveying dogma?"

"Aren't you? How are you any different from those mullahs, or priests? I mean, where's your curiosity? Where's the desire for discovery? Or does that only happen in, say, the Physics Department?"

Melissa grinned at that.

Diana let out a sigh. "Very well. I see your point. I heard that comment of Lewis's too, you know. About us being Academic Ayatollas and all. Very glib."

"Well, at least you didn't fire him for it. That's a start."

"Only because he had tenure," she retorted. Then she laughed. "Actually, he didn't."

"Didn't what?"

"Have tenure." She checked the rear view mirror once more. "All right, Mr. Journalist. Gatwick is two hours away. You've got two hours to make your case."

Jake glanced back at Melissa. "I may need a little help," he said.

Melissa, in the meantime, was looking out through the rear windscreen, squinting against the oncoming headlights. "Oh shit," she said. "There is someone back there. Go, go, go!"

Diana threw the old Jag into gear, and surged back onto the motorway, nearly colliding with an oncoming tractor trailer in the process. "Sorry," she muttered.

While Melissa kept rear guard Diana listened, tight-lipped, but to her credit didn't evict them from the car while Jake filled her in quickly on the Blodgett incidents, on his producer theory, that someone has a vested interest in preserving the status quo, and the unfairness of Marlowe's treatment by historians, including the Poet's Corner. She acknowledged he had a point there. After getting no response about Monsieur Le Doux, Jake was all out of arguments. Finally, he glanced back at Melissa, who shrugged. "It's in your court," he said. "Go ahead and tell her, if you want another go-around."

"No. Don't tell me." exclaimed Diana. "More Marlowe?"

"His son, actually," said Melissa.

"What? What are you talking about? Marlowe had no children."

"You know of. But I've seen evidence in Dr. Poulson's archives that suggest otherwise."

"Melissa found the 'Herb' on Lewis's list," explained Jake. "It stands for 'Herbert.' As in 'W.H.' "

Diana turned full around in the driver's seat to look Melissa in the eye. Jake grabbed the wheel. "Wait a minute. You're trying to connect Marlowe to the mysterious 'W.H.' by way of the Herberts?"

"It makes sense," insisted Melissa. " 'H' for Herbert. Hello?" She told a skeptical Diana about the Countess connection, and Mary's relationship with Marlowe. Diana listened in stunned silence to the dedication.

"And bear in mind, that no one–at least no one in Academe that I could find except Sunir–has ever looked at the Sonnets with this kind of love in mind–of a man in exile for a woman beyond his reach, and of a father for a bastard son whom he can never see or embrace and can only admire from afar. Then you see the implications, and it all falls together. Desmond Lewis was right, Professor Parker. And if anyone would let me, this would be my dissertation."

"Do tell," said Diana, eyes fixed grimly to the road. "I'm all ears."

"Marlowe wrote in his dedication to Mary how he shall on the very first page of a poem 'call on thee, Mistress of the Muses, and even to be increased by the praise of mortals', right? So, there's the perfect lead-in to the very first line of the very first page of this book of poems, in Sonnet One." She had brought along the Sonnets, apparently from the archives, and she opened it to page one. "Listen to this." Then she read, under the car reading lamp:

'From fairest creatures we desire increase,
That thereby beauty's rose might never die,
But as the riper should by time decease,
His tender heir might bear his memory:
But thou, contracted to thine own bright eyes,
Feed'st thy light's flame with self/substantial fuel.' "

"Certainly sounds like the same author," agreed Jake.

"The first lines are a man's most basic wish—to have 'increase,' Melissa went on, with a blush. "In other words, to father a child. Exactly like in his dedication to Mary. And with whom do all men, especially romantic, poetic men aspire to have such 'increase?' " She gestured, matter-of-factly. "With 'fairest creatures.' A beautiful, gifted woman. Like Mary Sidney, the most beautiful and gifted of them all. 'Thereby beauty's rose might never die.' Compare that to Shakespeare and his poor unlucky wife Ann Hathaway."

"Well, she did get his 'second-best bed,' " Jake pointed out.

"Shut up," said Diana. "Let her talk."

Melissa stuck her tongue out at him. "In any case, the next lines reveal what men fear most: *'as the riper should by time decease,'* in other words the young grow old and die, all men hope their *'tender heir might bear his memory.'* That couldn't be any clearer: *tender heir*? Shakespeare had no heir. His only son died in his teens. He then goes on to admonish the boy—from a distance—for childish offenses he'd only just heard about."

Diana continued to drive, in silence.

Jake checked the side mirror, then looked back over his shoulder. "You sure you saw someone back there?" he asked Diana.

She checked both mirrors, then shrugged. "Maybe not." She turned back to Melissa. "Go on," she said.

Melissa plunged ahead.

"The first ten sonnets and a lot of others suddenly make all kinds of sense if addressed to this mysterious son," she went on, "and not some unknown gay lover, like people have always assumed and couldn't explain. Even the dedication page itself speaks plainly of a father to his son, wishing him well as he sets forth in his life. And telling him, among other things, *that his father still lives*. It isn't only the first ten sonnets either, that talk about the pain of an estranged father." She picked up the book again.

"Sonnet 35 (last six lines):

I may not evermore acknowledge thee,
Lest my bewailed guilt should do thee shame,
Nor thou with public kindness honor me,

Unless thou take that honour from thy name:
But do not so; I love thee in such sort
As thou being mine, mine is thy good sport.

"See? He can't acknowledge his son. And again, Sonnet 124:

If my dear love were but the child of state,
It might for Fortune's bastard be unfather'd."

She put the book down and looked at them for a reaction. "Dad, remember I was wondering about 'Fortune's bastard,' before? *I may not evermore acknowledge thee, Lest my bewailed guilt should do thee shame*?"

Jake scratched his head and finished a notation. "I see what you mean. It's amazing that it can just sit there in plain sight for centuries and no one noticed."

"No one noticed what? That if you take sand, and apply enough heat, you get diamonds?" snapped Diana.

"No one noticed because they didn't want to notice, including Chambers," Melissa practically spat back. "Or you, no offense. Did, or did not Shakespeare abandon his wife and family in 1587, and show no remorse, no concern or care for any of them that can be demonstrated anywhere? He refused to even pay their bills or give them money. It's in the public record, Professor Parker."

"So, you think Marlowe is communicating with Mary and William by way of these sonnets?" asked Jake, still shaking his head in astonishment.

"Isn't it obvious? It's so sad, really. And it goes on and on. You can tell that the years are passing and he's giving up hope. A lot of the later sonnets were probably written in the waning years of the poet's life, dealing with other personalities and other conflicts. But the whole series begins with the sonnets addressed to William Herbert, 'Mr. W.H.' and to his mother, Mary Sidney Herbert, urging the young heir William to marry quickly and secure his inheritance as the Third Earl, something Marlowe could never give him and could only have ruined."

"So that's your Dark Lady?" Diana shook her head in incredulity.

"It's a pretty cool theory, I must say," said Jake.

"It's the only one that makes sense," Melissa insisted. "And Dr. Lewis must have reached the same conclusion. William Shakespeare was never estranged, exiled, or forcibly separated from anyone. The man who suffered and expressed those feelings again and again could only be Christopher Marlowe. The lost poet in exile."

Diana finally spoke up. "All right. I will admit your theory is intriguing, and better than a lot I've heard. And for your information," this was addressed to Jake, "I am not as completely close minded as you imagine. So just for the sake of argument. Let's assume that William Herbert was the son of Christopher Marlowe. How could you prove it?"

"By mitochondrial DNA testing of the mother's line, or if we can get some Marlowe bone marrow fragments, we could trace the Y chromosome. Aren't there survivors of these families?"

"I checked," said Melissa. "There are numerous Marleys, which is Marlowe's original family name, who still live in Kent. Some of them have got to be descendants of Marlowe's father John Marley. And the descendants of William Herbert are still around, right?"

Diana laughed. "Of course. The current one is Earl of Pembroke and Montgomery, as I recall. Shall we traipse over to Wilton and ask for a blood sample? I'm sure they'd love that."

"But," Melissa pointed out, "it would also entitle the Herbert family to a strong claim to the Shakespeare Canon. It seems to me that would be a far greater gain than any possible losses to the family in terms of titles or embarrassment."

"Well, there were plenty of kings descended from 'commoners,' none of whom were the genius Marlowe certainly was," conceded Diana. "By the way, the Marley family name used to be 'Merlin.' So, while you're at it, maybe you could claim your Kit Marlowe is descended from the court of King Arthur."

Jake laughed. "Maybe that would entice the Herberts."

"Hmmm," said Diana. The car fell silent, but for the sound of the wind, and the engine, and the traffic on the motorway.

"In any case," said Melissa, "the man who would wistfully write to his son to *'Look what is best, that best I wish in thee,'* and the one who ditched his family, never wrote a known letter and would not even bother to educate his own children are not the same man. I rest my case."

They rode in silence for a while. Diana checked her watch. "All right. I admit that was impressive. You may have a good subject for a dissertation there, and if you were in my college, I'd probably have to allow it."

"Really? I may hold you to that," said Melissa, gleefully.

"And she managed all that in just over an hour," added Jake.

"Don't press your luck, sir," said Diana. "We are still headed for Gatwick."

"All right. So what would it take to convince you to open your mind just a nudge further, allow academic freedom and free speech to flourish, and take us to Oxford?"

She laughed, wryly. "I see. Well, I suppose you could try bribery. A tank of gas, loaf of bread, and—" she cut herself off, and blushed.

"How about I buy you dinner, for starters," proposed Jake, with a grin. "Maybe ply you with a roast loin, bit of claret, and some spotted—never mind, scratch that."

"Yes, you'd better. Better not! Some things don't translate well to that foreign tongue of yours." But the tension in the car had eased considerably.

In the back, Melissa blushed hotly, not sure she liked the new direction this was going. Still, on the plus side, she saw no further indication that they were being followed. Or, equally important, deported.

Diana pulled off at the next service exit. "I don't know about you, but I am ready for that dinner you promised. I'd been looking forward to Sam's venison, you know. And a quiet evening by the fire convincing you of your folly. Instead, well, here we are. And we'd better find an inn. We won't make Oxford tonight."

After a short drive down a dark, fog-bound Kent country lane towards a town called Sittingbourne, she spotted a two story Tudor farmhouse sporting a white wooden sign with "Rooms and Dinner" in ornate black and gold-trimmed lettering. "All right," she said. "Will this do?"

There was no need to ask.

The innkeeper, an elderly white haired gentleman clearly of the old school, regretfully informed them dinner was over, but he might be able to put together "a snack." They expressed gratitude, especially Melissa, who had also missed out on Sam Poulson's cooking and was vocally "starving to death." He also assumed that Diana and Jake were married. Jake was about to dissuade him when he said, "You're in luck, I only have two rooms left, a double and a single."

"You two can have the larger room and I'll take the single," said Jake quickly, as they headed for the stairs.

Melissa tilted her head mischievously. "What if we don't get along?"

Two of a kind, he thought once again.

It was the old gent, the innkeeper, who actually broke the ice in terms of easing their mutual discomfort. After they'd set down the bags in the hall and were standing around feeling awkward, he announced, "Drinks and a light supper by the fire, if anyone's of a mind."

Jake, for one, was of a mind. Thank God for lonely geezers, he thought. He was a long way from forgetting the sight of Sunir falling, and then so soon afterwards Sam Poulson getting killed before his eyes. As luck would have it, the two women felt the same way. Soon they were sitting around a roaring fireplace in the common room enjoying excellent leftover salad, cold roast duck and pound cake, and sipping some wonderful Bushmill's Irish whiskey (which Melissa admitted she actually liked).

Before long, they had forgotten most of their troubles, the world's troubles, even Marlowe's troubles, and begun to unwind.

And unwind.

Somehow Diana and Jake were soon occupying the same couch, her skirt askew as usual, brushing each other's legs by accident, occasionally touching the other's knee after a good joke. The innkeeper was full of them, mostly of the bawdy 'man and his wife in a pub' variety. Melissa tried not to notice what was going on, but even she seemed to accept the inevitable after a while.

"Did you hear about the nuns at the abbey clinic? The Mother Superior tells them: 'I want you all to know that today we have acquired our first case of syphilis.' There's a gasp around the room, then Sister Mary Margaret speaks up and says 'Oh, good. I was getting so tired of that same old chablis.' " He almost fell off his chair in the telling of it.

Around the third drink, Melissa yawned dramatically, arose, and announced that she was going to bed. Jake worriedly wondered where that might be, but there was no graceful way of raising the question. He guessed he would find out before long, and the rest would fall in place accordingly. Or not.

Diana was getting a bit loopy, and Jake decided enough was enough. "I think I'd better get the lady to bed," he told the innkeeper. The old man looked disappointed at losing his audience, then grinned in approval.

"Yes, of course, you'd best take care of the lady," he said. "Have a good evening, sir and madam," he added, gathering up the glasses and dishes and scurrying away with a chuckle.

Melissa had deviously occupied the single room, leaving Diana and Jake to fend for themselves. Diana threw herself onto the bed and fell instantly asleep. Jake collapsed into the armchair. So much for sex and the single scholar, he thought, woozily; then thought no more.

The threesome in the Jaguar had just turned in when the late arrival entered the inn. He was a thin, gray-haired, sour looking man with no luggage. The aging proprietor didn't like him at all. "We're full up," he told the man, in some relief. The man reminded him of a gray wolf, somehow, and he did not like wolves.

The Learned thin man, for his part, had held his tongue, battled back the phantoms whispering and goading him, and stifled a disturbing impulse to exact righteous punishment on the arrogant old fool. Instead he had managed to control himself and taken up quarters at the less elegant rooming house across the road. It was better that he kept his distance anyway, he decided, and avoid recognition until he could find the right moment, once again. Plus, there were several serviceable knives in the dingy kitchen that would service further needs and purposes.

The bad news was that he had no new insights as to who the large chap was who continued to plague him. That was discomfiting, because he was still out there, somewhere. Still, with any luck—and he was due for some—he could bring down the whole flock of birds with one well-aimed stone. *If you have tears*, he thought, acidly, *prepare to shed them now*.

With great effort, he once again warded off those clawing fiends that still lurked in his head, ever more demanding of his full attention and obeisance. Once more he brushed them back and the pain they inflicted, and reason took hold. He had an appointment in Oxford two days from now. He knew that Desmond Lewis's trail pointed inevitably to Oxford. The Flemings would have to go there, no doubt were heading there now. Why not let things fall as they may, and surely they would?

Kent County, England,
Thursday, mid-November, 7:15 a.m.

Jake was awakened from fitful dreams of sex and violence by a knock on the door.

"Dad? You up?"

"Yes," he called out, unwinding from his painful position of semi-repose on the chair. "I'll meet you downstairs, Melissa."

Diana, also awakened by the knock, sat up in bed and looked around in momentary confusion, spotted Jake in the chair, and blushed hotly.

Melissa joined them in the lobby, some residual resentment mixed with devilry in her eyes, and made a big deal out of being nonchalant, oblivious, and totally naive about any hanky panky that may or may not have occurred in the room next door. Jake, in the meantime, could think of no graceful way to assure her that nothing had happened. At least, he thought, she seemed willing to be mature enough not to hold her mother's memory over his head. It was enough to live with already. Whatever happened with Diana (or any new relationship that might or might not come along), he would always love Beverly, and cherish her memory. Maybe, he hoped, their daughter understood that. Even though, as he knew, he had a lot to atone for.

Diana, for her part, acted as though of course nothing out of the ordinary had occurred, since it hadn't, and they departed the inn with well-wishes all around.

Once they were in the car, however, Melissa turned morose, and Diana wanted to talk.

"I know I agreed to take you to Oxford, but I think it's time we call in the police," she said. "I hate to belabor this, but three people may be dead because of this crazy quest of yours, Don Quixote. And they are going to catch up to you sooner or later—or us, now that I'm involved—and the piper will demand to be paid."

"Maybe four people," Melissa spoke up from the back. "Don't forget Sunir."

"Oh, thanks for that helpful reminder," grumbled Jake.

Melissa had no better answer. Diana just shook her head and drove on in silence, unaware of the man in the Passat a quarter mile or so behind her on the highway, whose disposition had not been improved by the lumpy bed he'd been forced to recline on for the night.

An hour later they had bypassed London and turned north on M-1. Then, with one of those flashes of insight that leave indelible scars on the interior lining of the skull, Jake knew what he had to do. There was still one more thing they needed, before pressing on to Oxford.

They needed to exhume Kit Marlowe's supposed grave.

He told the others. Melissa was both thrilled and appalled. Diana wanted no part of it, and brusquely declared that he was insane, and the most she would do would be to drive them to Deptford. Then they were on their own. In any case, they would need some tools. She grudgingly stopped at a garden center at the edge of the southeast suburbs, and Jake bought a serviceable pair of shovels, two pairs of gloves ("in honor of John Shakspere the glover," he joked to Melissa) and a flashlight. They were as ready as two amateur grave robbers were likely to be. Except that now they had to wait until dark.

Chapter Thirty-Eight

Alas, Poor Yorick

London, Thursday night, mid-November, 11:35 p.m.

It was time to move at last. After spending a restless day hopping from library to coffee shop to pub, ever watchful and fearful of pursuit, Diana long gone in a huff, the two trespassers emerged from their place of waiting in a harrowingly decrepit nearby park, pulled black stockings over their faces and approached the churchyard from the south, away from the church and rectory. Jake boosted Melissa, now in jeans, handed the shovels up to her, and clambered over the wall after her. They could just make out the bronze plaque in the pale moonlight. The sky shone like the tentacle-scarred underbelly of a great, lost manta ray. The graveyard was a forlorn clutter of monuments ancient and new, straight and askew.

"Tis now the very witching time of night, when churchyards yawn and hell itself breathes out," breathed Melissa, in a low voice.

"Don't talk like that," Jake scolded her. "I'm very superstitious."

"I doubt that. Anyway, it's from *Hamlet.* You should genuflect."

The hard-scrabbled area beneath the plaque, as expected, was unmarked, except from the activity of the nearby Lewis funeral several days before. At least Desmond Lewis, unlike Christopher Marlowe, had a stone. They began to dig. Melissa made up in endurance what she lacked in sheer muscle power. Jake had been running on empty for so long he was accustomed to getting by on fumes alone.

Their plan was simple: dig until they found bones or were deep enough to know that none were there. If they found bones, they would take them to the University, and using Diana's contacts (with her blessing or without), hope to find traces of marrow and compare the DNA to any living Marleys they could find, which surely they could, since they were ubiquitous, Poulson had told them, in Canterbury. If there was a way to compare them to the Puritan martyr John Penry, all the better. They could go there if they had to. If some random body or bodies had been thrust into the ground at this spot, so be it. So long as the DNA was not that of a Marlowe.

It was also an opportunity to say one last goodbye to Desmond Lewis, whose new granite marker and freshly compacted grave site stood close by.

They had found several bones of various sizes, somewhat to Jake's chagrin, when, at half past midnight he struck something with a loud clunk and held his breath. It was a skull. "Speaking of *Hamlet*," he muttered. "I think I just found Yorick." With a cringe, he tossed it in the bag.

"Oh shit. C'mon, hurry, please." Melissa called out, anxiously. "I think someone heard us."

"Hang on. We have to know one way or the other."

A light went on upstairs in the rectory, to the far side of the church. "Damn!" he muttered and dug faster.

She stopped digging, more urgency in her voice than before: "Come on. Someone's coming."

He heard a door open in the distance. He heard it slam, and footsteps approaching. The shadows came alive, as a lantern bobbed and weaved toward them.

"Who's there?" a gnarled voice shouted out.

That was when Melissa decided it was time to go.

And so Jake hastily agreed, scrambling hastily out of the hole, pulling her after him. But by then he knew they'd been seen. His heart picked up speed, even as his feet seemed to slow down. Frantically, they grabbed the bag and their equipment and ran for the wall. As Jake threw the bag and shovels over the wall and clambered after them, he heard a sharp scream behind him, followed by the almost identical pitch of a distant, wailing siren.

"Melissa!" he called out, turning back, fearing the worst. There was no sign of her, and his heart sank like Faustus into the pits of hell. He waited a horrifying moment, steeling himself to go back over the wall after her, come what may.

A hand appeared, then another, followed by an uncharacteristically tousled blond head. "I'm all right," she gasped, finally appearing at the top of the wall, breathless. "I caught my foot and twisted it." Quickly, he reached up and helped her over the side. As they reached the ground on street level, they were brought up short by the presence of a large man in a London Fog, waiting on the sidewalk. He didn't look happy to see them, if not in the least bit surprised.

"Evening," he said, curtly.

"Oh. Shit," said Jake, reaching for the nearest shovel. With sudden, and startling speed, the big man punched him, hard, in the last place he needed such treatment—his gut—and Jake doubled over in instant agony.

"That's for all the grief you've put me through," growled The Watcher, seizing Melissa by the arm. "And you can come with me, Miss."

Jake decided that this might be an excellent time for the church watchman to overtake them after all. Unfortunately, the watchman showed no inclination towards further pursuit beyond his brick boundary. In dismay, Jake could hear him muttering over the wall, finally shuffling away mumbling curses at "bloody vandals and thieves."

"Let go of me, you creep." cried Melissa, struggling.

"What do you want?" Jake managed to gasp, at last.

"Get in the car. Over there." Maintaining his grip on Melissa, he gestured towards a black car parked across the road. Melissa glanced at Jake, as though looking for a signal. She knew, because he had taught her so as a young girl, that abductions must be fought with every last breath like your life depended on it. Because, as Lewis' case had clearly shown, too often it did.

Jake feigned injury just long enough to cause the big man's attention to waver, which was just long enough for her to break free. Jake, still too busy recovering his gut to do much more than watch, stared in amazement as, with the practiced motion of someone who has not wasted her aerobics classes in mere foot-dragging and who has also taken Tai Kwan Do, Melissa brought her knee up sharply, kicked out with crippling accuracy, and delivered a foot directly into the center of the big man's crotch.

As The Watcher gasped and doubled over, she shouted: "Dad, run!"

Jake needed no further persuasion or encouragement. Especially when, up ahead, a police car rounded the corner in the direction of the front of the church. Melissa grabbed the bag and, abandoning their tools, they broke into a run, moving with adrenalin-charged speed and the agility of phantoms, which they must have resembled. One old vagabond roaming the neighborhood saw them whisk past and let forth a fearful banshee cry of his own, which melded with the wail of the approaching siren.

The darkened Jaguar slid out of the night like an apparition and pulled up beside them. The car window slid down as Jake stared in astonishment.

"Get in," ordered Diana.

They tore off the stocking masks and jumped into the car. For the second time in twelve hours, Jake had never been so happy to see anyone in his life, although he was not about to admit it.

"This is getting to be a regular thing," she said, wryly, as she threw the car in gear and took off.

"So, what brought about this unexpected surprise?" Asked Jake. Then he looked at Melissa suspiciously. "Did you have something to do with this?"

Once again, Diana Parker was a mixture of contradictions. "I changed my mind," she said with a shrug. "I promised to take you to Oxford, and a promise is a promise. Besides," and here she forced a laugh, "it's obvious someone still needs to keep an eye on you two, and it seems it will have to be me."

"Thanks for coming back," said Melissa, for both of them.

Diana put the car in gear and headed for the motorway. "What happened?" she asked. "I thought I heard sirens again."

Jake looked innocent. "Sirens? I didn't hear any sirens. Melissa, did you hear any sirens?"

Diana made a face and stepped on the gas. "I'm sure I'm going to regret this. Did you find what you were looking for?"

"Not exactly," said Jake.

"We got some bones," said Melissa, holding up her backpack.

"Along with nearly getting killed," mentioned Jake. "Again."

"Always an adventure, with you two. I assume you are being dramatic."

"No, we bumped into your old friend, Big Brother," said Melissa, matter-of-factly.

"My God." She looked around anxiously. "Where is he?"

"Presently indisposed," said Jake.

"Could we just get out of here?" suggested Melissa, nervously.

Diana looked at her sideways as she drove. "So, who called the police?"

Melissa let out a laugh. "I think we aroused the sexton."

Jake pulled out the skull, feeling much like the gravedigger in *Hamlet*.

"Dr. Parker, meet John Penry," he said.

She blanched. "John Penry? Are you serious?"

Melissa told her about the curious overlap of events in the late May of 1593, and Diana listened with continuing skepticism. She might be their accomplice now, but they had not succeeded in winning her over to the Marlowe camp.

"So," said Jake, at last, putting the skull away. "How far to Oxford?"

She glanced at him sidewise. "Frankly, I don't think you're quite ready for that scene." She laughed. "You're going to need to stop somewhere and clean up, for one thing. And get some decent clothes for God's sake."

"A bath would be really welcome, right about now," agreed Melissa.

They drove on in silence. As Diana turned north onto M-40 she sighed. "Good thing I'm not teaching this semester. Although I am supposed to be working on a book. Can you contribute for gas and tolls?"

"Of course," said Jake, embarrassed. "Meals, hotels, bribes, whatever it takes. Besides, I think a real Shakespearean in my story would provide a lot of authenticity to the whole authorship thing," he teased.

"Leave me out of your bloody story. I am not about to let go of four centuries of scholarship and tradition just because you people showed up."

"Tradition," echoed Melissa. "There's a keyword for you."

"And yet part of you is glad we did and at least suspects that we are right," said Jake.

Diana blushed and brushed a lock of hair out of her eyes. "Absolutely not. But tell me, young lady," she said, turning to Melissa. "Since when did you make this radical jump from Shakespeare's bed to Marlowe's?"

It was Melissa's turn to blush. "Over the last two weeks. Since I've actually gotten to see the biographical material and sources. And since I actually got to know who and what each of them really was."

"She's in love," explained Jake.

Melissa hit his arm over the seat. "Speak for yourself, Jake Fleming."

"Maybe you'll find something new for your book," suggested Jake, to Diana.

"I just finished working on a book," mentioned Melissa. "For one of my professors at Berkeley. Actually, I finished last term. I did most of the grunt work and a lot of the writing and editing."

"What's your book about?" asked Diana, conversationally.

"It's called *The Sonnets of Shakespeare, Revisited,*" said Melissa, matter-of-factly.

Diana stared. "You're joking. You worked on Scofield's book?"

"Yes. You know about it?"

"Of course, it's in all the bookstores. It just came out this week."

Melissa leaned forward, eagerly. "Really? You've seen it? He was supposed to tell me."

"Indeed, I have. It has excellent reviews, I might add."

"Did you read the introduction?"

"Indeed, I did. That's always quite telling, in regards to sources and so on."

Melissa smiled. "So, you must have seen it."

"Seen what?"

"My name. He said he would acknowledge me as his virtual co-author." she said, proudly. "Melissa Fleming. Maybe you didn't notice, since you don't really know me."

"No, I would have noticed." Diana frowned. "I'm sorry, but there were no acknowledgments at all. Just a foreword, which, come to think of it, was rather fawning about how wonderful Shakespeare 'undoubtedly' was as a Renaissance man and all that."

"Did he actually use that word? 'Undoubtedly'?" asked Jake.

Melissa stared at her, accusingly. "You're saying there were no acknowledgments at all? What about co-authors? Did he list me as co-author, like he promised?"

"Sorry. He was sole author."

Melissa's jaw dropped open, then snapped closed again. Jake looked at her. "Melissa, I had no idea. You want me to call him on this? I'll be happy to kick his figurative ass for you when we get back to Berkeley. His literal one too, if you want."

"Don't worry about it. I'll deal with it," she said, grimly.

Diana looked back at Melissa, sympathetically. “Look, I know how you feel. Luminary professors are notorious for exploiting young graduate students and then dumping them.”

“How about you?” snapped Melissa. “How many grad students have you exploited for your fucking books?”

“Melissa, easy,” cautioned Jake.

“What? Sorry if I offended your little love interest here, Dad. Fuck you. Fuck both of you.”

“You can stop with the suppositions,” he warned her. The shock subsided into silence, and Diana drove on, trying to remain calm, while Melissa sat stonily in the back. Jake’s head spun with misgivings and apprehension.

“Maybe we should just turn back, and I’ll go talk to Scotland Yard, like you suggested,” he said, at last. “Maybe this whole thing has gone far enough.”

“No, it hasn’t,” came from the back seat, to his surprise. “What, are you just gonna dump Lewis and those guys and forget about it? As a matter of fact, I’m glad Scofield stiffed me. Now I won’t have any compunctions about blowing him out of the water with my own book.”

“That’s my girl,” said Jake. “What’s it about?”

“Ha ha. Anyway, I intend to confront him about this as soon as I see him. He’s like *the* expert on Shakespeare, and I’m sick of it.”

“So, are we still on for Oxford, or what?” asked Diana.

Chapter Thirty-Nine

The Tyger's Heart

Nearing Oxford, England,
Early Friday, mid-November

Jake spent most of the trip north into the heartland in the back seat of the Jaguar dozing, while Melissa, now in serious discussion about the roles and status of women in the Plays sat up front. At least the two women got along now, he thought, gratefully.

After Melissa had apologized for her earlier outburst, that is.

Diana had not seen any cars following them in quite some time, much to her relief.

Stopping twice to rest, they reached Oxford just before dawn, found an all-night coffee shop on the outskirts, and waited there until the other shops were open so they could buy some clean clothes and 'necessaries,' as Diana put it. They also needed a place to clean up, and settled on a modest hotel near the railroad station, where Diana negotiated a room for the day only (she had no wish to spend the night in such a place) with two queen-size beds, while the others waited, still grubby, in the car. The room had a clean bath and towels, a phone, and that was enough.

A quick trip to a small mall nearby did the trick clothes-wise, and while Jake and Melissa were buying their various and sundry items, Diana walked over to a newsstand. She rejoined them a few minutes later, flush with excitement.

"You're not going to believe this," she said. "Guess who's in town as we speak, for a big book signing and reception?"

Jake looked at her blankly for a moment. Then glanced at Melissa, whose jaw dropped, then closed again firmly.

"John Scofield," she said.

Jake looked at her in surprise. "Scofield is in Oxford?"

Diana nodded. "Right. He is tenured here, you know."

Jake looked at Melissa. "I thought he was at Berkeley. Isn't that where you—"

"He's a visiting professor there, Dad. He's from here, originally." She glanced at Diana. "Right?"

"Yes. He's here for his book tour," explained Diana. "In fact, he's staying at the Oxford Inn on High Street and then will be giving a talk later at the university."

"But if he's from here, doesn't he have a house or something?"

"I believe it's faculty housing, and since he's taken a two-year sabbatical in the States—"

"I get it," said Jake, with a sigh.

"So, shall we pay him a visit?"

"No, let me," said Melissa, setting her jaw. "I intend to give him a piece of my mind, and it's not going to be pretty."

Jake frowned. "You sure about that? I mean, your degree and everything depends on his good will, doesn't it?"

"Not any more it doesn't," she declared, and there was no changing her mind.

Diana dropped Melissa off at the Oxford Inn, after she had changed and showered. "Good luck," she said, calling after her. Melissa didn't even look back.

For a moment Jake thought about going after her, then decided he was just being foolish and parental. She's a big girl, he reminded himself.

Diana drove them back to their hotel and they took turns cleaning up and rested fitfully for a half hour or so, fully clothed.

Diana got up after a while, feeling agitated. "I'm going out for a walk," she said. "I can't sleep. You go ahead and relax. I think I saw a Blackwell's bookstore down the way."

Jake nodded drowsily, turned over, and fell asleep in an instant.

He awoke from a dream involving a moaning skull in a backpack, with someone shaking him.

"What? What?" he murmured in a panic, prying his eyelids open and sitting up.

"Jake," said Diana, urgently. "There's something you should know."

"What? Where's Melissa?" he asked, looking around. "She back yet?" He rubbed his eyes and squinted at her, doubtfully.

"That's just it. I can't find her. But I did find a copy of Scofield's new book, and you're not going to like this."

Now he was wide awake and swung his feet over the side of the bed. "What is it?"

"Richard Scofield taught Desmond Lewis. Here at Oxford."

He frowned. "Oh, really?"

"Yes, he was Lewis's mentor. Right here, at Oxford."

Jake put his hand to his forehead. "Oh God." He scrambled to his feet grabbed for his coat.

"Apparently they had a major falling out over the Shakespeare biographical material some time back. Jake, if Desmond Lewis was trying to upstage Richard Scofield with his book, Scofield would not take it kindly, from what I've heard. He would absolutely flip."

That, thought Jake, might be putting it mildly. And Melissa was walking straight into the tiger's lair. "Let's go," he said, tersely. "We've got to find her."

Diana was already out the door.

Melissa had located the Scofield book-signing event without any trouble. It was the hottest ticket in town at the moment, and the crowd of mostly ladies that waited outside the hotel lobby chatted eagerly, all anxious to get a glimpse, if not a signature, of the famed Shakespearean scholar.

Melissa, after waiting for more than forty minutes, was too steamed to have any further patience for any of it and elbowed her way through the crowd determinedly.

Scofield saw her coming and smiled confidently when she marched up to the table. "Excuse me," complained the next woman in line, busy in the middle of fawning over the 'greatest Shakespearean writer of all time.' "Miss? You have to wait your turn."

"It's all right," said the famous author, reaching for her book. "This is my personal assistant, Miss Fleming."

"Oh my," said the woman, stepping aside with a facetious near bow to the intruder. "How lucky for you."

Melissa didn't feel lucky. "We need to talk," she told her work-study employer and faculty advisor.

"Well, my dear, as you can see, I'm rather busy. But I've been expecting you. Perhaps you could meet me at this spot, in, say, half an hour?" He slipped her a piece of paper, which she quickly pocketed.

"You got it," she said, turned and wheeled away, her head still spinning with anger.

He looked after her and his body trembled. He felt heartsick at her disloyalty, so like her predecessor. And now her! And he had loved her like a daughter.

Once more he shook off the phantoms that screeched in his head and smiled up at his adoring audience.

"Next?" he called out, as the woman who'd been waiting stepped forward.

Once back in the hotel lobby, Melissa unfolded the paper and glanced at the message. *The Bridge of Sighs* was all it said. Ordering a coffee from a lobby waiter, she pondered what to do. Am I crazy? She thought. Could Dr. Scofield have had anything to do with the death of Desmond Lewis? She shook her head. Impossible, she thought. She'd known him for almost four years, since her undergraduate days when she'd sat in awe in the fiftieth row of one of the huge auditoriums at U.C. Berkeley and listened, rapt, as he effused about the marvelous imagery, lyricism, and inventiveness of the greatest writer in the history of the world. She could hardly disagree, and certainly had no cause to question anything—*anything* he said. And of course, the plays are not in question, she quickly had to remind herself. Only the authorship.

But why would Dr. Scofield, or indeed anyone, including Professor Parker, or for that matter until recently even herself, be so adamant about that identity and its importance? Many long-held beliefs have been challenged successfully in the past, in her own experience. Poverty is a virtue, for example. Or that women were not capable of leadership roles. She herself had disproven this on more than one occasion, and not just while playing roles on the stage. And had women not even been permitted to perform on stage in Shakespeare's time? Even women's roles? So now the question became: why the vehemence when questioned, by Scofield and indeed, others. Why the intense righteousness? Why couldn't there be a rational, open debate?

She knew the answers of course. There were two of them: religion, and money. Shakespeare had become a religion to the Academics and their followers, as well as the people, especially of Britain. And as for the money? She could only guess. Billions, hadn't Professor Parker said? But she felt her father was onto something there. Follow the money. Scofield should understand this. Surely he was rational and sensible enough to talk to.

Her choice was simple: should I go to meet him? Or not? And if I do, to what end?

Putting down her napkin and a fiver, she reached a decision and arose from the table. There was only one way to find out what happened to Desmond Lewis. She would have to ask him herself. She hurried to the concierge's desk for directions to The Bridge of Sighs. What a name, she thought. Was Scofield being ironic?

"Let me out here," shouted Jake, as Diana pulled the Jag up to the front entrance of The Oxford Inn. "I'll meet you inside."

"No, wait—" she shouted, but he had already sprinted for the door and was out of hearing. Cursing to herself, Diana pulled around the corner, looking for a parking space.

In the lobby, Jake spotted the signs at once: "Dr. Richard Scofield and *The Sonnets of Shakespeare, Revisited.* Book Signing 10:00 to 11:00 a.m." He checked his watch. It was11:05. "Shit," he muttered, elbowing his way through the already dissipating crowd of fans, most of whom were greedily clutching their newly inscribed treasures.

He rushed over to the front desk. "Excuse me," he interrupted a busy clerk. "Where can I find Dr. Scofield?"

The clerk gave him a look of annoyance, then nodded towards a placard on the counter in front of him. "If you'll check the schedule, sir, you'll see that the luncheon is at twelve thirty. Then he'll be giving a talk at the Camera at 2:00 p.m., if you've registered."

"Never mind that. What room is he in?" snapped Jake, in exasperation.

The clerk bestowed him with his severest, most condescending look possible. "Sir, you appear to be intelligent and well-traveled enough to know that reputable hotels, most certainly ours, do not give out that sort of information."

Jake had had enough. He reached across the hotel counter and grabbed the starchy young man by the necktie. "And you look intelligent and well-traveled enough to know this. My daughter is twenty-three years old. She may be in Dr. Scofield's room. She shouldn't be there, and I am going to get her out of there, now. Do you get my drift?" The clerk's eyes were bulging now, and rolled right and left seeking help, which thus far was not forthcoming. He nodded, gasping.

As she approached the end of Broad Street and looked up ahead, Melissa wondered if she'd made a mistake. Professor Scofield had already excluded her from recognition in his book, which decision had to have been made months ago. So, all that bullshit about her being his "near co-author" was just that. Bullshit. No doubt as were the promises of help to get her some parts in forthcoming festivals, including Stratford. He had spent the last ten days trying to keep her in line, to prevent her from pursuing the line of questioning Desmond Lewis had followed. And what had happened to him?

But then again, wasn't she being presumptuous? Whatever happened to "innocent until proven guilty?" Scofield had treated her as someone—something special, from the very beginning. Certainly, like a protégé, almost like a daughter at times. Shouldn't she trust and honor such consideration as genuine and sincere? She didn't know, couldn't know for certain, that Dr. Scofield had done anything to Dr. Lewis, or his book. Or arranged for the shooting, or indeed did the shooting, of Balsavar and Poulson. How could she even think such a thing?

True, the circumstances of his increasing agitation and irrationality were troubling. It was almost as if he were suffering delusions, at times, or some kind of illness. In which case, if anything, he needed help. And if so, as his favorite student, as he'd so often said, wasn't she obligated to help him?

And what if their enemy was someone else entirely? For example, that big guy. Who the hell was he? Might Dr. Scofield, like the others, be just another victim in all this? Or even be in danger himself? If so, then she must warn him! She felt torn to the verge of tears. If only she could know for certain.

She pulled her collar tighter. The narrow cobbled road seemed nearly abandoned, and while she could now see the famed bridge up ahead, stretching between two buildings like the Italian *ponte* it had been modeled after, she would need to find a way in. She stopped and asked an aging porter for directions. After studying her with bemusement, he advised her to approach by way of the Radcliffe Camera.

"Is that a camera store?" she asked, in confusion.

She learned quickly, and bluntly, that it was not.

"Jacob, you stop that!" A voice spoke up behind the frantic Jake Fleming, at the hotel desk. "I'll handle this."

It was Diana. With a warning look, she nudged Jake aside and smiled apologetically at the ruffled, but now liberated desk clerk. "I am so sorry. My husband can be so rude at times, but our daughter is terribly vulnerable, and has such a crush on that man. And surely you know that even the most well-meaning celebrities are often tempted, shall we say, by young girls in ways that can too often compromise everyone, and even lead to litigation against all parties involved, including hotels."

The clerk nodded, uncertainly, with an apprehensive sidewise glance at Jake, who, helpfully, had stepped away from the counter.

"Er, right," he began. "But she is adult-age—" he began, until he caught Jake's eye again.

"So," she continued, lowering her voice, "if you would be a darling, and just let me go up and speak to them, I'm sure I can bring Melody to her senses and Dr. Scofield can go about his business without any further trouble."

The clerk gulped. Further trouble was the last thing he needed, just now. He'd only just been hired to help handle the overload and overbooking this event had caused. He nodded, agreeably. "Right," he whispered, with a glance to be sure his superiors weren't watching. "That would be room 912."

"Thank you so much," said Diana, turning, grabbing Jake by the elbow, and hurrying towards the elevator. Unfortunately, there was a crowd waiting for it, busily chatting about their recent acquisitions and encounters with literary greatness and fame. And both cars were at present stuck on the ninth floor, going nowhere, slowly.

Melissa crossed through the portico of the elegant round auditorium-tower so oddly named and found her way onto New College Lane. A student had told her the bridge linked two buildings of Hertford College, so the trick was to get into one of them and get to the bridge there. As she approached the entrance to the nearest building, she spotted a grizzled man in a doorman's uniform watching her. A porter, she thought. Or warden. She went up to him, anxiously.

"Excuse me," she said. "How do I get onto the Bridge of Sighs?"

"Sorry Miss," he said. "Students and faculty only."

She thought quickly. "I'm a graduate student. I'm supposed to meet my professor there," she explained. "Dr. Scofield?"

The man raised his eyebrows. "Ah, now that's a camel of a different color, isn't it?" He motioned for her to follow him and opened a side door into a building off the lane. "The famous professor returned from the New World and all. He's up there now," he told her. "Told me you were coming, in fact."

She hesitated at that, then turned and looked up at the Italian arch, so reminiscent of Venice, or Florence. It made her think, for a moment, of Marlowe, alone and exiled in Italy.

After wasting precious minutes banging on Scofield's door at the Oxford Inn, then returning to the lobby, Jake and Diana accosted the concierge, Jake bordering on frenzy. The concierge, having been alerted by the desk clerk, was already summoning hotel security.

Diana tried one last time. "Please," she said. "Our daughter is in trouble."

The concierge, a woman old enough to have grown daughters of her own, relented and flipped shut her cell phone. "Is she a blond girl, early twenties, hair pulled back?"

"Yes." exclaimed Jake. "Do you know where she went?"

“Well,” said the concierge. “She did ask directions to the Bridge of Sighs.”

She had a city map on the desk, and quickly showed them the shortest way. “Take Catte Street,” she said. “It’ll save you five minutes at least. You can’t miss it. It looks like *La Rialto*.”

Jake was already out the door.

As she stood at last on the illustrious bridge and faced her mentor, Melissa realized now that she had made a terrible mistake. She could see, plainly, and tragically, that her once beloved employer and professor had now gone stark, barking mad. He had locked and chained the hallway access door the moment she’d entered the archway, placed himself between the exit and her, and immediately launched into a long soliloquy, which she recognized to be an erratic mixture of lines from *Hamlet, King Lear*, and occasionally, *MacBeth*. He seemed to be working himself up to something, but the message in his eyes was clear enough. He was beyond reason, in a place of rage, of pain, betrayal, and indignation.

“ ‘For it is, as the air, invulnerable, and our vain blows malicious mockery!’ ” he was ranting.

“Dr. Scofield,” she began, but he silenced her by producing, with harrowing speed, a long kitchen carving knife, which he began waving about like a conductor’s baton. She turned to run the other way, but the exit was blocked by an iron gate.

“ ‘May not an ass know when the cart draws the horse?’ ” he asked, angrily.

“Dr. Scofield, please, let me help you,” she pleaded, holding out her hand. “Give me that.”

“ ‘Beat at this gate, that let thy folly in,’ ” striking his head, *“ ‘And thy dear judgment out.’ ”*

At that moment, there was loud banging at the hallway door behind her, which gave her hope.

“Dr. Scofield! Dr. Scofield!” It was Diana, calling out anxiously.

He stopped, alarm in his eyes. “Who speaks?” he shouted. “Go away. Begone, lackeys. *Come not between the dragon and his wrath!*”

Outside in the college hall, Diana looked at Jake in alarm. "He thinks he's Lear," she said.

"Melissa." shouted Jake. "Are you in there?"

"I'm OK!" she shouted back. She hoped. So far. She held her hands out towards Scofield, who looked at them, askance.

"OK? I don't think so," Jake muttered, and threw his shoulder against the door. Unlike in the movies, the door didn't shatter or burst open. Unlike in the movies, it was made of heavy wood and well reinforced, and securely locked. He bounced off, hit the floor, and nearly broke his shoulder. "Shit," he muttered, painfully pulling himself together.

Meanwhile, that action had been enough to snap Scofield out of his apparent delirium. He turned to face this new attack, and as he did so, Melissa sprang for him like a she-tiger protecting her cubs (or in this case, herself), and was on his back, screaming and straining to get at the knife, still being waved, but now being brought, with surprising and dismaying force, to bear, back over his shoulder like Frizer in Deptford, to rid himself of this new bane.

Meanwhile, the noise had attracted a crowd of students in the hallway, and someone had called campus security. A guard came hurrying down the hall.

"Melissa!" Jake shouted once again. But inside she was too busy fighting for her life to respond. The screaming and banging noises intensified, and Jake and Diana could only look at each other in horror. Jake decided to make one more try at the door and braced himself for one last all-out charge.

"Just a moment, sir." The porter called out, hurrying up the stairs. "I'll handle this."

"You have a key?" Diana asked him, quickly. "He's gone crazy. He has a weapon!"

"I doubt it, Ma'am," the porter told her, taking out his master pass. "We don't permit weapons." At which moment there was another scream from up on the bridge, and all went silent.

The porter hesitated, and Jake took over. Seizing the key, he plunged it into the slot, turned it, and pushed the door open. Diving through, he raced onto the bridge, shouting, "Melissa!"

The bridge was still and silent. For a long moment, Jake feared the worst. Finally, peering up along the arch, he could see his daughter where she stood at the top, holding the knife in both hands, having finally wrested it away from Scofield. The professor, in the meantime, sat on the bridge in lotus position, rocking back and forth.

" *'Nothing out of nothing.'* " he moaned. "First I made Desmond, then I made you, and now you are nothing to me."

"Easy, Dr. Scofield," said Jake, as Diana, and then the porter, and then the security guard hurried onto the bridgeway.

"Someone call the police!" A student shouted, from the hallway. "She's got a knife!"

Indeed, Melissa would have some explaining to do.

Jake gently took the knife from his daughter and handed it to the guard. "Here, you better take this."

"Professor Scofield, are you all right, sir?" asked the porter.

Scofield was too preoccupied to answer. " *'Is it not a lamentable thing?'* " he moaned, " *'That the skin of an innocent lamb should be made parchment? That parchment, being scribbled over, should undo a man?'* " He covered his eyes, ignoring the gathering crowd. Then he curled up in the middle of the Bridge of Sighs and began to weep, wailing, over and over again: " *'Howl. Howl. Howl!'* "

It was late in the afternoon by the time the college officials and the hotel manager were sufficiently convinced not to press charges against the Flemings. That their guest celebrity had gone over the top and needed to be hospitalized, however, was beyond question.

Diana Parker played a major part in the negotiations, smooth-talking the police and then university officials into explanations regarding Melissa (whose name, indeed, was not in the Scofield book, which would have supported her case) and her relationship to the professor back in Berkeley. Melissa had actually been handcuffed at first, which had enraged her so much, after her ordeal, she'd been too incoherent to make much of a defense for herself. As for

Jake, having more or less assaulted the hotel desk clerk hadn't won him any marks of favor either.

By the time they were all free to go, they were too exhausted to sleep, and more than ready for a diversion, if not a beer. Maybe two.

"So, what will happen to Professor Scofield?" asked Melissa, still not satisfied with the outcome. "They just going to give him some pills and send him home?"

"I hope not," said Diana. "He definitely needs medical attention, to say the least."

Melissa frowned. "Shouldn't someone be talking to him about those other murders? I mean, if he's gone off the deep end, he's dangerous. You saw what happened back there."

"It's quite possible he's just been overstressed. Book tours can be like a pressure cooker, I know," said Diana. "Anyway, believe it or not, we have an excellent health care system and I'm sure the professor is in good hands. If I were you, I'd leave well enough alone."

"The cops are talking to him now," said Jake. "If they have a warrant, and I sure as hell hope they do, they can keep him under guard until they can press charges. Odds are he's our killer."

Diana pursed her lip. "It's hard to believe."

"Anyway, it's out of our hands now."

Melissa looked disconsolate. "Can we just get out of here and go someplace?"

"I have an idea," said Jake. "I'd like to have a look at the remnants of William Davenant's pub. I understand it still exists."

"Davenant? The man who claimed to be Shakespeare's illegitimate son?" asked Diana.

As it happened, a conversation with the first local wag they encountered was sufficient.

The Crown Inn?" he chortled. "Yes, it's still there, up on Cornmarket Street. Just bring money." He laughed.

As was the case with so many of England's historic places, the inn had long since succumbed to the lure of the tourist trade. If Shakespeare, or Davenant, had left their mark here, it had long since faded. The historical blurb offered no new knowledge, the prices were high, and while the beer and food were adequate, something about the place struck Jake as though a ghost had walked on his shadow. They finished dinner and got out of there as quickly as they could, staying just long enough to solicit from the one sober person on the premises the location of a respectable small hotel.

"There's a decent bed and breakfast out on the edge of town," the Oxford man advised them, giving them a name and address. "You might try there."

They found it with little difficulty. There was room at the inn, and they checked in, weary and not in great spirits, taking two adjacent rooms on the second floor. Diana went upstairs while Jake and Melissa brought in the luggage from the car. Once again there was the awkward decision to be made about room assignments. They were in a sophisticated university town now, and the innkeepers were a gay couple who couldn't care less who slept where or with whom.

But the threesome by no means felt the same way.

"Have a nice evening," said the taller of the two partners, evidently the manager, as father and daughter trudged up the stairs with their bags. Bellhop service was definitely not included.

Somehow, Melissa once again secured a room of her own, leaving the other two to fend for themselves. Diana and Jake, both being grownups, took it in stride, and settled into the remaining room as though nothing was amiss. Diana took control of the bathroom while Jake turned on the TV, curious to see if there had been any report of the dust-up earlier here in Oxford, or even the Poulson shooting in Canterbury–still a rare event in the U.K. The commercial stations were as obnoxious as the ones back home, so he tried BBC, hoping to settle in with a small dose of normalcy while they took turns using the bathroom to undress and prepare for bed, each still uncertain as to the wishes or intentions of the other. The news came on, which reminded him that he hadn't contacted his paper yet and was long overdue to check in and face the music, as it were.

Diana emerged from the bathroom wearing a bathrobe, and Jake got just enough glimpse of one perfect breast, and just a flash of thigh and black bikini panties as she climbed into the nearest bed, to get an instant erection, which was sufficiently distracting that he almost missed the TV announcer come on the air to inform them that there had been a last minute change in programming. Due to popular acclaim, so the broadcasters claimed, instead of the usual episode of Mystery they had decided to treat their loyal viewers to a "special event:" a rerun of the film *Shakespeare in Love.*

"I don't believe it," said Jake, with an accusatory look at Diana. "Did you hear that?"

"What? Are you blaming me for something? And what are you still doing over there, by the way?" At that the robe fell away, and so did most of his inhibitions.

But still he could not quite let go. Not only had Shakespeare dominated his life for the past two weeks, but now the Bard was interfering with his sex life!

"It's probably just a coincidence," she assured him, reaching for his belt. Soon the boxers had been discarded, a condom had been located, and they were busy kissing, caressing, and penetrating every available orifice with every possible protuberance, almost as if venting days of so much stress and pressure all in one outburst of energy; devouring and consuming each other, mouths, tongues, arms, legs a frantic and urgent tangle of bodies intertwined, leading to a mutual heaving, sweating climax that, if Melissa couldn't hear it next door, meant she was wearing headphones, earplugs or holding her ears with her hands. Which, of course, was a possibility.

"Thank you, that was wonderful," she breathed, after managing a second orgasm for good measure.

"The pleasure is mine," he assured her, as Diana rolled over and pulled the covers over her head. Jake, still wide awake, scanned the channels with the remote, wondering if it was just sex, or could he possibly have suddenly fallen in love with this beguiling and maddening woman? Another channel was running reruns of an old BBC special called *In Search of Shakespeare*, entirely based on surmise; then they were treated to a commercial: Shakespeare's Globe Theater in London was offering free passes to seniors and students.

"My goodness," said Diana, sleepily nuzzling up against him. Could she feel the same way about their sudden intimacy? He didn't dare hope. It was risky enough just to fantasize about where this might be going. But suddenly he wanted it to go somewhere; to mean something. And he saw just enough in her expression to hope it might be mutual.

"Must be Shakespeare night," she murmured. "Among other wonders."

Apparently so. There was Shakespeare on almost every channel. This was no coincidence, he was certain. It was too much. Could the Foundation be behind this? They certainly were well connected, including some major corporate sponsors. Was Scofield a blind alley, even a red herring? The old warnings flashed in the back of his mind once again: *follow the money*.

"You don't suppose someone's trying to send us a message?" he asked, half in humor.

There was a knock at the connecting door. It was Melissa. Wrapping himself in Diana's discarded robe, Jake went to unlock it. Melissa stood there looking forlorn and outraged, and not just by her father having sex in the next room, which, if she'd noticed, was beneath comment, at least for the moment. "Dad. Have you seen what's on TV?" she demanded. Glumly, Jake confirmed that they had.

"All of it based on lies," she cried, bitterly, with the certainty of a True Believer.

But oh, how slick were the production values, thought Jake. It was amazing what money could buy. And how quickly it could be bought, in an emergency? He wondered. But again, if so, what emergency? Were they close, too close to something that was pushing panic buttons somewhere, even in boardrooms or high places?

Melissa finished venting and returned to her room with a terse good night over her shoulder.

Turning off the offending appliance, Jake contemplated the elegant shape outlined on the bed, and considered waking her for another go, if not conversation. Diana really was a lovely and sexy woman, for all her annoying obstinacy. Even her occasional episodes of awkwardness were endearing. He tried to dismiss the thought and failed. He just couldn't sleep, more and more bothered by a troubling idea. Discussions about Shakespeare's veracity were nothing new. They'd probably been going on for centuries, or at least since Twain and Greenwood's time. Coleridge, Emerson, and Henry James had also expressed disbelief about the Bard, he'd read. Even the great Prussian Emperor Bismarck had found reason to question his authenticity. He could use a Bismarck in his camp right about now, he thought. Calvin Hoffman had apparently caused a stir, but it had died down and long since been swept under the table and forgotten. So, what was different about this time?

As quietly as possible, he went over to the coffee table where he'd left his notebooks and switched on the small table lamp. He studied the Lewis list once more. Desmond Lewis had been eliminated, he now felt certain, for something he had discovered hidden in this list. As had Balsavar. No one had stopped Hoffman, though. Or Ogburn, or the numerous other published de Verians. They had simply been dismissed as fringe elements or crackpots. The Stratfordians, he realized, had the tremendous advantage of tradition, which they'd established before there ever was an issue, and clung to and successfully buttressed ever since. Skeptics and doubters and those with alternative theories were forced to cross the deepest of moats, climb the highest of barricades, and against overwhelming firepower, somehow penetrate the castle.

Small wonder it hadn't happened before. So again: what was different now?

And then it struck him like a sucker punch. *The audience*. The audience had changed. This was no longer a dispute between scholars vying for space amongst the academic journals and the respectful ear of the Dons. This was about a product and its consumer market. The audience had changed. It was now the ticket-and-e-book-buying general public.

Could that be what had pushed Scofield over the edge?

Jake dug out his tablet and started typing in deep agitation.

What Desmond Lewis had dared to do, been about to do, was bring the actual facts about Shakespeare not to the mahogany tables in the ivory towers, but directly to the Court of Public Opinion, and in so doing expose the man behind the curtain to the public itself. That had not been done before. Even Mark Twain had kept his views under wraps until he felt safe to speak from the grave. Lewis was about to expose a deity, an icon, but most importantly a money machine, as a fraud. The academics, as self-appointed apologists for the vast status quo, had always been able to suppress or dismiss such charges in the past as "baseless," all the while zealously protecting an increasingly powerful economic base. But the public had no vested interest other than those with jobs at hotels and bookstores and theaters and granted, a fierce tradition–a tradition no doubt forced down their throats over time by overbearing teachers and professors from grade school onwards through graduate school.

But how powerful is tradition, in such a case, he wondered? The Chinese once had a tradition of binding women's feet. The Hindus had a tradition of burning widows. Muslim tradition required women to remain in ignorant servitude, and American tradition glorified violence. Some traditions are well rid of, he thought. And the people were sensible enough, once given the facts, to make their own decisions: a situation that the powers-that-be could not risk allowing to happen. It was the people themselves who finally tore down the Berlin Wall. Not Reagan or Gorbachev.

Desmond Lewis had been about to give them cause to tear down The Bust if for no other reason than that people hate learning they'd been duped. So, he had been stopped.

Jake thought about waking the women and sharing his epiphany. He decided not to. Diana wouldn't appreciate it anyway. It wasn't, he felt sure, what she wanted or needed to hear from him just now. And no sense worrying them any more than was necessary. It didn't change anything.

Once again Jake fell asleep in the armchair and was awakened from a nightmare sometime in the middle of the night. He'd been dreaming that there was a tiger on the loose, snatching people in the most horrible ways. The community had gathered in a large auditorium to deal with the growing menace. They made much noise and hoopla. Meanwhile, he was trapped in the very next room. Alone. With the tiger. Which crouched to attack. Desperately he fended it off with a bartender's whisk, slapping it on the floor between death and himself. He called out for help, but the braying mob next door was too noisy to hear him. "The tiger is here!" he shouted, to no avail. *"The tiger is here!"*

He must have yelled in his sleep. The next thing he knew he was being nudged awake by a beautiful if somewhat disheveled dark-haired woman who looked vaguely familiar, wearing practically nothing at all, and apparently most anxious to soothe his fears away. As nature intended.

"Whaaa?" he murmured.

"Shhhhh, no discussion, please," she responded, pulling him down next to her on the counterpane. Reaching over, she took him in her mouth, and by this time Jake was sufficiently aroused, so to speak, to assist. He then set about applying kisses to clearly needful places, and just being helpful in general. Diana seemed more than ready for another, if possible, even more frantic bout of lovemaking, and to his own surprise, Jake was managing to stay on board, as it were.

Happily, there were no further interruptions or commentary from the room next door.

When it was over, he felt her looking at him, and met her eyes. "Is this going somewhere?" she asked, finally. "Because if it isn't, I'd like to know now."

"Where would you like it to go?" he heard himself asking, and immediately knew it was the wrong thing to say. "I'm sorry," he quickly backtracked, when she caught her breath. "I am not good at this. I hope to get better. The way I feel right now I would like very much never to lose sight of you again." Better, but not good enough.

"Jake Fleming," she said, at last. "You are a piece of work. But I will say this," she added. "You do have potential." With that she kissed him, and her kiss spoke volumes.

When they had reached the peak of their encounter, the ride back down was gratifyingly slow, for both of them.

Finally, at least for the moment contented, Diana lay back on her pillow and gazed at the ceiling, which displayed a few chips and cracks in the white paint, but nothing serious. There was a ceiling fan that might actually be useful on this occasion.

"Did you I know I was married once?" she asked him, after a while. "And divorced. It was *not* a good experience."

"I didn't know, and I'm sorry to hear it wasn't, but it doesn't matter. I would have been surprised to hear otherwise."

"And you?" she asked. "Are you divorced?"

"Widower," he told her, finding the word both painful and yet somehow comforting to be able to say, at last. "Melissa's mother died two years ago, of breast cancer."

"I'm sorry." She said. "Really. That must have been hard."

He fought back a tear and shook his head. Was he being disloyal to Beverly's memory now? And yet she'd told him in so many words that he should love again, implying, without saying so, that maybe he'd do a better job of it the second time around. Had that time come, then? It was a frightening thought, and yet an enervating one as well. And at the same time, he realized that he was entering new, uncharted, and perilous territory. So be it, he thought. He was ready. He looked at her, and she met his gaze, expectantly.

"I guess it's a little late to say we should take it slow," he teased, getting a poke in the ribs in response, albeit quickly followed by a long, deep kiss.

"Was that slow enough for you?" she breathed in his ear.

Morning came, and Jake was still asleep when Diana got up and went out on errands of her own. Then they gathered for breakfast in the cheery Tudor dining room as though nothing had happened, and for all Jake knew, maybe it hadn't. Maybe he'd dreamed the whole thing. Except he had not forgotten his epiphany.

***

Jake made his announcement, even as the women were initiating discussions as to when and whether to return to London.

"We need to go to Stratford," he informed them.

Melissa was pouting, and not paying attention. Jake assumed it was about him and Diana. Then she surprised him yet again.

"You know it just occurred to me," she said, "that, technically we're homeless. Not you," she added, to Diana. "I mean here in the UK."

"It doesn't matter," Jake repeated. "We need to go to Stratford."

"Stratford?" exclaimed Melissa. He could see her eyes light up. "Stratford-Upon-Avon?"

"I see no other choice but to take our fight to the seat of the Empire," he said.

"What fight?" Diana demanded to know. "Your killer has been apprehended, hasn't he?"

"Maybe. But in any case, I still need to finish what Dr. Lewis started."

"It's finished," Diana insisted. " 'Herbert' was your final code word. So now we can go home, and you can write your article."

"No. The point is, Stratford is the keystone, the lynch-pin, the still-missing link in this riddle."

"Dad, can you think of any more cliches?"

"I want to know why the Foundation was involved, for one thing. And who invaded our flat, or Lewis's for that matter? Scofield was still at Berkeley at the time."

"Actually, he wasn't," said Melissa. "He's been in London since I got there."

He stared at her.

She stared back. It was a stare-off.

Finally, Jake forced himself to speak. "So, he was your secret connection?"

"He was here about the book, you know? And I still work for him. Or did."

He put his hands to his face. "Oh, God, Melissa. The man is a psychotic."

"I didn't know that, OK? He didn't used to be. Jesus." She was ready to leave, like back in Bloomsbury. Diana put her hand out and touched her arm with a sympathetic nod, which calmed her down somewhat.

Jake stared into the distance, thinking out loud. "Stratford is where it all began. It's the headquarters of all things Shakespearean. More to the point, it's the headquarters of The Shakespeare Foundation. Also," he added, pointedly for Melissa's benefit, "there's a festival going. You did say you wanted to see some plays?"

"Dad—"

"Maybe even some tryouts? You never know—"

"Dad!" she nearly shouted.

Diana just shook her head. "So, you want to go to the mountain, like Mohammad? And do what?"

"See some plays?" said Melissa, with an edge of sarcasm.

"For one thing, I want some closure for Desmond Lewis and his still missing book."

"Yeah, right," said Melissa. "OK, so in a just world Stratford would return to dirt farming, the Foundation would be dissolved, The Globe renamed The Rose, and the theme park moved to Canterbury. Good one, Dad."

Diana shook her head. "I'm sure they'd love that, there. You saw how much Canterbury adores their hero."

"They'll change their tune when they know the truth," insisted Melissa, seemingly coming back around once more.

"Spoken like a true believer," Diana told her, with a smile of her own.

That seemed to help. Melissa rewarded her with a smile.

"More like a convert," said Jake, and immediately wished he hadn't. Why did he keep doing that? Shoving his parental foot down his gullet.

Melissa gave him his just desserts with a punch on the arm, but mostly symbolically. Then she gave him a wry grin.

"Maybe when all those Shakespeare Incorporated industries are countered by a growing Marlovian Restoration movement—"

"Inspired by my new book. Our new book," decided Melissa, nudging her father.

"And see all that green," added Jake, getting simultaneous punches on both arms.

"Have either of you ever actually been to Stratford?" Diana asked. "Talk about the tiger's lair."

But she grudgingly agreed to take them there; it wasn't far. "Besides, maybe it might not be such a bad idea to take in a play or two, whoever wrote them," she added, with a meaningful glance at Melissa. "Assuming you still want to be an actor."

"Of course, I do. Why would that change now that I have so much *experience*?"

Jake could tell she wasn't just being ironic.

And so, the matter was settled. By ten o'clock they had checked out, piled into the Jag, and were on the road northwards towards the county of Warwickshire and the once-rustic farming village on the meandering River Avon, where an enterprising upstart had become a legend, four centuries before.

They'd been on the road for just over an hour when Melissa spotted the first billboard–a rarity in itself in the relatively pristine hinterlands of Europe. Her spine stiffened at the sight, and she heard a grunt from her father. The billboard displayed a larger-than-life reproduction of the ubiquitous Drushout portrait of 'Shakespeare,' now serving as the corporate logo that Jake felt certain it was. In large print it read: **Shakespeare**. Then underneath: **He's One of Us**. The message was only too clear: that this down-to-earth working-class kind of guy was a regular person, not some effete, snobbish Cambridge phony like all those university-educated eletes.

"Yeah, right. If only," Jake heard Melissa mutter, from the front passenger seat.

Just then the view of the billboard was cut off by a fast-moving semi-truck overtaking them on the outside lane. "Christ." muttered Diana. "What's your rush, buster?" It was a four-lane highway, and they were in the fast lane: a bad idea. The truck surged past, then pulled directly in front of them, nearly cutting them off. It had a single name emblazoned across the rear: AVENA.

"Bloody hell," exclaimed Diana, hitting the brakes.

Jake glanced out to her left. "Watch it. Here comes another one." It was worse than that. In a matter of moments two more semis came seemingly out of nowhere and overtook them like hounds cornering a fox: one in front, another behind, and a third boxing them into the passing lane. All three bore the same legend: AVENA.

"What the f- hell?" Jake exclaimed. Then it came to him and he remembered where else he had seen the name. He glanced at Diana, whose knuckles were white as she gripped the wheel.

There was no shoulder to escape onto. They were trapped in a three-sided vice, each truck within a foot of them: front, back, and left, with a rail on the right and no room to spare.

Melissa shouted, "Omigod, they're going to kill us!"

Jake tried to roll down his rear seat window to shout at the nearest driver. But the noise and blast of wind were deafening. The trucks began to sound their horns: a ferocious, ear-splitting braying that continued for a half minute or more. Melissa covered her ears and Jake shouted vitriol through the open window but, like the spit blown back into his face, his voice was drowned out before it even left the car. There could no longer be any doubt that they had run afoul of someone, or something, a lot bigger and more powerful than a crazed, aging professor with an attitude. At the very least, they were definitely being given a message.

Diana clung to the wheel for dear life, trembling with terror, but there was nothing she or any of them could do but hold on. At a hundred and fifty kilometers per hour. And not dare flinch, sneeze, or make any sudden moves.

Then, as suddenly as it all started, it was over. The trucks in front and to the left accelerated on ahead, the one behind passed them with one last angry blast of its horn and was gone. Jake managed to memorize the license tag of the hindmost truck and jotted it quickly down. Diana was so unnerved she had to pull over off the highway at the next exit, where she sat and trembled for a full minute without speaking.

"It's okay," Melissa tried to reassure her, badly shaken herself. Jake reached over and put his arms around Diana's shoulders, as she began to cry. "Why?" She wept. "Why are they doing this?"

"I think I know," said Jake, at last. But he needed to be sure.

Chapter Forty

The Instruments of Darkness Tell Us Truths

Stratford-Upon-Avon, England, Friday, mid-November

The town of Stratford was exactly as Sunir had warned them it would be: a Disney World replica of "a typical Elizabethan village," managed by a benign-sounding operation known as the Shakespeare Birthplace Trust: a main source and purveyor of the sly conversion of "it is believed" into "established fact." Plus, now it had the added attraction of the Royal Shakespeare Theater, with year-round productions. According to the billboard at the edge of town, this week featured a star-studded *MacBeth*.

"Just what we need," grumbled Jake. "More daggers."

"Look at that," exclaimed Melissa, pointing off towards the river on the outskirts of town where a huge complex of buildings was under construction. "I wonder what that is?"

Jake looked closer and saw the answer on a large sign that proclaimed: "Coming Soon. Shakespeare Village: Condos and Townhomes for the Smart and Discriminating", then underneath: "prices from 500K." It also boasted a new half-finished high-rise hotel called The William Shakespeare, and a large office and retail complex. Fields and meadows that Shake-scene himself once owned were being cleared for an adjacent planned housing tract. It was the onset of suburban sprawl, Stratford-style. Then he saw it: a modest declaration: "Brought to you by Avena Global Partners, Ltd." printed on the bottom of each sign in gold letters with a neat logo of a sailing ship.

Jake pointed, a new warning roaring in his gut. "There. That's the name that was on those trucks." He glanced at Diana. "Is that a common brand name here?"

She shook her head, then shrugged. "I don't pay much attention to that sort of thing. Maybe. I don't know."

Melissa sat forward suddenly. "I know that name. Avena Global Partners. I saw it somewhere else recently."

"So did I," said Jake. "Twice. At the Globe. And on the Foundation website. This is no coincidence."

As they entered the busy town center, Diana pulled up alongside a large lorry that was presently occupying four metered parking spots. "Speak of the devil," she muttered. AVENA was imprinted right in plain sight on the side. It was one of the same trucks that had recently terrorized them. There was no sign of the driver, and Jake was tempted to let the air out of the tires, except that there were eighteen of them and it would take hours and he'd probably be arrested, beaten, and gutted before he even got started.

"Avena sounds almost, like, religious," said Melissa. "Like the liturgical 'ave' with the initials 'n.a.' for 'North America.' Ave North America."

"So, we nearly got run off the road by renegade clerics?" said Jake, dubiously.

"Something with Avenue, perhaps," suggested Diana. "An amalgam of some kind?"

"I'll run a check on it," said Jake, making a note. "And I'm gonna report these creeps."

The latest reconstruction of the "New Place" had a line around the block, so they passed on that for now, and reconnoitered the area. Even though it was November, the town was crowded with all shapes, colors and sizes of visitors: students, sightseers, tour groups, families, Brits and foreigners, and the idle curious. Jake even noticed a monk in a black friar's robe, complete with hooded cowl. He began to feel like a commando who had infiltrated enemy territory looking for the best place to plant explosives. And with that feeling came the certainty that someone, perhaps many someones out there were bent and determined to stop him at any cost.

Like they had stopped Desmond Lewis? Jake was still not ready to conclude that Richard Scofield was acting alone.

As they entered the town, one of the first things they saw was a huge Ferris Wheel, which reminded Jake and Melissa of The London Eye. It wasn't a happy observation.

"Talk about a tourist trap," muttered Melissa.

The Shakespeare Foundation was ensconced in an understated but clearly expensive faux-Tudor style building near the river at the edge of town.

"Look," said Melissa, pointing. There, parked in the back of the lot behind the building, was another of the Avena trucks that had nearly killed them. Jake considered marching through the front door and demanding to see Harold Sherwood, if only to discuss freeway etiquette in regards to the truck parked out back, and have a word with the driver about attempted murder, intimidation, and harassment. Not to mention do his best to kick the fucker's ass. The women convinced him that this wouldn't accomplish much. But what would?

"We have to think about this," he said. "These people have obviously been monitoring our research and Sunir's before us, and probably Lewis's. They know what we have, so there's no point trying to bluff them. And given their reaction, what we have is more than enough to put fear in their hearts."

"Which leaves us where?" Diana wanted to know.

"Up shit creek?" suggested Melissa.

"You Americans are so quaint. I still think if I were you, I'd go home, forget about all this, and let the police handle it."

"You brought us all the way up here to tell us that?" Jake shook his head. "You should know me better than that by now."

She laughed. "I'm not sure I know you at all."

After a so-so lunch in a tourist trap café featuring Bard Burgers de Luxe, they found an out-of-the-way hotel and checked in under Mr. and Mrs. Parker and Ms. Parker, but this time there was no aura of romance, and the tension had not dissipated. Diana used her credit card so the names would match the registry. Jake checked his watch for the time. Two p.m. That meant it was opening time in New York.

"I'll be right back," he told the two women. Not wanting to use the hotel lines, he went to the quaint old pay phone in the lobby and used his calling card to ring an old colleague at *The Wall Street Journal.*

"Sarah Collins, please," he told the newspaper operator, bypassing the voice mail system by pressing "0": an old, mostly reliable trick. "Tell her it's Jake Fleming, from *The San Franciso Tribune."*

A husky voice came on the line a moment later. "Jake Fleming, as I live and breathe," she bellowed, across five time zones. Sarah had once had a crush on Jake, who'd been smitten by Beverly by then. They'd both worked at the *Chronicle* at the time, and Sarah had left for New York a year later when Jake and Beverly got married. Beverly Stiller had given up a promising Broadway career of her own to marry him, and gotten neglected and ignored in return, which he would regret to his own dying day. But he and Sarah had remained friends and proven useful to one another on occasion.

"Glad you're still living and breathing," he told her. He lowered his voice. "Listen, I need some information."

"Are you in New York? If so, there's a killer opening tonight at the Met. *'Picasso's Children.'* "

"Picasso had children?"

"Ha ha."

"Actually, I'm in England. Stratford, actually."

"England? In November? You are a brave soul. What's up?"

"What can you tell me about a company called Avena Global Partners, Ltd.?"

She paused. "I'll have to get back to you on that. As the saying goes, 'still waters run deep.' "

"These waters haven't been so still lately, but I get your point."

"Uh oh. Do I smell a rat?"

"I don't know yet." He gave her the hotel number and waited in the lobby under the watchful eye of a prissy silver-haired desk clerk, who clearly suspected him of skullduggery.

"We're going out for a while," Melissa told him, heading for the door. "There's a pub where the actors hang out. Maybe I can talk to some of them." Diana was already outside, restlessly pacing the sidewalk. Jake didn't like it but knew better than to object to them going without him.

Sarah called back a half hour later at the switchboard, and the desk clerk grudgingly patched the call through to the courtesy phone. "Interesting outfit," Sarah told him. "It's an IBC, privately held, which means it's an offshore corporation. My guess is they're a shadow subsidiary of something bigger."

"Is that why I haven't heard of them?"

"They have a Bermuda Charter, which means a lot of secrecy. They have, as far as I could find in one outing, at least a dozen OFCs, or Offshore Finance Companies, and a ton of shell corporations of their own. A lot of big-name companies do this with impunity to avoid taxes, you know. Enron comes to mind. Or KBR."

Jake jotted some fast notes. "Go on."

"I can tell you this. Whoever is behind this little operation, or not so little operation, is deep under the covers with some major players. These shell banks and shell corporations are SOP for people who have something to hide and are pretty commonly used by high-rolling tax evaders and so forth from all over the world."

Tax evaders. Like Willy the Shake? Did his legacy still exist in more than name? Jake's thoughts raced.

"So, who are these guys?"

"I'll have to get back to you, this could take some digging. People who want to stay out of the limelight, shall we say? At least when it comes to business."

"Limelight. Interesting choice of words." He hung up, wondering fretfully what Melissa and Diana were up to. Hanging out with actors? Hard to imagine. And yet hadn't he done the same, in his fateful New York years when he'd met and courted Beverly?

Catching up with the women at a pub that was indeed crowded with such a varied assortment of characters and faces that they well might be right out of Shakespeare, he told them what he'd found out so far about Avena.

"So, what's that got to do with Shakespeare?" wondered Melissa, exchanging cards with a woman who looked an awful lot like Gwyneth Paltrow.

They took their leave from the pub crowd and browsed through a nearby bookstore while Jake collected his thoughts and considered their options. He noted, with a certain degree of irony, that almost an entire shelf in one corner of the store was dedicated to books by Desmond Lewis. And there was Professor Scofield's new book, on bold display in the window. He wondered if Scofield had planned to come here next and asked the clerk.

"Oh yes, in fact he was expected today, but he's been delayed," she said, apologetically. Sure enough, he noticed, there was a sign lying on its side on the floor behind the cashier's desk that said: "Today at The Royal Shakespeare Theater: Richard Scofield Reads from His New Book, *The Sonnets of Shakespeare, Revisited*." With a subtitle that made him smile, in spite of it all: *"Is there a Deeper Meaning Implicit in the Subtext of the Sonnets?"* He looked around for Melissa, but she'd disappeared. He wanted to ask her about that 'deeper meaning.' He spotted the robed monk again, perusing a book in the mystery section. Different strokes, he thought, idly.

He decided to tell Diana about his conclusions from the night before.

Melissa, who'd drifted off to peruse an alternative news magazine, suddenly laughed out loud. She hurried back to them, waving the paper. "Hey you two. Did you know that in 1847, none other than P. T. Barnum actually bought Shakespeare's house?"

"I'd read that somewhere," said Diana. Jake hadn't, and looked up in surprise.

"It was Barnum who really put this town on the map. It was falling down until then, and nobody cared. Obviously, he recognized a kindred spirit here."

"The man knew a quick buck when he saw one," acknowledged Jake. "So, what happened?"

"He wanted to move it to New York, every last board and shingle, and the Brits suddenly got all righteous about their 'holy national treasure,' as they called it and bought him out."

So, we *are* up against a religion, thought Jake. "They seem to have recouped their investment," he noted.

"But here's the funny part: none of it was original anyway."

"What do you mean?"

"I mean not one board or shingle in this town existed in 1616, when Shakescene died."

"So, it *is* a theme park."

"You Americans are unbelievable." complained Diana. "Let's get out of here."

Jake pretended to be busy studying a rack of postcards at a sidewalk kiosk depicting all the Shakespeare Birthplace sites, trying to ignore hard stares from several browsers nearby who'd overheard their banter.

They spent the remainder of the afternoon meandering along the river, and perusing Anne Hathaway's fairy-tale cottage in Shottery. Jake insisted on taking a look at the infamous gravestone and altered bust in the Trinity Church; then, towards tea time they returned to the hotel and suffered through a dismal 'early bird' dinner: 'The Shakespeare Special,' of rancid boiled mutton and cabbage. They still could not decide on a plan of attack.

There were no performances this evening, and the women were in the mood to step out on the town. Jake wasn't. Instead, he went up to the hotel room, tossed his coat on the bed, and collapsed into the standard-issue vinyl armchair. He'd just turned on the TV when the room phone rang.

Resisting the urge to ignore it, he finally reached over and picked up the receiver, deciding it was probably Melissa.

The voice on the other end was one he'd heard before. "Mr. Fleming? This is Harold Sherwood, from The Shakespeare Foundation. Welcome to Stratford. We hope you are enjoying your stay and had a pleasant journey." The mountain, it seemed, had come to Mohammad.

Jake's pulse quickened. "I've had better. How're things with you, Mr. Sherwood? Still showing people the proverbial door?"

"First of all, my condolences for your, ah, mishap in Oxford. I trust you are well?"

"Never better, thanks for asking." Jake decided this was a fishing expedition, as well as another warning that they were being watched. He was more troubled by the fact that their movements had been so easily tracked. The women were out there somewhere, vulnerable and exposed, he realized. He'd already lost one love of his life and would not lose another. Let alone two. Maybe he could stall for time and to think. "How did you know we were here?"

"We have friends, shall we say?"

"Do they drive eighteen wheelers?"

"I beg your pardon?"

"Look out the window, there's one in your lot."

"Ah, I see. Well, I'm sure you know, The Foundation has many sponsors."

"Sponsors who kill people?"

"Pardon? I don't get your meaning."

"Forget it. So, what can I do for you or is this just a courtesy call?"

Sherwood forced a laugh. "Yes, quite. Listen, Mr. Fleming, we need to talk, preferably as soon as possible. Can we please sit down like civilized people, and see if we can discuss this situation before it spirals any further out of control?"

It was pretty well out of control already, to Jake's way of thinking. Where the hell were Diana and Melissa? Then a terrible thought struck him. What if they were already held in captivity somewhere, as a final trump card of some kind? He made a decision.

"Where and when?"

"Can you meet me at the Royal Shakespeare Theater, in one hour?"

Jake remembered seeing billings about town that the next performance of *Macbeth* would not be until the weekend. Which meant it would be closed, other than for possible tech rehearsals, but due to unions even those were unlikely after hours. "If you're talking about the Scofield poetry reading, he won't be making it," Jake mentioned.

"No matter, all the better for privacy."

"I see. Will this be a private presentation, then?"

Sherwood laughed. "I'll see you there. One hour." Then, as a seeming afterthought: "Shall I expect the women to be joining us?"

So, he doesn't have them, thought Jake, in relief. "That's up to them, of course," he said. "But I don't think so." Over my dead body, he wanted to add. No way was he going to put them in danger again if he could help it. If he could even find them before then.

"Very well. I was merely offering you the chance to safeguard your companions. I'll see you shortly then."

So much for the safety argument.

In the corner office of The Shakespeare Foundation, Harold Sherwood hung up the phone and glanced across his highly polished rosewood desk at his visitor. "All right?"

The large man seated opposite him in the oversize leather wing chair nodded.

"You know, we were perfectly prepared to make a reasonable offer of settlement in this matter," noted Sherwood, regretfully.

"You needn't bother," The Watcher said, with a growl. "We'll take it from here."

As he hung up, Jake remembered that his daughter had a cell phone. Wishing he still had some Mylanta, he dialed her number. Melissa answered with the raucous noise of a pub in the background. "Hey. What's up?" she asked, cheerfully.

"I need you both to get back here to the hotel right away. And hurry."

"Why? What's going on?"

"Just do it. Please. I'll tell you when you get here."

Melissa and Diana arrived within fifteen minutes, brimming with annoyance. Jake told them about the call. Both women became instantly sober.

"I want you two to remain here until I find out what they want."

"No way," declared Melissa, at once. "I'm in this all the way, I told you."

Diana nodded in agreement. "If waiting in a chilly hotel room is your idea of safety, I beg to differ. Besides which, I'll be damned if you get to have all the excitement."

As usual, Jake gave in.

As he'd expected, the huge theater parking lot was dark and empty. Not another car was visible, which was worrisome. The main entrance to the theater complex was closed up tight, and the theater lobby was blacked out. Crew and construction people were union workers and would be home with their families or out on the town on a Friday night between shows.

"Turn off the headlights," said Jake, scanning the area.

Diana complied. "Now what?" The only lighting came from the emergency floodlights on the periphery of the property.

"Let's check around the back," suggested Melissa. "I don't like the looks of this. There's nobody here."

Jake didn't like it either. It looked too much like a setup. "He said he'd be here," he said, knowing that was less than reassuring.

Diana drove around to the back of the theater, pulled the Jaguar up to the stage entrance and turned off the engine. Then they saw it: the double stage door stood open, the blackened interior daring them to enter.

Cautiously, Jake got out and scanned the area. He gestured to the two women, who joined him on the pavement. At his insistence, they'd all put on soft-soled shoes, and walked in silence towards the gaping doorway. The only sound was the swaying of distant trees in the cold November wind. As they walked, Jake had the distinct, gnawing feeling that they were not alone. He'd had this same feeling in London two weeks before, when it all began. It was as if the whole town, the whole country was against them. It was not a comfortable feeling.

"Mr. Sherwood?" Jake called out, as they edged cautiously toward the open stage entrance, staying close to the wall. There was no answer.

"Something's wrong," said Melissa.

Suddenly a gust of wind slammed the heavy steel door shut with a nerve-jarring bang. The suddenness of the movement and the crashing noise caused both women to jump. The door creaked slowly ajar once more. Jake reached out and pulled it open again. "Hello?" he called into the theater's black interior. "Anybody here?"

"You'd think there'd be a guard, or someone," noted Diana.

"Mr. Sherwood?" called Jake, once more. They stepped into what was plainly a workshop area and squinted into the darkness. The only illumination came from a single dim lamp in a far corner, that cast little more than shadows.

"Well, at least they have the traditional ghost light," said Diana, in a low whisper. "It's supposed to keep out the ghosts."

"Let's hope it's working," said Melissa.

Jake immediately regretted not bringing a flashlight. "Hello?" he called once more.

So where was Harold Sherwood?

Diana located and threw on the nearest light switch. Nothing happened. "Bloody hell," she muttered. "Someone's turned off the power."

Again, thought Jake.

Diana rummaged into her purse and found a small emergency penlight, which she switched on. Thus armed, they proceeded to search the backstage area, picking their way through, among, and around racks of medieval weapons, rolling turrets, movable battlements, and other props and set pieces that sat menacingly in the darkness, awaiting the forthcoming bloody spectacle of *Macbeth*. There was even a recognizable black cauldron, which Melissa could almost see bubbling over with dark evil portends.

As they entered the theater proper, they found themselves on the main stage, the black tower of Dunsinane Castle looming above them, a realistic jagged profile of a painted Burnham Wood in the background. Melissa took in the stage and premiere auditorium at her literal feet, perhaps imagining herself one day standing on this very spot, brandishing daggers of her own or sharp pointed words to thunderous applause. Now it was she who called out once again: "Hello? Anyone here?"

Again, no answer. A cold wind came wafting from backstage, as if the stage door had blown open once again. There was no sign of Sherwood, or anyone else. Nothing but darkness and malevolent unwelcoming spirits, thought Jake. Diana and Melissa looked more than ready to leave.

Suddenly a deep, hollow groan seemed to fill the auditorium like a heavy groundswell, coming from somewhere out in the center orchestra.

"What's that?" cried Melissa, with a shudder. Diana shone the light around and finally located, hunched in the fifth row, a large hulking shape, slumped in a seat, only half-conscious.

Jake recognized him at once: The Watcher.

"Wait here," Jake told the women, as he clambered down onto the auditorium floor and made his way through the seats to where the big man slouched. The Watcher groaned once more, stirring as Jake reached him. His eyes opened, then widened as though seeing something dreadful in the distance. Jake could now see that he had been tightly bound and gagged.

Jake reached down to remove the handkerchief that had been stuffed in his mouth, asking him: "What the hell? Where's Sherwood?"

Just then Diana cried out behind him. "Jake!"

Jake jumped up and spun around, to find himself confronted by the specter of a ghostly black profile framed in center stage, a cloaked hand holding a very real Scottish dagger to the throat of a now thoroughly terrified Diana Parker.

"*By the pricking of my thumbs*, what have we here?" Snarled Richard Scofield, the famed author and scholar. "My wayward colleague, and Mr. Fleming, And my little protégé, as well. So good of you to come. I've been waiting for you."

Jake stared at him in horror, his head whirring.

"So. The prince of darkness is a gentleman,' " Murmured Melissa in equal dismay.

The large man emitted a muffled roar, the look in his eyes now recognizable as rage.

"Let her go!" shouted Jake, lunging back towards the stage.

Scofield tightened his grip. "Stop right there," he hissed. "This may be a prop, but it is very, very sharp. Don't be a fool, Fleming."

Diana, recovering, now struggled defiantly, and cried out: "Tell him: *'I had rather be any kind o' thing than a fool: and yet I would not be thee.'* "

Jake raised his hands, warily. "Take it easy, Scofield. Just let her go, and we can talk."

Scofield cast his eyes about: *" 'The thane of Fife had a wife: where is she now?' "* he snarled, mockingly.

Jake decided to stall. "You did this?" Jake asked him with a note of incredulity, indicating the furious, still-trussed-up Watcher.

Scofield nodded, with a dismissive shrug. "He's but a man, like any other man."

"But you were in the hospital," protested Melissa. "How did you get here?"

Scofield shrugged again, as if it was the most trivial of matters. "The guard was inept, it would seem. And the night nurse was easily persuaded. *'For mine own good, all causes shall give way!'* "

"Persuaded how?" Jake asked, desperate for time, edging closer.

"I told her who I was." Suddenly his eyes blazed and his lips curled as if he were another man, entirely. "Stand back. *'Come not within the measure of my wrath!'* "

"All right, all right," said Jake, trying his best to sound reassuring. "Don't hurt her. Besides, she's on your side! I'm the one who dragged her into this. What is it you want?"

"You know very well," said Scofield. "I need the notes. All of them. Yours and your daughter's. She has written a new and blasphemous dissertation. I want it. Now."

That was news to Jake. He wondered if it was true. "We don't have them," he said, truthfully. He'd left their notes in the hotel, sensing even at the time that it was one of those decisions from which there was no turning back.

"Oh really. Such a pity." Scofield pressed the knife point just enough to draw a small drop of blood. Diana cried out. "So," he whispered, in her ear. *" 'Art thou not, fatal vision, sensible to feeling as to sight?' "*

"Stop! He's telling the truth," Melissa shouted.

"Then get them," The professor said icily, tightening his grip. Diana now stood deathly still and didn't make a sound. Once again her captor leaned toward her ear: *" 'I see thee still, and on thy blade and dudgeon gouts of blood, which was not so before.' "*

"God, now he's Macbeth," wailed Melissa.

"That's enough!" shouted Jake. "Let her go!"

"The notes, Mr. Fleming. You haven't got much time."

"All right! I'll get them." Jake's mind raced, searching for a way out of this.

"Don't do anything foolish, such as call the police. You are *non grata* with them anyway, you should know. If you do not do exactly as I say, I will kill your traitorous two-faced girlfriend." He glared at Melissa meaningfully. *" 'Better be with the dead, whom we, to gain our peace, have sent to peace, than on the torture of the mind to lie in restless ecstasy!' "*

"You're crazy," she responded. "You need help. Dad, don't do it!"

Scofield shook his head. "He'll do it." He then looked at Diana and said: "Be still, Dr. Parker. This will be a while. Oh," he added, nodding towards Melissa. "And the girl stays."

Diana went pale, but Melissa glared, and sat down cross-legged on the stage, in defiance. Jake wanted to reach out to each of the two women, to apologize for dragging them both into this situation, for jeopardizing their lives, not to mention careers and everything they believed in. Diana looked at him with a secret message in her eyes he couldn't yet fathom. "Go ahead and do what the good professor says, Jake," she said, firmly. "We'll be all right."

"How do I know that?" he asked, heart pounding and thoughts in turmoil.

"You'll have to accept my word for that, Sir Journalist," snarled Scofield. "I'll give you thirty minutes. Am I understood?"

"What about him?" Asked Jake, pointing at the still bound and even more furious Watcher.

"Leave him to me. Now go!"

Jake backed away slowly, toward the stage exit behind him. His eyes swung from his daughter, whose expression was one of combined fear and rebellion, to Diana, who looked determined, and finally to the still-tied-up Watcher, slumped in the fifth row in helpless rage. Then a strange calm came over him. He would do what had to be done. He spun and raced for the exit.

"Thirty minutes!" Scofield shouted after him.

The waiting began. The big man in the fifth row had gone silent. Scofield pulled Diana to the floor and sat, fidgeting erratically, glancing now and then at his watch in growing impatience. Melissa was trying to count the minutes down in her head, praying hard, even though she was an agnostic. Diana sat nearby, now stoic, struggling with her own thoughts.

Five minutes went by.

Outside in the darkened parking lot, Jake raced to the Jag, found the door open, scrambled inside, and quickly turned the ignition. The in-line six complained, coughed discreetly, then roared to life. Diana had taken good care of it, it seemed. He put the manual shift in first, and pulled forward into a wide turn towards the exit. At that moment, another car pulled into the lot and approached rapidly, its quartz headlights blinding him. Jake tried to swing around it, but it cut him off, braking to a stop. That's when the blue roof light went on: a Stratford city police car, probably on routine patrol, thought Jake. Scofield had said he'd kill Professor Parker if he went to the cops. Instead, the cops had come to him. Two patrolmen got out, and Jake shut off the Jag. He had at most twenty minutes to get to the hotel—at least a mile away across town—get to the room, find the notebooks, and bring them back. It wasn't possible.

As the first police officer came around to the driver's door on the right, Jake pressed the button and the electric window—once ahead of its time—slid down. The officer leaned in and shone a light into his eyes: "Are you Jacob Fleming, sir?"

Inside the Royal Shakespeare Theater, Scofield's movements and mutterings were becoming increasingly erratic. " *'Ere the bat hath flown his cloister'd flight, ere to black Hecate's summons,'* " he intoned, to no one in particular, " *'the shard-borne beetle with his drowsy hums...'* "

Melissa, who had now counted at least twenty-five minutes, had regained her courage and called out: "Dr. Parker, you OK?"

"Silence, you ingrate bitch!" snapped Scofield.

"Fuck you," she muttered.

"Where is that fool?" demanded Scofield. "If he has betrayed you as well as me, then how can I be blamed for the consequences that heaven itself will surely unleash? *'Come, seeling night, Scarf up the tender eye of pitiful day; And with thy bloody and invisible hand Cancel and tear to pieces that great bond which keeps me pale!'* "

The two women exchanged looks, now both fearing the worst.

Scofield looked at his watch. "Time is up."

Just then they heard the stage door open, and footsteps approaching quickly.

Diana stiffened as Scofield turned toward the sound, knife still firmly at her throat.

Melissa called out: "Dad, hurry!"

Scofield tensed as Jake rushed onstage, looking flushed. Scofield followed his movements, looked at his empty hands, and shouted in rage: "Where are the notebooks?"

Jake raised his hands, apologetically, with a quick glance at Melissa. "I'm sorry. The car wouldn't start, and I started to walk, but then I realized there wouldn't be time." He glanced again at Diana in silent signal. "I need more time."

Scofield's eyes narrowed, and he stared at him for a long moment. Then he looked momentarily at his captive, his eyes wavering between daggers of vengeance and grudging forgiveness.

Just then an authoritative voice shouted out: "Richard Scofield! You are under arrest!"

Scofield blinked in surprise and his hand wavered.

That's when Jake made his move. Springing like an aging cat, he managed to get his hand on the professor's arm and pull it away from Diana's throat. But fatigue had weakened him and slowed his timing, and in a flash it was back. But as he and Scofield struggled over the knife, Diana, in the meantime, narrowly avoiding death with repeated near misses at the thrashing hand of her adversary, was able, with a desperate twisting motion, to break free.

A uniformed policeman hurried to her side joined by Melissa, while another rushed to free The Watcher out in the auditorium.

Jake finally overcame the insanity-driven older man, who collapsed onto the floor and was quickly seized and handcuffed. The professor began to shake and weep once more.

" 'Canst thou not minister to a mind diseased, pluck from the memory a rooted sorrow?' " he wailed. *" 'They have tied me to a stake; I cannot fly!' "*

The large man, once freed, was livid with rage and indignation. "About bloody time," he growled, working his jaw and rubbing his head, which bore a large red welt. "He sneaked up behind me and hit me with a frigging mace, the bleedin' lunatic," he growled, picking up a dented piece of theatrical weaponry from the floor by his seat. "Good thing it was only wood."

Jake stepped back and eyed him warily as the weeping professor was led away. The big man got slowly to his feet and tested his aching head and limbs. "So, where's Sherwood?"

"Back in his office. He couldn't make it, I'm afraid."

"I see. So, who the hell are you, really?"

The large man came forward, reached into his pocket, and pulled out his wallet. He flipped it open and extended it to Jake and the two women. "Hume Crawford, Scotland Yard," he said, as though disclosing valuable information he was loath to divulge.

Probably just embarrassed at being bested by an aging psycho, figured Jake. "You're Scotland Yard?" he intoned disbelief, glancing at the wallet then back at its owner, although not consciously trying to rub it in.

"That's him," said the nearest cop. "Seen his picture in the papers."

Why hadn't I seen that? Jake fretted. "And you've been following us all this time?"

" 'Fraid so. We had some concerns about Dr. Scofield there–"

"Jesus Christ," muttered Jake. " 'Concerns'?"

"According to the doctors down in Oxford, he's suffering from some kind of paranoid schizophrenia. Also, they found a vial of a dangerous substance in among his possessions, which put him at further risk of suicide."

"What substance?" Jake snapped, quickly.

"Some kind of antiquated poison."

"Hebenon," breathed Melissa.

Crawford looked at her sharply. "How did you know that?"

"I bet it was on those arrows back there in Canterbury, too," she added, with a glare.

"You do know that same substance was found in Professor Lewis's remains?" Jake mentioned.

Crawford blinked, disconcerted. "We'll have to check on that. In any case, something pushes him over the edge, and he loses it, as happened yesterday, apparently. He slipped past our guard last night and made his way up here, it seems."

"So, are we under arrest, or what?" Melissa wanted to know.

Crawford shrugged. "I could probably think of some pretty reasonable charges. Assaulting a police officer, for one," He glared at Melissa at that. "Resisting arrest. Obstruction of justice for another. Shall I go on?"

"I think we get the picture," said Jake.

"As I was saying, we had some concerns about Dr. Scofield ever since he arrived back in England. We'd linked him to the Desmond Lewis case ten days ago, then your daughter threw us for a loop when she took up with the gent, beggin' yer pardon, Miss. But tryin' to keep up with you is one reason we slipped up with Dr. Poulson and the assistant, I'm afraid."

Melissa, momentarily speechless once more, finally managed to explain: "He was my employer, as well as my faculty advisor, in Berkeley."

"So how are you connected with the Shakespeare Foundation?" Jake demanded.

"Similar interests, you might say. National security and such."

"Shakespeare is national security?" asked Melissa, in bewilderment.

"Ten billion pounds a year to the economy says it is," said Jake, with a tight nod of recognition. Crawford looked at him circumspectly but didn't respond.

"So, what do you want from us now?" asked Jake.

Crawford perched on the edge of the stage. "We make a deal. We'll forget you ever came to England, and you do the same. Dr. Scofield won't be going anywhere. I can assure you he will remain safely in custody this time and will be charged with the murders of Desmond Lewis, Gloria Peckham and Samuel Poulson. Especially if that hebenon stuff matches up. So, you needn't worry further on that score."

"I doubt he'll stand trial, he's completely insane," noted Diana.

"Be that as it may, we'll keep him safe and let justice take its course," said Crawford. "Now, as for you folks, as I said, we'll be more than happy to let bygones be bygones. However, there will be one condition."

"And what might that be?" asked Jake, dubiously.

"There's a British Airways flight to San Francisco tomorrow noon from Heathrow. We'll expect you to be on it. Tickets will be waiting for you at the counter."

"That's it?"

"That's it."

"What about my daughter? She was hoping to study theater in London, you know. And see some plays, and work on her dissertation or something."

Crawford looked at Melissa and bit his lip. Then he smiled. She had that power over people, Jake realized. "She," he said, "can stay."

"What about Dr. Balsavar?" Melissa spoke up. "Who shot him? We were there, and please don't deny it happened."

Just then, Jake sensed a movement in the corner of his eye, and heard Melissa let out a cry of alarm. As he turned and looked around in confusion, a second black shadowy figure emerged from the castle gate and lurched on stage towards them like a vengeful Shakespearean wraith. The women both gasped, and Jake stared in disbelief as the phantom materialized into a black hooded monk: the same Monk Jake had seen twice earlier that day in town. The monk drew closer, and the women stepped back in horror. Then he threw off his cowl. "Nice of you to ask," commented the voice of Sunir Balsavar.

"Sunir!" Melissa shouted, and ran to hug him in a moment of uncharacteristic spontaneity.

"Acting Deputy Balsavar, at your service," grinned the Pakistani, with an embarrassed blush.

"You're working with the police?" she drew back and stared at him, horrified.

Crawford spoke up. "He didn't have much choice, once we finally caught up to him. He was next on Scofield's list, and as you saw, we couldn't keep track of him, and The Professor, and you lot as well. We did our best, but it still wasn't good enough, sorry to say."

"So, you told them we were going to Canterbury?" asked Melissa, indignantly, with a glare at Balsavar.

"You were in great danger, or did you forget?"

Now it was her turn to blush. "That's true. But how did you know?"

"Actually, you told Chris, remember? And he told me," explained Sunir. "But it was too late, by then."

"What about at Deptford? Were you trying to arrest us there?" Melissa turned back to Crawford.

"Well, you were trespassing, weren't you? You still need to explain that little escapade."

Like hell we will, Melissa was thinking.

"In any case, we wanted to ask you about what happened in Canterbury. And also about Gloria Peckham. You do know about her?"

"I told them," said Diana, stiffly.

"By then Scofield had eluded us once more and was already in Oxford, but we didn't want to arrest him until we were sure."

"Wasn't witnessing him murder Dr. Poulson sure enough for you?" snapped Jake.

Crawford looked defensive. "As I said, we arrived a moment too late, and when you fled, we lost him in the confusion. Then, with no witnesses and no suspect, and only a stolen museum artifact from the 16th century to trace, we had some delays, to put it mildly. And meanwhile he was long gone."

"Lucky for me," grumbled Melissa.

"Well, we knew where he was heading," Crawford responded, defensively.

After statements were taken and warnings given, the Flemings and Diana Parker were finally permitted to leave. "Just be on that flight," Crawford advised Jake once more, before departing in his black car with the tinted windows, followed by the police car with John Scofield handcuffed in back, staring disconsolately out at his receding lost kingdom as he was driven away.

More than happy to go somewhere warmer and more welcoming, Jake, Sunir, Melissa and Diana piled wearily back into Diana's Jaguar. As they pulled into the now-empty street, Jake turned and regarded the resurrected Pakistani like a long-lost friend. "So, Sunir, you crafty devil. How did you do it? The Lambeth thing?"

Sunir smiled broadly. "Well, when the threats from Dr. Scofield got serious enough to the point that I felt my life was in danger, I asked myself 'what would Marlowe do?' And the answer was clear. So I did what he did."

"You staged your own death," Jake said, in admiration.

"Then became a secret agent. Like Monsieur Le Doux," added Melissa, with a happy laugh.

"No wonder we couldn't find any trace of you." Jake shook his head, in bemusement.

"So, who were those cops at Lambeth?" asked Melissa.

"Some unemployed actors, basically. You should meet them. They had blanks, and I had a blood capsule for realism."

"It worked," admitted Jake, although he felt a little miffed that Sunir hadn't trusted him. But then, why should he? The mistrust had been mutual. "And the archivist?"

"Brother Michael was in on it too, of course, although it may have cost him his job. And now I've proven how easily it could be done, haven't I?"

"So, what about the death mime at the Widow Bull, the other night?"

"I don't know. It wasn't Scofield, but the police wouldn't tell me any more."

"Maybe another actor?"

"Probably. My guess is it was someone sent by the Foundation just to scare you off. I believe they support a lot of actors, with their various theater projects."

"Or their sponsors do," said Jake, thinking once again of Avena, the limo at Blodgett's, and the skinheads.

They rode back to the hotel in silence, each lost in thought. Jake gazed out the window towards the river. The unfinished tower of the new William Shakespeare hotel was clearly visible in the distance, lit by the lights of the town and the construction floodlights.

Diana spoke up. "I still don't understand what this Avena firm has to do with anything."

"It's clear they have a vested interest in the Shakespeare name, from an economic perspective. It's also clear they are behind the Foundation. Or vice versa," replied Jake.

Melissa shook her head in disgust. "You're saying they got to Scofield, somehow?"

"I don't know about that. They may have simply been using him or taking advantage of his madness."

"So, who are they, exactly?" Sunir asked.

"My colleague in New York is still working on it. But these offshore conglomerates answer to no one, basically."

"And that's legal?"

"Yes. For the most part it is." He stared balefully out at the distant, rising tower. "These multinationals are deliberately structured so as to be above the law, or rather, untouchable by the law. In my country they pretty much write the law or own the judges. So, you can bet shillings to donuts they'll leave poor Richard Scofield twisting in the wind."

"Serves him right," said Sunir.

"Not if he wasn't in his right mind," insisted Diana.

"Scholarly types like Dr. Scofield and you, my dear Diana, don't deal with such banalities as corporate profits and the need to protect them at all cost. But Big Business has no such compunctions, as we all know. And Desmond Lewis put it all at risk."

"You put it all at risk too," Diana pointed out.

"True. And you can safely bet they were behind that visit from Harold Sherwood after the scare tactics didn't work. But we're not just talking about one corporation, here. The fact is that if Shakespeare's name is discredited, a big portion of the English tourist economy will go down the toilet. Bye bye New Place. Bye bye a million tourists a year with bulging wallets and all those ex-urban Yuppies soon to follow. Bye bye profits. And the same again for the other sites, like the Royal Shakespeare back there, The Globe, and all those fancy books and DVDs and the rest of it. Bye bye Shakespeare, Incorporated. And that's what Scotland Yard was worried about, more than anything."

As they reached the hotel Jake reached out and took Diana by the hand. He hoped she would forgive him in time, for turning her world topsy turvy. And the way she looked at him, he thought, she just might.

"Tell me something," he said to her, as they got off the elevator. "Were you really going to take us to Gatwick?"

"Absolutely," she said, firmly. Then smiled. "But I was hoping you'd talk me out of it."

Sunir, who had been living the life of the monastic hermit, agreed to join the others for a nightcap. Jake unlocked the door to Diana's and his room and stepped inside, reaching for the light switch. "Come on in, take a load off. I'll call room service."

He stopped short. Something was wrong.

"Hold on." He held up his hand to the others and moved cautiously into the room, his gaze sweeping from side to side like a harbor searchlight. Something had changed. But what? Then he saw it, and his heart plummeted. The table and dressers were bare. His valise, containing all of the research notes and documents, was gone.

Melissa dashed to her room and returned with fresh pain and rage in her eyes. "Bastards!" she cried. "They took all my notes and laptop too. All that work. The one time we left it behind." She threw herself on the bed, her body shaking with fury. But as he moved around the room, Jake noticed something the intruders had failed to discover: a small duffel bag on the floor next to his suitcase. "They missed the bones from the Deptford cemetery," he said, opening it and taking out the skull. "They missed Yorick."

"Or John Penry," sniffled Melissa, taking it from him like a long lost friend. "Or missed their significance."

"So, we're still in the game, and they don't know that yet. At least it's something."

They returned to the hotel bar to reconnoiter, and Diana ordered a round of whiskeys. Jake had one last card to play and made one more call to Sarah Collins at *The Wall Street Journal*, figuring she would still be at work.

When she answered, she sounded strangely subdued. "Oh, Jake. Hello."

"Did you get any more background on Avena?"

There was a pause. "It's interesting. The usual avenues seem pretty well blocked, on that one. But I did find something."

"C'mon, out with it."

"Well, this outfit goes way, way back. It's older than the Hudson Bay Company, and almost as old as the British East India Company. And there may be some tie-ins. From what I could find, they had a Royal Charter dating back almost to the 1620s."

"1620s! You've got to be shitting me." He thought hard. "Do you know who the original partners were?" Oddly, his stomach was growling again, for the first time in quite a while.

"Some old theater cronies, some New World and East India speculators, and a printing company. Headed up by a minor nobleman, apparently, but get this: he claimed to be descended from William Shakespeare, no less."

Jake took a moment to absorb this shocker. "You're kidding. If so, that means this company goes back to the original Shakespeare himself!"

"Could be. The founder's name was Davenant. Sir William Davenant. Sometimes spelled the French way, 'D'Avenant."

"Jesus. Sir William Davenant?"

"So, there's your 'Avena.' Avena means 'oats,' actually, but no matter."

So, he thought. The illegitimate son, feeling his oats. Poor Anne Hathaway, once again. Was it possible he'd been right all along? That this really was Shakespeare's own company?

"Quite an interesting character, apparently, this D'Avenant. Good in business too. He had major interests in the London theater. He gets credit for the first movable sets, by the way. And also for putting the first woman on stage in England, bless his heart. He was also into finance, import-exports, and was heavily involved with the English Civil War. Even got to be Poet Laureate of England for a time."

"A regular Johannes factotum."

"Excuse me?"

"Jack of all trades. Go on." Like father, like son?

"Well, in addition to producing plays and publishing, the principal holdings of the company then, as now, were real estate. So far as publishing, apparently they were among the originators of the so-called 'Pattern Books.' These were the first books explaining how to make quick money in real estate, commodities and so forth."

"Jesus, so this guy invented the 'how to get rich' book?"

"They also had extensive interests in the New World: a major stake in sugar plantations in Haiti, early on. Big slave holders and tobacco growers in Virginia and Georgia in the colonies. You know Davenant was Treasurer of the Virginia Colony for a time, and also Lieutenant Governor of Maryland in 1650, until he got arrested at sea and thrown in the Tower by Cromwell. Yeah, this guy got around."

"So, can we pin any current names to this donkey?"

"I doubt it. The top shareholders are anonymous, for one thing."

"I see." So, thought Jake. Willy the Shake. And his illegitimate son, Willy Junior, following in his father's footsteps, creating, manipulating, and controlling a new industry for the New World. Setting the stage for Hollywood, Wall Street and Broadway alike. And now come full circle, like Edmund, in Lear.

Jake wondered how he was going to break all this to Flannigan, back in San Francisco. “If someone were to find a connection to certain criminal activities here in the U.K., can they at least take them to the IMF? Or the Hague?”

“Yeah, sure. Good luck.”

“OK,” he said, writing furiously. “Thanks for checking.”

“No problem. But you owe me a dinner, next time you’re in New York.”

“Deal.”

When he rejoined the others in the bar and told them what Collins had said, they sat in stunned silence and pondered what it might mean. Sunir was circumspect as he bade them goodnight. “Never mind,” he said. “We still know what we know, and where the truth lies. We still have the List. We can gather it all again.”

Jake hoped so. He’d had more than enough of spooks for one day and was ready to call it a night.

Except for the message waiting on his voice mail from Tom Flannigan in San Francisco. Fearing the worst, he returned the call, wondering where to even begin. “Jake,” shouted the editor, mouth full as usual. “If you ever decide to get your ass back here to the Coast, there’s a letter for you from someone named Gloria Peckham. She says there may be another copy of the Lewis book out there. Apparently, your friend wasn’t so trusting after all. She says she’ll tell you more when she gets back from her holiday.”

Ah well, thought Jake. “Thanks for opening my mail,” he said.

When he promised a full report in the morning and ended the call, Melissa stopped by his side and managed a smile. “I’m going to bed. Good night Daddy,” she said. “I love you.”

“I love you too, Sweetheart,” he replied, a tear welling up in the corner of one eye. “And thanks for all your help.” He hadn’t heard or used any of those words in a long time.

He returned to the bar and invited Diana for dinner. Jake had some more bad news for her, however, and didn’t pull any punches. “You know what all this means, don’t you?”

“Do tell,” she insisted, squeezing his thigh under the table.

“You’re going to have to throw out all your books and start over.”

He ducked as she aimed a carrot stick at his head.

Late that night, his dispatch written and faxed from the hotel desk, Jake curled up at last in exhaustion, Diana at his side. As he gazed at her sleeping profile, he felt an almost forgotten sensation welling up inside, in the vicinity of what he now remembered to be his heart. He wondered if it was possible for a man of his age to fall in love again. Did he even deserve another woman as lovely as Beverly had been; as Diana, sleeping peacefully at his side, was now? He hoped so. In the morning he was going to ask her to marry him. In a world of crumbling beliefs and shattered dreams and lowered expectations, such an opportunity, such a gift might not come again.

Besides, it was the right thing to do. He only hoped she would agree.

Wilton House,
Near Salisbury, Wiltshire
England
Late summer, 1620

The traveler approached the ancestral home of the Pembroke bloodline without fear or trepidation, only hope: something he'd clung to all these years and never quite given up. Careworn and weary, he had gone so far, remained so long, and the journey home so fraught, that he had no idea whether he would be welcome or not, but it didn't matter.

He had a delivery to make. Tied behind the saddle of his horse—a black Arabian who had carried him almost as long as his fractured memories—was a small wooden casket: the same one he'd had and treasured during his escapades as Monsieur Le Doux, the Huguenot spy he once had been. He'd left all those books and materials in the care of Walsingham ages ago; they no longer mattered. What he had now, and all he had left in the world, was the manuscripts: the plays, the Sonnets, all. He had come to present them at last to the woman he loved: Mary Sidney Herbert, Countess of Pembroke.

The boy had grown up by now and done well, with a career of his own as a man of letters, busy at Oxford, where he had by now founded his own college: Pembroke. His personal life, the traveler had heard, had been less fulsome and rewarding: a failed marriage to the Earl of Talbot's daughter, then an affair with his Sidney cousin that had produced two unwanted children.

The rider understood all too well the pain of doubtful parentage, even of doubtful nationality, and had dedicated his own life to protecting young William's true identity. And the old Earl, of course, had been oblivious, abandoning his wife to their country estate, busy in London with enabling Shakespeare's own usurping ways, unaware of this, or perhaps any truth.

Only Mary had known—had ever known—and she, too, had guarded their secret. And she had kept it in isolation, almost an exile of her own, alone in this once bustling house for all these years where, in her glorious youth, she had been hostess to the finest minds, greatest writers, artists and poets in all of Europe, celebrated and toasted as one of their best, their own. He wondered if she would receive him, if she still loved him, if she even remembered him. But no matter. He could not turn back now, after all these miles, and years.

He didn't even need to conceal his identity anymore. All of those who might have wished him harm, or feared, or pursued, or persecuted him were long gone: Whitgift, Warwick, the Queen herself, even that usurper Shake-scene. His friends and protectors, of course, were long gone as well: Burghley had died long ago; Raleigh and Essex had been executed twenty years nigh, and Walsingham grown old and gray in Chiselhurst.

"And what name should I give Her Ladyship?" the wizened gatekeeper demanded to know, unimpressed with the visitor's dusty, well-traveled, time-worn looks, although he had to acknowledge that the man might well have been handsome, once.

The rider hesitated. "Ah," he said, with a laugh. "Therein lies the rub." He scratched his chin, as if trying to recall. "Tell her it's Amyntas, come at last," he said. "She'll know."

THE END

Acknowledgements

I could not have written this work without information provided by my eldest brother Robert, who first discovered the Calvin Hoffman book *Murder of the Man Who Was Shakespeare* in 1955, while earning his Doctorate in Physics at the University of Chicago.

Bob passed this on first to our youngest brother Alex, who was developing a screenplay on the subject. I eventually acquired this book and information from Alex and wrote the novelization of his screenplay which was optioned three times, including by Jude Law. Sadly, the film was never produced. Alex passed in 2018 and I went ahead with this novel.

A Shakespeare Timeline

Year:	Event(s):
1564	Birth of William Shakespeare At Stratford-on-Avon, Eldest son of John Shakespeare, April 23rd.
1581	A "Will Shake-shaft" is mentioned as working as an "Antick" or puppeteer in Lancaster.
1582	Marriage of William Shakespeare to Anne Hathaway, license issued November 27th to marry Anne Whateley. License issued November 28th to marry Hathaway.
1583	Susanna, their oldest daughter born, christened May 26th.
1585	Shakespeare twins, Hamnet and Judith born; christened Feb. 2.
1586	Shakespeare leaves his home and family around this time (some chroniclers suggest a year earlier) and goes to London.
1587-92	Robert Greene and others describe Shakespeare establishing himself as a player, horse-handler (groome), puppeteer, userer, broker and "Johannes Factotum."
1589	In the above capacities, Shakespeare becomes affiliated with the amalgamated Lord Strange's and Admiral's Men (continuing until 1594).
1592	Robert Greene publishes A Groats-worth of Wit warning his fellow playwrights not to do business with the "Upstart Crow" named "Shake-scene." Greene dies.
1593	Venus and Adonis, registered anonymously in April, is published in June, one week after the 'death' of Marlowe. Shakespeare claims it as the "first heir of his invention" in his dedication to the Earl of Southhampton in September.

1594	Shakespeare described in Willobie his Avisa as having been involved in some way with someone named "W. H.", presumably Henry Wriothsley, the Earl of Southhampton.
1595	Shakespeare living in Bishopsgate, now listed as a partner ("sharer") in the Lord Chamberlain's Men.
1596	Shakespeare's son Hamnet dies.
1597	Richard II published, first quarto published under Shakespeare's name. Shakespeare fined in conjunction with his purchase of the New Place in Stratford. Shakespeare cited for tax evasion in St. Helens parish, London.
1598	Frances Meres, a part-time minister, publishes Palladis Tamia and mentions plays ascribed to Shakespeare on p.281. Shakespeare indicted for hoarding grain ("malt") during a famine in Stratford.
1600	Shakespeare sues John Clayton for seven pounds lent in 1592, the year of Greene's invective against Shake-scene the "userer."
1601	Essex Rebellion occurs in London. Participants and authors of the performance of Richard II indicted. Essex executed, Augustine Phillips arrested. Shakespeare ignored by authorities because as the Queen stated in a deposition to her barrister, she knew the playwright to be the "atheist."
1612	Shakespeare gives deposition in Mountjoy lawsuit, regarding a fiscal dispute in a household where he had been a lodger in 1604. He can't remember anything.
1613	Shakespeare leases lands to a neighbor for sheep-grazing, in the "Shakespeare-Replingham Agreement."
1616	Shakespeare writes his will, has a "sound memory" and leaves his "second best bed" to his wife. No mention of plays, poems, books, or writing materials of

any kind. Stratford resident John Hall notes in passing that his father-in-law William Shakespeare "died on Thursday."

These are the only known facts about William Shakespeare, of Stratford-upon-Avon.

The rest is surmise. MT

Facsimile from the First Folio:

The Names of the Principall Actors in all these Playes.

William Shakespeare.
Richard Burbadge.
John Hemmings.
Augustine Phillips.
William Kempt.
Thomas Poope.
George Bryan.
Henry Condell.
William Slye.
Richard Cowly.
John Lowine.
Samuell Crosse.
Alexander Cooke.
Samuel Gilburne.
Robert Armin.
William Ostler.
Nathan Field.
John Underwood.
Nicholas Tooley.
William Ecclestone.
Joseph Taylor.
Robert Benfield.
Robert Goughe.
Richard Robinson.
John Shancke.
John Rice.

Bibliography

Aesop, The Complete Fables Ed. Robert and Olivia Temple NY 1998

Bakeless, John, The Tragical History of Christopher Marlowe in two vols. Harvard, 1942.

Birch, Thomas, Memoirs of the Reign of Queen Elizabeth 1754.

Brooks, Alden, Will Shakspere, Factotum and Agent, NY 1937

Chambers, Sir Edmund K. Shakespeare: A Study of Facts and Problems, in two volumes, Oxford University Press, 1930

Champlin, Charles, The Great Shakespeare Mystery Caper

Davies, John The Scourge of Folly, 1610.

Eccles, Mark Christopher Marlowe in London, 1934.

Evans, G. Blakemore, et. al. Ed. The Riverside Shakespeare NY, 1974.

Fleay, F.G. Shakespeare Manual, 1876.

Greene, Robert, The Life and Complete Works in Prose and Verse of Robert Greene, M.A. Cambridge and Oxford, Ed. George B. Harrison, NY 1964.

Greenwood, Sir George, The Shakespeare Problem Restated, London, 1937.

Greenwood, Ben Jonson and Shakespeare, 1921.

Hamilton, Charles, In Search of Shakespeare, San Diego 1985.

Hazlett, William, Lectures on the English Poets, NY 1968.

Hoffman, Calvin, Murder of the Man Who Was Shakespeare NY, 1955

Hotson, J. Leslie, The Death of Christopher Marlowe, 1925.

Lewis, Roland, The Shakespeare Documents; Facsimiles, Transliterations and Commentary, 2 volumes, CT 1940-41.

Magnussun, Magnus Ed. Chambers Biographical Dictionary Cambridge, 1990 (5th Edition)

Matus, Irwin Leigh, Shakespeare, In Fact, NY 1994

More, David, The Marlovian , "Drunken Sailor or Imprisoned Writer?" Fall 1996.

Noble, Robert C. Shakespeare's Biblical Knowledge, 1975.

Nicholl, Charles, The Reconing: The Murder of Christopher Marlowe, Orlando 1992.

Robertson, J. M. The Shakespeare Canon, 1922-30

Rowse, A. L. What Shakespeare Read and Thought, NY 1981.

Ridley, M.R. Ed. Othello, Moor of Venice, 1958.

Schoenbaum, S. William Shakespeare, A Compact Documentary Life, NY 1977.

Simpson, R.R. Shakespeare and Medicine London, 1959.

Steiner, George, The Death of Tragedy, NY 1963

Stopes, Charlotte, Shakespeare's Family, 1901

Tarloff, Frank, Jarrico, Paul, "Blacklisted...Fifty Years Ago Today" in Written By , The Journal of the Writers Guild of America, LA, October 1997

Twain, Mark, The Complete Essays of Mark Twain, NY 1963

Urry, William, Christopher Marlowe and Canterbury London, 1988.

Ward, B.M. The Seventeenth Earl of Oxford, 1550-1604, from Contemporary Documents, London 1928.

Webster, Archie, "Was Marlowe the Man?" in National Review London, 1923.

Willoughby, E. E. A Printer of Shakespeare

Wraight, A.D. Shakespeare, New Evidence, London, 1996.

Wraight, The Story that the Sonnets Tell Publications: Merriam, T.V.N. and Matthews, Robert A.J. in Literary and Linguistic Computing "Neural Computation in Stylometry II: An Application to the Works of Shakespeare and Marlowe" Vol. 9, No. 1, 1994

Author's Note

The Shakespeare Foundation, Avena Global Partners Ltd. and the present-day characters in this novel are figments of the author's imagination. Likewise Blodgett's Books. All other historical and factual institutions, references and character descriptions are real and accurate. Sir William Davenant was real, as were his claims, and his life and career as described.

On Sale Now!

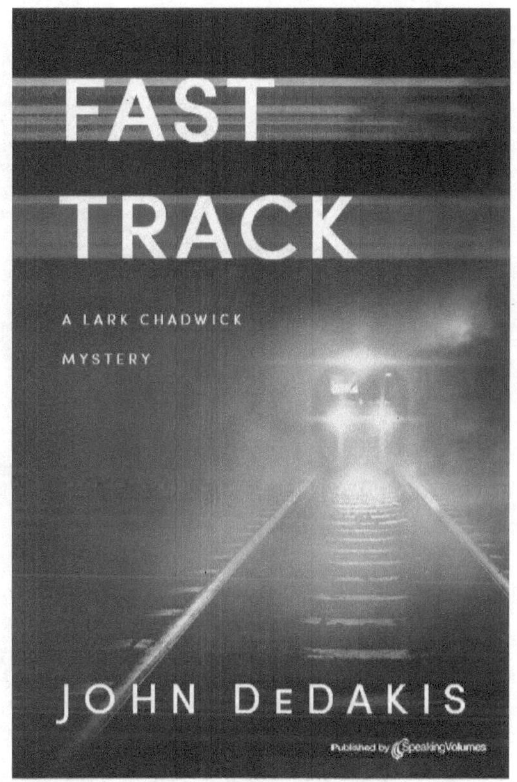

For more information
visit: www.SpeakingVolumes.us

www.ingramcontent.com/pod-product-compliance
Lightning Source LLC
LaVergne TN
LVHW050914080826
845145LV00001B/86

* 9 7 8 1 6 4 5 4 0 3 5 5 5 *